UNINVITED GUEST

Her eyes were a deep midnight blue that showed she was of the Blood—a Darklander. I was a half-breed Darklander myself. If she sensed the Blood in me, my business would be in jeopardy, along with my life.

"Kamus of Kadizar?" she asked politely.

I nodded, and before I could stop her, she raised both arms in a summoning gesture and spoke in the language of Darkness. There was a clap of thunder, a billowing of foul dirt-colored smoke and I had an uninvited guest.

It stood almost three meters tall, with skin the color of dried blood. It was bald, with pointed ears and yellow eyes, and antlers protruding from its shoulder blades. It was fanged and taloned and hugely-sexed, and it stood near the window poised to spring on bird-claw feet . . .

DARKWORLD DETECTIVE

J. Michael Reaves

BANTAM BOOKS
TORONTO · NEW YORK · LONDON · SYDNEY

DARKWORLD DETECTIVE
A Bantam Book / June 1982

Parts One and Two appeared, in different form, in Weird Heroes, Vol. 8, *Jove Books and BPVP, November, 1977.*

Map by David Perry.

ISBN 0-553-20672-9

Published simultaneously in the United States and Canada

Bantam Books are published by Bantam Books, Inc. Its trademark, consisting of the words "Bantam Books" and the portrayal of a rooster, is Registered in U.S. Patent and Trademark Office and in other countries. Marca Registrada. Bantam Books, Inc., 666 Fifth Avenue, New York, New York 10103.

PRINTED IN THE UNITED STATES OF AMERICA

0 9 8 7 6 5 4 3 2 1

To BYRON PREISS
A Weird Hero

I would like to thank Evelyn Sharenov, cartographer and musicologist; Terry Blass and Marc Scott Zicree for the title and opening line of Part Two; Steve Perry for skeletal suggestions, and Arthur Byron Cover for a fateful remark several years ago.

A human steeped in the Dark
arts is greater than a devil . . .
you shall carry that knowledge
with you to the Dark Land.

—ROBERT E. HOWARD

The streets were dark with something
more than night.

—RAYMOND CHANDLER

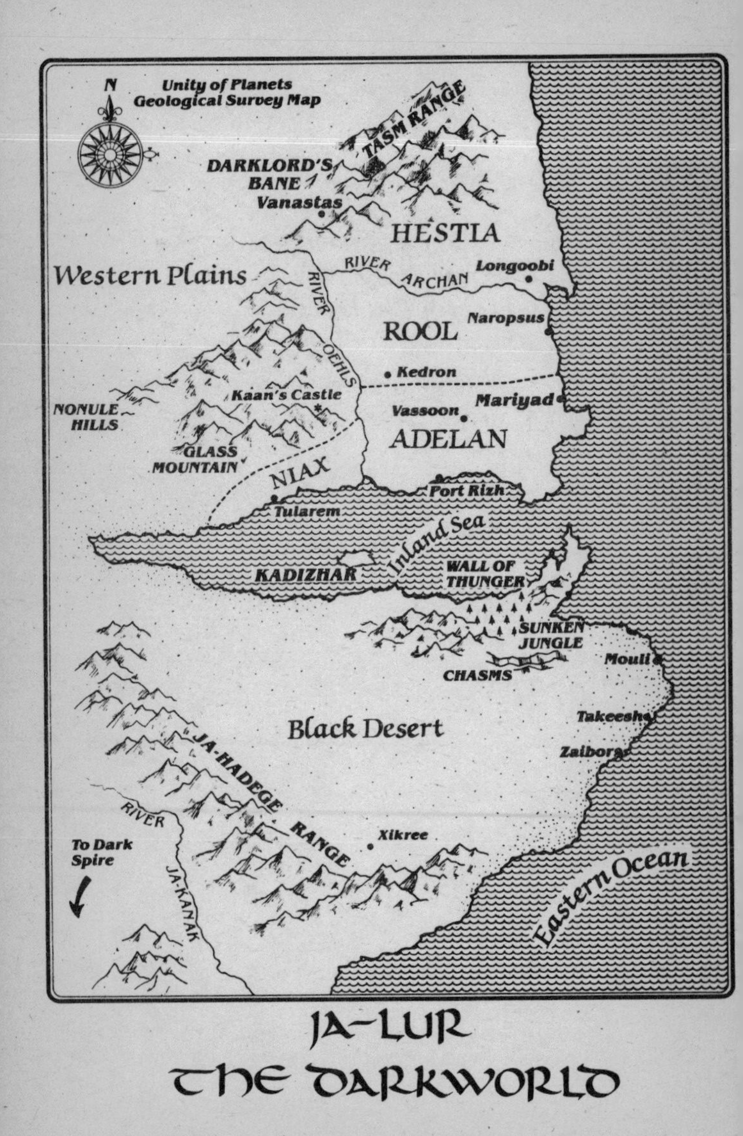
N
Unity of Planets
Geological Survey Map
TASM RANGE
DARKLORD'S
BANE
Vanastas
HESTIA
Western Plains
RIVER
ARCHAN
Longoobi
RIVER
OEHLS
Naropsus
ROOL
Kedron
Kaan's Castle
NONULE
HILLS
Mariyad
Vassoon
ADELAN
GLASS
MOUNTAIN
NIAX
Port Rizh
Tularem
Inland Sea
KADIZHAR
WALL OF
THUNGER
SUNKEN
JUNGLE
CHASMS
Mouli
Black Desert
Takeesh
Zaibor
JA-HADEGE
RANGE
RIVER
JA-KANAK
Xikree
To Dark
Spire
Eastern Ocean
JA-LUR
THE DARKWORLD

PART ONE

The Big Spell

I

My sword needed polishing. The swivel chair creaked as I leaned back and put my sandals on the glass that covered my stone desk. My blade was serving as a paperweight at the moment; it did a poor job of reflecting the amber sunlight. Noon on Ja-Lur is a little brighter than twilight on Earth. I had been thinking about Earth a lot lately; mostly wondering why I had left it to return to my home planet, the Darkworld. Business wasn't good.

My office was hot and quiet, the oil-lamp flame unmoving. Through the narrow window I could see the slums of Thieves' Maze, and beyond that the towers and ships of the Unity Spaceport. If the other wall had had a window, there would have been a view of Overlord Kirven's palace. I was just as happy that there wasn't.

Dash, my phonecub, was folded like an old wineskin in one corner of his cage. He looked hungry; I knew the look well from my mirror. I squeezed my moneypouch and felt the round outline of one thin dechel. With one dechel I could insult a beggar.

Dash stirred, then unwrapped his two tails and sat up. He perked pointed ears, his black fur bristled, and those solemn silver eyes grew large. I sat up—somebody was calling. The phonecub's small body went lax and his mouth opened.

"Kamus of Kadizhar?"

I didn't recognize the voice, but it belonged to a woman. It had that carefully casual tone that usually means a job. I quit fondling my pouch. "At your service."

"You are the one who solves problems for a fee?"

"I could be an augur or a procurer and do that," I said. "My specialty is investigative work."

"I see." Her voice grew slightly colder. "My name is Valina," she continued, "and I want you to find someone for me."

"My fee is seven hundred wechels a fortnight, Valina," I said. "Plus expenses." No surname and no name of origin usually meant a slave—I wanted it clear that I didn't work for grain. At least not until that last dechel was spent.

"Fine," she said smoothly. "How do I reach you from the Marketplace?"

"Take the Avenue of Columns west to Manthion Tower. Turn left on Cartrattle Street, right on Whores' Path. I'm in the third room on the second floor of the last building before you reach Thieves' Maze."

She said nothing more. Dash shook his head and yawned. I tossed him the last sweetmeat in a dish on the bookcase, one I'd planned on eating myself, and thought about the call.

A slave with seven hundred wechels? Perhaps she was a front for a wealthy, anonymous master. I glanced around the small chamber I called an office. In one corner was a pile of papers awaiting a filing cabinet from Earth. A chipped wine jug and a few mismatched mugs sat on a wobbly table, flanked by two clients' chairs. My trenchcloak hung behind the door. A slight breeze was now bringing ripe scents from the Maze through the window. Not very impressive, but, since I was the only private eye on the planet, I couldn't see any reason to be impressive. Valina would have to take me as I was.

* * *

She walked in like she owned the place and wanted to sell it. She wore a simple slave's tunic of purest silver, and a turquoise-inlaid dagger that looked like it could open more than letters. Her figure was nice, not outstanding, but her hair definitely was. It was gray, not the gray of age but a gray like the heart of a cloud, which came to silver even in Ja-Lur's dull sun. It swooped back and curled past her shoulders, making a net that caught an interesting face. A high forehead, small nose, and cheeks that were almost gaunt. Her mouth had a slight curve that didn't remind me of a smile.

Then I saw her eyes.

They were deep and midnight blue, with a look in them as subtle and indescribable as it was unmistakable. If most eyes are mirrors of the soul, then these were still wells reflecting incredible depths. By those eyes I knew she was of the Blood—a Darklander. Like hunger, I knew the look, and it meant trouble for me. I was a half-breed Darklander, and Darklanders aren't welcome in the Northern Nations. If she sensed the Blood in me, my business could be in jeopardy—along with my life.

If she did, she gave no sign. "Kamus of Kadizhar?" she asked politely.

"We went through introductions once," I said, watching her. "Let's try something new."

"As you wish," Valina said, and smiled. Then she raised both arms in a summoning gesture before I could stop her and spoke in the language of Darkness. "*Rylah Tobari, ke'n Sorgath!*" The oil lamp guttered and went out. There was a clap of thunder, a billowing of foul, dirt-colored smoke, and I had an uninvited guest.

It stood almost three meters tall, with skin the color of dried blood. It was bald, with pointed ears higher than its crown. The lobes were pointed, also. From its shoulderblades rose antlers like the twisted limbs of a hanging tree; they seemed to join with the roiling smoke. Its eyes were yellow against black. It was fanged and taloned and hugely sexed, and it stood in a shaft of dim sunlight from the window, poised on bird-claw feet. It grinned. I didn't. Dash shrieked and tried to crawl into his food dish.

"I think you have the wrong place," I told Valina. "A charlatan lives three houses over in the Maze . . ."

The darkling laughed. "Creature of a moment," it said, "you have lost your life. Prepare yourself."

"What is this?" I asked. In the dimness they did not see me slip a vial of sleepweed powder from my potion pouch. I stared at Valina. "Return this thing to the Dark and let's talk. We might like each other."

Valina smiled again and said, "Since your powers are halved by nature, the darkling's will be also, to make a fair fight." She spoke a Phrase, and the darkling seemed to dwindle slightly. It looked reproachfully at her and I took advantage of that to cast the vial their way. "*Nithla,*" I cried, "*vorst enyon!*" My pronunciation was terrible, as always. But the powder ignited in midair nonetheless, and the darkling blinked as golden smoke mingled with oily brown in the rank breeze from the window. It swung one arm backhanded through the mist.

"Such a puny spell," it said contemptuously, in a voice like grating metal. "Did you seriously think it would affect me?"

I shrugged. "Not really, but it was worth a try." I took up my sword and stepped from behind the desk, taking care to stay upwind. "What would you have?" I asked.

"Your soul for sustenance."

"Come and get it, then."

At that it howled and leaped forward, its heavy claws digging into the wooden floor. It lifted a chair and flung it at me. I dodged and heard it smash to kindling against the wall. I swung my sword and drew a black line across the darkling's thigh. The wound hissed and steamed, and three stony talons just missed the side of my face; the thing had a reach on me. I lightfooted backwards to the bookshelf and heaved a bookend at it. The darkling caught and crunched it in its mouth, yellow gaze mocking, then stalked forward, casually lifting one end of the heavy stone desk out of the way. That impressed me, the more so since its strength had been halved. Of course, it had to be powerful to survive in direct sunlight. But I was hoping it was not powerful enough to survive without help.

I glanced at Valina. She was watching me, oblivious to the faint golden wisps drifting toward her.

I dove forward as the darkling set the desk down; I rolled beneath its slash and tried to hamstring it. It danced back and I saw its leg coming at me; I fell back with the kick but was still knocked breathless into a corner. It leaped to straddle me—and I heard Valina cough.

I thrust upward and skewered an obvious target—the darkling squawked indignantly and jerked away, tottered, and went down with a crash. There was a sigh, and Valina collapsed behind me as the compound had its effect. Simultaneously the darkling, lying in dim sunlight, gave a whinnying cry and turned to dust.

I rolled over and sat up. I felt as if I'd been racked, but

fortunately I hadn't been scratched or bitten. I looked at the fragments of the bookend. They were acid-eaten.

I pulled Valina to her feet and sat her in the remaining client's chair. I slapped her once on each cheek, not gently, and let her head loll forward. She took a deep breath and shuddered. "Head down," I said. "Breathe deeply. And don't move or I'll break your neck."

She believed me. I sat down behind my desk. After a moment she lifted her head and smiled at me. I wasn't growing fond of that smile. She did not seem at all tired; to cast a spell that strong would have exhausted me. "Very good, Kamus," she said. "Tell me; how did you know I was binding the darkling to this world?"

"It made sense. If it had been strong enough to survive direct sunlight on its own, you wouldn't have been able to control it."

She nodded and ran fingers through streamers of hair. "I had to know if you could battle things of the Dark and live."

"You could have asked, and saved us both a lot of trouble," I told her. Then I caught the look she was sending across the still-dusty air. "All right, so we're both Darklanders. I won't tell if you won't. Now stand up, turn around and walk out."

Something that looked bad in eyes as blue as hers flashed. I leaned forward. "You wouldn't get past the first syllable." I meant it. I'm not as casual about killing as are most people on my world; after all, a private eye should have a basic moral code. But I wasn't about to give her a second shot at me. This lady was dangerous. I had stronger stuff than sleepweed in my pouch.

She settled back, fingertips smoothing her tunic. After a moment she said slowly, "Kamus, I ask your help."

"Why should I help you? I've had furniture smashed, the office is filled with darkling dust, and those potions don't come cheap."

"I'll reimburse you for everything, and a considerable amount besides. Only let me tell my story, and then tell me if you will be of help.

"I am late of the entourage of the Lord of Vassoon."

That was supposed to intrigue me. It did. Vassoon had been until recently a small province around two hundred kilometers southwest of Mariyad. More recently, within the past week, it had become a blighted land with a large crater where the lord's keep had stood. There had been a plague, and quite a few dead peasants. The story was that the Keeplord had been a Darklander, had gotten ambitious, and the Darklord had smote him down, along with castle, servants, and the general countryside. It could be true—but if it was, how had Valina escaped?

I unwrapped a stick of imported chewing gum while watching her. Some private eyes smoke, but that habit isn't popular on the Darkworld—polluting someone else's air is a good way to get hurt. I stuck the gum in my cheek and motioned for her to continue.

"Do you know," she asked, "who 'the Brothers Below' are?"

"I've heard the term in the Maze. It's supposed to be another name for the Kakush, a legendary oligarchy of criminals that have their fingers in all the illegal and most of the legal businesses in Mariyad."

"It's the only clue I have to finding Kaan," she said. "If he's learned too much of the Darklore . . ."

I held up a hand. "The beginning," I suggested.

She stroked her cheekbones with those long, ringless fingers. "I'll start before the beginning" she said.

"Edward Knight came to Ja-Lur from Earth seven years ago. He was not an ambassador from the Unity of Planets; rather, he was a renegade, a scientist who had discovered that some secrets need more than science for their explaining. So he stole a spaceship and sought a world where magic worked.

"He landed in the Black Desert, north of Ja-Agur. He feigned amnesia and became a slave to a local wizard in one of the coastal towns that trade with the Darkland."

"A charlatan?" I asked.

"You used that word before. I'm not familiar with it."

"A Northern term: a human who claims to have Dark powers."

"I see. No, this man was of the Blood. I was part of his household. I watched Knight as he learned speech and custom—and Language."

That called for a reaction. "An outworlder learning Language? That's unusual."

"There is Dark Blood on other worlds," she said. I had known that, but my powers had not worked on Earth. "It is common on Earth still, though Earth has almost left the area of overlapping cosmos that we call the universe of Darkness. Because of this, the Blooded on Earth can mate with humans and be fruitful, not sterile as they are here."

That made me relax somewhat. Valina had recognized me as of the Blood, just as I had known her—one Darklander can always recognize another. But she knew nothing of my human heritage. Not all matings between Blooded and human are sterile.

"There are few pure lines left on Earth," she continued. "But in Knight the Blood ran clean, and he learned—behind my master's back at first, later at his feet."

"And he killed your master," I said.

"Yes," she said calmly. Sweat was collecting along my headband. If what she was telling me was true, then this could be big. Big enough to forget about very quickly.

"My master never suspected. He died unknowing, his soul plucked and flung to darklings. There were others with power in the village, including me, but Knight was more powerful. He made himself lord. He was arrogant beyond sanity, but the Darklord did not crush him—even when Knight chose to bring a plague upon the town. One dark night, the wind came roaring with pestilence through the small village. The next morning there was no living soul left, for Knight had gone north, taking me with him, and all the rest were dead."

Dash was whimpering in his cage. I watched Valina. The depths of Darkness had left her eyes; now they were as flat as that turquoise blade she wore. I went to the wall lamp and relit it—the shadows were getting too thick.

"We crossed the Inland Sea and came to Vassoon, where Knight took the Keeplord's throne. It was easy for him. He commanded more of Darkness than even a full-Blooded outworlder had a right to. There have been waxings and wanings of Darkness of Ja-Lur in recent times, no doubt because Shadownight is only two months away."

I nodded. Strange things happen on Shadownight, when the two moons of Ja-Lur eclipse and form the Bloodmoon. They don't roll around too often; the last time one occurred was when I was conceived.

Valina looked troubled. "I feel that this Shadownight will be a bad one, if only because I know that some of the Elder Spells, long lost, have been found—because Knight found one."

"He *what?*"

"In an ancient crypt, in a skeletal grasp, he found a single Phrase of the *Synulanom*, an ancient scroll of spells hidden there by Mondrogan the Clever, during the Dark Wars, powerful enough to grant control of all the Northern Nations from Hestia to the Inland Sea. When Knight finds the rest of it, he intends to speak it, and with the power gained he will conquer the kingdoms.

"Then he intends to challenge the Darklord."

"I swallowed my gum. "That settles it," I said. "This is out of my league. I've gone up against quite a bit for my fee, but not someone who's crazy enough to challenge the Darklord."

"Don't be foolish," Valina said with a flash of teeth. "Knight is walking dead—the Darklord will crush him. It's Kaan I'm worried about."

"I'd almost forgotten about him."

"Four months ago two Unity agents, Daniel Tolon of Earth and Kaan Ta'wyys of Thanare, made planetfall. Knight caught them entering his keep. He sentenced Tolon to be a galley slave, but offered Kaan a chance to learn and rule by his side. Kaan was also of the Blood; he and Knight had dabbled together in Darklore, but the evil of it had repelled Kaan. Still, they were linked, and so Kaan had sensed Knight's plans to conquer Ja-Lur, and had come to stop him.

"He refused Knight's offer at first, but later decided he would need knowledge as a weapon. So he learned, and he used his new spells to help me escape, last week. I heard the next day that the keep had been destroyed and that all within it had vanished." She took a deep breath. "I'm afraid for Kaan. I know how easily the Dark secrets can corrupt even those of pure Blood. I want you to find him for me, Kamus, before the Darklord destroys them."

The she joined me in being quiet. I picked up a stick of gum and toyed with it, ran a finger along the flat of my blade, and in general pretended to think about it. I'd already thought about it, and I knew I didn't want to touch this case with a ten-foot battle lance. All I wanted was to break it to Valina in a way that would avoid more unpleasantness.

"What makes you think the destruction wasn't the Darklord's move?"

"If Kaan were dead, I would know it," Valina said flatly. I didn't argue with that; they were both of the Blood.

"But I've tried to contact him through the Dark," she added, "with no luck."

"Any idea where they've gone?"

She shook her head. "It couldn't be far; Knight wanted to start his rule in this nation of Adelan. I have nothing but that cryptic phrase, 'the Brothers Below,' which Kaan whispered to me just before I escaped. He did not have time to tell me more."

I looked at her. She had told me all of this without a hair losing its place. Her eyes were still flat, oddly lacking. "Why do you want to find Kaan so badly?" I asked.

"Because I love him," Valina said coolly. "I thought that was understood."

"Not by me. You could have been reciting a history lesson."

That was my second mistake of the day. Valina's eyes suddenly got very nasty—so nasty that I gripped my sword in case she was thinking of another test. Instead, she stood, pulled seven large gold coins from her moneypouch and tossed them on my desk. They cracked the glass desk cover. "You'd better know something in three days," she said, each word cold as a snake's hiss. Then she turned and left, quickly, before I could tell her I had no intention of taking the case.

I looked at the cracked glass and the shambles the darkling had left. Seven hundred wechels to start me on a case involving outworlders and Darklanders, a case that could bring both the Unity of Planets and the Darklord himself down on me.

I sighed, swept the coins into my hand, pulled out a sheet of parchment, and began an expense account, starting with the bookend.

2

I fed Dash and told him to take any messages. Then I took the quick route to the Unity Spaceport, through the heart of Thieves' Maze. Dank Lane was a street I usually avoided, but I wanted to reach the Spaceport before Customs closed. I still had no intention of getting involved in this case to any great degree; I merely intended to give Valina an idea of where to look for her outworld lover. I wasn't going to invade any sorcerer's citadel to carry him out—that was definitely not in the league of a half-breed Darklander barely able to keep the few spells he knew from backfiring.

Dank Lane was narrow and high-walled—the slender strip of sky above was dark, dark blue, with a smear of honey to the west. Mariyad traffic grew thick toward the streets near the Spaceport, as outworlders foolish enough to enter the Maze were fair game and easy marks. This deep in the Maze, however, few bothered to keep up appearances. Cripples sauntered by me with crutches slung over their shoulders, on their way to beg at the gates. Blind men eyed me suspiciously. I didn't fit—I wasn't burly enough for a footpad, nor tattered enough for a beggar. Were the lane less crowded, I would have had trouble. But too many thieves spoil the taking, so I thought myself safe.

Until I noticed that I was being followed.

Suppertime in the Maze; I could smell lentils, boiled meat, and cheap wine. Dank Lane twisted between rickety, gap-boarded houses, jammed together and piled at overhung angles. Rail-less stairways hung like gray cobwebs down high brick walls that made night out of evening. At times the lane was almost ankle-deep in cess, save for a narrow path of foot-polished cobbles at the center. Not everyone bothered to keep their feet dry. The one following me didn't—I noticed him trying not to be noticed, dodging from one clot of people to the next. I studied him from the corner of my gaze: a small, stooped figure in rags the color of wormwood. No threat by himself, but if he were in league with others...

Then I caught another glimpse, and noticed the familiar cadence to his limp. A motley group passed between us, and I ducked for the shadow of a doorway. As he passed I put out an arm and grabbed his grime-stiff cloak, regretting the probability of fleas, and pulled him in.

"What news, Ratbag?" I asked him.

He squealed, of course, and stared at me. His eyes were stitched with red, and set barely wide enough for a nose the shape of a cornerstone. Scabs and burst purple veins littered his face. "Kamus!" His voice was as shrill as a cart axle. "I wanted to warn you—I—"

"Of course you did." I shoved that last dechel between his crusty teeth to stop their chattering. "You always have my welfare at heart. Who are you selling out this time?"

He spat the coin into a black-lined palm and stopped shivering. "No gossip. Word is that someone is looking for you—a savage, it's told. A skin-clad outlander with murder on his breath. He's sure been told where to find you by now."

I looked at him suspiciously. "This out of the kindness of your heart, Ratbag?"

"You always pay top for news of the Maze, Kamus." He glanced pointedly at the dechel.

"That's all I've got right now. You'll get more next time." I thrust Ratbag and his urine-sharp smell away from me, watched him scuttle into alley dimness. Then I headed for the Maze exit, holding my breath like a man in a slaughterhouse.

I didn't recall offending any savages lately.

* * *

The Spaceport was a kilometer from the city wall, surrounded by knee-high savannah grass. It was small, not over an acre in size, and the only one permitted on the Darkworld by the Darklord. Though he rarely spoke to anyone on the planet, and technically ruled only the Darkland, the Darklord had his ways of indicating edicts. After several attempts at building other spaceports in other major cities had been met with plagues, quakes, spontaneous human combustion, and other setbacks, the Unity of Planets had decided to be content with the one outside Mariyad.

Once I stepped from grass to plasticrete and passed the sleek, gleaming weapon detectors, I was considered subject to Unity law. Once inside the boundary, the little Darklore I was capable of would not work, just as technological devices did not work outside—again, the Darklord's will.

I entered a public gate guarded by two crewcut Earthlings wearing the form-fitting white uniforms of the Unity Service. Muscular knuckles gripped rayguns as I passed. They looked as if they wanted me to try something, just to relieve their boredom.

I walked down the wide white concourse toward the Terminex, next to the Galactic Arms Hotel. The Unity symbol—twenty melded golden globes with a ring about the whole—shone over the irising doors. Past the low roof, against a purple sky, a polished silver globe of a ship descended toward its berth without a sound.

Some of the more humanoid Spaceport employees were busy behind ticket counters as I entered the large hexagonal chamber. The only non-military entity was something green and webbed, dozing in a force chair. I cross the resilient, cream-colored floor, had my sword taken from me at the weaponcheck counter, and floated up a tube to Customs and Acculturation. I always felt uneasy in the Spaceport. Everything was hushed and whispered, and the creak of my leather trappings and empty scabbard made me feel like an easy target. I reminded myself that I was, after all, a private eye, and private eyes are supposed to feel out of place everywhere. It didn't help.

An information-retrieval robot waited behind the Customs counter. It was a dull gray cylinder the size of a crystal ball pedestal, with a sensor screen, delicate as a spider web on top. A function light eyed me as I leaned on the imitation solebanite counter and popped my gum.

The robot whirred and said, "*Ssssp*. May I help you, sir? I must warn you that there has been a dysfunction in my primary-unit continuity circuits within the past seventeen minutes. This may interfere with optimum performance and efficiency. *Kzzzt*."

I sighed. "Customs information, month of Telander,

local calendar. I need a list of those outworlders entering Ja-Lur during that period."

"This information is restricted to Beta-Twelve Unity personnel or Ja-Lurians of comparable author-*click*-author-*click*-authority. *Nnnnn*." The function light flickered and the robot said politely, "*Ssssp*. May I help you, sir? I must warn you . . ." and went through the entire speech again.

"Ah—I'm Sergeant Sumak of the Mariyad garrison, here on city business," I told it. "I just showed you my papers. On authority of Overlord Kirven Saculas, I request a list of outworld entried during the month of Telander."

"I regret I must request to see your papers again, sir." Its light blinked again and it added, "*Nik-nik*." I waited a moment, then demanded, "Well?"

"Your papers, Sergeant?"

"I've showed them to you twice, Darkbegotten! That does it. I'll tell the Overlord of the Unity's lack of cooperation and violation of treaty immediately." I turned and started for the tube.

"My apologies, sir. The list." It gurgled, and a small cassette dropped from an aperature onto the counter. I pouched it and headed for the reading room as the robot blinked and asked if it could help me again.

* * *

It was quite late by the time I reached the Marketplace. The crowd had thinned—a few baggy-robed crones pinched pears at fruit stands, some beggars and street musicians whined, each in their own way, for alms. Streetwalkers whispered silkily as they walked. The usual.

I went into the Blue Lotus Tavern and took a high-backed corner booth, away from the sound of ale slopping from tankards and the smell of old barracks jokes. Quite a few guardsmen hung around the Blue Lotus. I usually overheard interesting things there. They might not have anything to do with whatever case I was on, but they were interesting.

Slave girls danced, bells tinkling, in each of the tavern's corners. A eunuch and a panderer were harmonizing badly at the bar. I ordered a stew—the scents of the kitchen had reminded me how hungry I was. It would be my first good meal in several days.

I sat there and thought about what the cassette had told me. *Daniel Tolon, Earth citizen, Age 34, Height 1.5m, Weight 85.7kg, Blood Type 0+. Occupation: Freelance trader (perishables). Arrived 0900 Twelfthday, Seventhmonth, U.Y.125.* His visa had been optioned to own-risk upon planetfall, which meant he was free to leave Mariyad and the Northern Nations, and if he died as a result he got an unmarked grave (if lucky) and his family a short condolence form. The form was marked sent as of a week previous, as he had not been heard from since planetfall. So much for Daniel Tolon.

But there had been no listing of a Kaan Ta'Wyys of the planet Thanare. He had forged his name . . . which meant he wanted no one to know of his coming to Ja-Lur, not even his next of kin. Which was interesting.

I had some sour wine and thought about Valina. Her knowledge of the Dark Language was more extensive than mine, and her Blood, the power behind the Words, obviously purer. To summon a darkling at noon was impressive. She had evidently studied for years before Knight killed her master. Then he had kept her as a slave, while she bided her time, waiting for an opportunity for revenge.

I could not help wondering how Knight planned to challenge the Darklord. It was quite a jump from deposing a Keeplord to overthrowing the nameless supreme Darklander who ruled all of Ja-Agur, and, in indirect ways, much of the rest of the planet. Even with the *Synulanom,* it seemed impossible. I had heard of it; a collection of powerful rites used by the Darklord during the Dark Wars in an attempt to conquer all Ja-Lur. Mondrogan the Clever had hidden it, and the Darklord had returned to the Darkland. I had thought all that legend, like the Black Mask, which supposedly allowed one to see into the realms of Darkness, but now I wasn't so sure.

The serving girl set a tureen full of stew in front of me, and I shelved speculation. The Darklord could wait; I was ravenous. I picked up my spoon—and a hand slightly smaller than a saddle came down on my wrist.

My eyes followed the hand up an arm an ogre would have envied, and I was starting at a tanned, impassive face. Looming over my table was a character out of place even in the melting pot of Mariyad: almost as tall as a darkling I'd met recently, and seeming nearly two axe-hafts across the shoulders. He was coffee-colored, and naked save for a loincloth of spotted junglecat hide. A totem-tattoo of the same beast was over his left breast. He was covered with scars, and missing most of his right ear; his eyes had the color and expression of obsidian, and his hair, also black, was a long mane bound by a leather thong. He wore leather armguards as well, scuffed with bowstring marks. I figured him for a barbarian.

"Kamus of Kadizhar?" His voice was pitched lower than a quake. He didn't wait for an answer. "Come." He hoisted me away from my stew. I grabbed the booth with my free hand. "I'm eating," I said. "Interrupting a meal isn't civilized."

One corner of his mouth lifted slightly; I expected to hear it creak. "I'm not civilized," he said.

"You're not someone I want to know, either. Go slay a dragon or something, and let me finish my stew."

The corner lifted a bit more. It would be a half-smile in a hundred years or so. The arm at my wrist flexed slightly; and suddenly I felt like I was on the rack. I gasped, let go, and staggered toward him. The tavern had grown fairly quiet. Guardsmen nudged each other and pointed, grinning.

"Will you come?" the barbarian asked quietly. "Or be carried?"

Since chances were good that this was the savage about whom Ratbag had warned me, it seemed suicidal to leave the Blue Lotus with him. I shouted at the guardsmen. "What's it come to when a citizen can't even have a meal in peace!" One guardsman there was more drunk than the others. He bellowed, "Outlander pig! to dare annoy a taxpayer!" and drew sword. He was a very large guardsman, also very drunk, and surrounded by drunken friends who urged him on. None of that helped—the barbarian took the edge of the guardsman's blade on his leather armguard at just the right angle to deflect it without injury, though it shaved hairs from his arm. Then one massive sandaled foot caught the guardsman in the stomach and sent him across the tavern like a crossbow bolt, to splinter a table and die coughing blood.

The barbarian released me. "Fight," he told me, and unsheathed a broadsword that looked as long as a rafter beam.

I wasn't on his side, but that made little difference—the

killing of their comrade had brought the rest of the guardsmen to the attack with a sotted roar. Slaves and dancers vanished with the ease of long practice. A guardsman made a blind-drunk thrust at me; I parried it with a chair, grabbed the tureen of stew and threw it in his face. Wine pitchers shattered mirrors and windows, tables were overturned, tapestries rent, and patrons slashed while I headed toward the door. Silos, the tavern owner, crouched behind the bar with a look of weary resignation—this was probably the third fight in a fortnight. And guardsmen never pay for damages—one of the advantages of being a guardsman.

I retreated before a relatively concerted attack by three more of them, kicked a table in their faces, and dove for the door. Everyone was fighting indiscriminately by now, guardsmen and outraged civilians. If I didn't get out of there fast I would be forced to kill someone, which I didn't want to do. The barbarian wasn't bothered by such scruples; I could see him fighting, head and shoulders above the crowd. It would have given me a hernia just to lift that broadsword, but he swung it onehanded, mowing down guardsmen right and left.

Just as I reached the door, it swung open and a captain rushed in, sword ready. Behind him were five or more men. The captain thrust at me, and I barely had time to draw sword and parry. I brought the flat of my blade down on his neck—he bent double and I stepped on his back and went out the window. I landed, rolled to my feet, and leaped. A swordslash whistled beneath my sandals as I scrambled up the steep, shingled roof and leaped across the alley to the next building. I ran rooftops for several blocks before pausing to remove my identifying trenchcloak. Then I dropped to the pavement.

I was on Cobbleweave Street, a good distance from the Blue Lotus, and I was in trouble. I had probably been recognized, and I had attacked a captain of the guard—at least, that's how it would be reported. My first day on a case usually goes better than that.

Whoever that idiot of a barbarian was, he had probably ruined my career in Mariyad. Most of the Guard knew me and had little love for me—this would be all they would need to put me underground. I started back to my office. I had a friend at the Garrison; a lieutenant named Sanris. Perhaps he could help me, somehow. . . .

I turned a corner and a grip gentle as a sea serpent's asked me into a recessed doorway.

"You fight well," the barbarian said.

I simply stared at him.

"Follow me," he said, and turned toward the street, his grip on my arm like a lead tourniquet. I pulled my dagger and he flicked it from my hand as if it were a toothpick. I spoke three Words and he staggered, looked vaguely ill, then straightened and shook off the effects of the spell. He turned to face me and shifted his grip from my arm to my neck. There was a battlefield roar of blood in my ears, and the street darkness about me broke into bright colors and ran into blackness.

3

There was a chariot race being held in my head. I was glad I hadn't eaten the stew—I would have lost it. My body was one solid ache—even my hair hurt. I blinked, and candle light seared my eyes.

"He's awake." The barbarian's gravelly voice.

"You shouldn't have been so rough, Ult." Another voice, much lighter but still male, with a curious accent.

"He used Darklore. He comes from beyond the Black Desert." The usual barbarian paranoia for anything that smacked of horns. Every Darklander had a pickled human heart personally autographed by the Darklord, and a penchant for sacrificing virgins. I had never been south of the Inland Sea, and I'd never even met any virgins. I didn't correct him, however, it being all I could do at the moment to squint my eyes and make out two forms standing over me. I concentrated on the smaller one, and eventually it developed a face.

It was a lean face, with long, straw-colored hair and pain lines too new to look at home. He was recently tanned, the skin along his hairline still peeling. There were pouches of weariness around his eyes the same storm gray of Valina's hair.

He wore a slave's tunic of light brown. The hints of whip welts laced his upper arms and shoulders.

He squatted beside me, looking concerned. "Kamus, I apologize. I merely told Ult to fetch you . . . I should have made it clear he was to bring you in one piece."

"What do you want?" I croaked.

He grinned uncomfortably. "I want to hire you to find somebody."

That struck me as funny, too. I might have laughed, if my throat hadn't hurt so badly.

He offered me some wine; it went down as gentle as lava and stunned my stomach. Then he taught me how to stand again. My tunnel vision widened, and I saw we were in a small, stifling garret room with one round, unglazed window, gray-curtained with spiderwebs. Two pallets lay at opposite ends of the room. The feeble dawn light and the single candle showed me that the wooden walls were rotten and termite-gnawed, and the floor sagged dangerously under the barbarian's wide stance. Faintly below I could hear the scrabbling of rats, and I could smell grain and meal through various other reeks, not the least of which was barbarian body odor. This was a warehouse attic, and they had been here for some time.

"My name is Danian," the straw-haired one said. "That's all you need know—and that we're willing to pay you this." He handed me a moneypouch that I almost couldn't lift. The leather bulged with a thousand tiny flat planes; I tugged open the drawstrings, and tipped precious stones into my hand. They caught the dim light and played joyously with it. I was meeting quite a few rich slaves lately.

"They're all yours," Danian said. "Enough to relocate you anywhere in the Northern Nations, and keep you fed for years to come. And all you have to do for them is find someone."

I looked over his shoulder at Ult. "You can keep them if you'll spit him over a slow fire instead," I suggested.

The big man made a sound like an avalanche and started toward me. Danian whirled, put both hands against the massive chest and snapped, "No, Ult! Back!" He looked like he was trying to hold up a toppling tree. "We need his help." Ult subsided slowly, glaring.

"That wasn't bright," Danian told me.

"So? If I was bright, I wouldn't be here. Thanks to your

brass-brained friend, what little business I had in Mariyad is no doubt ruined. You think I feel like helping you now? Why didn't you must come to my office and ask?"

"There are people looking for me," Danian said.

"Considering your friend's manners, that's understandable. Look, pretending for a moment that I'll help you, I still don't know nearly enough. I don't know what your interest is in this person, or what you intend to do with him—"

"Her," Danian said.

"Whatever. I expect honesty from my client. I give him honesty in return. Those are the terms I work by."

"These are our terms," Danian replied. He put a hand on his sword hilt. Now I was being threatened. "You really don't have a choice. You know Mariyad much better than we do—both of us are foreigners. We need to find a woman named Valina, and you're going to help us."

"Valina," I said. Things began to connect.

"I say kill him," Ult suggested. "You can't trust Darklanders." He pulled his sword halfway clear.

I kept a pensive look while I checked out Danian again; the hints of whip marks, the recent tan, and his outrageous accent, which I now realized was outworld. Things were definitely beginning to connect. I pulled out a stick of chewing gum, slid it into my mouth, rolled up the foil and snapped it into a spiderweb. "Tell me about this Valina," I said to Danian.

He told me. It wasn't news. She was a slave from a northern province who had escaped from her master with important knowledge. Her master wanted her back, and had sent Danian and Ult to fetch.

"Bring her to us, or tell us where she is, in a day's time. Once we have Valina, you have this." Danian held up the pouch again.

"One day!" I said. "It will take longer than that just to find a lead, unless I'm lucker than I've ever been before. And what about the guardsmen? How can I hunt while I'm being hunted?"

Danian shrugged. "I didn't say it would be easy."

I raised my hands helplessly. "Considering the alternative, what can I say? I'll try."

"Excellent," Danian said, and smiled. "Tomorrow dawn we'll meet you at the intersection of Butcher and Mace

Streets, in the heart of the Maze. I'm sure you'll have good news."

Ult smiled also, and popped one massive knuckle. It sounded like a neck snapping.

I started to leave. "Wait," Danian said, and before I could turn he flipped a blindfold over my eyes. "We have to take precautions," he said as he led me down a flight of rickety wooden stairs. "You understand."

He opened a door and we stepped out into morning coolness. I smelled damp alley garbage. Danian led me down twisting streets; I was in Thieves' Maze, no doubt of it. After much doubling back and path-crossing we stopped.

"Remember," Danian said, "Butcher and Mace, tomorrow at dawn," and I felt him start to unknot the blindfold. Then there was a shout from one side and the sudden rush of booted feet; Danian's hands tore away from my head and I heard a broken curse. I reached up to rip the blindfold away, but a fist against my cheekbone sent me stumbling into the wall.

"Take them!" someone shouted. There was the heavy steel sliding of swords from scabbards.

The rough brick tore the blindfold free. I was sprawled by a low wall. Ten guardmen had surrounded Ult and Danian, who stood back to back under a wooden balcony. Ult swung a two-handed massive stroke that slammed into one guardsman's armor hard enough to knock him off his feet. Danian handled his smaller blade awkwardly, trusting Ult's gigantic swaths to protect him as well.

I saw all of this in an instant, as two guardsmen pulled me to my feet and pinned my arms. I was headed for the gibbet anyway, so: *"Dammi gwil, sinald pai!"* I shouted. It was supposed to stiffen the guardsmen's leather cuirasses and leggings, immobilizing them. Evidently I mispronounced something, because the balcony above Ult and Danian abruptly collapsed with a rending of wood and a shattering of pottery. Ult pushed Danian free and dived to safety, but I saw five guardsmen caught beneath the debris. One of the two holding me clapped a hand over my mouth, and they dragged me around the corner while Ult hoisted Danian over the low wall and leaped after him.

I was dragged through a low, skull-leering gate and out of the Maze on Blackmark Street. Ahead was a barred guardwagon, into which I was tossed. A filthy rag was stuffed in my mouth, and one guardsman lashed the beasts into a clattering gallop down the street. I lay twisted in stinking hay with the other guardsman's sword poised over me. The hay stank because previous prisoners had tried to escape and blood had soaked the chaff. I didn't move, save for bouncing about as the wagon careened on. I didn't even turn around to see where we were going. I knew all too well: we were headed for the City Garrison and the Dungeon. I had been there before.

* * *

Captain Thoras had sandy hair; the sands of the Black Desert. Every time I saw him it was sweat-damp, even in winter. I saw him much too often. He had eyes as kind as pit vipers, and a habit of baring his teeth as he talked. It was hard to feel confident around him. He was a large man, starting with his bones and including, according to the wenches at the Blue Lotus Tavern, not quite everything else. Thoras was also one of the few guardsmen I knew who had a mind of any dimension. His hobby was collecting antiques and curiosities, and I had just been added to the list.

At the moment, he was sitting in a wide, high-backed chair in a narrow, high-ceilinged room. There were some barred windows, a stone desk bigger than mine, a mangy phonecub in a dirty cage, and little else. When I shifted my feet the room echoed. The oil lamps had been turned off. I was sitting on a small stool, surrounded by three guardsmen who held torches over my head. I was sweating. I was supposed to.

Thoras had his scuffed boots on the desk. He balanced a chipped dish on one knee, on which were some lonesome, sharp chicken ribs, ivory-clean. A row of red knuckles next to his mouth hid most of a chicken leg, which he was polishing to match the ribs. I watched those last bits of fowl vanish, swallowing in time. My stomach was growling, but I couldn't have eaten even if Thoras had felt like tossing me a bone. My arms were manacled and a bronze clasp covered my face from nose to throat.

Thoras eyed the bone and belched at it. "Kamus," he said, in a voice his children probably thought was jolly, "I don't understand your continuing antagonism toward the Guard. Haven't we bent over our swords to be nice to you?

When you returned from Earth with your crazy idea of becoming some sort of mercenary for private hire, we let you do it. And though we've crossed purposes once or twice, I've never had you on the rack."

He began to beat out a slow tempo with the leg bone against the heel of his hand. "But now... as if attacking Captain Sarya wasn't enough—though privately I wish you'd killed the crystal-sniffer—you've shown yourself to be a Darklander, and proven it by killing five good men. Not to mention helping that murdering barbarian and his friend to escape." Thoras shook his head. "Bad, very bad. But because I like you, Kamus—or did before you showed your true colors—I'll let you speak your side." He waved the bone at the three torchbearers. One of them released the clamp, while the other two pricked my throat with daggers.

"If you try to speak Language," Thoras cautioned me, "they'll cut out your voicebox. Now—tell me about it."

I told him how the fight in the Blue Lotus had come about. "The savage took me back to his friend, who offered me jewels to take a case for them. They weren't giving me much choice, so I agreed. Then your men attacked us."

"At which time you called upon the Dark and killed five of them," Thoras said. His voice had lost its jolly.

I took a deep breath. "I'm only half-Dark, Thoras. My mother was human; she was... raped on Shadownight by an exile from the Darkland." The words came hard—I felt as if I was insulting my mother by telling Thoras how I had been conceived. "So my powers are uncertain. I was trying to bring down the barbarian and his friend when I shouted that spell. It backfired."

Thoras stared at me. "A half-breed Darklander," he murmured. "Like Mondrogan the Clever, I suppose, in old legendry. Well, old One-horn supposedly made up for his lack of power by his wits, which is more than you've done." He slapped the bone against the desk as though it were a gavel. "You spoke Language; that makes you a Darklander, and that means you die."

I was afraid he would look at it that way. Now my only hope was to gain some time by playing on Northern superstition. "Killing a Darklander can have serious consequences, Thoras."

The man with the clasp slapped it over my face hastily,

before I could try any kind of death curse. Thoras nodded at my words, setting the dish carefully on his desk. He kept playing with that bone; it was beginning to bother me.

"Should I slay you by force of arm, your spirit will haunt me by day; should I slay you by force of nature, your spirit will haunt me by night," he said, quoting an ancient saying. "Still, I understand there are ways to deal with your kind." He posed the bone between two fingers. "I could ruin your eyes, ears, and sense of smell by delicately using a sharp-filed dead man's bone, and thus render your spirit senseless and harmless. Or I could have you buried alive beneath another's grave, so that your spirit would be unable to pass the body above you." He pulled his lips back from his teeth and snapped the bone in half. "Just to be on the safe side, I think we'll do both of these, and burn your cadaver to boot. Sentence will be carried out at dawn, between day and night." He gestured and they pulled me to my feet. "Find him a cell. Keep him gagged, but do him no violence—if a drop of his blood touches you or your weapons, you're in for a lifetime of ill luck. Take him away. Tomorrow dawn he dies."

It didn't look like I would be keeping my appointment with Danian and Ult. I wasn't sure if I had the power to return and haunt anyone after death or not; I had never given it much thought. But I would certainly make an effort as far as Thoras was concerned.

Two of the guardsmen hustled me from his presence and along the dingy, bare corridors of the Garrison. We went down an iron stairwell that coiled in the center of the building, its lower depths lost in blackness. A clammy breeze hushed about us as we descended. The guardsmen said nothing. The only sound was the flat clanging of their boots against iron as we hurried to meet the rising echoes.

There were no grinning death's-heads over the Dungeon gate, no signs to the effect of *Abandon All Hope*, et cetera. None were needed. Beyond the gate, recessed, iron-bound wooden doors lined a chamber, dimly lit by two guttering torches.

"Here's an empty one," one of the guardsmen said, pushing the door open. They led me into the cell respectfully, and left me there.

It was Shadownight black inside, save for faint phosphorescent tracings of slime on the ceiling, which illuminated nothing. I shifted my shoulders experimentally. The manacles binding my arms were locked just above my elbows, preventing me from slipping my arms over my legs in a contortionist's trick. I tried scraping the back of my mouth-clasp along the stone wall. No good. I backed up to the door and explored it with my fingers. Cold iron, moldy wood. But one of the iron strips near the bottom stood away from the wood.

I lay down and worked my head into position. My neck was in knots of agony by the time I hooked the lock on the strip and tugged. The clasp unsnapped, and the thing fell away from my face with a dull clank. I lay on the slick, damp floor, exhausted; I had fought for my life three times within the past two days on nothing but wine and chewing gum. After a while I began to shiver, and I dragged myself to my feet.

I could speak Language now—for what that was worth. The guardsmen had taken from me the potions I carried, which enhanced and stabilized my badly-spoken spells. Without them I might turn myself into a frog. Possibly I could summon up a Darkling powerful enough to free me from the Dungeon—but one that powerful, I would be unable to control. They would burn and bury a mindless, soulless moron at dawn.

I leaned against the wall and thought about it.

That door, despite its mold and rust, was strong, as were the walls. There was a good chance of backlash from any spell powerful enough to shatter them. But a door was only as strong as its latch. I crouched before the lock and began to speak.

I could not gesture with my hands behind my back. The Words sounded garbled and unfamiliar as I spoke them. My foot slipped once, and I lost the cadence. Still, at the end of the spell I could smell the thin tang of newly rusted metal.

I stood and hurled myself against the iron-bound wood. The door creaked, but did not give. I ruined my other shoulder, and this time the lock gave way. I stumbled out into the corridor, exhausted; even that small spell had drained me.

My arms were still manacled, but I managed to reach through the bars of the gate and unlatch it. Now all I had to do was fight my way through the entire armed Garrison with my hands tied behind my back. Simple. I put a foot on the stairs, intending to have a cautious look. As I did so, I heard the stairwell echo dimly to a tread far above. I hurried back into the chamber, pulled the two torches from their niches with my teeth, and doused them in a slimy puddle. Then I closed the door of my cell and hid in the corridor just outside the chamber. I hoped there wasn't more than one coming. The strain of the past few hours was starting to make itself felt. I leaned against the wall until a wave of dizziness passed.

Yellow, flickering light began to illuminate the stairwell. After a moment, a single guardsman came into view, his face in shadow. He paused at the chamber entrance, then stepped in cautiously. He stopped at my cell, sword unsheathed.

I slipped into the chamber behind him and opened my mouth to shout a spell. He heard me and turned quickly, and I saw his face. I swallowed the first Words of the spell, grinned instead, and said, "Hello, Sanris."

4

Sanris of Taleiday and I had been friends for over a year, even since my first case, in which I'd saved him from being eaten by the giant rat of Solipta. Since then, Sanris had been my inside man at the Garrison, and we had helped each other professionally and personally many times.

He was far too intelligent to be a Guardsman, and claimed he only kept the job because it attracted women. In that area, he was certainly enjoying his work. He liked taking risks if the stakes warranted it, and was not above taking graft; still, he was by far the most honest Guardsman I knew. I trusted him.

He led me out of the Dungeon by a secret passage that was an escape route in case prisoners ever got out of control, and hid me at the house of one of his many lady friends. This one was a rich and more-than-slightly kinky noblewoman who lived at the north end of Mariyad. She put me in a bed that felt like a cloud and was bigger than my office. I slept the rest of that day and most of the night, and woke up ready to eat my sandals. I didn't have to; I was served a seven-course breakfast, and Milady made it clear that the feast need not stop there if I so desired. I declined, not because she was Sanris's lover—he wouldn't have minded—but because I needed all my energy for something else.

After she left, I closed the heavy fur curtains, rolled up the plush and flammable rugs, and started work. Sanris had returned my possessions, including my potion pouch. I mixed compounds and ignited them, and eventually sat in the center of a circle surrounded by flames that ran the gamut of the spectrum. I started to speak a Calling Spell.

The dark room grew darker, until I seemed to be floating in the middle of space, and the flames grew brighter. It took some time to get an answer. I kept wondering what Milady would think if she stuck her head in to see if I'd changed my mind. The sight would probably make her more determined than ever to get me into her bed. Northern women have certain myths about Darkland men.

I had almost given up, when suddenly the Darkness shattered soundlessly, then whirled together into a fiery wheel that blurred and became Valina's face. The image faded away below her shoulders, but it looked like she was naked.

I hope I'm not interrupting anything, I said. She shook those beautiful gray curls and looked at me thoughtfully. *This must be important*, she replied, *for you to call through Darkness to me*.

It would have saved me a lot of trouble if you had left the name of your phonecub. But you're right—this is important. I'm off the case. I have some information for you, and once I give it, we're quits. You can pick up your seven hundred wechels at Pallas the Moneyholder's. He's open until sundown. I saw her nostrils flare and her eyes blaze, and spoke quickly so she couldn't get a word in. *Don't bother threatening me, Valina, because it won't work. You couldn't possibly hand me more trouble than I'm in already. The Guard knows I'm a Darklander, and they've sentenced me to death. I'll be lucky if I can save myself, let alone help you*.

You incredibly clumsy dolt, she broke in, her voice seething. *You bungler! By the Dark Spire, I ought to—*

Your sympathy's appreciated. Now here's the information: Daniel Tolon, the Earthling, is looking for you. He's calling himself Danian. He has a fistful of jewels and a large, unfriendly barbarian named Ult to persuade people to talk about you. I gave him no leads. Now it's up to you.

She was silent for several seconds. Her voice was acid fire the last time she spoke—this time it was pure ice. *Hiring you was quite probably the biggest mistake I've made in this entire affair. I only wish I had the time to make you regret your incompetence. You've wasted valuable time, led my enemies to me, and given me nothing helpful.*

Maybe I'm not coming through clearly, I said. *They found me. I didn't find them. They're waiting for me to meet them with information about you—an appointment I have no intention of keeping. I'm going to be quite busy with my own problems for some time.*

She wasn't listening. *Kaan could be anywhere in Adelan by now. Could be anywhere . . . but how to . . . the Kakush . . .*

She broke the connection with an impatient gesture. The room returned to normal darkness. I drew the curtains and opened the windows, then lay back down, had a stick of gum, and brooded.

Her last thoughts had been fragmentary, and obviously not directed at me. It takes concentration to keep private thoughts separate while speaking through Darkness. She had made her feelings quite clear in the thoughts that had been meant for me, however, She was right—I had bungled. I had made few moves worthy of my profession. I had become overwhelmed by the rapid sequence of events, and things had gotten completely out of control. But I couldn't think of a way to remedy it. I'd be lucky if I thought of a way to save my life.

Sanris arrived later, bringing Dash with him, and we split a bottle of wine. I noticed him watching me from behind his drinking mug. He had been studying me whenever he thought I wasn't looking ever since he rescued me. I pushed my hair back from my forehead and said, "No horns, Sanris."

He grinned and emptied his mug. "I don't know much about sorcery or about Darklanders, Kamus. I'll confess it frightened me when I heard you were one of them. But I know you, and I'd trust you if you told me you were Jann-Togah, son of the Darklord, himself. If you say the spell you used on those men wasn't meant to kill them, I accept that. Still, I'm glad I knew none of them personally."

"I had no intention of killing them." I felt badly about those five deaths; it wasn't the first time my incomplete abilities had caused others harm. For better or for worse, however, I had the Blood in me. A Darklander can no more resist using Darklore than a human can resist using any of his five senses.

I cracked a chestnut on my swordhilt and asked, "What does the Guard know about the Kakush?"

"The Mazelords?" He chuckled. "Periodically some pompous undersecretary from the palace issues memos ordering a full-scale investigation of them, and then someone else countermands it as a waste of time. If you want my personal opinion, with the slipshod, graft-ridden way this city is run, Overlord Kirven himself could be one of the Brothers Below."

"Do you believe there is some sort of organized criminal elite that influences city government?"

"I believe it's possible. Why?"

I didn't answer. "The Brothers Below," Kaan had told Valina just before her escape from Vassoon. And she had mentioned the Kakush just before breaking contact with me earlier. How did they figure into this case? I wondered, then remembered that I wasn't on the case anymore. I had other things on my mind.

"I've got to figure out some way to get myself reinstated as a citizen," I murmured out loud.

"There is no way," Sanris said. "The Blood is anathema in Mariyad, Kamus, and you know it. When the Overlord hears of this, there won't be anyplace for you to hide in the entire nation of Adelan. You've got to get away; Rool, maybe, or Hestia. I have a friend on the balloon-boat lines who can smuggle you out. You can join one of the crystal caravans that cross the Nonulé Hills. No one will suspect you in that company; crystal runners have all sorts of strange people with them."

"Thanks," I said. "But I don't want to leave Mariyad. If only—"

Dash leaped to his feet abruptly and began lashing his tails frantically against the cage bars. "Kamus! Kamus!" There was no mistaking the shrill voice that came from the phone-cub's mouth, just as there was no denying the panic in it.

"Ratbag! What's wrong?"

"Kamus, I saw him kill Gallian! The hooded man—he

spoke three words, and Gallian's skin shriveled and broke, and blood—"

"Ratbag, calm down! Where are you?"

"At a public phonecub in the Rusty Sword Tavern, in the Maze. Kamus, I'm scared! There's Darklore in the Maze . . ."

"Just stay where you are," I ordered him. "I'll be right there."

"All right, Kamus." The reedy voice sounded relieved. Dash shook himself as the connection broke and chittered for a sweetmeat. I gave him the nut I'd cracked and looked at Sanris.

"The Rusty Sword," I said. "It's a sleazy dive in the heart of the Maze." I buckled on my swordbelt.

"You're not thinking of going there?"

"Ratbag is a ferrett, I admit, but he's always dealt fairly with me." I was out the door by this time, tossing words over my shoulder. "If he's in trouble, he deserves my help."

"You're insane," Sanris told me, following at a run. "If Thoras gets his hands on you again—"

"That's my worry. You stay here."

"If you haven't any more sense than to go bulling into the Maze in search of a flea-ridden crystal-sniffer, you at least need eyes behind you."

We stopped arguing at the street. I hailed a passing carriage. "The Skull Gate," I said. "And hurry."

We ran from there. Fortunately it was early morning and most of the Maze's inhabitants were still asleep or hung over, else our obvious urgency would have brought us trouble. When we reached the Rusty Sword, however, there was no sign of Ratbag. The tavern was not even open, and wouldn't be for another three hours. All around us were the crowded, tumbledown buildings of the Maze, standing only because they had no place to fall. There were few people in the street, other than a few bodies in doorways. It was as tranquil a scene as the Maze had to offer.

"You see," Sanris said. "He's played you for a fool."

I examined the phonecub in its cage outside the tavern. No clues there. "Who is Gallian? Or was, rather."

Sanris thought. "Possibly Gallian of Port Rizh, a merchant who fronts for much drug traffic. Quite a few Guardsmen are on the take from him, in various ways. But why would he be a Darklander target?"

I shrugged. "Is there any proof Gallian was connected with the Kakush?"

"Rumors only, just as there are rumors about every unscrupulous businessman and politician in Mariyad."

"Well, let's go look for Gallian, then," I said.

"This is folly," Sanris said sadly, but he followed me.

Gallian did not live in the Maze, of course, but he transacted some of the shadier aspects of his business within its boundaries. It was here that Ratbag must have seen him. There was a huge crowd about his building when we got there, however, and it included a number of Guardsmen. I saw Thoras bending over a mass of bloody pulp that bore a faint resemblance to a human being. The crowd was becoming unruly at the presence of the Guard in their domain. There was no way I could learn anything here, not with Thoras and his men about. It seemed that everywhere I turned in this case, I ran into a stone wall.

We faded back quickly into the Maze, walking slowly down Dragonpock toward Blackmark. After a few blocks Sanris said, "Kamus, it must be obvious to you now that this is too big for you. Darklanders, outworlders, the Kakush . . . even if you weren't a hunted man in Mariyad, you'll only have your head handed to you if you persist in unravelling this. Take my advice: Get out of Mariyad."

He was right, and we both knew it. This was a case that Mondrogan the Clever himself would back away from. I sighed. "What time does your friend's balloon-boat leave?"

"In time for you to pack some belongings and food." He put an arm across my shoulders. "I will miss you, my friend."

I would miss him, too. And my work, and this city. I hated to leave Mariyad; for all of its corruption and cruelty, it fascinated me. But he was right—I was in over my head. Nothing I had worked on before had ever come close to this.

We were approaching an intersection; suddenly, on the other street, two unmistakable figures came into view. I recognized them at the same time they recognized me. The four of us stopped. Ult saw Sanris and his hand went for that broadsword again. "Betrayal!" he growled to Danian. Danian stopped him with a gesture, and they approached us slowly.

"Do we fight?" Sanris asked softly.

"Are you kiding? I've seen Ult in action. He'd make

basket cases out of us. We'll try talking first, then running."

They stopped out of reach of our swords, but within easy reach of Ult's. "You're late, Kamus," Danian said.

"I've been busy. A little matter of escaping from the Garrison."

Danian nodded. "And so you have no news. I thought so. Well, despite being fugitives, Ult and I are honest men. I feel it was our fault you were captured, and we owe you for that." He handed me another pouch, smaller than the first one he had tempted me with. "A portion of the jewels, to make up for the trouble we've caused you. If you run across any information and want to let us know, Silos at the Blue Lotus will put you in touch with us. Good luck, Kamus." He turned and walked away. Ult gave me a final superstitious glower and followed. I stood tossing the bag from hand to hand, watching them disappear around a corner.

"Finally a bit of good luck" Sanris observed. "If that pouch really is full of jewels, you've got enought wealth to see you safely through your relocation."

"Let's get out of the Maze," I said.

It wasn't easy; Guardsmen were all over the place, and we had several narrow escapes. I could not return to my office or home to pack, of course—the Guard had both under surveillance. Sanris persuaded a few ladies to shop for some traveling needs while I lay low until time for the balloon-boat to leave.

I felt uneasy about Ratbag; he had seen something he wasn't supposed to, and this mysterious hooded Darklander might be looking for him. Sanris promised to look for him after I was safely out of town. I was feeling rather heavily indebted to Sanris.

Finally everything was ready at the balloon-boat port. I was currently hidden in a special room on the top floor of one of Mariyad's largest brothels; the owner was another of Sanris's friends. The room was an overdressed, fetish-filled chamber, replete with leering, well-endowed statues, a tiled ceiling mosaic depicting one hundred and one different positions, and red drapes hung in vulva folds. There was also an enormous waterbed; this last had been an Earthling suggestion. It was made from the rubbery skin of a giant sea slug.

I was relaxing on it when Sanris came in. "I'll not be able

to see you off," he told me. "There's a rumor that you've been seen by the docks, and Thoras wants every man available at that end of the city."

"Who started the rumor?" I asked. He grinned. "The men need exercise on occasion." He gripped my hand. "Good luck and goodbye, Kamus. May we meet again some day. There's a eunuch downstairs named Yesh who will take you to the balloon-boat port. He can handle anything up to and including Ult."

"You'll be hearing from me, Sanris."

He turned toward the door, and I started to get off the bed.

The attack came totally without warning. There was a loud crackling noise all about us, and the red draperies suddenly writhed and turned black, like flower petals on fire. Darkness descended with a rush, before we could even draw swords. The walls and floor of the room seemed to fall away, to sink and stretch in a strange new perspective. I grabbed Sanris's arm and pulled him onto the shaking waterbed. There was a feeling of rushing upward, as though the outer edges of the room were streaming away from us, as though we were erupting toward the ceiling. But there was no ceiling above us—only Darkness.

"*Salan mach torrad!*" I shouted. The spell worked somewhat; the dreadful soundless rushing slowed a bit. Sanris crouched on the bed next to me, sword drawn, trying not to be affected by the apparently bottomless depths that now surrounded us.

"Don't panic!" I told him. "It's only an illusion, to disorient us!" Actually, I wasn't sure. I had never seen a spell like this before.

Sanris pointed upward. "Kamus, look!" The blackness overhead, an inverted bowl of night, was cracking. Veins of red and yellow shattered over the surface, like tinted lightning. Bolts of fire began to crackle toward us. I smelled ozone. It was no illusion, that was for sure.

I shouted another spell which slowed our ascent again, but not as much or for as long this time. Fire bolts were hissing all about us now; the ruptured sky was very near. The furs and silks were already smoldering, bits of them dropping like meteors into the blackness below. The thunder and crackling was deafening. I couldn't hear the spells I was shouting. Sanris grabbed me and pulled me across the quaking bed, and a fire-bolt struck near where I had been, burning a hole in the bedskin and releasing a cloud of steam. It also gave me an idea.

"The water!" I shouted. "Of course!" I gripped the waterbed frame and shouted, "*Tilye maldaz, bol!*" In response, a geyser of water erupted from the center of the bed and poured upward into the raw heart of the fire. Sanris stared, wide-eyed. The bed should have been emptied in an instant, but the spell kept the jet of water pumping thousands of liters at the fire. We wrapped ourselves in furs to keep from being blistered by clouds of steam. But it was working—the bolts were weakening, and our rate of ascent was slowing as well. The spell wasn't broken yet, however. I fumbled potions from my pouch, mixed them as best I could—I would need all the help I could get to break this one. Incense mingled with steam as I chanted. The thunder grew muffled and distant. The steam had a reddish tinge now, but we felt no heat. The Darkness was fading—I could see hints of the walls about us. The constant shouting of spells was beginning to exhaust me, but I managed to grin at Sanris and give him a thumbs-up sign. He wasn't familiar with the Earthly gesture, but he could see the spell was fading. He grinned and sat up, letting the blanket slip from his shoulders.

Then one final bolt of fire stabbed through the steam and enveloped him, turning his flesh and clothes into an explosion of cinders, freezing his grin into the leer of a naked skull. A cloud of greasy smoke mingled with water vapor as his bodily fluids evaporated. The skeleton hung together for a moment, then clattered into a pile.

An instant, one horrified instant, was all I had to see his death. Then the lights went out. There was a moment of whirling vertigo, and when I opened my eyes I was back in the boudoir. The room was undisturbed, tranquil. The draperies were unburned. Only two things kept it from being a dream: the empty and ruined waterbed I sprawled upon, and the baked bones that had been my friend, Sanris of Taleiday.

5

I went back to the Maze.

It was evening of the day after Sanris died. Ater leaving the brothel I had gone back to my home, and by a combination of spells and luck had gotten past the Guardsmen and inside. I found my few volumes on Darklore still where they were hidden, and some research provided me with a disguise spell. It was only effective at night—Ja-Lur's dim sunlight would evaporate it, and it required periodic repetition. But it got me past the patrols and back to the Maze.

Before I left the brothel, I had made another call to Valina. There was no answer.

From what I had seen of Valina's powers, she wasn't capable of such an attack as the one in the brothel. But if she had found the missing Phrase of the *Synulanom*, she might have used it to supplement her Darklore and so form such a spell. Given the power, the motivation to attack was certainly there.

But there was another possibility to be considered: Edward Knight. He probably had the power, but what was his motivation?

Once in the Maze I started some elementary detective work. If I'd done that three days before, it might have saved a life. Now I had the feeling it would cost more lives before I was through.

I dropped the disguise spell at first, as there were no Guard patrols in the Maze at nighttime. After a few hours, however, I spotted someone following me. I spoke the spell and left him watching a tavern while I walked out in front of him to continue my search. It didn't take very long. I made a few threats, bruised my knuckles once, and soon had a trail that led me to a hidden chamber in the basement of a gambling house. In the chamber was a straw-tick mattress that stank of offal, and crouched on the mattress was Ratbag, and he stank of fear.

I dissolved my disguise and entered, closed the door, and put my back against it.

"Kamus, I had to run. That hooded man, the Darklander —he's after me, I know it. I saw him kill Gallian without a touch, just words that made the blood burst from his pores." Ratbag was shivering convulsively. His skin looked even more jaundiced than usual in the glow of the single oil lamp.

"Calm down," I said. "If a Darklander wanted you dead, you'd be dead by now. You help me and I'll protect you."

"Why should I trust you?" he whined. "You're a Darklander too, they say."

"But that's exactly why you should trust me, Ratbag. Who better to keep you safe from Darkness? Listen to me. What do you know about the Kakush?"

"Not to talk about them, that's what I know. They got eyes and ears everywhere. They own the Maze, and a good deal of the city too. Cross them and you wake up dead."

"Do you work for them?"

"Everybody works for them, Kamus, whether they know it or not. Out of ten things you buy in a day, eight of them brings money to the Brothers Below."

"Was Gallian of Port Rizh one of them?"

"I think so," he said, his teeth chattering.

"Do you know where and when they meet?"

"Kamus, *please* . . . I'd sooner take my chances with Darklanders than the Kakush . . ."

I put my hand under his pointed wet chin and lifted him to his feet. "that's just what you're doing. Ratbag, I've no time for your paranoia. *Do you know where and when they meet?*"

His shivering had increased to the proportions of a seizure, but he managed to say, "I delivered a message there once . . ."

"Very good." I changed the subject before he lapsed into catatonia. "Now, about this Darklander . . ."

"He—he was slight-built, that's all I can say. I couldn't see his face, just his hand when he spelled. A small, pale hand, like a child's."

A child's . . . "Did he wear rings?"

"No, not a one."

"Did you notice anything else? Any glimpse of his face, or hair?"

"Hair—I did see a curl of hair under the hood. Gray, it was. He must've been a little old man."

"No doubt," I said. "Now, there just one more thing you can do for me, Ratbag. Take me to the Kakush."

It took some time and the promise of a handful of jewels to persuade him. He followed me back to the tavern, where the lad who had been tailing me—a thin Maze urchin—was still waiting for me to exit. I watched him, judged his price, then came up behind him and caught him by the neck, slapping a few dechels into his palm.

"Who's paying you to follow me?" I asked him.

"Two men, sir, if it's pleasin'. A giant in skins and a—"

"Good enough. You carry a message to the smaller of the two. Tell him to stop wasting time this way and meet with me at the Rusty Sword Tavern right away. Got that?"

He got it. Off he scurried, sniffling.

Ratbag looked at me. "I've never seen you like this, Kamus. You're all orders and threats. What's happened?"

I didn't answer him. I started for the Rusty Sword.

Valina's search for Kaan was somehow tied up with the Kakush, and she had been wandering around the Maze in hood and cloak, attacking possible members. Her temper wasn't serving her well; spelling the blood out of people isn't the best way to keep a low profile. I thought I knew why she was looking for the Brothers Below. If I was right, and I survived, I might be one step closer to revenging Sanris's death.

We waited in a secluded booth for them. The Rusty Sword was a much dingier place than the Blue Lotus. It boasted one bored dancing wench, and most of the customers were under the tables. I spent my time reassuring Ratbag, and getting him just drunk enough to be brave.

At last Danian and Ult joined us. Ult squeezed his bulk between bench and table and aimed a dirk-sized finger at me, saying, "I've got protection against your spells now." He was wearing a necklage of kallith bulbs, the smell of which was supposed to repel Darklanders. It was one superstition which worked; kallith bulbs repel anything with a nose, except barbarians.

"Keep him quiet," I told Danian, "and listen. I know you're really Daniel Tolon of Earth. I know you're a Unity security agent, and that you came to Ja-Lur with Kaan

Ta'Wyys to find Edward Knight. I know you're looking for Valina now in hopes she can put you back on Knight's trail. Well, I'm looking for her, too. She's directly or indirectly responsible for the death of a friend. I propose we join forces."

"Why should I trust you?" he asked.

"Because it's easier than playing stupid games of tag in the Maze. I'll admit I wasn't entirely honest with you when we first met, by not admitting I knew Valina. But you weren't honest in your reasons for wanting her. These games get us nowhere. I'll find her, with or without your help. What's it to be?"

Ult, for once, kept his mouth shut as Daniel Tolon considered. "What's your plan?" he asked.

"Are you with me?"

"We are."

"We're going to invade the inner sanctum of the Kakush," I told them.

* * *

Torchlight glimmered in rainbows from stagnant, greasy puddles. The jagged skyline of the Maze rose against the golden lights of downtown Mariyad to the east and the harsh white light of the Spaceport to the west. Ratbag led us down an alley and into a narrow passageway between two buildings. He stopped at a boarded door, counted off paces and knelt to hook his fingers under a large flagstone in the center of the passageway, leprous in the light of Bellus and Jaspara, Ja-Lur's two moons. I looked up at the full moons, noting that they were slightly closer together than seemed right. Their orbits would grow closer still, until, less than two months from now, Jaspara would eclipse Bellus—on Shadownight.

Ratbag pulled the flagstone up, revealing a dark hole. Then he looked at me. "Don't make me go down there with you, Kamus," he pleaded. He was in bad shape. Terror was part of his life, but he had had a lot lately, even by Maze standards. "All right," I said. I paid him the jewels he'd earned and he ran like a spider. "Good luck, Kamus," came floating back on the thick night air.

"You're not worried about betrayal?" Ult asked.

"You have betrayal on the brain. As long as his pouch jingles, Ratbag's trustworthy."

"I hope so," Tolon said.

We started down. We descended by means of niches carved in the rock wall. I had no way to measure the distance; the pivoting flagstone had closed above us, leaving us in total darkness. But it must have been at least a hundred meters before my sandals touched bottom.

Once down, I dared not make any kind of light. Ult led us, using his barbarian's sense of smell and hearing. We followed a twisting corridor for quite some time without encountering branches or forks. Then at last we came to another pivoting section of stone, this one at the end of the corridor. Ult pushed it open a crack, and light made us blink. When our eyes were adjusted, we went through the revolving door.

We were in another corridor, large, with an arched ceiling. The light came from oil lamps set at intervals. A steady breeze kept the air in motion. We followed the breeze. There were doors set in the walls, most of which were locked; the few that weren't showed only sparsely furnished living quarters. It was like being in an underground hotel. We saw no one.

I had disguised Tolon and myself with a spell when we entered the light corridor. There wasn't much I could do for Ult—the spell only changed features and gait, and did nothing for size. He wouldn't have stood for a spell being put on him, anyway. Tolon and I looked like typical Maze cutpurses, a relatively common sight in this underworld.

We came to a fork in the corridor, and Ult stopped. "We're out of the Maze by now," he whispered. "We must be under downtown Mariyad—I'd say the Marketplace, or the Garrison."

"And not a sign of a soul," Tolon said. "A place this size wouldn't be completely deserted."

"Listen!" Ult said sharply. Faintly, behind us, was the sound of several sets of footsteps.

The lamps in the left-hand fork had been doused for some reason, so we chose the right-hand. "Let's find an empty room and wait for them to pass," I said, trying doors, all of which were locked.

"Can't you cover us with some sort of invisibility spell?" Tolon asked.

I shook my head. "It would take too long, even if I got it

right." I tried another door, which opened. I looked in cautiously—it appeared to be a large auditorium, with other doors at the far end. "In here!" They followed me, and I shut the door.

That was a mistake. The footsteps grew louder, until they were right outside the door, and then stooped. We drew swords as we hurried toward the other doors. They were flung open when we were halfway there, and in rushed at least twenty swordsmen, while behind us entered ten more.

"It appears that we were herded into a trap," Tolon said.

I nodded. I had anticipated as much, the Kakush probably had this procedure down pat. But they would not expect a small-time Maze beggar to use Darklore. I had a spell rehearsed for just this occasion. As the swordsmen closed on us, I opened my mouth to shout it—and something, probably a dagger thrown hilt-first, hit me at the base of the skull. I saw the floor coming my way, but didn't feel it hit.

* * *

Again my head felt like ice giants were playing handball with it. Again there were faces hovering over me as I opened my eyes; quite a few of them, this time. Faces and knives... I was surrounded by men who held blades next to my body.

I recognized many of them as influential and respected businessmen and officeholders, and others I had seen in the Maze, dressed in filthy rags. The Kakush, present in all its subterranean glory.

And then one more face moved before my eyes: a flat, cold face with snake eyes and black hair. Captain Thoras, commander of the Mariyad Garrison. The Kakush ran Mariyad, no doubt about it.

Thoras bared his teeth in his version of a smile. "Kamus, you're as much a half-wit as a half-breed." He recognized me, of course; my disguise spell had vanished when I was knocked out.

I looked about me—I was strapped to a cot in a small chamber. The crowd kept me from seeing if Tolon and Ult were there too. There was no gag to prevent me from speaking Language—just those thirty-odd knives, all an inch from my skin.

"So tell me," Thoras continued, sitting on the edge of the bunk and tickling my nose with a dagger, "to what do we owe this visit?"

"You should know," I said. "That fragment of Darklore is yours, isn't it?"

He leaned back, eyes wide. Murmurs of surprise came from the assembly. "How did you know that?" Thoras asked.

"It makes sense," I said. "You're an avid collector of strange and esoteric things. Furthermore, it occurred to me when you sentenced me that you knew a lot about Darklanders. Those two interests made you the natural one to buy such a curiosity if it was offered to you."

He nodded. "I'm impressed. Yes, I acquired the parchment from a Southern trader some months ago. On the chance that it was something important, I donated it to the Kakush. We hoped that we would somehow, some day be able to translate it."

"Why didn't you tell me about it when you had me?" I asked. "I could have told you if it was more than just someone's grocery list."

Most of them laughed at that. "Hand a possibly-dangerous spell to a Darklander?" Thoras said. "That stupid we're not, Kamus. No, we've managed to obtain some Darklore books, and we have the parchment partially translated. It is a spell, isn't it?

I sighed and nodded. "It's part of an Elder grimoire called the *Synulanom*. But even if you translate it, Thoras, what good is it to you? You need someone of the Blood to get results from it."

"It's a bargaining point. You're the second Darklander it's lured here. Someone wants it badly, and might be willing to pay quite a bit for something big like this."

So they had managed to catch Valina . . . either that, or someone entirely new had entered the picture. I hoped not. "You've got hold of something big," I told Thoras. "Too big. If you advertise possession of the *Synulanom*, you'll attract the attention of someone who wants it badly, sure enough. But he doesn't have to bargain. What he wants, he takes."

That put a chill on the party. People looked at each other in apprehension. "The Darklord," someone murmured.

"That's it," I agreed. It was the best way to convince them what a sandcat they had by the tail. It made an impression, judging by the worried whispers now circulating.

"Quiet!" Thoras bellowed. "You all knew tampering with Darkness was risky!" He turned to me again. "If it's the

Darklord who wants this *Synulanom*, then so be it. He's not a god, and we'll deal with him if we have to. And we can. You're looking at the Kakush: the real rulers of Mariyad, and all Adelan. We can resist any pressure he puts on us."

"Enough of this," someone else said—I recognized him as Oreus Bodag, Chief Adjutant to the prime minister. "We have nothing to gain from bragging, Thoras. Dispose of him, and let's get on with the translation."

Thoras grudgingly agreed to this, and fitted me with another bronze mouthclamp and manacles. Then he led me through the crowd and down a series of corridors. At last we came through another revolving wall section and into a chamber that looked vaguely familiar. After a moment, I knew why: it was similar to the cell chamber I had been in before as Thoras's guest. We were in the Garrison Dungeon, on the bottom level. I realized that the Mazelords were using the cells for their own purposes.

As he pushed me into an empty cell, I caught a glimpse of Valina, also gagged, and Daniel Tolon, in separate cells. Thoras slammed the door shut.

"This time, Kamus," he said, "I promise you'll die at dawn. Slowly."

After he had gone, Tolon called my name. "Ult fought his way free and escaped," he said. "Do you want to know how they caught us?" He sounded disgusted. "They smelled that damned kallith bulb necklace he was wearing. The superstitious idiot.

"I suppose you're wondering why he and I are working together. You know that Knight sentenced me to one of his galleys on the Eastern Ocean. Ult was my oar-partner. We led a slaves' revolt and took over the galley, during which I saved his life. We sailed north, and on an island we found an ancient shipwreck and a chest full of jewels. The rest of the slaves are now living high in other countries, but Ult insisted on helping me find Kaan. He's as faithful as a hound. And about as intelligent."

He sighed. "Kaan's probably long dead by now. I don't know why he insisted on trying to stop Knight himself, instead of telling the Unity. I didn't even know what he intended until after planetfall." He laughed shortly. "I thought it was a vacation."

I could see Valina through the grids in the cell doors. I

was grateful for her mouthclamp, considering the glare she sent my way. She was obviously blaming me for this, which was no surprise, as she had been blaming me for everything so far. I watched her, wondering if she was the one who had attacked me and killed Sanris. Had she gained access to the *Synulanom* just long enough to send that spell my way? It didn't look like I was going to find out.

I examined my cell, but there was nothing that suggested an escape plan. It seemed I could only wait for morning and death. But I hadn't entirely given up hope. I had known Thoras for some time; he was as fond of torture as a cat. He would have to come back and taunt me some more.

He did. After a few hours he returned to my cell, carrying a large, brittle scroll. I stared at it as he unrolled it and held it up, grinning. It had to be the fragment of the *Synulanom*. One end was frayed, as though a piece had been torn off. In one corner was drawn in faded ink a stylized grinning face, with one horn rising from the left temple; the sigil of Mondrogan the Clever. He had no doubt affixed it when he had hidden the scroll.

In the doorway leading to the stairwell, a shadow moved. I kept my eyes on the scroll, which Thoras rolled up again.

"It's translated," Thoras said. "Except for one key Phrase, it's complete—and full of spells that could make some Darklander ruler over all the Northern countries, and grant power beyond compare. I just wanted you to rest assured, Kamus, that we'll put it to good use."

The shadow in the doorway moved into the torchlight and became Ult, with a dagger in his hand. He took two long steps and was behind Thoras. I looked away. Thoras quit talking; a second mouth across the throat doesn't make anyone more talkative.

Ult!" Tolon cried.

A second shadow, scarcely as tall as Ult's waist, turned out to be Ratbag. He deftly picked the locks of our cells and then picked my mouthclamp and manacles, chattering an explanation as he did so. "It was Ult's idea," he said, his eyes darting everywhere for more of the Brothers Below. "He found me and told me what had happened. He made me—I mean, I volunteered to help. I told him that the Garrison was over the Kakush underworld. We picked a fight with some guards—" he had to gulp and close his eyes at this memory—"and got ourselves thrown in the Dungeon."

I looked at him closely. His pupils were pinpoints, and his skin was flushed. He was packed with dream crystals. It had been a hard night for Ratbag.

"Ult," I said, as I picked up the *Synulanom*, "I've underestimated you."

"I didn't do it for you," he growled as he tore the lock off Tolon's cell.

Ratbag opened Valina's cell and saw her dark cloak and hood. He let out a squeal like steam escaping and hid behind me. I looked at Valina. "We'll have to work together to get out of here," I told her. "Agreed?"

She nodded, slowly.

"Pick her locks, Ratbag. She won't hurt you."

"What do we do now?" Tolon asked.

"Now we get out of Mariyad," I said. "Our lives won't be worth a dechel if we don't."

"We still don't know where to look for Knight and Kaan," Valina said.

"True. But we have this," I said, holding up the *Synulanom*. "And I think it's going to be our ticket to them."

6

With my abilities backing up Valina's, we had no problems sneaking out through the Garrison and across town to the balloon-boat port. Ratbag did not go with us. He hadn't been seen aiding us, he said, and he wanted to keep it that way. I couldn't blame him.

Valina did not speak to me any more than was necessary during our escape, which suited me. I still wasn't at all sure how to react to her presence. She was my prime suspect for the murder of Sanris, but she was also my client. I wished I had had a chance while in the underground to ask how long she had been locked up with metal around her mouth; that would have helped. If she had been caught by the Kakush before the attack on Sanris and me, she would have an alibi. I could ask her, of course, but she would be smart enough to lie if it wasn't true.

As the amber sun rose, we caught a southwest-bound balloon-boat. My plan was to stop close to the ruins of Vassoon, which was now a thriving tourist attraction, and look for clues. I would follow any I found, wherever I had to, to find out who killed Sanris. And I would keep a close eye on Valina while I did so.

The balloon-boat lines of Mariyad were the best in the Northern Nations. Each craft was supported by four huge, gas-filled pods of the balloon tree, and pulled by teams of twenty kragors, flying reptiles of a breed similar to but larger than those used by the Flying Guards. The boats were built of light, strong emsam wood, and carefully ballasted to provide stability even in high winds. They were capable of carrying over thirty passengers at once.

I stood at the stern, watching Mariyad and the coast fall away behind. The farmlands and patches of forest were still misty with morning fog. The purple sky looked like a deep, still lake, and it was easy to want to somehow fall upward into it, to lose myself in it. I wasn't happy with the way things had turned out. My best friend was dead, and I was in exile. Not the best foundation for a good reputation as a private eye. I hoped Milady would give Dash a good home.

Daniel Tolon came to stand beside me. He clipped the lifeline every passenger wears while on deck to the wooden railing, and contemplated the view.

"You're from Kadizhar . . . where is that?" he asked me.

"An island in the middle of the Inland Sea. It's a sleepy little place; the most exciting thing to happen there in the past thousand years was when Mondrogan the Clever, according to legend, fought a darkling there. They put up a statue to it."

Tolon nodded, his gaze introspective. "Darklings," he said, and shook his head. "I never thought I would encounter a world where magic worked." He looked at me. "You can really perform magic, can't you?"

"Not magic," I said. "Darklore. There's a difference."

"How does Darklore work?"

I hesitated, unsure how to verbalize things I knew instinctively. "Darkness—by which I mean much more than just the absence of light—is a realm, a cosmos, a universe, in which the ability to influence situations and outcome by will power and ritual is much greater than it is elsewhere. Those who lived there wanted something to unify those chaotic powers, and so they evolved the language of Darkness. It's an idiom of cantrips and rituals, and some names strong enough to conjure by, such as Jann-Togah, the Darklord's son."

"Could you conjure by the Darklord's name?"

"Not really, because no one knows it; 'the Darklord' is a title given to him by others."

"It seems to me that this world somehow exists tangentially in both universes," Tolon said. "Is this really the case?"

"Yes. According to legend, the Darklord and his kind first appeared during the first Shadownight, a thousand years ago. There was a long battle between Darkkind and Humanity. Humanity won some battles; they stole from the Darklord powerful spells, like the *Synulanom*, and talismans, like the Black Mask. Without them, the Darklord did not conquer, but was never really defeated. An uneasy truce has existed for centuries."

"And other worlds have been touched by this Dark cosmos," Tolon mused.

"Earth and Thanare seem to have been, though not as strongly as Ja-Lur. But they've had their Shadownights, or Halloweens, or whatever, when Darkness encroaches." I was silent, thinking of what Valina had said about this coming Shadownight being a bad one. Did it, I wondered, somehow have a connection with the discovery of the *Synulanom*, with Edward Knight coming to Ja-Lur?

Tolon said, "I've never looked upon good or evil as anything more than abstract concepts; I've always thought that it lay within a thinking being's power to choose one or the other. But now I have to tell you, Kamus, that I think this Darkness that is a part of you, and Edward Knight, and maybe Kaan as well, is evil." He turned and looked at the Nonulé Hills, a band of darker purple against the sky. "This is a strange world," he said. "Lovely, in a dreaming, bemused sort of way. I have the feeling it's very, very old."

I shrugged. "What world isn't?"

"Thanare, for one. It's a terraformed colony world. A hundred years ago it had a poisonous atmosphere and a decaying astroid belt that kept dropping meteors on it. Then the Unity made a paradise of it. You should see it. I don't know how anyone born there could ever want to leave."

The next line was obviously mine. "Kaan Ta'Wyys did."

Tolon sighed. "Yes. Yes, he did. I don't know why. I've been his closest friend in the Unity Service for seven years, and I've never known what motivates him. He hated being an agent, never talked about his reasons for being one. Yet he was a good one, better tham me—he's saved my life many times. But he had no pride in his work, no love for it." He was silent for awhile, then said, "He's absent without leave here. That's why I havent't reported what's happened . . . why I'm trying to find him myself. Once I get him off this world, maybe I can find a way to keep him from being court-martialed . . . I owe him that much." He looked at me. "Do you know what I mean?"

"Close enough. I owe some things myself. A friend of mine died because I took this case."

"I'm sorry to hear that."

"He was trying to get me safely out of Mariyad. His reasons weren't completely altruistic, I'm sure. He was a Guardsman, and crooked, though not as much as most. His commander—the one Ult killed—was a Mazelord, one of the Brothers Below, and my friend must have known it. You should have heard him trying to talk me onto a balloon-boat." I sighed. "He died trying."

"People do strange things for friendship," Tolon said.

I felt the outline of the scroll sewn into the lining of my trenchcloak. "They do, for a fact," I agreed. I untied my lifeline and started forward, but Tolon's voice stopped me.

"Kamus—I shouldn't be telling you this, but—even if we manage to find and defeat Knight, that won't be the end of this as far as the Unity is concerned."

I waited, but he said nothing more. "What do you mean?"

"I can't say any more; I'm still a Unity agent."

"Come on," I said, "I've had clearer warnings from oracles."

"I can give you a code word: Boreas."

"Is it a man?"

"Outwardly." He looked out over the rail, his light hair blown by the wind. "Don't ask me to say any more, Kamus. I could be wrong, and I must protect myself. I'm sorry. Paranoia is an occupational hazard in my line of work."

"Why did you say that much?" I asked.

"For friendship," he said softly.

I hesitated, then turned toward the cabin. I would go into this further with him later. Right then, quite honestly, I didn't feel up to it.

I found Valina the only one inside the cabin, asleep on a bunk. I watched her for a moment, then lay down on the next bunk, hands behind my head, staring at the ceiling. She claimed to be motivated by love, yet she was the coldest, hardest woman I'd ever met. If only I had some idea of what went on inside her. Of course, her coldness and hardness didn't mean she wasn't capable of love, any more than it would keep some poor fool like Kaan Ta'Wyys from loving her, if he did.

If he did . . .

Right about then she landed on my chest.

My lungs collapsed and the world went red. Through a roaring in my ears, I could hear Valina speaking Language, and knew I wouldn't live past the final Word. I kicked out at her with both legs, and it felt like my ankles were tied to my insides with a very short cord. But it kept her from completing the spell. I rolled over on top of her, trying to keep her occupied while I wrestled air back into my lungs. She wriggled out from underneath me and grabbed my trenchcloak, pulled it off my shoulders fast enough to spin me around on the floor. Somehow I got my legs in a straight line between my head and the floor and pushed; I half-leaped, half-collapsed on her. She had torn open the lining and found the fragment of the *Synulanom*. She was hissing, and her eyes looked like two flat blue stones. I slapped her, hard. It did no good. She started to toss another spell my way; I wrapped part of the cloak around her head and spoke first.

"Dulemeen ghoor, tas zule gen!"

It was a simple Sleep Spell; I hadn't time for anything fancy. But instead of putting her out, it put her in a trance—she stood relaxed, eyes open and empty. I went over the Words again, mentally. I had pronounced them right. Which meant that my spell had combined with . . . another.

Valina's motivation. It had been staring me in the face every time I saw her. Her eyes; the flat look that came and went. She was ensorcelled, under a geas, and had been since I first met her.

But I didn't have a chance to question her. Now that our fight was over, I could hear shouting from outside, on the deck. I looked out one of the windows; a bat-winged shape carrying a rider flicked past. I ran up the steps to the deck, and saw the sky filled with flying guards on kragors. Two of them had already landed on the wide forward deck, folding their wings and diving under the curve of the balloons, then breaking their fall at the last moment by flapping their wings. It was a dangerous and difficult maneuver. I saw Ult come charging around the corner of the cabin, brandishing his pigsticker. The wind from another landing knocked him sprawling. He almost went over the side. One of the kragors casually brought the knobbed end of its tail down on Ult's head, and the barbarian was out of the fight.

Passengers were running and screaming. The cold air from the kragors' wings buffeted us, and their hoarse croaking made it hard to think. Another kragor landed, and the wind flung an old merchant off the deck; he dropped with a thin scream toward the ground, a thousand meters below.

Valina had followed me to the deck. She stood behind me, watching everything impassively. I pulled my sword, and one of the kragors stretched out a sickle-shaped head split with gleaming teeth and snapped the blade with a bite.

"*Dammi gwil, sinald pai!*" I shouted. The spell worked this time; unfortunately, it worked on me and Tolon, who had just arrived from the rear deck. Our tunics and leggings stiffened until we could move only with great difficulty.

"Don't you know any other spells?" Tolon asked me.

There were four kragors and riders on deck, now. The flying guardsmen, small, incredibly strong men bred for their job, all wore black tunics. "No one moves!" one of them shouted. A sky sailor didn't listen—he tried to jump one of the guardsmen. The small man knocked him completely across the deck and over the side with a casual backhand blow. One of the guardsmen circling the balloon-boat put a crossbow bolt into the deck at another crewman's feet as a warning.

The guardsman spoke again, pointing at Valina, Tolon

and me. "You three—mount behind my men." Tolon and I did so, moving with dream-like slowness. Two guardsmen slung Ult's bound, unconscious body across one of the kragors' humps, and another fetched Valina from the cabin.

"Don't bother trying any more Darklore," he added. "As you can see, we're protected. Your spells will only backfire." I was glad that at least I had gotten the Words right this time.

We were strapped into the second seats of the saddles.

The kragors fell away from the deck, caught the cold air under their wings, and flew toward the west. The balloon-boat disappeared quickly behind us. We flew over forest that gave way to rough, uneven ground that rose toward the Nonulé Hills. Occasionally, below us, I could see flashes of deep, iridescent green, much brighter than the dull foliage; the flashes moved like large, quick amoebas. I don't know what they were; there's still a lot on my world I haven't seen. I also saw a rare water sloth in a small lake; a huge, furry island with teeth. It would have been a nice ride if I hadn't been so worried about my destination.

The guardsman I rode with said nothing. We had only one nasty moment, when Ult woke up and insisted on trying to kill his guardsman and himself in some sort of dramatic escape attempt. My captor circled in close, drawing a bead with his crossbow. I solved the problem by speaking the few Words that put the barbarian to sleep again. This was no time for heroics.

We flew for two days. We ate and slept under sword-point; our captors seemed to have no need for food or rest. We crossed the River Oehls. The hills grew rockier and more inaccessable, until eventually we were flying over a landscape that looked like it had been hacked with an axe. The hills were mountains now, with steep cliffs and narrow passes. We went through a final pass so narrow that the tips of the kragors' wings almost touched the walls. It opened into a cloud valley; we dropped through the gray mists, and I saw what had to be our destination: a gray, rocky castle in the center of the valley. It had towers and parapets of ancient design, and looked like it had been hastily occupied after centuries of disuse and ruin. Surrounding it at the base were crude huts and livestock pens, and a few hectares of tilled land.

We spiraled to a landing on the flat surface of the tallest

tower. It was less than ten meters across, with stairs leading down into the center. It was wet and slippery, scraping the bottom of the clouds, and strong gusts of wind blew from all directions. I was never happier to be taken inside an enemy fortress.

Within, the walls were hung with fabrics of muted tone, with occasional braziers that gave a smoky light. We passed several heavy, bolted doors. The guards led us down wide, sweeping stairways of marble and through several sparsely furnished chambers. We saw few servants.

Valina was still in her trance, but Ult had regained consciousness and was occupying most of the guards' attention. Eventually we were deposited in the most comfortable cell I'd seen during this case; a large room draped with tapestries and cured skins, and a window set in one stone wall. There was a thick rug, and soft, feather-stuffed couches and chairs. There was also a table with a meal set for four, which Ult promptly ate.

Tolon and I sat down to wait. "This is Knight's castle," he told me. "I recognized some of the servants. Congratulations to us; we made it."He snorted. "I wonder if Kaan's still alive. Not that it matters now, I guess."

"We still live!" Ult said with his mouth full.

"Oh, shut up," Tolon replied tiredly.

The door opened. A tall man with a red mane of hair entered. He was dressed in silver robes that made his pale skin look almost sickly. His face was serene, and his green eyes had that Darkland look in them. He wore no weapons. He nodded to each of us with a faint smile.

"Surely most of you recognize me?" he said softly.

"Knight," Tolon said, using the name like a curse.

Ult said nothing; he just picked up a hambone from the table. "Don't be foolish," he was warned. "I could turn that into a tricorn snake, and you'd be dead in a second." Ult dropped the bone hastily. The red-haired man inclined his head toward Valina's blank stare. "Even colder than usual, I see. You appear to be in a sort of thrall, my dear. *Pansa mach tas zule.*" Valina shuddered, and new depths suddenly appeared in her open eyes. She was even less happy to see him than Tolon and Ult were.

He turned toward me. "Kamus of Kadizhar, I presume. You are the one I want to talk to."

I stood up. "I've been wanting to talk to you, too."

"I knew it!" Ult said. "Dogs of the same leather stick together."

Ignoring that, the red-haired man said to me, "As Daniel said, my name is Edward Knight."

"You can make them believe that if you want," I told him, "but don't try to play it on me. You're Knight's acolyte, Kaan Ta'Wyys, and you can drop the disguise spell any time."

He looked at me in surprise, then threw back his head and laughed. He spoke three Words, and his face wavered like rippling water, to be replaced by thinner, sharper features, blue eyes, and pale green hair. Kaan stopped laughing and grinned at me.

"You *are* astute," he said.

"*Kaan!*" Valina was on her feet and in his arms in an instant, or tried to be. He did not respond to her embrace, except to pat her lightly on the shoulders once and then let his hands fall to his side. "You should have told me!" she said accusingly. "You defeated Knight! That means we've won. I've brought the *Synulanom*, and together we can rule all of the North, we can challenge the Darklord himself!"

"Ah yes, the *Synulanom*," Kaan said, turning toward me. "I believe the sword-wielding sleuth has it, am I correct?" He held out a hand. "It would be useless to resist, of course."

I ignored his hand. "You've kept close watch on her," I said.

"She had an important task," Kaan replied, "although she didn't know it." He made an impatient gesture with that outstretched hand, which I continued to ignore. I clasped my hands behind my back and started a slow stroll around the room.

"Find the Kakush, steal the *Synulanom* and return to Vassoon. That was the geas you laid on her, right?" I kept my eyes on Valina. Kaan did not. She looked from him to me. "Kaan?" she said, uncertainly.

Kaan folded his arms and smiled. "You fascinate me, Kamus, truly you do," he said. "How did you guess I had killed Knight and taken his place?"

"I didn't, until just before your men captured us. That was when I saw the spell you put on Valina. You had learned somehow that the Mazelords had the *Synulanom*, but you couldn't escape Knight with the missing Phrase to search for it. So you helped Valina to escape, gave her money, and commanded her to find the *Synulanom*."

I wasn't looking at Valina either, now. I hated to put her through this, but she would learn soon enough. The sooner she became Kaan's enemy, the better it might be for us.

"Maybe Knight caught on, or maybe an opportunity presented itself—I don't know," I continued. "But your battle with him took place the next day, and caused the destruction of Vassoon Keep."

"Enough of this," Kaan said. "The scroll, Kamus, if you please."

I stopped across the room from him and pulled it from the lining of my trenchcloak. "You underestimated the power of her love for you," I said to Kaan. "She searched for this under your geas, thinking it was her idea, intending to bring it back to liberate you from Knight's rule. But to increase her chances of finding you, she hired me."

Kaan snapped his fingers. "*G'nai!*" he shouted. The *Synulanom* leaped from my grasp and slapped into his hand. "You will regret forcing me to do that," he told me softly.

"When she hired me," I said, "the first thing I did was go to the Spaceport and check the entry records. I found Tolon's, but not yours. Which meant you'd entered under an alias. Why? Because you had no intentions of leaving. Tolon told me you were unhappy with the Unity Service. Valina told me you were linked with Knight because you had both studied Darklore together offplanet. You knew what he was doing, and you came to stop him.

"But only because you intended to take his place."

Kaan turned toward the door. "You're a witty and erudite conversationalist, Kamus, but I really have no more time for this."

I glanced at Valina. There was agony in her eyes, but she still did not quite believe. I gave it one last try. I told Kaan, "Valina wanted to find you before the Darkness corrupted you; not everyone of the Blood can handle it. You couldn't; you had been corrupted years before. You used her as a tool to find the *Synulanom*. And now she knows it."

"*Kaan!*" This time it was a cry of pain. She rushed toward him again; I wasn't sure whether she meant to embrace or attack him this time. The move wasn't completed; Kaan paralyzed her with a Phrase, then turned to me.

He chuckled. "Very good, Kamus. Excellent, in spots. You would have made a good detective, I think. Pity . . ."

"Kaan." Tolon stood up. "You're saying he's right?"

"For the most part, Daniel. I was bored with the Service, with risking my life for low pay. I'd helped depose enough tyrants on various worlds to wonder what being one might be like. Now I'm on the verge of finding out, and no one will depose me, I guarantee you that. The Darklord would never ask the Unity for help, and he can't stand alone against a unified North. I will lead my empire against him when Shadownight comes, when Darkness and chaos flood all of Ja-Lur. I will turn his own powers against him."

The pain in Tolon's face was as great as Valina's. He took a single step toward Kaan.

"Now, don't make me paralyze you, too," Kaan warned. "You'll all be my guests for a short while. I might need some experimental subjects to test various aspects of the *Synulanom*, and servants are hard to find out here." He turned toward the doorway. "If you'll excuse me, I have a date with destiny."

"One last thing," I said. He raised an eyebrow at me. "I still don't know if it was you or Valina who killed my friend Sanris of Taleiday. It doesn't matter. If she did it, it was while she was spellbound by you, so I hold you responsible."

Kaan looked puzzled. "Whatever are you talking about?"

"You attacked me two nights ago in a Mariyad brothel with some sort of fancy brimstone spell, to scare me off the case. Don't try to deny it."

"I'm afraid I'll have to. You were wrong on some parts of your deductions, Kamus; you're a bit too eager to make up facts when you don't have enough evidence. Knight destroyed Vassoon to cover his tracks, not in battle with me; I didn't know enough to challenge him safely then. In fact, our battle took place only two nights ago."

"Wait a minute. Are you saying you were fighting a Dark duel with Knight when Sanris and I were attacked?"

"It certainly appears that way."

"I don't believe it," I said.

Kaan shrugged. "Suit yourself. But think it through, Kamus: Why should I try to scare you off the case? From what I could tell by watching Valina, you were already off the case—in fact, you made a considerable point of having never taken it. If you hadn't seemed like such a bungler—though I admit you have more talent than I thought—I would have wanted you *on* the case. I *wanted* Valina to find me." He smiled then and left.

I spoke a spell to release Valina from her paralysis. She collapsed into one of the chairs, sobbing. The room was very quiet. Tolon sat looking at his hands, and Ult watched him in concern. I had nothing to say to any of them.

Kaan's alibi made perfect sense. There was no reason for him to have been behind the attack in the brothel. Which meant that I was going to die without knowing who had killed Sanris.

7

I stood at the window and stared at the ground below. The clouds filtered the already-dim sunlight, making it always evening in the valley. I could see a few peasants' fires, like orange dots. The only way out of this chamber was through the window, and I didn't know any spells that would grow wings on me. Not that it made any difference.

Even if we did escape from Kaan's castle, where did that leave us? In a mountain wilderness, hundreds of kilometers from the nearest city. And very soon Kaan would begin his reading of the *Synulanom*, which would change the world, and not for the better.

A flying guard passed by the window. He had been circling the tower at this level for the past few minutes, evidently under orders to keep an eye on the window. Kaan was taking no chances. We were going to die here; it was that simple. There was no way out.

That was the way I had felt in Mariyad, and it had taken the death of a friend to snap me out of it. I couldn't let myself sink into hopelessness again. Ult's philosophy, simplistic as it was, was right. I looked at him, then out the window at the passing guard on his kragor.

"There's a way out," I said. The only problem was, it was certain suicide.

"What did you say?" Tolon asked.

"I said there's a way out of here, just maybe. I'm going to try it. If it works, I'll have us out of this room. If it doesn't, I'll be dead, which might not be such a bad idea either."

"What are you talking about?" Ult demanded.

I told him.

"You're insane," Tolon said.

"Granted," I said, "but I'm going to try it. I'll need your help, Valina."

She did not answer. She sat on a corner of the couch, hugging herself, rocking slightly back and forth. I crossed the room and pulled her to her feet. "Remember me, Valina? I'm the person you love to hate. Have you forgotten how much fun it was?" Then I slapped her. She drew back from me, and her blank eyes filled first with shock, then anger. "You—"

"That's better. Show a little life. After all, it's only the end of love, not the end of the world."

"You have no right to—"

"I have every right to. I'm about to risk my neck for you, so show some interest." Then I led her to the window. The flying guard passed by again.

"Let me get this straight," Tolon said. "Ult is going to throw you out the window and you're going to try to land on the kragor?"

"It's impossible," Ult said. "He's going too fast. If you managed to do it, the guard could still rip you in half. Those little men are strong."

"Under normal circumstances, yes. Now, here's my plan: when he comes around again, Valina will recite a spell to slow down the reaction times of both the kragor and the guard. When he comes around after that, Ult will give me a leg out the window and I'll jump him. If I'm lucky, I'll take him by surprise."

Valina nodded, slowly. "It might work . . ."

"It has to work. You can't get his attention long enough to enthrall him, but you should be able to slow him down. Get ready; he'll be coming by again soon."

The flying guard passed the window again, and Valina started chanting. We waited. I was posed across the room, and Ult stood by the window, hands formed in a stirrup. Tolon watched from the other side.

"Here he comes!" he said. "Ready . . . now!"

I ran, leaped, put one foot in Ult's hands and felt him launch me, like a stone from a catapult, out the window. The ground below blurred past. I did a mid-air flip and came down, feet first, into the second seat of the saddle just as the small man started to turn slowly toward me. The sudden weight caused the kragor to squawk and drop several meters, which didn't help his confusion. I pulled his dagger from its sheath, had it tickling his ribs and my arm around his neck by the time his eyes got wide.

We were parallel to a balcony. "Land your beast there," I told him, pointing. I spoke slowly so that he could understand me; to him, the rest of the world was accelerated. He had no time to think about a counterattack; the kragor was down before he fully realized what had happened. I put him out with the pommel of his dagger then. I was taking no chances; he could have torn off my arm and beaten me to death with it. I shooed the kragor back into the sky with its unconscious cargo. The saddlebelt would keep him safe. I wished I had the time for a reaction of fear and nausea to what I had just been through as I ran back down the corridor to the door. In a moment, Valina, Tolon, and Ult were free.

Ult gripped my shoulder like a tree grips the soil. "That was a brave gamble, Darklander. I'm impressed."

"Thanks." I pried his fingers loose. "Do you mind? I plan on using this arm."

"How do we find him?" Tolon asked.

"I don't know," I admitted. "But we'd better hurry, before—" Then I stopped, and stared at Valina. She stared back. "Yes, I feel it too, she said.

There was no way to describe it: a soundless, vibrationless tension that charged our minds. Kaan was beginning his recital of the *Synulanom,* and Valina and I could feel it in our blood, by our Blood.

"We can find him now," I told Tolon. Valina and I started running, pulled like iron toward a lodestone. Tolon and Ult followed, down those ancient corridors. We didn't meet any servants or guards; they had probably all taken a holiday while their master became ruler of the North. The feeling grew stronger as we approached the center of the castle. I ran until the walls looked red instead of gray. If Kaan finished speaking the spell of conquest, there would be no reversing it. I could hear the Words echoing now.

We rounded a corner. Ahead of us was a barred door. Tolon passed me, and suddenly the floor beneath him opened up—a pivoting stone, like the one that led to the Mariyad underground. His cry echoed for a moment before the stone slapped back into place. I was going too fast to stop, so I jumped it. Ult stopped by bracing his arms against the corridor walls and used his body to stop Valina. "Daniel!" he shouted, pounding at the floor with his fists. The trapdoor would not open. "Daniel!"

"There's no time, Ult!" I shouted. "Break down this door before Kaan finishes the spell!"

Ult left the trapdoor and hurled himself at the wood. The latch held, but the hinges splintered, and we tumbled inside.

We were in a large chamber, filled with statues of Darklings, altars and burning incense holders. Kaan stood at an altar near the far wall, in front of a door. The *Synulanom* was before him, illuminated by a single candle, and I could see that it had been joined with another piece of parchment. It had been made whole; the missing Phrase had been added.

He saw us, and his expression would have frightened a darkling. It didn't frighten Ult; the barbarian ran toward him, bare hands outstretched. Kaan kept chanting, his voice filling the room with pounding, echoing Words. He gestured without losing a syllable, and a whirling cloud of amber smoke appeared, condensing into a scorpion three meters long. Ult tried to stop, slipped on a rug and sailed beneath the monster on his back. It struck at him with its stinger and missed. Ult leaped to his feet and began throwing statues at it, which bounced off its exoskeleton.

I threw the dagger at Kaan—it curved around him and hit the floor behind him. "Valina!" I shouted. "Do something!"

She stared at Kaan. "I—can't . . ." she whispered. Her love had shackled her better than any spell could.

"Great," I said, as Kaan turned toward me.

He didn't have to stop reciting. The Words of the *Synulanom* had charged him with enough power to cast spells at me by gestures alone. But he had to keep glancing at the parchment; the more powerful a spell, the harder it is to remember and pronounce, and the more effort it takes. His divided attention was the only thing that kept me alive. I shouted the most powerful spells I was capable of unassisted, and his voice drowned them. The Phrases were the only sound in the universe:

"DAMATH UMAL RANIBAR PAI K'CHEN, SHILYEAH CTHUL TAND MACH SORBAEN . . ."

I could *see* the spells he cast—the air was so charged with force and so full of incense smoke that the spells were visible as brilliant bolts and waves streaming from his hands. That helped me avoid them, but not for long. He hurled a latticework of green, glowing bands that wrapped around me, pinning my arms. He was nearing the final Phrase now; I could feel it. The room crackled with energy as Kaan lifted his hand to hurl the bolt that would finish me. His fingers glowed crimson, and I tried one last trick. As he looked again at the scroll I chanted the simple disguise spell both he and I had used before. Kaan looked up again, saw the face I had taken—and faltered. The thunder of his recital faded. He had lost the cadence!

In that single moment of weakness, before he could recover and before I could press my hopeless advantage, the pulsing energy in the room combined in a blinding rainbow flash, and vanished. Suddenly everything was quiet, and the smell of ozone mingled with incense was all that was left of the battle. Kaan stood with arms outstretched, mouth open and eyes empty. He swayed and then collapsed on the altar, knocking over the burning candle. It rolled across the surface until it hit the scroll. There was a thin crackling as the dry parchment began to smolder.

The flying guard's dagger was now planted between Kaan's shoulder blades. I looked beyond it, at Daniel Tolon framed in the open door behind the altar.

Valina began to sob quietly as the small fire flared and then burned out.

Tolon kept his eyes on the dagger. "There were passages under the floor," he said. "Stairs. I followed the sound of the fighting." He looked at me. "You have my face," he said in dull wonderment.

I spoke the Words that dissolved the disguise spell, barely able to stand; my defenses had taken a lot out of me.

Then I heard a step behind me and turned. There stood Ult, bloody, disheveled, and grinning. He held the huge, knob-shaped end of the scorpion's tail in one hand, the stinger still dripping. "I think I'll make a helmet out of it," he said proudly.

I sighed and shook my head. "It'll turn to dust when sunlight hits it," I told him. "It's made of Darkness." Ult dropped it quickly and kicked it away from him.

I held my fingers against the vein in Kaan's neck, just to be sure. He was dead. I wondered if it had been a moment of concern that had made him hesitate when he saw his former partner standing before him, or only surprise.

"I knew who I was killing, Kamus," Tolon said pleadingly.

Valina was still crying for something that had never been. I looked at the body of Kaan Ta'Wyys, lying in the ashes of the *Synulanom*.

"I wonder if you did," I said to Tolon.

* * *

I went back to Mariyad. I knew it wasn't a bright move, but I had my reasons.

I had taken Kaan Ta'Wyys's body from his citadel and buried it the following day, saying Words over it to insure a peaceful rest; though I doubted if they would have any effect. Still, it never hurts to try.

When I re-entered his chamber a final time, I saw that even the ashes of the *Synulanom* had vanished; some might say it was as though the spell had never existed. I would never be able to look at it that way, however.

We had no trouble leaving the deserted citadel. I put a docility spell on four kragors and they carried us northeast to Kedronj; from there we caught a balloon-boat, and arrived in Mariyad two days later.

I said good-bye to Daniel Tolon at the Spaceport. He had decided to report that Kaan Ta'Wyys had died in an attempt to prevent Edward Knight's gambit to overthrow the Northern Nations. I suppose it made him feel better.

Before he left, I asked him about his cryptic warning concerning the man named Boreas.

"You said the Unity has plans for Ja-Lur," I reminded him. "What kind of plans?"

After a long moment he said, "The Unity is a government, Kamus, and, like most governments, it is not wholly benevolent. Have you heard of Devil's Asteroid?"

"In passing."

"The purge of the Vehn Dom system? The support of the dictatorship on Murphy's Planet?"

I hadn't. He nodded glumly. "There could be worse things than Darkness, Kamus," was all he would say. Then he entered the lift tube, leaving me to wonder what new problem might be around the corner.

Ult was going west, as there was a rumor of war among the Plains tribes and fighters might be needed. He shook my hand in farewell, almost taking some of my fingers with him. By jumping out of a window onto a flying kragor I had earned his respect and friendship. That and a major miracle would put my life back the way it was before he ruined my dinner at the Blue Lotus.

As for Valina . . .

"I'm going north," she told me. "The cold and the snow may be a kind of cure for the pain. And the further I get from the Darkland, perhaps the less I'll feel like a Darklander. I hope so."

I said I hoped so too, for her sake, although I had the feeling it wouldn't take her too long to recover. Valina struck me as a woman who landed easily on her feet after any disaster.

"You do believe that I had nothing to do with your friend's death?" she asked me.

"That's the only part of this case that's unsolved," I admitted. "But I have a theory that I don't like."

"And it is?"

"Now that Kaan and Knight are dead, there's only one other I know of who has the power to cast such a spell."

"The Darklord," Valina breathed. "But that's absurd! Why would he want to scare you off the case?"

"He wouldn't. But Kaan's reading the *Synulanom* was a good reason to keep me on the case, and what better way to keep me on than to give me a revenge motive?"

"But if he were going to interfere, why didn't he simply kill Kaan?"

"Who knows the Darklord's motives? Like I said, it's only a theory. It'll need a lot of proof, which I'm not likely to find."

She nodded. "Take care of yourself, Kamus," she said. "Things are happening. I think we are already into the eve of Shadownight."

I watched her balloon-boat leave, then used my disguise spell to go to Pallas the Moneyholder's and pick up my fee. I found Dash still at Milady's, and collected a few other things that I'd need for my trip west.

The last thing I did was go to the graveyard, where I paid my respects to a slab with Sanris' bones buried beneath it.

I still intended to avenge my friend, but it would have to wait a while now. I needed to make a new life before I could think about devoting it to revenge. I was fairly sure that Sanris would think it a stupid way to spend one's time, seeking absolution from a pile of bones. I half thought so myself. But even if Sanris' life hadn't had any particular meaning beyond wenching and wassail, his death still deserved meaning. Or at least revenge.

I was the only private eye on the planet, and I couldn't let anyone cross me, not even the Darklord. Valina had said that Darkness can corrupt, no matter how powerful the Darklander, and Daniel Tolon had spoken of its intrinsic evil. I had given a lot of thought to that over the years. My job was more than just a job—it was my way of keeping Darkness at bay. A private eye should have a basic moral code.

I suddenly realized that the night was almost gone. I had stood brooding too long over Sanris's grave; the sun was rising. The balloon-boat port was halfway across Mariyad, and my disguise would disappear in sunlight. I ran for the street, pulling my hood up. There wasn't a carriage in sight. The first faint rays of the sun touched me, and I felt the disguise spell evaporate. To make matters worse, a trio of guardsmen came around the corner just then and saw me.

Before I could shout a spell and run, they recognized me. One of them nodded curtly. Another, a young private I had seen at the Blue Lotus, said pleasantly, "Hello, Kamus, how's business?" Then they passed me and continued down the street.

I stood staring. Surely every guardsman knew I was wanted by now. I started walking, slowly. I saw other guardsmen; none of them tried to arrest or attack me. I went to my office. Sanris had told me it had been ransacked by the Guard. If so, there was no sign of it now. This was no trick of the Guard's, I was sure; they weren't subtle enough for that. Either I was going crazy, or—

—that major miracle had happened.

It had. I visited my old haunts, the Blue Lotus, the Maze, over the next few days. Ratbag had no memory of helping me invade the stronghold of the Kakush. Beggars and businessmen whom I remembered as being Mazelords brushed past me without a sign of recognition. I even visited the Garrison; Thoras was still dead, but evidently I had nothing to do with it. Somehow, all knowledge of my participation in the events of the past few days had been erased. My business in Mariyad was as healthy as ever, for what that was worth.

It was the proof I needed. Only the Darklord could have spelled the memory out of so many people. He had made it safe for me to stay in Mariyad, and I had no idea why.

Evidently, he had some sort of plan. But I had plans too, and they didn't include being part of his plans. The Darklord had killed Sanris, casually, and ripped my life apart, and now, just as casually, he had put it back together again. I couldn't let him continue manipulating me—but how was I going to stop him?

I had no idea. But one thing was certain: I couldn't be his pawn. I had to have free will, to make my own decisions, to solve cases on my own. A private eye can't be a puppet. It's bad for business.

Some day, I would have to explain that to the Darklord.

PART TWO

The Maltese Vulcan

I

It was the ugliest creature I had ever seen. It was also the richest.

It was also annoyed with me. "I am not used to waiting," it said—or rather, the intercom over my head said. I was sitting on a folding seat in a clear oval bubble. The bubble floated in a tankful of murky water, as did the creature, whose name was Stam. Stam looked like a large, brownish-yellow barbell with two half-flaccid sacs, the smaller containing brain and sensory organs, the larger containing everything else. Three tentacles radiated from the head sac, with a sphincter mouth centered at their base. One tentacle had a prehensile tip and suckers, one was bifurcated to provide an opposable grip, and one had a serrated chitinous claw like a lobster's chela on its end. The eyes were at the ends of a Y-shaped stalk which sprouted above the tentacles.

Stam was the high priest of a religion about which I knew nothing save that its churchly coffers were bulging with money. That was enough to bring me to the Mariyad spaceport, and to this murky tank in which I now floated.

The murky tank was Stam's private quarters aboard the *Yith'il*, a ship that looked like a fishbowl with tachyonic thrusters. It was compartmented by milky crystal walls, and filled with water. Stam's quarters were furnished somewhat better than my room above the Demons' Dance Tavern in Mariyad: a few slimy rocks, some strands of kelp, and a couple of iridescent crab-creatures thrown in for atmosphere. On a rock beside Stam was a control console consisting of several glowing, shell-shaped objects. Occasionally the cephalopod would fondle one with its bifurcated tentacle, and the shell would ripple through various colors.

The water was murky because Stam communicated by releasing clouds of ink in various patterns, which were translated into words for me. The patterns that meant it was not happy about waiting were being dispersed by the circulating pump. When they were gone, I said, "I came as soon as I got your call. Security's tight around the Spaceport today; they almost didn't let me on board. Now that I'm here, what can I do for you?"

Stam tickled one of the shells, and a curtain of kelp parted to reveal an inset screen. It lit up with an image that was somewhat distorted by the currents in the chamber; a lean, muscular humanoid almost two meters tall, wearing a pair of green trunks. He stood with his arms crossed in a regal pose that was about as unselfconscious as a darkling learning to knit. Stam turned one eye toward the picture and kept the other on me. More ink stained the water, and the translated words were hushed and reverent. "This," the cephalopod said, "is my god."

A snappy comeback to that seemed inappropriate, so I kept quiet.

Stam stroked the shell again and the picture dissolved into a closeup. The face was lean and aristocratic, with arched cheekbones and even more arched eyebrows. He had a widow's peak of blue-black hair that shone like wet fur, and pointed ears. He was amphibious; I could see parallel slits of gills in both sides of his neck, under the jawline. His expression was supercilious, but there was also danger in it. I wouldn't want to meet him in a dark alley. Or on a lighted boulevard.

"You will meet him soon," Stam said. "He is Taqwatkh, the Bringer of Lightning, the Glorious Redemption, the One, the Only. It is for him that the Spaceport security has been increased—for reasons which need not concern you, our god has found it necessary to leave our world and grace the Unity of Planets with his presence."

"Great," I said. "How do I fit in?"

"We have heard of your success in a matter involving Earthlings and the Unity," Stam said. "Because you have had previous dealings with outworlders and matters of interstellar diplomacy, I decided to contact you."

Word of mouth is the best advertising—even for sapients who don't have mouths. I tried to look modest. Actually, I was wondering how much Stam had heard about Kaan Ta'Wyys and the *Synulanom*. I had tried to keep it quiet, since there were aspects of it that still worried me.

A blare of sound similar to a siren from the translator jerked my attention back to the tank. Stam glared crossly at me from within a thinning cloud of black ink.

"*If* I may have your undivided attention." The voder's reproduction of his communication sounded decidedly petulant. I realized I was beginning to think of Stam as "he" rather than "it".

"We have a layover of three days before conditions will be right for a hyperspatial voyage to Centrex, the Unity homeworld. During this time, I have reason to believe that there will be an assassination attempt on Taqwatkh. I want you to help protect him."

One thing about being the only private eye on the planet—I got all the cases, big and small. This one didn't sound small. Before I could ask questions, however, Stam said, "You must prepare to meet Divinity; Taqwatkh will return soon," and reached for his shells again.

"Wait a minute," I said. "I haven't decided whether or not I'll take the case."

Stam's totally nonhuman face somehow managed to look shocked. "There is no question! Taqwatkh needs protection! He is the Bringer of Lightning, the Glorious—"

"I remember," I said. "But with all due respect, he's not *my* Bringer of Lightning. And if I'm going to help protect him, I'll have to know a lot more than you've told me so far."

Stam twisted his tentacles into knots. "It was only with the greatest difficulty that I convinced Taqwatkh of your necessity. It is not meet that I should discuss sacred things with a human."

I decided this wasn't the time to mention that I wasn't entirely human. "It's also not meet that I should take a case blindfolded." I watched my words puff like smoke signals of ink from the translator. "Why don't I make it easy on you? I'll tell you what I know—which isn't much—and you can fill in the blanks. I know that you come from a planet whose Earth colonists call Malta II. I've heard that there's been some conflict between the colonists and the cephalopods, and I assume the assassination threat has to do with that. Now I'll ask some questions."

"I could be boiled alive if Taqwatkh learns how I am overstepping my authority."

I folded my arms. "If you want me to work for you, I need facts. Do you fear assassination from the Earth colonists?"

Stam's body rippled nervously. "Yes. The colonists, who inhabit the many archipelagos of our ocean world, are members of an old Earthly religious sect known as the Knights of Malta, or Knights Hospitalers. They are best known now for their advances in biology and genetics, but they are also a fanatically religious group. They have made several attempts to convert us by force to Christianity. Since they are colonists from a Unity planet, Taqwatkh is going to Centrex to protest. I believe some of the Knights are fanatical enough to attempt to kill him to prevent this."

"If he's a god, why does he need my protection?"

"Do not confuse our god with theirs, or yours. Our god had the ability to cast bolts of power and to lift great weights, but he is not omnipotent. Like some ancient Earthly gods, he has foibles and faults. Nevertheless, he is our redemption."

I believe in never arguing theology with an intelligent octopus. "I'll take your word for it. Now—what makes you think they'll try something while you're on Ja-Lur?"

'While we were landing, a message from Malta II was broadcast to a personal receiver somewhere in the Spaceport. Security personnel were unable to locate the receiver, though everyone was searched thoroughly. The message was: 'The Vulcan has landed.'"

That meant nothing to me. "So?"

"Vulcan is the name of an ancient Earth deity, a mythological god of fire who forged thunderbolts. I believe it is a code word chosen by the Maltese to describe Taqwatkh and alert the assassin. We cannot take chances. We have only one god."

"I still don't understand why you need me. Isn't the combined security of the Spaceport and your own personnel enough to—"

"But Taqwatkh refuses to remain on board! He insists on entering Mariyad to pay periodic visits to one Apolgar Zad, a local chemist. For this he should have the protection of someone who knows Mariyad. He refuses to take any guards with him—he leaves the ship incognito."

"I get it. When does he make these little excursions?"

"Usually in the afternoons—he has just left, in fact. You may name your price to protect him."

That did a lot to influence my decision. I was wary of taking this case—if anything happened to this Taqwatkh while he was on the Darkworld, it could cause a serious diplomatic crisis. It wasn't the first potential worldbreaker I had handled, however; if I did it once, I told myself, I could do it again. Besides, how many private eyes could say they had once been bodyguard to a god?

"You've got a deal," I said.

Stam unwound his tentacles with a snap that rocked my bubble. "Excellent!" he said. "Now you must meet arrgghhh..."

"Who?" I asked. Stam said nothing. His ink slowly dispersed in the current. His eyes stared, and his tentacles floated loosely. From somewhere behind his head sac, red streams began to streak and stain the black clouds.

I pressed the "emergency" button.

* * *

Stam was not dead. He had been given a near-fatal dose of Niotrinaline, a chemical which caused fibrillation in Maltese cephalopods. The blood I had seen came from a burst artery in his headsac. How the Niotrinaline had been added to the water filter of Stam's quarters was the subject of considerable controversy over the next few hours. I was cleared of any suspicion immediately; I had been in a bubble of unbreakable plastic, constantly monitored by an automatic life-support.

The doctors at the Spaceport infirmary said Stam would remain in a coma for several days, but, barring complications, he would live. I left the infirmary intending to return to the *Yith'il* and wait for Taqwatkh's return. Though my client was in a coma, I still felt I was on the case, and I wanted to talk to the god of the cephalopods. His absence during his high priest's mysterious malady had put the entire Spaceport in an uproar. I was on my way back back to the ship when Taqwatkh saved me the trouble of waiting for him; as I stepped out of the lift tube toward the slidewalk, something uncomfortably like a small bolt of lightning scorched the pavement too near my feet. I reached to my belt for a sword that was still at the weaponcheck counter as I whirled around. Standing at the top of a ramp was Taqwatkh, who had just proved he deserved his first title. He descended the ramp like a parade and stopped in front of me, arms folded.

"Very impressive," I said. "Is that your whole act?"

He let a sneer lift his lip. "You are Kamus of Kadizhar," he told me.

"That's amazing. Now try this one: I'm thinking of a number between—"

He grabbed the front of my tunic and suddenly I was dangling in the air at the end of an arm like a steel beam. "I will not have this," he said between his teeth.

"Neither will I." I grabbed his arm and swung my legs to the side, then jacknifed them above his head. My tunic ripped, but the unexpected movement overbalanced him, as I had hoped it would; he was incredibly strong, but his mass was little more than mine. We landed in a heap, and I was up first. I was saved from dismemberment by a security team, who respectfully restrained Taqwatkh.

He gestured imperiously and they released him. He had the power of command, no doubt about that; it radiated from him. The security team, who had been hunting for him, now melted back, looked about nervously, and quickly found something else to do. I noticed that several of the team were Mariyad guardsmen; part of a cultural exchange program, according to their badges.

After they had left, Taqwatkh said to me, "I will control my temper," in a voice quiet as ten sandcats after a large meal.

"Good of you."

He gave me a look that made me feel like a child with a runaway mouth. I kept my eyes on his.

"Stam hired you to protect me," he said. "I tell you that this will not be necessary. I am Taqwatkh. If a god cannot protect himself, he does not deserve the title."

I replied, "Stam hired me with your best interests in mind. The Darkworld isn't a member of the Unity of Planets yet; once you leave the spaceport, you leave the Unity's protection. Mariyad can be a dangerous city, and a lot of its people don't like outworlders. I think you could use someone who knows the streets." And I could use that blank check Stam had promised me.

"I am a god," he said slowly. His flat expression could have been painted on his face.

"I won't argue with that," I said, "at the moment. But your own high priest admitted you're not omnipotent."

He took a deep ominous breath. "It is not for my subjects to question my motives, intentions or whims; I am absolute. How then should a human and an alien dictate to me? Stam was mistaken: you are not needed."

"Stam is in the infirmary," I reminded him. "Aren't you interested in learning who put him there? I am."

"You—are—not—needed," Taqwatkh repeated. "That is all." He made a slicing gesture with his hand, turned and walked away without looking back.

Religions on Ja-Lur include polytheism, monotheism, pantheism, and deism. Many worship the Darklord as a god, but there are also plenty of anthropomorphized animals, masochistic martyrs, and elevated ancestors. Some of the more esoteric deities include Rumulund, the earth god of Rool, best described as forty acres of living land, and Skalos, the spider god of Niax—every world has at least one spider god.

But Taqwatkh seemed an odd candidate for godhood. He was only a humanoid, with limited powers probably no greater than mine. Yet I scrabbled for a living uncovering fixed duels and poisoned goblets while he was the absolute ruler of a world. Not that I felt like an underachiever; I was satisfied with my life. Usually, anyway. As far as I could see, the only thing that had put Taqwatkh in his position was his powerful personality, and I couldn't even be sure it was that—what was impressive to me might be laughable to a cephalopod. I wondered how Taqwatkh had come to be the god of a species different from himself. Not that it was unusual—most gods on Ja-Lur were nonhuman, there was the Cthulhu cult on Earth, and so forth. But I was curious as to how it had happened. I watched Taqwatkh returning to his ship, and admitted to myself that I was fascinated by him and his position, though I was less than enchanted with him personally. I wanted to learn more about the Maltese cephalopods and their god. I also wanted to know who had tried to assassinate Stam, and why. But it didn't look like I would be doing any of these things, as Taqwatkh had just taken me off the case.

2

I met Lohvia of House Zad the afternoon of the next day. The sun was a dark brass smear that could be stared at for minutes without blinking. Shadows were blurred at the edges and black in their hearts. A few stars still glimmered around the edges of the indigo sky. All in all, it was a bright, clear day.

I was walking through the wealthier part of Mariyad, along Taafite Street. Behind low, wide walls broken by ornate gates, beyond cropped grass and sculpted shrubbery, were the manses of shipowners, generals, and statesmen. Even the air was sweeter here, laced with salt from the sea breezes that washed the soot and smoke toward the poorer parts of the city.

There were a few people on the street; noblefolk who walked with the rustle of silk and satin instead of the scrape of coarse cotton and leather. The men wore court daggers the size of nail files, and looked uneasily at my sword. I seldom passed through this part of Mariyad. I stopped even less seldom. But I had a reason for being here today. Out of curiosity, and because I had nothing better to do, I had decided to take a look at the house of one Apolgar Zad.

The address surprised me—chemists and apothecaries seldom make the kind of money Taafite Street demanded. When I saw the place, I was even more surprised. The building was in an awkward stage between house and castle, and had more wings than a flock of bloodbirds. Any room in any of the sections would be twice the size of my office. Gables and peaks made the whole thing look like a mountain range with windows.

As I approached the open gate I heard the faint melody

of a lute. I stopped just inside the grounds and watched. A woman with long, bright hair was leaning from a window in one wing, listening to a minstrel who sat crosslegged on the grass beneath her. He was a tall, thin lad, on the edge of gangliness, dressed in black and gray. He had a pleasant peasant face, much too full of innocence. He was not singing, only playing light and cheerful notes. As I watched, he bounced to his feet and began skillfully pantomiming a story, using his hands and still keeping the tune on his lute. The lady above smiled at him and clapped her hands, though there was a slightly worried look on her face. Still, it was a nice, pastoral scene, and those don't come often to a private eye. I couldn't tell what story the minstrel was miming, though it seemed to have something to do with Mondrogan the Clever.

I'd had my look at Apolgar Zad's mountainous mansion, and so I turned to head back to my office on the edge of Thieves' Maze, hoping I'd get a call to a less-complicated job than protecting a god. But just then a heavy oaken door bound with iron opened directly below the window. It didn't open slowly, for all its weight; it flew wide and smashed against the gray wall, drowning out the minstrel's lute. A small, wiry man in green tunic and leggings ran out. He had a flying kragor emblazoned on his cuirass. He was slightly over one meter tall, but seemed built of pure fury. He reached the minstrel in three long steps, wrapped a fist in the baggy gray blouse, and lifted him completely into the air. The woman in the window above screamed. The lad, balanced on the small man's fist, kicked and waved, trying to brain his attacker with the lute. The small man seized and crushed it in his free hand.

About this time, I noticed that I was running across the grass toward them. I knew it wasn't a bright move. I didn't need the symbol on his green uniform to tell me that the man was one of Mariyad's elite Flying Guards; his size and strength were clues enough. He was capable of bending my sword into a plowshare, or around my neck. My only chance against him would be to try a spell and hope it worked, but I couldn't do that with witnesses about. I realized all this, but still I ran. I knew how it felt to hang like laundry from someone's upheld fist, and I suspected that the minstrel didn't like it any more than I had.

The Flyer saw me coming, and whatever mayhem he planned was suspended, along with the minstrel. The lady stopped screaming. I came to a stop before them. Everyone waited to see what I would do, including myself.

I didn't draw sword—one of the few smart ideas in me this morning. I expected to see the Flyer's arm begin to tremble—not even a Flying Guard can hold a man heavier than his own weight one-handed in the air for more than a few minutes. But the Flyer's arm remained as stiff as a Guardsman on a three-day leave.

"Why not let him live to learn from his error?" I suggested. "He's only a boy."

The Flyer looked at me and smiled unpleasantly. Then, instead of lowering the minstrel, he simply opened his fist and let him drop, heavily, completing the destruction of his lute. During all of this the lad had remained silent.

The small man somehow managed to look down on me, though his eyes were level with my chest. His expression was two parts anger and one part disdain, but I had been stared down by an expert yesterday; I wasn't bothered. He was as lean as dried meat, this Flyer, with eyes like hot black cinders. Tension showed in every tight muscle; even his hair seemed clenched in tiny black curls.

"Who are you?" he asked.

"Kamus of Kadizhar. I'm an investigative mercenary."

The flyer nodded. "I've heard of you. The fool who charges a fee to mind other peoples' affairs."

"I wouldn't describe it quite that way . . . let's just say I'm a music lover."

"So am I," retorted the Flyer.

"I liked his playing, before you broke his lute," I went on doggedly. "Why not let me take him to some street corner where people have poorer taste in tunes?"

"Why should I not kill him? I think it would be a favor to the world of music." He was one of those who won't let go of a joke after snagging it by accident. I was spared any further variations on the theme by the appearance in the doorway of the lady from the window.

"You won't kill him, Xidon," she said. Her words fell on him like stones, and he suddenly looked his height again.

This was my first good look at her. She was an impressive woman; tall and thin, with hair long and full enough to make her blue lace gown seem almost superfluous. A brooch about her neck held the three horns of a tricorn snake against a dark background. Her face was of the sort that gives itself fully to whatever emotion possesses it. Such a face can be as smooth and pale and hard as frozen milk, and does its most harm that way.

She reminded me of someone I had known.

Xidon's fury melted like bogmist. He tried to recapture the scene by pointing indignantly at the minstrel, who now sat sadly inspecting the wreckage of his lute, and saying, "Lohvia, the squawling of this begpenny—"

"At the moment," Lohvia said coldy, "he carries much more favor with me than you do." I winced—I couldn't think of a better way to see the poor lad pounded into pemmican. But the Flyer was beaten by now. He said pleadingly, "He should at least learn to play decently before—"

"Leave, Xidon—you're only making matters worse."

His jaws snapped shut and he turned away from her, raked the minstrel with a look that should have left scars and, ignoring me, pulled a whistle from his beltpouch and blew.

"Your father must hear of your indiscretion," he told her. By that I assumed she was Apolgar Zad's daughter.

"And your commander of yours," she replied, sweetly. Xidon's hard brown face drained of all expression then, and became an earth-colored mask. Any further words were cut short by the arrival of his kragor, which landed with an explosion of wind that tore at the grass and bushes. Xidon put one hand on the saddle pommel and gave me a glare that belonged in a furnace. I was still smiling—now didn't seem like a good time to stop. He vaulted into the saddle and shouted, "Ho!" The kragor lashed its barbed tail, sprang from the ground, caught air beneath its wings, and hurtled away in thunder. In a moment it had vanished into the soot-dark sky; Xidon had at least managed a dramatic exit.

Lohvia paid no attention to his departure. Instead, she went to kneel beside the minstrel.

The lad held his shattered instrument, his lower lip trembling. Lohvia spoke soothingly to him. "I can give you money for a new lute, Niano," she said. "I feel responsible for what happened." He looked at her with a flash of indignation in his eyes, then touched her cheek with the tips of his slender fingers and shook his head.

I watched Lohvia's movements and mannerisms, and remembered someone else.

Niano stood, clutching the remains of the lute. He offered me a grip that was weak, but firm and cool. I said, "Xidon won't forget." It would do no harm for him to be wary. He pointed to himself, then to the sky and shook his head. He did not intend to forget Xidon, either.

I watched him leave, and decided that I respected Niano. The fact that he was a minstrel did not impress me in itself. The cobbled streets and roaring taverns have always been filled with itinerant singers and poets, grubbing a meal for a song or story. Some of them are good; most think they are. Nearly all lead a starveling, hand-over-lute existence, sleeping with vermin more often than each other. But that never stops new romantics from taking to the road with their songs, usually to die of malnutrition or other stomach disorders, such as a swordthrust. Niano was a romantic to the core; that I could tell. But what really impressed me was that he had become a minstrel despite the considerable setback of being mute.

"He plays beautifully," Lohvia said, more to herself than to me. "He mimes the legends of Mondrogan the Clever with such verve and expertise that words are not necessary." The tone of her voice said that she was in love with this voiceless vagrant, just as Xidon was obviously taken with her. A pretty triangle: no one could have anybody. I was sure Apolgar Zad would as soon see Lohvia wed a Darklander as a penniless minstrel. And Xidon was forbidden by law to marry outside his race. For centuries the Flying Guards had bred selectively to produce a race light and strong enough to ride and control the kragors. He had less chance of her hand than Niano.

I watched her watching Niano, and I tried to decide what it was about her that reminded me so strongly of Thea Morn, an Earthwoman I had once known and loved. Thea had also been tall and blonde, but there the resemblance ended. In subtle ways, however, Lohvia reminded me of her.

It had been a while since I had closely inspected my feelings about Thea's memory, and it was something of a shock to realize that she had been dead long enough now for me to feel only a quiet sadness and a kind of enjoyable nostalgia as I watched Lohvia. Part of me was glad that it had finally come to that, and part of me regretted the loss of pain.

Lohvia interrupted my thoughts by turning to me. "Thank you for stopping Xidon," she said. "I'd like to do something to repay you, Kamus."

"You can," I told her. "Invite me in for a few minutes' talk."

She hesitated, then smiled and nodded. She led me inside and into a sitting room hung with tapestries that must have used up five generations of weavers. I wasn't completely sure why I wanted to talk with her, but my reasons had nothing to do with Taqwatkh's visits to her father. I asked her to tell me about herself, and settled back to listen. Lohvia was in her middle twenties, bored with being a rich merchant's daughter and fascinated by the carefree, footloose life she imagined Niano led, which was about what I had expected to hear. I watched her talking, the way she lifted her chin when happy and quirked her lips when exasperated. I listened more to the tone of her voice than her words, and remembered . . .

When a limited cultural exchange program was announced between Earth and Ja-Lur five years ago, I had put in my application along with thousands of others, not really expecting to be one of the few chosen. I had no idea why I was granted a visa—the qualifications were complicated and secret, requiring approval by a quorum of Lords and Overlords, and, according to rumor, the Darklord himself.

While on Earth I traveled, attended special acculturation classes at the finest universities, and in general experienced the luxuries and pains of an advanced and decadent civilization. I had to have genetic adjustments to shrink my pupils and protect my skin from the powerful sunlight, but other than that I fit in well on Earth. They had cleaned up the cities centuries earlier; now, solar and fusion power supplied the decadent population of three billion with everything they needed. It was so peaceful that it didn't take long for me to become bored, and I passed my time reading books about Earth's past. The late nineteenth and early twentieth centuries seemed much more alive and interesting times than the present.

"Of course," Lohvia was saying, "I realize it would be a radical change in my lifestyle to marry Niano. But I think I'm adaptable enough. He has enough talent to be the court minstrel of Overlord Kirven . . ."

I had met Thea at a luxurious vacation resort in the Iberian States. I asked her if she came here often, and she said she owned the resort. Like Lohvia, she was the daughter of a rich man: Strangland Morn, Chairman of the board of directors of A.S.T.R.A., or Associated Simulacra Technologies and Robot Analogues. He had more millions than the Maze had roaches; it was literally impossible to spend them all. Before he died in a spaceship collision, he had bought each of his seven children thousands of incredibly expensive gifts, including terraformed planetoids complete with gravity generators.

Thea did not hate being rich—she loved it, and although she gave much of her money away to charities, her extravagances were still enough to make me lean heavily toward socialism. Despite my aversion to her unearned wealth, I loved her. And she loved me, although her big mistake was trying to show it with money; she spent more on me than the gross planetary product of Centauri IV. We would have breakfast on Luna, brunch on Mars, tiffin on Titan, and dinner on Halley's Comet. Finally, guilt made me call a halt to the high living. I was beginning to feel like a gigolo. I told Thea I wanted to go back to Ja-Lur, to try making it on my own as a private eye.

"I'd be willing to give up my fortune," Lohvia said. "It doesn't mean anything to me. If Niano doesn't become court minstrel, I'd try living on the streets with him . . ."

That was what Thea had said. She even proposed for us a trial period of roughing it in a dangerous prehistoric wildlife preserve on her planetoid, to see if she could stand the primitive life. She endured the danger and dirt for two days; then, after a tearful confession that she couldn't take it and didn't want to hold me back, she ran into the Transportal and teleported back to her automated castle on top of the planetoid's highest mountain. I tried to follow her, but the portal wouldn't work, leaving me to hike through twenty miles full of saber-tooth tigers, tyrannosauri and other genetic backbreeds.

"I love him," Lohvia told me, her eyes shining. "And he loves me. So nothing can separate us. Nothing."

When I got back to the castle, I found Thea lying dead before the portal. There wasn't a mark on her—evidently the malfunction had killed her in transit. I carried her up to the highest bedroom tower, which overlooked half the planetoid, and strapped her in the bed. Then I put on an airsuit, went down to the underground control complex, and shut off the gravity generators. Instantly the atmosphere, rivers, forests, and lakes exploded into space, forming a beautiful ring of ice around the planetoid. The castle's foundations shook with the quakes, but held. I went back and looked at Thea, now a frozen beauty who would sleep forever in her airless castle. Then I flew back to Earth, caught a spaceship for Ja-Lur the next day, and tried to forget the pain and still remember Thea. It seemed I'd finally begun to . . .

. . . I realized that Lohvia had asked me a question and was waiting politely for an answer. I smiled while replaying the part of my mind that had been listening to her.

"Yes," I replied, "I think true love is a wonderful thing. It happens about as often as a snake wears sandals, but when it does, it's always worth waiting for."

"That's exactly how I feel," she said breathlessly. "And I'm seriously considering running away with Niano. What do you think of that?"

She was everything that age hates youth for: vibrant, innocent and almost bursting with love. I thought of Niano's performance for her, and the look on her face as she had watched him leaving. They would make quite a couple. I realized I wanted to see in their happiness an echo of what I had had briefly with Thea, but I didn't want to encourage Lohvia to do something that would change her whole life just because it had almost worked for someone else. But wouldn't it be better for her to take such a chance—what could she learn about life, protected in this mansion? I opened my mouth, not sure what I was going to say—and was saved by a young slave woman who entered through some drapes the size of stage curtains. She bowed and said, "You have a visitor, Milady."

"Yes, I do, Janya," Lohvia snapped. "He sits beside me now." She waved her fingers in dismissal, but the slave didn't leave. Instead, she said, "Your pardon, Milady, but there are visitors and visitors, if you take my meaning."

Lohvia turned and stared at her, and all of a sudden she was nervous. She nodded quickly, then turned to me and said, "It seems I must play protocol for a moment, Kamus; please excuse me," and was up in a swirl of silk and out of the room, her thin pale fingers combing at her hair as she left.

The slave—a small lady with brown hair and an almost childish figure—looked at me coolly for a moment, then turned and followed Lohvia.

I leaned back on a couch soft enough to swim in and put my feet on the rim of a plant pot the size of a well. Luxurious as the place was, it couldn't hold a taper to the least of Thea's many mansions. By Darkworld standards, however, it was almost as impressive as Overlord Kirven's palace. I started to wonder about Apolgar Zad—he was obviously an important man in Mariyad, and, according to Stam, he had dealings with the god of another world. I wondered if he was reasonably close to honest, or if he was a member of that oligarchy of crime, the Kakush. I shrugged. It was none of my business. I wasn't on a case here; I was merely indulging myself in what suddenly seemed a not-entirely-healthy invocation of the dead. I decided it was time to go. When Lohvia returned, I would leave. I had no business casting her and Niano in a remake of my love affair with Thea. They had their own dream to make come true.

Lohvia entered through the drapes then, and I stood. But instead of saying good-bye, I said, "What's wrong?" Because she was obviously very upset. Her hands fought with each other and she didn't meet my eyes as she replied, "Nothing. I must ask you to leave now, Kamus. It's been a pleasure chatting with you." She took my arm and steered me toward the door. I stopped and faced her. "Lohvia, you're not a very good liar."

She let a smile flicker on her lips—it died fast. "Please, Kamus. Believe me, it has nothing to do with Xidon or Niano. But your presence here would complicate matters. Please?"

It looked like the only direction left to me was down the hallway and out the door. Once outside, though, I stopped on the lawn and looked back. I had planned to leave anyway, but not under circumstances like these. I didn't have to be a great judge of ladies in distress to know that something was wrong. I reminded myself that this woman was Lohvia of House Zad, not Thea Morn, and decided that I had a firm grip on that. Whatever was going on was none of my business. So I started prowling around the shrubbery that surrounded this wing of the mansion.

Before long I found an open window which let me into a

bedroom. The door was open, and I slipped into the hallway and tried to find my way back to the sitting room. In no time at all I was hopelessly lost. Then I heard footsteps. I hid behind a stuffed snowcat, near a door. Around the corner came the slave who had announced Lohvia's visitor. When she passed me, I quickly opened the door beside me and slipped into the room.

I was in a laboratory, full of benches lined with stoneware beakers, retorts, and dishes. I looked around. It was quite impressive. But what impressed me the most was the body lying on the floor, beneath a window.

It wasn't easy to recognize, though I'd seen it alive and happy not an hour ago. It was Niano, the mute minstrel, with his chest and head crushed, just like the lute still strung across his broken back.

3

I didn't move. Some half-filled beakers still steaming over just-extinguished candles told me that the laboratory had been used quite recently, which meant someone might return at any time. A shattered container had left a slight dusting of white powder over most of the floor, disturbed by footprints near one workbench. A single set of bare footprints led from the bench to the body, and a set of large sandaled prints went from the bench to the door. Niano wore sandals, but his feet were too small to have made those prints. It looked like two people were in the room when Niano entered through the window—the barefoot one had killed him and left by the window, while the sandaled one had left by the door through which I had just entered, and only a moment before.

That was all I could see. I could feel more, however; a disturbance, an uneasiness similar to what Valina and I had felt when Kaan Ta'wyys had begun speaking the *Synulanom*. Darkness had come into this room, and recently.

I needed to make a closer examination of the body, but I didn't want to leave my footprints in the dust. So I took some potions from my beltpouch, mixed them, and cast the result—a fine transparent powder—into the air. "*Tanna ennay simald doon esson*," I said. The powder spread through the air, condensed into a flat layer of mist about the thickness of a fingernail, and settled over everything in the room except Niano and me, clinging to contours and outlines without disturbing anything. I stepped onto it, crossed the room without touching the floor, and bent over Niano.

His blood had not yet begun to clot; another sign that it had just happened. There were no clues as to who had done it, other than the fairly obvious fact that it was someone with superhuman strength; his skull had been caved in by a single blow and his ribcage was splintered, probably from a bearhug. Then I noticed two odd things. The first was that a round area the size of my hand on Niano's tunic over his chest was singed slightly.

The second oddity was more impressive. As I straightened and turned to look around, I saw several small plumes of mist rising from the shield spell I had laid on the floor, as though the spell was disintegrating. I started back quickly toward the door, assuming that, as usual, my uncertain half-Dark powers had improperly cast the spell. But then I saw that the tendrils of mist were curving together, forming an oval outline in the room's center. The oval, perhaps a meter across at its widest point, hovered in mid-air. I could see the room through it, but the view was blurred, and not simply by mist—Darkness clouded it as well.

I stared at it and felt cold, as though a breeze had blown from the oval and chilled me. There was only one explanation for it: like iron particles arranging themselves along lines of magnetic force, my spell was reacting to the presence of another, more powerful spell cast earlier.

Then I did feel a breeze, from the window behind me. It dispelled the mist pattern, and I was left wondering if I had imagined it or if my earlier instincts had been right.

If they had, that meant there was another Darklander in House Zad. I sighed. Another complication was all I needed.

I turned and looked out the window. It opened onto a large balcony. From there I could see that this side of the mansion was quite close to the outside wall—about twenty meters of lawn separated them.

Directly below me was Janya the slave, approaching a row of rainbow trees that lined the wall. There was no sign of anyone else. Janya glanced up and saw me at the same time that I saw her. She shouted, "What are you doing up there?"

I was in it, now. "You'd better send someone up here," I told her. "There's been a killing." Her eyes grew big, and she ran back inside.

I walked back across the room and spoke Phrases that dissolved the protective shield spell, as well as the vestiges of the earlier spell. I was taking no chances. Then I looked at Niano. The moment I had recognized him, I had put aside the shock and sorrow I had felt—my professional side had taken over, looking for clues with an emotionless eye. A private eye can't help getting involved at times, but he can't let it interfere with his work. But now the facts had been noted, and now the only things left to think about were Niano, who had lost his life, his music, his stories, and all his chances at love—and Lohvia, who had lost him.

I went back into the hallway, closing the laboratory door behind me, and then I heard Lohvia's voice calling my name. I turned and watched her come down the hall, wearing an apprehensive face. Walking with her was Janya, and a man—

That was as far as I got before I realized what he was, and the shock of it made me forget what was in the room behind me. He was tall and wiry, deeply-tanned, and wore a short kilt of deep red with a sword hanging scabbardless from a strange feathered belt. And he was a Darklander. That in itself was enough to set me back; Darklanders aren't popular north of the Inland Sea. But his nationality by itself wasn't what had me gaping. It takes a Darklander to know a Darklander before a Word of the Language of Spells is spoken; there's a certain sense of recognition. It centers around the eyes, but it has to do with sight the same way color has to do with the shape or texture of an object. I can't describe it, but the strength of it varies with the power of the Darklander. I had *never* felt such power from anyone of the Blood before. On a scale of one to ten, he was fifteen and I was about negative five.

I scrutinized him as he approached with Lohvia. His hair

was long and straight, glossy black, and bound by a single leather thong. His face was lean and full of sharp angles—cheekbones, supraorbitals, and nose all jutted emphatically. His eyes were the color and temperature of interstellar space. His face looked oddly familiar to me; I decided that was because it was similar in both appearance and attitude to a god I'd met recently. He smiled at my surprise. I didn't say anything. I didn't know who he was, and wasn't sure I wanted to. I felt certain about only one thing: he had to be the one responsible for the spell upstairs.

Lohvia said, "Kamus, Janya said you told her there had been a killing. What do you mean?"

"I've had to tell people of death before, and I'll have to again. It's never easy. But I doubted if it would ever be harder than it was this time. I tried to make it as gentle as I could; my words sounded harsh and unfeeling to me. She tried to go into the laboratory, of course. I held her until her strength had turned to tears against my chest.

The Darklander watched me through the scene, his smile gone now, his face totally impassive. But I had the feeling that he was amused, deep inside.

He turned to Janya. "Call some slaves," he told her. "And Apolgar Zad."

* * *

Apolgar Zad was a tall, thin man, mostly legs, with a short torso and almost no neck. He stalked around the huge, lushly-carpeted main hall like a reed-bird through savannah grass, making dour expressions that tugged his long nose from side to side.

The main hall of his mansion was large enough to be a hanger for a Unity space cruiser, so the five of us weren't crowded. Besides myself, there was Apolgar, Lohvia, the Darklander (who had been introduced to me as Palos of Zaibor), and Captain Olarus of the Mariyad Garrison. Lohvia was very white and still. Palos of Zaibor was enigmatic. Olarus was bored. I could tell he was bored because he had just announced the fact.

Apolgar turned and pointed a carrot-shaped finger at him. "Bored or not," he said in a querulous voice, "I want you to take action on this. Precipitate though she is, my daughter still means much to me, and I will have the liquidation of her friend avenged."

Olarus spread his hands. He was younger than Thoras, the previous Garrision Captain, and even less likeable, if that was possible.

"All this fuss over a wastrel so poor he didn't even have a voice?" he asked languidly. "Come, Apolgar. The Guard has better things to do—"

"You have nothing better to do than react to my wishes," Apolgar Zad told him. "I am not without influence in this city, you know. My daughter has told you who murdered this Nolo—"

"Niano," Lohvia murmured.

"Quite so, quite so. All that is left for you to do, Captain Olarus, is to arrest the killer."

"Arrest a Flying Guard, one of Mariyad's finest fighting men, on mere suspicion of killing a beggar? Oreus Bodag would have my head! You have no proof, other than the traditional hot temper of the little men—"

"No proof? You say my daughter's hypothesis has no proof? Why, man, have you not listened to his testimony?" and he pointed at me. "The circumstances of the young man's death indicate an attacker possessed of enormous strength. You have admitted that there is room on the laboratory's balcony for a kragor to land. It had been substantiated that this Flyer was jealous of the chemistry between the minstrel and Lohvia. Add to this his volatile, unstable temperament, which you yourself noted, and the equation is complete, the reaction inevitable."

"What about the footprints?" Olarus asked. "The bare prints might possibly be Xidon's, but the sandal imprints must belong to someone else—why, they're large enough to be made by your feet," and he grinned as he looked at Apolgar's huge, ill-shined boots.

Apolgar glared. "I have reached my boiling point," he announced. "I have become saturated with your picayune protests. I say the analysis is correct; all that remains is for you to arrest the offender. I take full responsibility for this action."

Olarus shrugged. "That's different." He stood and straightened his headband. "I'll send several men to the

Flyers' barracks—I've a hunch this Xidon won't take kindly to being arrested." He turned and bowed to the Darklander. "An honor, Palos of Zaibor." The Darklander nodded and smiled that faint smile again. I wondered how honored Olarus would feel if he knew he was talking to someone from Ja-Agur. The Garrison Captain bid farewell to Lohvia, then looked at me and said softly, "If this causes me trouble, Kamus, I'll have your hide stretched between poles."

I smiled. "If this causes you trouble, Olarus, you'll be too busy worrying about your own hide." Olarus scowled and left, wading with difficulty through the rug. After he had gone, I stood and made my good-byes. Apolgar Zad thanked me for my noble efforts on behalf of his daughter. Lohvia thanked me, her voice fragile and ready to shatter; she turned away quickly and left the room. Apolgar started after her, saying hurriedly, "Janya will see you out."

I watched everyone leave, still unsure if I had done the right thing by not mentioning that a Darklander was somehow involved with the murder. Of course, I had little choice—if I had mentioned it, I would have had to explain to Olarus how I knew it, and that would require revealing my heritage. I had been unmasked as a Darklander once before, and it had taken a miracle to let me stay in Mariyad.I did not want to tempt fate, and the Darklord, a second time.

Janya watched the curtains swirl into stillness after daughter and father, then turned to Palos and me and said, "Gentlemen?" and made a gesture toward the exit, setting it off with arched eyebrows.

"You seem to take this quite calmly, Janya," remarked Palos of Zaibor as we walked down a corridor.

"One grows used to emergencies and calamities in Apolgar Zad's house," she said, "as one grows used to strange visitors." Her light voice had more than a touch of sarcasm to it. All Palos did was look at her and smile that slight smile of his, but it took the cockiness out of her. I was fascinated by this Palos. I was fairly familiar with the Who's Who of the Darkland, and I had never heard of anyone by his name with so much raw power. Just walking next to him kept me on overload; it was like standing by a furnace.

"Is murder an everyday thing around here?" I asked her. She looked at me. She had short brown hair and an elfin-thin face, one that looks all wrong without a smile and mischief in the eyes. Now it looked somber and more than a little scared. It made me slightly angry with this mystery man—who was he that he could cow Lohvia and this slave, anyway?

"No," Janya said. "Murder has never happened before, that I know of." Though she did not look at Palos, I had the impression that last was meant for him.

"At least we know who did it," Palos said as we left the mansion.

"Do you really think Xidon did it?"I asked him.

He grinned at me; he had an easy, open grin. It broke the ice of those eyes and made one forget how cold they had been. "Who else could it have been? He certainly had a motive. He flew his kragor to the window, killed the poor lad, and left by the same route."

"What about the footprints?" I asked.

"Well, one set of them had to be yours, of course—the barefoot set. For some reason, you took off your sandals when crossing the room—unless you floated across to the balcony." He grinned.

He was toying with me—he knew I had used a spell to keep my prints out of the dust. "It still leaves a number of questions unanswered. How did Xidon know Niano would be in that room? Why didn't Janya, who must have left the house almost the same time as the killer, hear the kragor's wings?"

"And what was Niano doing there? Talking to the owner of the sandaled prints? That means someone else knew of the killing." This came from Janya—I was beginning to admire her. Palos obviously wasn't. He flashed her the same grin as he had me, only somehow it was now as chilly as an ice giant's ankle. "You have quite a curiosity," he said in gentle warning, "for a slave."

Janya did not have time to react to this, because her attention was suddenly attracted by something overhead. She pointed at the purple sky and shouted, "Look!"

We looked—overhead, Xidon was spiraling toward the same wing where he had attacked Niano this morning. I looked at the window and saw Lohvia leaning on the sill, staring at the ground where the minstrel had played for her. The thunder of the kragor's wings made her look up, quickly, as Xidon came in for a landing.

Janya turned and ran back into the mansion. Neither

Palos nor I moved as the Flyer landed, the backwash from the wings ripping shrubbery to shreds. Xidon leaped from the saddle, looked at the window, and stopped, confused. Lohvia was no longer there.

"Lohvia?" he called uncertainly.

"Murderer!"

She flew at him fingernails first, through the door he had ruined earlier. Xidon's jaw dropped, but he was quick enough to twist out of her way and let her sprawl into a flowerbed. Palos and I charged to the scene. I had my sword out as Xidon leaped back into the saddle; I slashed the reins as he tugged them, and he sprawled backwards and almost lost his mount. But he recovered, shouted a command, and the beast took off.

Then I saw Palos of Zaibor extend one arm, his fingers crabbed in a Dark gesture. He spoke no Words, but the kragor jerked as though caught by an invisible lasso, and went into a steep dive toward a fandala tree. Xidon somersaulted free in midair and landed running, but I was running, too—I slammed into him, and we rolled across the lawn together until we hit the stone base of a statue. I came up on top, my fingers around his throat, and what I felt made me loosen my grip in surprise. He flung me off his chest like an empty tunic and leaped to his feet. The statue beside him was of an ice giant, solid marble and ten feet tall, but Xidon ripped it free of its pedestal as though it were made of dandelions and lifted it above his head to crush me. Fortunately, he was still standing on the soft lawn—the weight of the marble drove him into the ground up to his shoulders. At the same time, Palos knocked the statue from his grip with another gestured spell. Xidon tried to claw his way out of the soft ground, then collapsed as a final spell put him to sleep.

During all the spell-casting, Palos had not used a single syllable of Language, nor was he even breathing hard from the effort. I had seen power like that only once before—when Kaan Ta'Wyys of Thanare was filled with the power of the *Synulanom*, and even he had been speaking the Phrases of that spell. Palos of Zaibor, I concluded, was one powerful Darklander.

So powerful that his Bloodline had to come direct from the Darklord himself.

He helped me to my feet. "Congratulations," he said.

"We seem to have saved Captain Olarus the responsibility of catching the murderer."

"This was your idea of a criminal sneaking back to the scene of the crime?" I asked. I dusted myself off, and something tickled my hand; several strands of Xidon's hair had been caught on a ring I was wearing. I pulled them free and was about to cast them away, but reconsidered and put them in my potionpouch.

Palos watched me, with that smile. "Saving hair to build a spell around?" He asked. "I'm surprised at you, Kamus. That's a charlatan's trick."

He had finally acknowledged my Blood. I wanted to return the favor by calling him by his real name, but things were by no means settled down at House Zad; slaves were dashing about, helping a hysterical Lohvía and surrounding an unconscious Xidon, and Apolgar Zad was on the scene, shouting orders no one was listening to. I went back into the mansion to find a phonecub and call Olarus. If my hunch was right, the Garrison Dungeon would be a good place for Xidon.

I also needed a quiet place to think about the possible reasons why a living legend would be visiting Apolgar Zad. Because with such power as I had just seen, Palos of Zaibor could only be one person: Jann-Togah, the son of the Darklord.

4

There have been almost as many legends of Jann-Togah as there have been of Mondrogan the Clever. How he was exiled by his father from Ja-Agur, the Darkland, for trying to usurp his father's throne, and of his efforts to recross the Black Desert and break a barrier spell that kept him from his homeland. According to the stories, his power had been halved when he was thrown out, and even at full strength he had been no match for the Darklord. I didn't want to think about how powerful that would make the Darklord, as I intended—

somehow, some way—to make him pay for causing the death of my friend, Sanris of Taleiday, and for trying to run my life and career. True, since he had restored my secret life as a Darklander in Mariyad I had seen no other evidence of attempts to make me into a puppet. Sometimes I thought that my determination to confront this mysterious monarch was overreaction. I had attempted to contact him several times through Darkness, with no result; not surprising, since he never took calls. Still, I could not shake the conviction that the Darklord wasn't through with me. Being of the Blood, I've found my intuitions usually have some truth in them. Which might explain why I was instantly convinced that Palos of Zaibor was Jann-Togah.

He was one of the very few Darklanders in current times whose name was, in itself, a conjuration; one could summon darklings and intensify spells in Jann-Togah's name, though, of course, by so doing one ran the risk of making him mad if he found out.

Probably every mental case in Mariyad has at some time claimed to be Jann-Togah, just as they've claimed to be his father. Some of the more aspiring charlatans in the city have put his name on their shingles, and sold enough aphrodisiacs and death potions to retire as a result. I had also met several Darklanders who claimed to be him. I didn't believe them. But I was convinced that Palos was the real thing.

And that meant he was a likely suspect for Niano's murder. He was certainly capable of summoning a darkling who could have crushed Niano in its grip. The reason for it? Perhaps Niano had surprised him in the performance of whatever Darklore I had sensed there, and . . .

But so far, Xidon had the better motive. There was also the little matter of Palos's or Jann-Togah's, alibi; he had been with Lohvia since she left me, and in sight of servants since he had entered the house. But being in two places at once would pose no great problem to so powerful a Darklander . . .

It was quite late by the time I got back to my rooms above the Demons' Dance Tavern. I had waited for the Guard to come for Xidon, and Lohvia had sat with me and talked about safe, trivial subjects, such as what Earth had been like, and sobbed occasionally on my shoulder.

Though I was tired, I didn't sleep well that night. I kept seeing that brief, happy scene on the lawn between Lohvia and Niano—a happy scene that would never happen again. I finally gave up and waited for dawn to trickle in. While I waited, I decided to do a little research. From a hiding place beneath a floorboard I took several old scrolls and tomes on various Dark subjects. For several hours I looked through them, searching for a description of the spell I had seen in Apolgar Zad's laboratory. I was about to give up when, in the gray light of pre-morning, I found what I was looking for.

It answered an important question, though I didn't care for the answer at all.

Next, I headed for the Unity Spaceport. There I took a lift tube to the infirmary. After filling out hundreds of forms and getting enough paper cuts to warrant a medal, I was allowed to turn over Xidon's hair sample for cell analysis. The analysis would be instantaneous, but they wouldn't get around to doing it for several hours. While I was waiting, I visited Stam's room.

He was conscious and almost recovered. His room was a water-filled chamber with a bed that looked like a cross between a fishnet and an ancient Earthly moonshine still. Several tasteful arrangements of coral sent by concerned acolytes aboard the *Yith'il* were set about the room.

Again, Stam wasn't happy with me. "Why are you not with Taqwatkh, to protect him on his journeys into Mariyad?" His ink signals were hastily formed—they caused static in the airlock's voder translation.

"Take it easy," I advised. "You're not a well cephalopod. Taqwatkh hasn't left yet." I didn't really know if he had or not, and didn't mention to Stam that the Bringer of Lightning didn't want me anywhere near the case—the high priest had enough worries. "I need a few questions answered," I told him, "if I'm to do a good job as bodyguard. The first and biggest is: exactly why is Taqwatkh going to visit Apolgar Zad? Were they roommates at seminary school, or what?"

Stam was some time in replying; when he did, the answer was evasive. "If Taqwatkh has not seen fit to tell you, perhaps I would be overstepping my authority."

"He'll never know. The information could be important."

"In fact," he signaled slowly, "I do not know why he insists on these visits. There are many matters I am not fit to know—this, evidently, is one of them. I do know that, according to our scriptures, he made a similiar pilgrimage to this planet a thousand years ago, our time. This was long before the Unity was established, of course—just after we had developed space travel under Taqwatkh's guidance."

"Now we're getting somewhere. Do you know if this current trip has anything to do with someone named Jann-Togah?"

"I have heard the name—the exiled son of your mysterious Darklord, is it not? But I have not heard my god mention him."

"Has he mentioned the Darklord?"

"No."

"How about a Flying Guard named Xidon?"

"No, never."

So I thanked him, told him I was on my way to protect Taqwatkh from the forces of evil, left the water chamber, and stood around pulling my lip. I intended to do my best to protect the Maltese god from any assassination attempts—even if Taqwatkh didn't want me on the case, I considered myself on it for a variety of reasons, the biggest of which was that Lohvia had enough grief without an interplanetary assassination in her front yard. Another was that I felt Niano's death was somehow connected with Apolgar Zad's dealings with Taqwatkh, and with Jann-Togah, and that spell, whose origin I was now pretty sure I knew. But what was the connection?

I had no answers, yet. I decided a good place to start looking for them would be the Spaceport library.

* * *

The entire written history of Ja-Lur had been put into a memory cube one centimeter across. I dropped it into a scanner and started reviewing the scrolls written by historians, looking back nine hundred years ago, which corresponded to a thousand Maltese years. There was no mention of visitors from the sky or of a lightning-flinging, super-strong alien. That lead blocked, I decided to look into the history of the Knights of Malta.

That cube said the island of Malta, on Earth, had been ruled by a resurgence of the Knights Hospitalers for almost a hundred years. Their discoveries in genetic manipulation, cloning, and bionics were the most advanced on Earth, and eventually they developed an army of android angels (the

Seraphim Mark IV Class), which, along with the special effects department of a leading holofilm company, they used to stage a very convincing Second Coming. The android Messiah told the nations of the world to turn over leadership to Malta. Religious wars raged over the planet, until the deception was unmasked by a special missions team of the Roman Catholic Church, acting under direct orders from the Pope. As a result, the entire population of Malta was banished to Beta Draconis III, or as they renamed it, Malta II.

That was interesting, but it still didn't tell me why Taqwatkh was visiting Apolgar. I had the feeling that that information would be the link I was looking for, but I had no idea where to start looking. The entry on the native race of Beta Draconis III, the cephalopods, was quite general and sketchy, and all I learned from it was that they called their world by an ink signal meaning "Globe of Slime and Stench"—the cephalopod equivalent of "Paradise."

So I gave it up, and decided to see if I could go to the source of the problem and find any answers. I was fairly sure what Taqwatkh's reaction to my continued interest would be, and I wasn't looking forward to it. But I had reached a dead end.

As I was on my way to the landing plates, however, the P.A. system announced a call for me from Mariyad. I went back into the Terminex and found a public phonecub. I scratched its ear and said, "Kamus of Kadizhar here."

The cub refused to transmit until he was offered a sweetmeat; fortunately, I happened to have one in my pouch. I dropped it in his mouth; he chittered in thanks, then opened his mouth and spoke in Janya's voice.

"Hello, Kamus," she said. "I thought this was where you'd be."

"You're a better detective than I am today. What is it? Has anything happened at the house?"

"Nothing momentous," she said. "But I'd like to talk to you—I think I can clear up a few things for you."

"And why would you like to do that, Janya? Not that I'm counting the horns on a gift kragor."

"Kamus, being a slave for Apolgar Zad is a better life than most free folk know. So I'm trying to protect myself, as well as my master and mistress. Apolgar Zad is dealing with Darklanders."

I counted five for the proper effect, then said slowly, "That makes matters interesting."

"I can make them much more interesting, but not over a phonecub. Darklanders can tap their minds, you know."

I'd never been able to, but I didn't tell her that. "All right, Janya—I'll meet you at the Blue Lotus Tavern at noon." Taqwatkh habitually made his mysterious trips to Apolgar Zad in the afternoon, so there would still be time to get back to him. And I had the feeling I could learn more from Janya than from the Bringer of Lightning.

Before I left the Spaceport, however, I checked back with the infirmary. They had finally completed the analysis I had requested, and what they told me made a lot of the puzzle clear.

Janya was sitting in one of the high-backed corner booths of the Blue Lotus, as far away as possible from the ale-guzzling, joke-roaring Guardsmen, slavetraders, and other clientele. I felt guilty about asking her to meet me here—though she was a slave, she was used to much better surroundings, as she had pointed out. To me, the Blue Lotus was practically a second home. I apologized to her and she said, "Kamus, I once made my living belly-dancing in a much more disreputable tavern than this one. The only thing I find offensive about this place is the age of the Guardsmen's jokes. But we've better things to talk about." She leaned close to me and said, "Palos of Zaibor is a Darklander."

It was no act to look impressed, even though she was telling me news I already knew. What impressed me was Janya herself. She was as pale and fragile as a rainbow tree blossom, but she had a quick mind, a fine and facile wit, and considerable courage. She would make a good ally, I decided, as I ordered a mug of ale. I described Taqwatkh and asked Janya if she had ever seen him, without telling her who he was.

She nodded with excitement. "That's the other Darklander! Palos wants to abduct him; he's threatened Apolgar with financial ruin unless Apolgar helps him."

"How can Palos cause that?"

"Because he helped Apolgar move up in society years ago, by supplying him with Black Desert dream-crystals."

So Apolgar had made his fortune by supplying Mariyad with illegal drugs. I pulled out a pack of chewing gum and thrust a stick into my mouth. "You've spent a lot of time listening behind curtains."

"I told you—if Apolgar and Lohvia are ruined, I go back to belly-dancing."

"What is Apolgar doing for the 'other Darklander'?"

"I'm not sure; some sort of drugs, or chemical concoction."

I nodded. "In the laboratory where Niano died."

"Yes."

"Do you know if Palos has ever been in there?"

"Not that I can say. Xidon has—I surprised him lurking about there once."

Things were falling together, but I still needed a stronger motive for the killer. "Who do you think killed Niano, Janya?"

She looked surprised. "Why—Xidon, of course. Who else but a Flying Guard could have mangled him like that?" She sighed. "I miss Niano. He had so much talent. He knew all the tales of Mondrogan, including some that I'd never heard before."

A guardsman at the bar was talking about the extraordinary strength of the Flying Guard imprisoned in the Garrison Dungeon. I kept one ear on him while I said to Janya, "Such as?"

"Never mind that. What about Apolgar's—"

"What were some of the stories Niano told?" I repeated. I'm not sure why I asked—maybe just to keep her occupied while I listened to the guardsman's tale.

"Well, did you know that Mondrogan once saved all of Ja-Lur . . ."

". . . put him in our strongest cell," the guardsman told Silos, the tavern owner. "Jungan was on duty when that Flyer ripped that solid bronze door from its hinges and crushed poor Jungan beneath it like a scarab . . ."

". . . monster from the sky with the strength of a hundred men, who could cast lightning bolts from his fingers . . ."

". . . burst through the Garrison wall and was gone before . . ."

". . . come to Ja-Lur because his powers were waning, and there was a certain drug here that could restore them. Mondrogan—"

I slapped the table hard enough to cause whitecaps in my ale. "That's it!" I shouted. Those two stories had suddenly made Niano's murder clear to me, and also told me that I might be too late to prevent Taqwatkh's assassination.

Ignoring the bleary surprised stares of the tavern's occupants, I grabbed Janya and we ran out. The Marketplace was empty, except for a few pedestrians. "You can never find a carriage when you need one," I growled and started down the street at a run.

"Kamus, wait!" Janya ran to catch up with me. "What is it? What about—?"

"I don't have time to explain now, Janya. I've got to get to the Spaceport before—"

Just then I noticed a flicker of something at the edge of my vision, and I suddenly had the feeling we were being followed. But I couldn't see anyone behind me who looked suspicious. I kept one eye toward the rear as we hurried through the Marketplace. There were a few old women cackling over hens, one or two panderers and harlots advertising yards of flesh, but I could see nobody interested in Janya and me. Yet I couldn't escape the feeling that we were being shadowed. I ducked into a dim, unoccupied market booth, pulling Janya in after me, and watched the few passersby. No one glanced our way, but the feeling of being watched grew.

"Kamus, what—"

I laid a finger across my lips.

Then I saw it, as it slid into the booth, a darker outline against the dimness. It flowed along the wall, elongated by the angles of the wooden booth—a shadow, unattached to a body. Trailing from one heel was a thread of Darkness that ran across the dirt floor and out the door. The shadow hovered near us as Janya pressed her hand against her lips and shrank against me. It was ectoplasm in negative, a Body of Darkness. And I had a good idea who it belonged to.

I unsheathed my sword as it rippled along the gray, ill-fitting slabs of wood. I knew there was nothing I could do against it with unenchanted steel, but I had an image as an ignorant human to maintain. So I swung, uselessly, and watched the tip of the blade graze wood fibers and leave the shadow unharmed. It raised a shadow blade and swung—the black image left the wall like a ray of night and flickered quite close. Janya controlled herself with an effort that I felt as she pressed against me. I stroked her hair and said, "Don't worry."

"It's Darkness, isn't it?"

"I can't imagine what else it could be," I told her.

"Well," she said, "I've seen better shadow skits at a childrens' puppet show."

The shadow moved again, and its entire length stood against one wall. Previously, it had been too distorted to recognize—now, Janya gasped and said, "That profile! It's Palos of Zaibor!"

His voice spoke inside my head. *Well, Kamus. You and Janya just won't leave well enough alone, will you?*

Since he had contacted me, I could respond without setting up a spell, and without Janya realizing I was communicating with him. *I think you'll be sorry you're delaying me,* I told him, *if you want Taqwatkh's business with Apolgar Zad to be successful. And I think you want that, because I know who you are.*

"Kamus, he's just standing there," Janya whispered. "Shouldn't we try to run?"

"You can't run faster than Darkness," I told her. "Wait—I don't think he'll harm us."

His shadow rippled along the wall away from us like intelligent ink, causing Janya to breathe a sigh of relief. It appeared to cross its legs and lean against the wall with arms folded. *So tell me; who am I, and what do I want with the Maltese god?*

You're Jann-Togah, son of the Darklord, and you want to use Taqwatkh, the Bringer of Lightning, in your campaign against your father.

The shadow nodded. *Very good, Kamus. You just might make a better ally than an enemy.*

I'd make a better ally than Taqwatkh would. His power bolts are running low, aren't they? I don't know anything about the cephalopods' religion, but evidently the bolts are important—they call him the Bringer of Lightning.

His full power is beyond conception, Jann-Togah said. *He is the reason for the cephalopods' advanced civilization. Obviously, an aquatic race would have little heavy industry such as exists on other worlds. It is hard to make fire and, as I understand it, generate electricity underwater. Taqwatkh's power bolts fill these needs.*

But his power runs low every thousand years, their time, I said. *He has to come to the Darkworld, where certain chemicals or herbs exist that can pep him up. He must have made quite an impression the last time he dropped in; minstrels are still telling about his battle with Mondrogan the Clever. At least, one minstrel was. You knew his reason for being here—as soon as he's up to strength, you intend to use him against your father.*

He won't be up to strength this time, I'm afraid, Jann-Togah said with a sigh. *The secret of the elixir has been lost, and Apolgar has been unable to duplicate it.*

"Kamus," Janya said desperately, "has he got you enthralled? You're just staring at him—"

"It's all right," I assured her. "Somehow, he's talking to me, in my head."

"What's he saying?"

"Quiet—I can't hear." *Jann-Togah, Taqwatkh will be of no use to you or anyone if we don't get to him immediately. He's been under threat of assassination since his arrival on Ja-Lur, and I know who the assassin is. He may have already struck.*

By the Dark Spire!" Jann-Togah swore. *Who is it?*

Xidon.

The Flying Guard who killed the minstrel?

He's not a Flying Guard. The Spaceport Infirmary tells me he's a Knight of Malta who's been genetically altered to resemble a Flyer. He got into the Yith'il *as part of an exchange program with Unity Security, and tried to kill Stam, the high priest. He would have gone after Taqwatkh then, but the god was at Apolgar's laboratory. Then he was arrested as Niano's murderer. He's broken out of the Dungeon, and he's on his way to finish his mission. And he'll do it—he's been specially bred to kill Taqwatkh—unless we stop him!*

Jann-Togah's shadow had straightened up at this. I could hear him putting the facts together in his mind, just as I had—it didn't take him long. *I'll meet you at the Spaceport,* he snapped. *Get there as fast as you can!* His shadow vanished.

"Let's go!" I pulled Janya out of the marketbooth.

"But what did Palos say?" she demanded.

"We've even less time now than we did before," I said. "In fact, you'd better not come—"

"You're going to leave me here without telling me what's happening? Think again, Kamus."

I looked around desperately for a ride, and saw one: trundling slowly down the street in our direction was a racing chariot, its driver half dozing on his feet, holding the reins loosely.

"I hope you don't regret this," I told Janya. "Get ready to move fast," and I pulled two pinches of powders from my pouch and tossed them into the air. I muttered a Phrase—too low for Janya to hear, I hoped—and the powders ignited, causing a burst of crimson light. The two jemlas pulling the chariot reared and then bolted in panic, scattering what few shoppers there were. The charioteer, caught completely by surprise, went axe over armor and into a fruit stand. I grabbed the railing as the cart careened by me and managed to pull myself onto it. I grabbed the reins and pulled, slowing enough for Janya to leap aboard—then I speeded up. The jemlas—much like Earthly horses, except for vestigal wings and forehead horn, which have caused Earthly mythologists some sleepless nights—broke into full gallop, and we were off. We hurtled out of the Marketplace and headed up the Dragon's Back, a street named for its series of small, regular humps, like a serrated backbone. We hit only the high spots. The chariot wheels screeched, iron rims striking sparks, as I made a right on Blackbrine Street. Astonished faces flickered by. Janya sensibly clung to the sides of the chariot instead of me as we careened over the cobblestones. I hit a wet patch and the chariot slewed to one side, scattering a group of citizens and a few Guardsmen; the latter shouted for me to stop. I snapped the reins harder.

"Kamus, you're going to be in a lot of trouble," Janya said—one of the great understatements of the year. I didn't answer. We skirted the high wall that surrounds the Maze, roared by the building that held my office, and headed for the West Gate.

The gate detail saw and heard us coming. Fortunately, traffic was light at this hour. Peasants with pushcarts and litterbearers leaped out of our way. One litter overturned and pitched a fat woman, wearing more silk than a ship wears sailcloth, into a cartful of squealing pigs. I didn't stop. The gate's iron bars began to lower—the wrought emblem of Mariyad, a Flying Guard astride a kragor, came into view as we rushed toward it. "Hang on!" I shouted to Janya, "And keep down!"

The jemlas were well-trained—they didn't slow at all, though the teeth of the gate tore at my hair as we went under it. A few crossbolts shattered against the sides of the chariot, and the feathers on one tickled my ear. Then we were on the turnoff that led across the kilometer of savannah to the Unity Spaceport.

As I approached, I saw a kragor overhead, dropping toward the main entrance of the Spaceport Terminex. Janya saw it too; she grabbed my cloak and cried, "Xidon!" I had had the same idea, and was trying to think of a surreptitious spell that would protect us from aerial attack. But as the flying reptile came out of its dive and landed in a green explosion on the grass near the road, I saw that the rider was Jann-Togah.

By this time we had attracted quite a bit of attention. Guardsmen were charging from the West Gate towards us, and Unity soldiers were pouring from the Terminex. Janya and I tumbled from the chariot just in time to be seized by a white-uniformed native of the planet Moran—he was built for seizing, having four arms mounted on a snakelike body.

"Relaxxxx," he said. "I don't know what the idea wassss..."

"Arrest Xidon of the Mariyad Flying Guard!" I shouted. "He's going to kill Taqwatkh of Malta II!" but I couldn't make myself heard over the pandemonium. The Mariyad guardsmen were demanding custody of us, and the Unity soldiers were insisting the matter would have to be decided by their superiors.

Jann-Togah was being held by several soldiers. I saw him make a series of his sign-Language gestures. At first, I noticed no difference in the shouting madness; then I realized that, instead of speaking Adelanese, the Unity soldiers were all talking in their various native tongues. Communications quickly disintegrated. A scuffle between a soldier and a guardsmen broke out, then another. The Moranian released us as someone stumbled into him from behind. Jann-Togah pulled me out of the crowd. "That will keep them busy while we attend to Xidon! Come!"

We ran around the Terminex and along the boundary between grass and plasticrete, past the thin silver force fence projectors. There was little activity once we passed the hotel and the warehouses; all spaceport security was at the front gate. The landing field was quiet, with only a few ships on the landing plates. The *Yith'il* was berthed on the near side of the field, about fifty meters from the force fence. As we caught sight of it, Janya pointed and shouted, "Look! The other Darklander!"

Taqwatkh had just emerged from the ship. He was standing on the high hatch platform, hands on hips. He seemed to be looking for someone.

Jann-Togah pointed also, at a figure crouched on a nearby conveyor ramp. "Xidon," he said. "With a weapon."

5

The Maltese Knight was huddled on the arch of the swooping ramp, which stretched in a parabola from a warehouse loading dock and intersected several freight lift tubes. He rested a raygun against the railing, holding it aimed steady at Taqwatkh. The beam could puncture a meter of metal.

Which is what it did, instead of puncturing the Maltese god, because I yelled, "Duck, Taqwatkh!" The god turned, startled, as Xidon fired, and a stream of pressurized water shot from the ship's hull. The hull self-sealed as Xidon turned, saw us, and fired. He was above the level of the force fence, but he had forgotten the Darklord's mandate against outworld technology on Ja-Lur; the raybeam flickered out to the edge of the field and blinked out a meter short of us. Janya and I ducked reflexively; Jann-Togah slammed his hands against the invisible, unyielding force fence, searching for a way to climb or break through it.

What happened next surprised all of us: Xidon fired another rayblast at us, but this one, instead of stopping at the boundary, slashed into the ground between Jann-Togah and myself. We both jumped back, staring at the streak of scorched dirt. "Impossible!" Jann-Togah shouted. "My father's mandate—"

Whatever he was going to say about his father's mandate was left unfinished, because another rayblast from Xidon forced us all to jump for whatever cover could be found, which, on a savannah, was precious little. We waited for the next shot, but it didn't come; I looked up cautiously and saw the reason why. Instead of retreating into his ship like any sensible god, the Bringer of Lightning had decided to take the offensive. He tried to leap from the *Yith'il* to the closest arc of the ramp. He didn't quite make it, though he managed to seize the ramp's railing as he fell. The ramp shook, upsetting Xidon's next shot at us. The beam drilled into one of the fence projectors; there was a shower of sparks, and the section of force fence before us vanished.

Xidon screamed in rage. Jann-Togah ran toward the loading docks and the ramp's base. Janya and I followed him. According to the until-recently infallible mandate, Jann-Togah and I were powerless now, and vulnerable to Xidon's rayblasts. But Xidon was having problems of his own; Taqwatkh was on the ramp and coming toward him.

Several faces belonging to various species had appeared in the ports and hatchways of some of the ships, watching, but no one dared interfere in this battle of titans. Xidon fired at Taqwatkh, but missed; the beam sliced almost completely through the thin curving metal, causing the ramp to sag dangerously. Taqwatkh leaped over the cut and kept coming. Xidon fired again, and this time the Maltese god managed to deflect the beam with one of his weakened powerbolts. The beam shot off at a tangent and neatly sliced the top from one of the power silos near an Aldebaran cruiser, exposing a well of some sort of thick, viscous fuel substance.

Xidon was obviously between an asteroid and a hard place, with Taqwatkh coming from one end of the ramp and Jann-Togah from the other. He turned back toward Jann-Togah and fired at him again. The Darklord's son, hanging precariously from the ramp's scaffolding, instinctively made a defensive Gesture. Probably as much to his surprise as to mine and Xidon's, it worked—the power bolt was deflected, to cut a swath in the plasticrete. Not only did technology now function outside the Spaceport's boundaries, but Darklore functioned inside!

But there was no time to wonder why. Taqwatkh let fly with another bolt, which knocked the gun from Xidon's hand.

He expected the Knight to be stunned by the bolt, but Xidon showed no effect, since he was genetically immune to Taqwatkh's powerbolts.

Surprise made Taqwatkh hesitate. Xidon leaped forward and crashed into him; both of them tumbled from the swaying ramp. They landed on the cargo deck platform of the Aldebaran cruiser, and there the fight went on.

Xidon braced himself against the ship, tore free one of the hatch doors, and threw it at Taqwatkh, who dodged out of its way. He moved quickly behind Xidon, and brought both fists down on the small man's neck. Xidon staggered, recovered, and the two grappled again, their blows denting the spacecraft's hull.

Jann-Togah had stopped his ascent of the ramp when the others fell from it. I saw him Gesturing, but to no effect; the mandate was evidently working again. I started to run toward the Aldebaran cruiser when Janya shouted, "Here, Kamus!" She tossed me the raygun, which she had caught when Xidon dropped it. I aimed at the cargo deck. The angle from the ground was steep and I was afraid of hitting Taqwatkh, but I had no choice. Xidon's strength and his immunity to the god's powerbolts were giving him the upper hand—Taqwatkh was weakening. I fired, and as I did the entire conveyor ramp sagged again, directly into the path of the beam. The beam sliced through it completely. The partial cut Xidon had made earlier acted like a hinge, and the entire section, with Jann-Togah hanging on, dropped and swung toward the cruiser. Taqwatkh managed to break free of Xidon just as the severed end of the ramp crashed into the platform. The shock broke Jann-Togah's grip and he slid down the ramp, colliding with Xidon and knocking the Knight off the platform. Xidon fell with a wavering cry of anger and frustration and plunged neck-deep into the clinging fuel substance. For all his strength, he was helpless in the tarry mass.

Then there was silence, except for Xidon's thrashing and curses. Neither Janya nor I moved for a moment. Then Janya said, "Kamus, I hope you're not going to tell me you planned it that way."

I grinned at her and spun the raygun around my finger.

There were shouts in the distance, and I saw a small army come around the warehouses in our direction. "Here comes the Unity," I said. "And they're not happy."

Jann-Togah and Taqwatkh descended to the ground by a lift tube and joined us. Taqwatkh stared at me with that haughty look I had come to know and hate. "So, detective," he said. "I see you did not heed my order."

"Luckily for you," I told him. I didn't feel like talking to Taqwatkh. I turned to Jann-Togah and said, "You realize that we're guilty of breaking about twenty interstellar laws."

Jann-Togah nodded, and then the Unity surrounded us. An Earthling general, portly and red-faced, with enough stars to fill a globular cluster, was shouting, "Lock them up! I'll have them all on Devil's Asteroid for this! Illegal entry, unauthorized use of weapons, destruction of Unity property..."

"I think not," Jann-Togah said. And somehow his quiet voice doused the shouting completely. Everyone stared at the Son of the Darklord and the Maltese god. Separately, either one had enough sheer presence to cow a regiment—together, I truly think they could have challenged the Darklord himself.

"Do you know who I am?" Taqwatkh asked.

The general worked his jaw several times and managed to pump a reply up his throat. "The emissary from Beta Draconis III."

"More than emissary—absolute ruler and god. Do you wish your superiors at Centrex to know that you tried to arrest a visiting deity?"

"Ahem," said the general. "Well. Since you put it that way..."

* * *

The four of us were gathered in the airlock chamber before Stam's infirmary room. The high priest had just finished thanking me so effusively that the ink hid him from sight. Taqwatkh had come as close to thanking me as he could, saying, "You have done well in my service, Kamus of Kadizhar." I had said nothing to that. I didn't want to be reminded of it.

I had done my job, all right. I had saved the Bringer of Lightning from assassination. I had been on the wrong side, from the start.

"But tell me, Kamus," Stam asked, "How did Xidon manage to poison my water with Niotrinaline? Even if he was part of the security exchange program, they were constantly checked for concealed weapons."

"But Xidon *was* a weapon," I told him. "The Knights of Malta had designed him genetically to kill you and Taqwatkh. His body was capable of manufacturing and secreting Niotrinaline. He was amphibious—when I wrestled with him on Apolgar's lawn, I felt the gill slits in his neck. That, and his unusual strength, made me decide to have his hair cells analyzed for a genetic breakdown."

"He might have been planted here years ago, to wait for Taqwatkh's coming. He was undoubtedly under orders to destroy himself once his mission was completed, leaving the blame on Ja-Lur instead of the Knights. But he fell in love with Lohvia, and that ruined his cover."

"It was, of course, easy for you to deduce my reasons for wanting to abduct Taqwatkh," Jann-Togah said. "But how did you know Apolgar Zad was working to restore his powers?"

"I didn't, until almost too late. His first visit to the Darkworld and his battle with Mondrogan the Clever had been preserved in legend and song, instead of historians' scrolls. But Niano was a minstrel, and he knew the legend."

Taqwatkh kept his eyes on me. His face was impassive.

"It all makes sense," Janya said. "Except how Xidon killed Niano. He had the only motive, of course—jealousy. But I'm sure I would have heard his kragor landing on the balcony when I was outside."

"You didn't hear it," I said, "because it didn't land. Because Xidon didn't kill Niano."

Janya looked at me in shock. "But who else could it have been?" she asked. "Who else was strong enough—" and then she stopped. The room became very still. Even Stam's tentacles stopped moving.

I was very tired, very sick of the whole affair by now. I was tired of thinking about why I had done what I had done. But I had to put it into words, now. "Here it is," I told them. "Niano was worried about Lohvia. So instead of leaving, he re-entered the mansion, perhaps through the same window I used. He wanted to learn what Apolgar was up to. He hid in the laboratory."

I looked at Jann-Togah. "No one knew your real identity. You could have killed Niano easily and used Darklore to pin the blame on someone else." I looked at Taqwatkh. "Someone with great strength, and the ability to cast bolts of power."

"Kamus," Jann-Togah said. "Think well before you accuse me . . ."

"Darklore had been at work in the room," I told him. "If Niano had discovered that you were a Darklander, wouldn't you have killed him to keep it secret?"

"Quite possibly," Jann-Togah said. "But he did not, and I did not."

I looked at him for a long moment, then nodded.

"No, you didn't." I turned to Taqwatkh. "But you did."

No one said anything. Taqwatkh's expression did not change, but his eyes pinned me to the wall.

"Niano was a minstrel," I repeated. "He knew the legend of Taqwatkh and Mondrogan. He was in the laboratory when Apolgar tried and failed with his latest elixir. Maybe he became excited when he realized it was true, and you heard him. You wanted your presence there a secret; perhaps you were afraid that if your cephalopod followers learned your powers were fading, there would be anarchy on Malta II." I took a deep breath. "You tried to kill Niano with a powerbolt first. Your powers were very low, and so the bolt merely burned Niano's chest. So you finished the job by crushing him."

Janya said, "But why didn't I hear him leave?"

I said, "I'll get to that in a moment. Olarus was right; Apolgar left that second set of footprints. He ordered Olarus to arrest Xidon because he wanted to protect Taqwatkh." I turned to the Maltese god. "You must have promised Apolgar quite a fortune for his help. He was a wealthy man."

"I am the god of a planet," Taqwatkh said. "It is a simple matter to buy wealthy men." He added, quietly, "I could kill you."

"Your power is fading," Jann-Togah said. "You are dying. You cannot aid my cause. If you kill Kamus, I will kill you. I have killed gods before."

"Even if you somehow have powers here," Taqwatkh retorted, "I am still strong enough to destroy you all. But what difference would it make? Shall a god be punished for the death of a mortal outworlder? He was an insect—I crushed him. There was no need for Apolgar Zad to blame another to protect me. I am Taqwatkh. Neither the Unity of Planets nor the Overlord of Mariyad could question my act. I am a law unto myself."

"There are those," I said softly, "more powerful than you. And you know it. Shall I tell them how you escaped from the laboratory—or will you?"

For the first time, the Bringer of Lightning's proud and haughty look faltered. Taqwatkh looked confused, and angry at his confusion. "I do not know how it happened," he said at last. "One moment I was in Apolgar Zad's laboratory—the next, I was aboard the *Yith'il*. The transition was evidently instantaneous."

I nodded. "It was a spell of transport." To Jann-Togah I said, "The spell was so powerful, the residue of it was still in the room. It had been cast from a far distance—at least as far as the Darkland."

Jann-Togah nodded slowly. "Yes," he said. "It's my father's hand—there's no doubt of it."

"You are dying," I told Takwatkh. "Your search here is a failure. And when you die, Niano will be avenged," and I tried to believe it as I said it.

Taqwatkh laughed then. "There are other chemists," he said. "There are other worlds. Long ago, I gave the cephalopods civilization and spaceflight, that they might aid me when the time came for my quest. The search is not over. I will find the ingredients for my elixir; perhaps on Centrex, while I make my protest against those petty colonists." He turned to Stam. "You will be released tomorrow," he said. "And tomorrow we will leave."

Stam had sunk deep into his webbed bed. His translated voice was broken and halting. "My Lord . . . I . . ."

"You do not question."

"I—do not question."

Taqwatkh looked at me again. "You are but a mortal," he said. "I have watched the stars collapse. What are you to me?"

He left the room.

After a long silence, Stam said to me, "Kamus . . . you must understand . . ."

"I know," I said. "Whatever his faults, he's your redemption. Well, good luck."

"I—will see that you are paid whatever you—"

"Forget it," I said. I walked out, followed by Janya and Jann-Togah.

We left the Spaceport without talking. When we reached

the road to Mariyad, Jann-Togah stopped. "This is where I leave you," he said. "This plan to regain my homeland has failed me, but there are other plans."

"You've got my vote," I said. "I have a bone to pick with your father, too."

He looked thoughtful. "I know. It may be easier for both of us, now."

I knew he was referring to the inexplicable breakdown of the Darklord's mandate at the Spaceport. "There have been other signs of mystic turmoil in the world," he continued.

I nodded. "I know. I've seen some of them. Another Darklander once suggested that these happenings are because Shadownight is coming."

Jann-Togah said, "It will be a strong Shadownight, I think. Perhaps the strongest since the first one, a millenium ago. My father will try to use it, as he tried to use the first one, to make his dominion complete again. I think perhaps my chance is nigh." He spoke softly, his eyes fixed on something, a throne perhaps, in the far distance. Then he looked at me. "Kamus, I would leave this city and this land if I were you," he said. "There will be a scourge against Darklanders come Shadownight, if my intuition is correct. For my father fears the loss of his power, and he will do anything to prevent that. Also, I sense danger coming upon you; a danger from the north. Be wary."

He was silent then. I thought about what he had said. If this were true, then more than my personal vendetta against the Darklord seemed to be at stake here. If it were true . . . I did not know how much I could trust Jann-Togah, after all. Darkness was strong in his soul.

When he spoke again, it was on a different subject.

"Tell me, Kamus—you knew Taqwatkh had killed the minstrel, and yet you helped save him from the assassin's raybeam. Why?"

I had been asking myself that, over and over. I had thought that the only answer was the obvious one: there would have been interstellar repercussions and a possibility of war between the cephalopods and Ja-Lur if Xidon had succeeded. But was that the heart of it? It had been my job to protect Taqwatkh, regardless of how I felt about him personally. But he had countermanded Stam's hiring of me, so had it really been my job? It would have been justice to let Xidon kill him, I knew. But Niano would not have wanted revenge at such expense; at least, I hoped not.

There was nothing else I could have done, and yet I felt like I had betrayed Niano and Lohvia. I had wanted to see them happy. Instead of answering Jann-Togah, I turned to Janya and said, "Don't tell Lohvia the truth. Let her think Xidon killed Niano."

"You don't have to tell me that," she said softly.

Jann-Togah said, "I think you are a very sentimental person, Kamus of Kadizhar."

"Is that so? Then tell me, Darklord's son—If you knew that Taqwatkh was useless to your conquest of Ja-Agur, why did you risk your life to save him?"

He had been turning to go; that got him between the shoulders. He stiffened, turned and looked at me, eyes full of surprise at himself.

"I'll tell you why," I said. "Because you felt sorry for Taqwatkh. Because he was alone on a pedestal, lonely and frightened. And you know the feeling."

He closed off everything in his face; it became merely a mask of flesh. I had gotten to him, and he did not like it. Janya huddled against me under his gaze. After a long moment, he said simply, "We will surely meet again, Kamus."

Then he turned and started down the road toward the Southlands. Always toward the south, for Jann-Togah. I was as sure as he was that we would meet again—and I wasn't looking forward to it.

Janya locked her arm in mine, and we started back toward Mariyad. My head was full of thoughts about Lohvia and Niano, about a love that never had a chance. She was so beautiful, Lohvia was; so much like Thea had been.

I looked down at Janya. She was nothing like Thea had been, nothing at all. That made me surprisingly happy.

But it could not make me forget that once again the Darklord had interfered in my work, and my life. Because of his inexplicable aid to Taqwatkh, the Maltese god had almost gone unaccused of Niano's murder. As it was, he would go unpunished. I did not know why the Darklord had done this, but I intended to find out. Jann-Togah had indicated that there would be trouble on Shadownight. Perhaps it was time for me to take a trip—to the Darkland.

I decided that this would be the last case I took until I reached some sort of resolution with the Darklord.

It was evening; the sun was a lump of molten gold on the horizon. We strolled slowly toward the West Gate. "So tell me," she said, "what does the only private eye on the planet do for relaxation after he solves a case?"

I shrugged. "Well, sometimes I go to the Blue Lotus and watch the dancers."

She smiled. "How about a private show?" she asked.

PART THREE

Murder on the Galactic Express

I

The android walked into my office and asked, "Have you ever heard of the *Galactic Express?*"

I didn't answer him at first; I was busy packing. There wasn't a lot left in my office to pack, however; I had sold some of the furniture to a collector of Earthly memorabilia, and the rest to local merchants, and the rest of what I owned wasn't enough to fill a phonecub's ear. When I had finished stuffing one small bag with books and spell potions, I could no longer ignore the android, and he didn't look ready to leave. So I said, "Of course I have. The *Galactic Express* was a passenger ship that went off course several years ago during planetfall. The change in orbit caused it to crash, due to the Darklord's mandate, somewhere in the northern nation of Hestia."

The android nodded. "On the mountain called Darklord's Bane. And do you know of the cargo it was carrying?"

I sighed. I had no time for this; I had a reservation on a balloon-boat headed south in three hours. "Did you insist on coming here just to give me a trivia quiz, Mr.—?"

"My name is Orpheus. Orpheus Alpha." Androids have no more control over their names than most of us do. "Mr. Alpha," I said, "as I explained to you by phonecub—just before I sold my phonecub—I am not taking any more cases. I am leaving Mariyad immediately on personal business. I don't know, nor am I interested in, what cargo the *Galactic Express* was carrying when it crashed. I'm sorry you insisted on coming out from the Spaceport for nothing." I opened the door, which gave the smell of Thieves' Maze an excuse to waft through the window. I hoped it would usher him out.

It didn't. Instead he said softly, "Would you be interested in the Black Mask?"

He didn't waste words, this android. He was tall and slim, fair-haired and lean-featured, with a high forehead; the alpha class of androids were designed for brains rather than brawn. He was wearing a conservative brown one-piece suit, with a chest pouch. Despite his casual dress and attitude, he was nervous, which was unusual for an android. It showed in the set of his shoulders, the way he studied his hands when he wasn't studying me. There was nothing to indicate that he had come out of a Matrix like an assembly-line product except a stylized starburst imprinted on that high forehead. There was nothing to indicate that he knew I was a Darklander, except his reference to the Black Mask.

I said nothing, but my stomach began cannibalizing itself. I watched him warily. In the past several weeks I'd become more paranoid than ever of anyone discovering my heritage. Though Shadownight was still almost a month away, we were already into its eve, as Valina had said. There had been reports lately of darklings spontaneously manifesting without invocation, and staying. Nightmares and disturbing visions were common to everyone from Overlords to Maze beggars. Phonecubs spoke in tongues. Rains of frogs, stones, insects, and other, less wholesome objects occurred at inopportune times. On top of all this, the Darklord's mandate had definitely broken down; in the few days since Jann-Togah and I had fought Xidon in the Spaceport, all sorts of technological devices, from rayguns to pleasure plugs to rocket boots, had started to function outside the Unity's jurisdiction—sometimes. Just as Darkness sometimes failed to respond when Language was spoken. This was nothing new to me; as a halfbreed, my powers were about as uncertain as my next meal. But full-blooded Darklanders were finding it very disconcerting. There was no doubt about it—Shadownight was coming. Drape your windows in kallith bulbs, bolt your doors, say your prayers—and don't trust your neighbor.

In such a climate of supernatural fear, anyone could be accused of being a Darklander just by being in the wrong place at the right time. According to one popular myth, unsorcelled steel will not kill a Darklander, so there was a simple way to test a suspect's humanity, though it was little comfort to the suspect.

All this was added reason for me to leave Mariyad. Though the Darklord had, I suspected, protected my identity once when it was revealed, I couldn't count on it happening again. According to what Jann-Togah had said, now seemed a good time to go to the Darkland, both for safety's sake and to confront the Darklord.

My obsession wasn't improving my social life; for one thing, it had caused the breakup of a potentially interesting relationship with Janya. Nevertheless, I knew I had to go south. The only problem was that I had no idea what to do once I reached the Darkland. It had occurred to me several times that, by journeying south, I might be doing exactly what the Darklord wanted. If that was true, it might be a good idea to come with a weapon—and the Black Mask was a formidable weapon, even if I had to go in the opposite direction to get it.

If it existed at all . . . it was one of the talismans of the Elder Ages, brought from the Dark cosmos when the Darklanders established Ja-Agur beyond the Black Desert. Supposedly it allowed to the one who wore it vision into the realms of Darkness, access to and some control of the more powerful spells and Darklings. It also let anyone read and understand the grimoires of Darklore, and—perhaps most important—it showed the underlying reality of any spell. All in all, not a bad item to have handy when confronting the supreme sorcerer of a world.

But there were reasons against going, too; a potent one was a warning by Jann-Togah of a danger from the north. Also, time was growing short, and the journey I contemplated was long. Still, I was willing to listen to the android. "Go on," I said.

Orpheus Alpha steepled long, slender fingers, clasped them, interlaced them in a slow physical mantra as he spoke. "You no doubt wonder how I have my information. I know about your secret because I know Daniel Tolon; he suggested I contact you. I used to work for A.S.T.R.A. You are familiar with it?"

"'Associated Simulacra Technologies and Robot Analogues,'" I said. "They made you."

He grimaced wryly. "They did indeed. A.S.T.R.A. holds exclusive patents on pseudoplasm, the self-replicating gel which constitutes androids, and on the Matrix, with which the pseudoplasm can be genetically programmed and incubated. These secrets, you can well imagine, are protected zealously. The only other manufacturer of humanoids, the Homunculi Corporation on Malta II, produces androids of far less quality and applicability."

"In your unbiased opinion."

"I feel no loyalty toward A.S.T.R.A.; I am merely stating facts. To continue: It is common knowledge that the *Galactic Express* lies atop Mount Darklord's Bane. No real attempt has been made to reach it, because no one thought the salvage that the passenger vessel carried worth the expedition's risk. The mountains are, I believe, populated by lifeforms of a particularly threatening nature . . ."

"Ice giants," I said. "You could call them threatening."

"I see. Well, there is something there worth the risk—to me. It has been recently learned that one of the passengers had stolen a Matrix and a supply of pseudoplasm from A.S.T.R.A. They may still be on board. I have studied maps of the area; I can find the ship. But I am a stranger on this world; I need your aid, Kamus. In return for that, I will lead you to the Black Mask, which also is on Darklord's Bane, in an ancient temple."

He looked at me expectantly. I looked around the empty room to see if there was anything I had missed; not because that was a possibility, but to give his story a chance to settle. I had only spoken to a few androids before. They occupied an uneasy position in galactic society. Human nature does change, but very slowly, and so it was unfortunately true that androids were subjected to much the same prejudices and crimes that minorities of previous centuries have been. They were sexless; the Matrix was their only means of reproduction. They were not allowed a great range of emotion. And they were programmed with the ancient laws of robotics which had been conceived long before there were robots or androids, the laws that prohibited them from harming intelligent lifeforms or allowing them to come to harm. Whenever I had thought about this, I could not decide if this infringed the freedom due androids as sapient beings, or if it was justifiable. Is it a crime to program a computer? Was I feeling liberal guilt, or merely anthropomorphism?

Whatever the reason, I found myself wanting to help Orpheus Alpha, even though his expedition sounded like less fun than a hayride on a plaguecart. It was not entirely true that no expeditions had been made to the *Galactic Express;* I had heard of a few. None had been successful. The same mandate that had caused the ship to crash prevented the use of Outworld technology to reach it. One native expedition had reached it, but the hull had evidently survived the crash intact, so they were unable to enter.

All in all, it didn't sound promising, save for the possibility of the Black Mask.

I looked at him. "You haven't told me how you know where the Black Mask is," I said.

Orpheus Alpha hesitated, then said, "I'm afraid that must remain my secret."

I shook my head. "I'm sorry. I just can't see myself going on a long and dangerous journey in the opposite direction of my quest, all on your word that you, an outworlder, know the location of a legendary talisman that's been sought unsuccessfully for ages. Good day, Mr. Alpha."

The android sighed. "I can't say I blame you, really. I rather expected you'd see it that way." He then reached into his chestpack and pulled out a raygun, which he aimed my way. He looked apologetic about doing it, which did little to console me. He said, "You're aware, I assume, of the recent haphazard nature of your Darklord's mandate. Those who study such things estimate that the probability of this blaster functioning outside the Spaceport is well over fifty percent. And before you attempt to speak a spell, may I remind you that your abilities, never too reliable, are rendered even more questionable by the current state of things?"

So much for the laws of robotics, I thought sourly. I kept my hands away from my potion pouch. "What happens now?"

"Now we take a walk into Thieves' Maze, and I will introduce you to someone whom I hope will change your mind." He gestured toward the door. I picked up my bag and left my office for the last time. The android followed me, close enough to make the skin between my shoulder blades itch.

* * *

The dim sun of the Darkworld was just past zenith as we walked down Dragonpock Street. The Maze would not become active until evening. It was a crisp autumn day and black smoke, filled with sparks like darklings' eyes, rose from several chimneys. The lifting smell of baking bread mingled with the damp, gritty odor of garbage. It was fairly quiet for the Maze; occasionally we could hear shrill voices raised in argument behind sooty windows, and once, from beyond the curve of a narrow alley, the dim clatter of swordplay. We kept walking. Orpheus Alpha's raygun was small enough to be mostly hidden by his hand; not that the sight of an android herding a man along at gunpoint would have raised many eyebrows in the Maze. The few people we passed merely glanced incuriously at us before going back to more important things, like crystal-sniffing or coughing.

It had been some time since I'd been in the Maze; my adventures of the past few months, particularly the case involving the Kakush, had brought me something of a reputation, and not a popular one in some areas. I was even known off-planet; *Space-Time,* a news holozine, had featured a slight anecdote on my last case, fortunately not mentioning my Dark powers. Though the majority of my dealings with the Kakush and the *Synulanom* had been forgotten by the Maze's inhabitants, some residual suspicion must have been left, for I could no longer count on contacts like Ratbag and others for information. Or perhaps it was simply because the notoriety was setting me apart—that, and the general nervousness due to the approaching Shadownight.

The Mariyad Guardsmen were also aware of me to a greater degree now; I was no longer considered an amusing eccentric, but had now graduated to being a possible embarrassment. Even if the Darklord's actions had not forced my leaving Mariyad, it was entirely possible that I would have had to go soon. My new-found fame was beginning to backfire on me. The present case was a good example of that.

And, as if things weren't bad enough, I had the distinct feeling that we were being followed.

It was little more than a hunch, and before I had time to keep an eye out behind us to make certain we reached our destination: a flight of wooden stairs that had probably been there before Earth developed space travel. "Up to the garret," the android said.

I started to mention my hunch to him, but before I could

say anything he gestured sharply with the blaster. "Don't think I won't use it," he warned. "I assure you, Kamus, I'm not an ordinary android."

"Obviously," I said. "They broke the mold when they made you."

I started up the stairs. They shook like a knight in cold armor. Orpheus Alpha knew enough to stay a few steps behind me so that I wouldn't be tempted to play Darkworld roulette. "I wish you hadn't made this necessary, Kamus," he said. "You don't know how upsetting the use of force is to me."

"I take a rather dim view of it myself," I said as we stopped on a creaky landing before a small, rounded door. It was here that Orpheus made his mistake; he stepped close to me to reach the door's latch. I brought my fist down against his forearm, knocking the blaster away from me. He fired reflexively, and a lance of energy arced across the narrow street, incinerating part of someone's laundry line and dumping the rest onto the fetid street. I put Orpheus between my other arm and the door, and took the gun away from him, stepped back with it leveled at him. "You were right," I said. "It works. I'm lucky I didn't try anything."

He looked at me, thin shoulders slumped in defeat. "I should have known better than even to try," he murmured.

"You only made one mistake. Of course, that's all it takes." I glanced over my shoulder. The street was clear, but I still had the feeling that someone else knew we were here.

"Before you go, or shoot me, or whatever you intend," Orpheus said, "please come inside with me. Let me show you why I've resorted to such measures. Please, Kamus."

I could still walk out of it, I knew. I sighed. "Open the door," I said. "But remember, Orpheus—I'm not conditioned against pulling this trigger."

He said nothing, but the faintest of smiles touched his thin lips, and that said very plainly that he disagreed with me. Then he opened the door and entered. I followed.

It was very dark inside, save for one flickering candle that barely illuminated the small room. Near it, a robed and cowled figure sat on a stool, motionless. The sloping ceiling and the candlelight magnified and distorted the shadows. It was a scene to make even a Darklander nervous, and I breathed a sigh of relief when the figure stood and faced me, and I saw dimly within the cowl the white, still face of a woman.

Behind me, Orpheus said, "Here he is, Lady Thanatos."

The figure took a step toward me, then stopped, staggered slightly, and raised a hand hidden by the sleeve to her head. She lifted her head and I saw the face, calm as death, clearly. Then, as I watched, it wavered and rippled like a dissolving disguise spell, and a skull grinned at me from within the cowl.

2

"This isn't funny," I said.

The robed figure stood uncertainly for a moment, then shook back the sleeves of the robe, revealing finger bones yellow in the candlelight. "Malfunction, Orpheus," a hollow, sepulchral voice said. The jawbone moved vertically in a mockery of speech.

"Be thankful that only the holomask broke down,"Orpheus said from behind me. He stepped forward quickly. With his free hand he opened the robe, revealing a small, gray, oval mechanism with several buttons and a tiny calibrated dial attached to the skeleton's ribcage. He twisted the dial. "No power in the mask's generator. It must be that damned supernatural mandate again," he said.

"It could have been me as well, couldn't it?" The graveyard voice contained no human tones, but I somehow felt a strange eagerness behind the words. The thought was more chilling than the sound of her voice.

"Calm down, dearest," Orpheus said, though the voice had not sounded upset. "You know the stasis cell is there in case your power fails," the android continued soothingly.

"The cell is still experimental; it is not failsafe." An eerie chuckle. "There is only one way to learn if it works, Orpheus." Suddenly the skeleton's mood seemed to change; fleshless fingers grasped Orpheus' arm. "Let me go back to the spaceport, Orpheus. Please."

"It's too dangerous; you know that," he replied intensely.

"Danger? What can threaten me, Orpheus?" The skeleton turned away from him slowly. "I sat alone here, Orpheus; did you know that?" The voice sounded almost wistful. "They gnawed on the bones of my feet..."

Orpheus's features were gaunt; his face looked almost as skull-like as the cowled bone he stared at. "Hang on," he whispered harshly. "So much depends on you..."

It did not seem to hear him. "I don't know what I want," the voice said; "life—or the rest of my death..." It turned suddenly toward the door. "I'll go back alone. There must be an easier way to restore my body..."

"Don't go," Orpheus said in a warning tone as it, or she, turned toward the door. Then, as the cowled figure continued to move, he withdrew from his chestpack a small stringed musical instrument that looked like a miniature lyre. "Do I have to play for you, Lady Thanatos?" he said softly. The skeleton, by now almost to the door, stopped and turned back toward him. They faced each other, clearly in a contest of wills. Then, "No," the hollow voice said. The bones beneath the robe slumped slightly; Orpheus had won.

I sat my bag down on the floor and coughed politely into my hand. "I hate to interrupt a private conversation, but would you mind explaining this amusement ride, Orpheus?"

Orpheus sent a glare my way that could have stoked up the sun, then evidently remembered that he needed my help and calmed down with a visible effort. "Kamus," he said, "May I introduce the reason we need your assistance: the Lady Thanatos. As you can see, she has been the unfortunate victim of that maniacal cult known as the Order of the Osteomechs."

I had heard vaguely of the Osteomechs. "Some offworld group of religious fanatics, aren't they?"

"Obviously." Orpheus gestured at the skeleton, who stood motionless. "Their creed is to renounce all fleshly pleasures, pains, and distractions by the rather extreme expedient of renouncing the flesh entirely. As you can imagine, they are not overwhelmed with eager initiates, and so must kidnap people to swell their ranks. This is what happened to Lady Thanatos. She was forced to undergo a horrendous initiation: submerged in acid which disintegrates all but the bones, while her mind, enduring the agony, was not allowed to die, but instead recorded into a computer which controls—"

"Orpheus, *stop it!*" Lady Thanatos shouted. Again, though the voice had evidently been designed to sound hollow and emotionless, the agony in it came through loud and clear. The earlier morbid mood had obviously vanished.

Orpheus stopped immediately, looking contrite. "I'm sorry, dearest. I was merely trying to convey to our reluctant employee the seriousness of your condition." He turned to me again. "I'm sure you can see now why we desperately need the pseudoplasm."

"You want to create an android body for her." I'm not a detective for nothing.

"I apologize for using force to bring you here, but I think you'll agree that the situation warranted it. I helped her escape from the Osteomechs, and I've no doubt that they've pursued us. We need you as a bodyguard and aide, Kamus. Will you help us find the *Galactic Express*?"

They waited for my reply, the Osteomech's eyeless gaze somehow beseeching. A living skeleton who, by nature of her technological rebirth, was in danger every second of death from the Darklord's currently capricious mandate. Orpheus Alpha seemed to care for her, or for the person she had been, at any rate. This was intriguing in itself; androids were not programmed for passionate feelings. They could feel loyalty, and concern to a degree, but in general they remained in a state of artificially induced Zen. But, as I'd had cause to notice before, Orpheus Alpha was no ordinary android.

The Lady Thanatos was even more intriguing and upsetting. She was obviously trying to cling to her sanity, with varying degrees of success. It was quite a quest I was being asked to join. I was intrigued and sympathetic; perhaps I would have joined it, if I didn't have my own quest. But to take on a case like this now made about as much sense as playing leapfrog with a unicorn. I had to untangle my own life before I could try to help anyone else's, and the only way to do that was to confront the Darklord and at least try to learn what his purpose was. Until I knew what was real and what was his dark fantasy, I could not be my own man, and I couldn't be worth anything as a private eye.

I didn't look at them as I said, "I'm sorry. At another time..."

Lady Thanatos stepped toward me. I couldn't help my reaction—I retreated. She stopped abruptly, and that stop said as clearly as any expression she could not show that I had hurt her. After a moment, her eerie voice said, "Kamus, without the aid of someone like you, our chances are almost non-existent. I must remain hidden, and Orpheus is also marked for suspicion as an android. We've offered you the Black Mask—does that not sway you?"

Orpheus said, "He doesn't believe that we can find it."

I said, "It's not just that. This is all happening at just under light speed. You offer me no proof; you just walk into my office and walk me out of it. I'd have to hear a lot more about this before I agreed to help you."

Any reply Orpheus was about to make was stopped by a creak on the outside landing. We looked toward the door. The dim sunlight showed a shadow moving across the ill-fitting jamb. I had forgotten my suspicion of being followed.

"The Osteomechs," Orpheus said softly. "They've found us."

Lady Thanatos could not gasp, but the reflexive movement of her skeletal hand toward her jaws indicated it.

The latch began to move slightly. "Does this place have a back door?" I asked.

"No."

"It figures." I tossed him the blaster and took some recently purchased thunderdust from my pouch, hoping the spell would work for me. As the latch clicked, I spoke three words, "*Wolends ya pathak!*" and hurled the vial at the door. The thunderdust was supposed to explode the door outward; instead, there was a rather smoky *Pop!* and the door vanished, revealing two tall, thin figures in robes and cowls, with holomasks peering out. The door latch still dangled in one gloved hand.

"And I thought I had trouble with spells before," I said.

Behind me I heard a slight mechanical sound as Orpheus pressed the firing button of his blaster with no effect. Simultaneously, the holomasks on the Osteomechs faded away, to reveal two leering skulls. The Darklord's mandate had struck again; some, but not all, of the machines in the room had failed.

I drew my sword. The Osteomechs parted their robes to reveal swords hanging from their pelvic girdles. They pulled them from their scabbards and lunged toward me. I blocked one sweeping blow and countered. I struck instinctively to incapacitate with a thigh wound, but my blade simply passed through the fabric, encountering nothing where flesh would normally be, and I barely managed to parry the second one's thrust.

"Strike their heads off!" Orpheus shouted. "It's the only way!"

I struck again, but the second one had gotten inside my guard and I missed. I stepped backward and promptly fell over my bag, landing on my back. The Osteomech dropped on top of me; ivory phalanges tightened around my throat. I seized its wrists and pulled, with no effect—it was strong.

It was strong, but, without any flesh padding its bones, it was also light and fragile. Before it could throttle me, I heel-palmed its naked jawbone, knocking out a tooth and snapping the Osteomech backward hard enough to break its hold. I scrambled to my feet and looked around; the second skeleton had gone for Orpheus, who was trying to hold it off with the stool. He threw it at the Osteomech, sending the skeleton clattering to the floor, then reached into his chestpack. That was all I saw before I felt a bony hand grasp my ankle. I turned and swung my sword, felt it pass through dry vertibrae and jar on what seemed to be a thick cable inside. The Osteomech's head flopped to one side, and one of its arms collapsed with a rattle into separate bones.

The room suddenly filled with music, or rather, with the components of music: a monophonic series of notes plucked from strings, each tone swelling and reverberating in the tiny garret, then fading away to be replaced by another, different sound. There was no harmony to it, no relationships between the notes, but their regularity, like oil dripping into water, was hypnotic, almost soothing. The effect on the mechanized skeletons was considerably more than soothing; Lady Thanatos and the Osteomech facing Orpheus were motionless, as was the one kneeling and holding my ankle in a suddenly lax grip. I stepped away from it. Orpheus kept playing, face frowning in concentration. The music sounded vaguely familiar, and after a moment I realized it was similar to ancient Oriental music of Earth. The Osteomechs were beginning to move, very slightly, with tiny clicking twitches of bones. Then Orpheus plucked one final, shivering note, and the three skeletons dropped to the floor like marionettes with cut strings, the rattling crashes providing a discordant finale.

Orpheus put his instrument back in his chestpouch, turned, and picked up the pile of bones and fabric that was Lady Thanatos. "We must hurry," he said to me as he carried her out the door. "There will be more of them after us!"

Perhaps his music had hypnotized me slightly; at any rate, I asked no questions, but simply followed him. We moved quickly through the reeking streets of the Maze, Orpheus taking care that none of his lady love's bones showed.

At the corner of Guardslayer Street and Eunuch Avenue I saw five cloaked figures round a graffiti-covered cistern a few blocks away and follow us. "You were right," I told Orpheus. "But we should be safe while we're on the streets. Their disguises are too fragile for them to risk attacking in public." I hoped.

We exited the Maze through the Skull Gate, appropriately enough, and caught a carriage that would take us to the balloon-boat port. Halfway there I remembered that I had left my bag back in the garret. That didn't improve my mood any.

While we were in the carriage, Lady Thanatos regained consciousness; or so I assumed, since the skeleton once more moved of its own accord. The holomask began functioning again as well, and the calm, alabaster face materialized over the skull again. "So you played after all," she said hollowly to Orpheus.

"I had to," the android told her.

"I don't know why I fear the music so. Oblivion is preferable to this mockery of life . . ."

"Don't start that again!"

"Why not? Look how much closer I am to death than to life."

"You are *not* going to die," Orpheus said between clenched teeth. "You will live, and when you live, so at last shall we—" He stopped, then said in a soothing tone, "Believe me, dearest, all of this travail and hardship will be worth it."

Her holomask showed only resignation. An awkward

silence followed, into which I plunged with, "That was quite a tune back there, Orpheus. Where did you learn to play the lyre like that?"

"It's not a lyre," he said warily. "It's a miniature kithara. As to what I played . . . it is my own composition, a reconstruction based upon the ancient Greek Dorian mode. Within the framework of that scale, I plucked a pentatonic system. The music is powerfully soporific in its effect on the mechanized minds of the Osteomechs, much as other scales are tranquilizing to humans. I have my theories as to why, but I shall not go into them here. As to the potency of its effect . . . well, you have seen for yourself. It was with my kithara that I rescued Lady Thanatos from the Osteomechs."

He lapsed back into brooding then. I glanced back through a crack in the carriage's old leather canopy and saw another carriage following us, a thin, hooded figure holding the jemlas' reins. Whether I had agreed to help Orpheus or not made no difference now; unless I came up with an idea, those animated nightmares would see me more dead than they.

We moved on briskly down the streets of Mariyad, past the green and hedged esplanade and the crenellated outer wall of Overlord Kirven's palace, through the dusty chaos of the Marketplace and the warehouse district. The various stenches of Mariyad were washed away by the sea breeze here; by the docks, the air was sharp and thrilling as a succubus's kiss. The balloon-boat port was just inland from the docks, a large area of soft-plowed ground and a stone building. I could see the large gas bags looming over the roof, all painted with the flying guard emblem of Mariyad. They were an impressive sight against the indigo sky, but I was more interested in the crowds of people at the entrance. Quite a few tourists were there to see more of Ja-Lur despite the many risks, now that the technological aids and comforts so important to outworlders worked at least part of the time. Tourism was booming, especially in the larger cities, where fear and distrust of outworlders was still mitigated by the money they had. I looked at the potpourri while Orpheus paid the driver. At another time I would have been interested in seeing such things as a native of Wikerson's world, covered with a living fungoid symbiont, or a tenclone from the twin worlds of Romulus and Remus, each with a different glyph of the clone name glowing on their chests, or a tall thin insectoid wearing a hypoallergenic skinsuit to protect him from xenophylactic shock. These and many other outworlders mixed singly or in tours with Ja-Lurians from other cities and nations: Glass Mountain girls, Vermillion Asthetes from Port Rizh, crystal caravan leaders from the Nonulé Hills and various and sundry merchants, mercenaries, sailors, alchemists, charlatans, and others. As I said, it would have been a fascinating study in customs and culture shock, but at the moment I was looking for cowled and hooded Osteomechs only.

We moved through the crowd warily. At the ticket window Orpheus was told that the *Graywolf*, which was bound for Vanastas, the capital of Hestia, was leaving. If he could catch it he could buy the tickets from the captain.

We hurried through the crowd. As we walked out onto the field, Orpheus said to me, "Kamus, this is your moment of decision. Do you go north or south?"

The *Graywolf*'s lines were being released by the ground crew. On board, two sky sailors were hauling the rope ladder up; when they saw us approaching, they let it down again and shouted for us to hurry. I looked back at the crowd and saw five cloaked figures break through it, running across the field toward us. I turned and looked toward the other boats, one of which was supposed to go south, and which I was supposed to be on. There was no way for me to reach them; the Osteomechs could cut me off easily.

I turned and pushed Orpheus toward the rope ladder. He grabbed it and started up, as did Lady Thanatos. I followed, hooking the last rung over my sword hilt to carry it up with me. Looking down, I saw the Osteomechs reach the spot where the ladder had been, and look up. One shook a gloved fist. Then I was over the rail and onto the deck, and the *Graywolf* was rising rapidly into the air.

Orpheus came to stand beside me. "It seems you've made your decision."

On my other side, from within the muffling folds of her cloak, Lady Thanatos said, "Thank you, Kamus."

"Oh, my pleasure," I said. "I was wondering how to spend my vacation."

3

I stood at the stern of the *Graywolf*, watching the spires and towers of Mariyad vanish into the dark distance, realizing that it was entirely possible that I'd never see the city again. I was starting my quest to confront the Darklord the same way it seemed I started most things: backwards. I shrugged. I hadn't had much choice in joining them. All I could do now was hope that Jann-Togah wasn't very good at predicting danger.

I reminded myself of the possibility of finding the Black Mask, but I knew that that had the chance of a snowball in a supernova. Still, I didn't entirely regret coming. I wanted to see their quest succeed. The romantic in me took the lead at inopportune times. Orpheus's non-android characteristics intrigued me, and I felt very sorry for Lady Thanatos—mixed, I had to admit, with a certain understandable amount of uneasiness. I wanted to see their improbable romance succeed, as I had wanted Lohvia's and Niano's to succeed, as I had wanted Thea Morn's and mine to succeed. I hoped this one didn't turn out the way the others had.

I turned away from Mariyad to have a look at the other passengers. Orpheus had gone forward to seek out the captain and pay our fares, and Lady Thanatos had gone with him. I sat down and watched the show.

Most of the passengers were tourists from Earth and other worlds, which meant that decadence reigned. Ja-Lur had suddenly become chic to outworlders, particularly to the Hyperspace Set, those rich enough to loudly hate being rich, who spend their time jaunting between solar systems. They wandered about the boat, exclaiming over the quaintness and primitiveness of the architecture and apparatus, and generally getting in the crew's way. They laughed when a complicated aspect of someone's apparel or equipment failed at the mandate's whim, such as when the magnetic fields holding spinning rocks above an asteroid magnate's head stopped and gave him a nasty headache. It also amused them when a mind music hat on a Prime Mentor from the planet Maelstrom shut off, probably for the first time in decades, and he had to be sedated due to shock. There were lots of laughs on the *Graywolf* this trip.

Presently one of the other passengers sat down beside me. She was human, and either young or rich enough to look young. Her body could have been the crowning achievement of a genetics parlor. She was wearing a green spiral strip which looked like it had been sprayed on, which it had. She was also an albino, or had dyed her eyes red and her skin and hair the color of paper. "Hello," she said, in a voice that could melt a comet. "Aren't you Kamus of Kadizhar?"

I said I was. "We thought so! How nova!" she said, obviously proud of herself. I had seen her among the passengers before, and knew that by 'we' she meant her brother, apparently a fraternal twin who was covered with black skin dye. She grinned at me. Her front teeth had been microsculpted with tiny frescoes of questionable taste. She lifted one hand and twirled it about the end of her wrist; her little finger had been replaced with a multipurpose prosthetic plug. The attachment she wore currently was a drug inhalor. "We read all about you in *Space-Time* holozine. You prevented a war between your planet and Malta II, didn't you?"

"Some thought so."

"My name is Ivory." I didn't ask her where she got it. "I was wondering if you wanted to join us in our cabin? We could sniff plasma and warp into some hypersex."

I had already decided that this was a proposition. A witty reply seemed called for. " 'Us'?"

Ivory looked vaguely upset. "Oh, I'm very rude! I haven't introduced my brother, Ebony!" Then she looked straight at me and an odd change took place in her appearance. Her lips thinned and compressed slightly, her eyes grew wider, rounder, the muscles governing them relaxing and tensing in subtle ways. Her shoulders hunched very slightly. None of the changes was spectacular by itself, but together the effect was like the emergence of another personality.

The new face looked bored, and somewhat annoyed. "I must apologize for my sister," a voice that was Ivory's and yet different, deeper, said. "One would think that someone so well-versed in seduction would be more aquainted with subtlety."

"So you're mindswappers," I said. "Well, thanks for the offer, but in this case, three is definitely a crowd."

The slim shoulders shrugged. "Don't misunderstand me, Kamus; because I am mentally linked with my sister doesn't mean I share her desires or her insatiable appetite. Believe me, it's not easy living with her. Or in her, for that matter."

The change of expression came again, and Ivory was back. She looked angry. "Don't think I don't know what he said! If we weren't linked . . ." she looked at me, and the anger was replaced by disappointment. "I had hoped you might be more cosmopolitan, anyway," she said to me.

"What can I say? Ja-Lur is a backward planet."

She pouted, stuck that prosthetic pinkie in a nostril, and inhaled deeply. It looked like potent stuff; from the way her eyes unfocused and from the euphoric smile that replaced the pout, I was pretty sure that her mind was expanding like a fireball. She stood and wandered back into the crowd.

"Humans are so decadent," Orpheus's voice said from behind me. I turned toward another part of the cluster of frills, leather, plastics, feathers, and scales that marked the perimeters of the tourists. Quite a few of them were gathered near the cabins under the shadow of the balloons, laughing and talking and sniffing, swallowing, or otherwise absorbing a galactic variety of stimulants. It was getting to be quite a party. Making his way around the outside of it cautiously was Orpheus Alpha, the Lady Thanatos close behind him. "I've been looking for you, Kamus," he said. "There are no more rooms—oh, pardon me." This last was addressed to a large blue hairless Gelatinoid who was obviously, by its size, from a heavy-gravity planet. It had a sonic tattoo of a strange ideogram where a chest might be on a humanoid. Orpheus had just bumped into a pseudopod it was using to hold a stim-sponge and to gesture while it talked to an Aldebaran hydromorph. The Gelatinoid flushed an angry orange and turned toward Orpheus. Its amorphous shape snapped out two pseudopods, one a whiplike extension that pinned the android's legs, the other a blunt organic club that struck his solar plexus. Orpheus bent over double, gasping for breath. The Gelatinoid lifted him and dangled him upside down. Conversation died out; eyes and other sensory organs were all directed at the two.

I had started across the deck when the Gelatinoid attacked; its ideogram meant it was a seventh configuration of Ry'nl Fatagh, an extraterrestrial martial art that was particularly brutal. "Put him back on his feet, please," I said.

A small translator near the top of the amorphous outworlder spoke in a tinny voice. "He is only an android, why should I not dispose of him?"

It reminded me very much of the attitude Xidon had taken toward Niano, and it made me just as mad this time. But before I could do something foolish like draw my sword or speak a spell, Orpheus, hanging upside down, reached into his chest pack quickly and pulled out his blaster, taking advantage of the Gelatinoid's divided attention. "No matter how fast you are," he said, "You can't match the speed of light. Release me, or—"

The Gelatinoid was taken aback by this un-android behavior, as were the majority of the tourists there. "Faugh," it said, finally; "I would not soil my pseudopods on you." It dropped Orpheus, turned and squished angrily off toward the companionway. The majority of tourists drifted away from our location as well, seeking to re-establish the merriment elsewhere, as Orpheus picked himself up painfully. I saw Lady Thanatos out of the corner of my eye as I moved to help Orpheus. She had not moved; her holomask had shown no flicker of concern.

I tried to help Orpheus to his feet, but he shoved my hand away. He was seething with rage; a most unusual sight in an android. "Barbarian," he muttered, referring, I hoped, to the Gelatinoid. "'Only an android' indeed!" He glanced at Lady Thanatos. "They'll soon learn better," he said under his breath.

"Are you all right?" I asked him.

He visibly mastered his anger, as before, and nodded. "Yes, thank you. Now, as I was about to say . . . I am afraid there are no more cabins or rooms available. I was able to provide quarters for you, after a fashion, in a storage locker in the hold; it is big enough to sleep in, and will keep you warm. I can go several days without sleep; we will be in Vanastas before I tire. I hope that will be satisfactory."

"It will have to be," I said. I nodded to them both, and walked forward. The deck was fairly quiet, save for laughter and other sounds of the outworld tourists, the croak and flapping of the kragor team and the rubbery stretching of the huge balloons overhead. I breathed deeply of the thin, cold air, which was scented with the smells of tar and wood. I found a space near the prow that was relatively private, clipped my safety line to the rail, and looked down at the green patchwork of farmland passing beneath. Near a stand of timber was a small keep; the bastions and ravelins of its wall seen from overhead reminded me of the starburst on Orpheus's forehead. I had never seen an android protest unkind treatment before. Their genetic programming simply did not allow it.

It was then that the thought occurred to me: what if he were not an android?

It would be fairly easy to alter one's appearance to resemble an android, at least as far as facial features went. Removing the genitalia would be a bit extreme . . . all I had by way of suspicion was his non-android personality. Why would someone want to be thought an android?

I put a rein on speculation. I had no facts yet; all I could do was keep an open mind.

I had become involved in strange situations before, but this one slew the dragon. I knew nothing, really, about either of them; I was on the *Graywolf* by a combination of circumstance and hunch-playing. I wanted the Black Mask, and this entire affair was just mad enough to make me believe I might find it.

And when I did find it—what then? Catch the next balloon-boat south to the Black Desert, and then make my way into the Darkland to confront the Darklord. How could I possibly make the trip in time—me, a lone half-breed who couldn't trust my abilities to entertain children, much less save my life?

The breeze of the balloon-boat's passage stirred my hair. I looked down on Ja-Lur, the Darkworld, my world. This planet where I was born and, most likely, would die. Which would soon, if Jann-Togah and Valina were right, be innundated by chaos on Shadownight.

As a Darklander, I knew that I would not be popular on Shadownight. Still, it might work in my favor. Both Jann-Togah and Kaan Ta'Wyys, whose knowledge far exceeded mine, had indicated that Shadownight would be the ideal time to attempt to overthrow the Darklord. It seemed that even the Darklord would have his hands full when the eclipse of Bellus, the outer moon, by Jaspara, the inner, formed the Bloodmoon and the forces of Darkness were loosed. Maybe then, with more luck than I had any right to expect, I would somehow use the Black Mask against him.

But Shadownight was less than three weeks away. It would take two of them to reach by balloon-boat the far reaches of the Black Desert where the realm of Ja-Agur began. Beyond that, no map showed details. The few Darklanders I had met all came from the stark, moon-like mountains to the south of the Black Desert, or the coastal regions. I had met no one from the interior of the Darkland. I had heard vague legends of Ja-Kanak, the Dark River, which supposedly flowed upland from the sea into Ja-Agur and to the Darklord's citadel. But I didn't know how much was true and how much was myth. There was only one way to find out—go there.

And try to come back alive.

The wind was becoming chill; I went below decks. As I walked down the dark companionway, two cabin doors opened simultaneously; from one stepped Lady Thanatos, unmasked, her cloak open and her skeletal structure showing. From the other came a triped of Kilroy's Planet, wearing robes of optical fibers that glowed with ultraviolet light. The eerie radiance washed over Lady Thanatos, illuminating her bones, which were covered with green, glowing patches. It was a sight that couldn't be matched in a month of Shadownights, and once again, involuntarily, I stepped away from her.

Again, I could sense that she was hurt. "I did not mean to frighten you, Kamus," she said.

"I didn't mean to be so jumpy." I gestured at a wooden bench nearby. "Would you care to sit?"

"If you care to. I do not grow tired standing." She folded the bulky creases of her robe about her and sat down, her black-gloved hands motionless on her lap. I sat beside her.

She was as still as the victim of a Gorgon's glance; no twitches, no slight movements designed to settle flesh comfortably into a new position. It was disconcerting.

"I hope you don't mind," I said, "if I ask you some questions. Though I'm employed primarily as a bodyguard, I can do a better job if I know more about you."

"I don't mind." Impossible to tell from the unearthly timbre of her voice if she meant it.

"First, just to satisfy my curiosity—could you explain the mechanics of your state?"

She hesitated. "Orpheus went into this partially. Briefly: my mind has been encoded and encased within an electronic brainbox, a computer that now sits where my brain and spine once did. I see my microcameras and hear through microphones, all implanted where eyes and ears once were. I speak through a vocal device. My skeleton is articulated and mobile due to tractor and pressor beams which operate between source points on my joints and perform the functions of musculature and cartilage; all are powered by a hyperfield generator implanted here." She indicated her sinus cavity.

"I take it, then, that you can no longer feel, taste or smell."

"No longer," she said distantly.

"I'm sorry to dwell on such painful subjects," I told her.

She was silent for a moment. "Painful . . ." she said at last, slowly. "No, they are not painful—not any more. When I was transformed, I thought I would go mad—perhaps I did go mad—if so, madness is a boon. I do not really remember having a body. Sometimes I look at others and think: how bulky, how cumbersome. How inefficient. Sometimes I wonder if I really want a body again . . ."

She fell silent once more. I sat beside her, feeling decidedly uncomfortable; watching someone's humanity slipping away has never been one of my favorite pastimes. I cleared my throat and said, "About your life before you became an Osteomech—"

"I can only tell you what Orpheus has told me of my past. As far as I am concerned, I was born in the acid bath; the trauma of my conversion wiped out any previous memory. But Orpheus says that the Matrix can restore my memory, if I so desire."

A Zane Seneschal from Niquos staggered past us, stumbling over its six legs but not spilling a drop of the Liquid Light in its goblet.

"Do you believe Orpheus?" I asked her.

The holomask looked shocked. "Do you think I should not?"

"Just asking. I like to know where everyone stands."

The naked skull showed no expression; I wished she would re-activate her mask. "I believe him. He loves me."

"Is that not unusual in an android?"

"I would not know . . . as I said, my memories and experiences are relatively new. But I think it may be more common than A.S.T.R.A. would care to admit."

"I would still like to hear what you know of your past."

"I was a young woman, in my early twenties; the daughter of a quantum engineer on the planet Carcosa. We lived in the capital city, King-In-Yellow, by Lake Hali; a beautiful area before the disaster, I am told. My father worked for A.S.T.R.A. Orpheus also worked there, and he says that he saw me often, and came to fall in love with me.

"I was kidnapped by the Osteomechs not long before the hyperpower plant disaster that destroyed King-In-Yellow and my family. Orpheus had already left Carcosa in search of me. That is all I know of my past; all I care to know, really. What is the point of remembering more? I already feel sorrow at the thought of my family's death; how much more would I feel if they were real people to me instead of abstractions?"

There was a sort of logic to that, if I didn't examine it too closely. I asked her about her captivity by the Order of the Osteomechs. She described a horrible existence; living in caves on a barren world, studying and meditating constantly on the inevitable heat death of the universe. They had given her the name of Lady Thanatos. She had evidently been intended to be an important part of their theocracy; she did not know what, however, because Orpheus had rescued her before she was to learn.

"How did he manage that?"

"I do not really know . . . his music put me to sleep as it did my captors. The sounds lull me into a sleep-like state. Orpheus does it to me on occasion, to calm me, when I become too upset with my state. It is pleasant, yet I fear it at times. Other times I long for it."

"And he brought you here to search for the *Galactic Express*. It's a dangerous quest," I said. "You realize that at any time the mandate could shut off the hyperfield that powers your computer. That would not be the same as the unconsciousness that his music causes. Instead, it would wipe your memory banks and force fields; destroy your personality. In effect," I said, watching her, "it would kill you."

She showed no signs of desiring that. All she said was, "Orpheus has thought of this. He has added a stasis cell to my brainbox. In case of a power failure, my mind and memories will be dumped into the cell, which requires no power to store them. When the mandate fails again, normal functioning will continue."

I thought about that. It sounded risky; if the contents of her mind were not all dumped in time, she could suffer the electronic equivalent of brain damage. "It seems there should have been an easier way. Couldn't A.S.T.R.A. have provided you with an android body?"

"Orpheus says the cost would be too much."

At this point footsteps echoed down the companionway; I looked up and saw Orpheus Alpha standing before us. He looked angry. "You are unmasked!" he snapped at Lady Thanatos. "Activate it immediately! We must take no chances—the Osteomechs may still be pursuing us!"

"I'm sorry, Orpheus. You're right."

He looked from her to me. "What were you two talking about?"

I smiled. "Just chatting."

He hesitated as though about to say something further, then motioned with his hand to Lady Thanatos. "We must talk in private," he said to her, and led her toward the cabins. I leaned back on the bench and thought about it.

Lady Thanatos seemed to me to be trying to hold on to her humanity, but it also seemed to be a losing battle. I hoped Orpheus and I could reflesh her bones before she lost it. But I was beginning to wonder if we would.

4

The *Graywolf*'s course from Mariyad to Vanastas took five days. They were fairly uneventful. The locker Orpheus had rented for my quarters would have cramped a corpse, and in addition it was next to the cabin of a Green Vaul from the Swofford System, so the smell was enough to sicken a scavenger. I burned a lot of incense.

On the second day one of the few Ja-Lurians on board, a taciturn Plains tribesman, hurled overboard a hermaphrodite who propositioned him. That put a damper on the debauchery for a time. By the fifth day, however, the party was going strong again. Three other outworlders died: Dan Dostoyanovitch, GFL star player and winner of the Hyperbowl trophy, dissolved from an overdose of Ultra Dust; Tal Grigor, a native of the planet Phoenix, fell to his death because he was too drunk to remember that his wings were vestigal, and a Borealis Dancer was killed by a snow cat which she tried to pet during one of the landings made to rest the kragors.

On the third day, as we crossed the river Archan, I saw Orpheus alone at the rail and decided to try to get some answers to my questions about him. He had been friendly enough when we had spoken before, but evasive about his past. I joined him and asked, "Why are you masquerading as an android, Orpheus?"

He looked startled, then laughed. "Is that what you think?"

"I'm not sure what to think. But I'd have to be as dense as a neutron star not to notice a difference between you and your average android."

He looked off into the distance. "I am an android," he

said after a moment. "I am, and yet I am not. According to the scientists at A.S.T.R.A., I am the result of faulty Matrix programming—in other words, a mutant. How it happened, they are not sure, nor have they been able to duplicate it. Or so they tell me. Rather than return me to the vat, they decided to study me, no doubt to learn how to turn this to their best advantage. They were in something of a quandary; they did not want to destroy an example of an android with free will, which they might wish to use someday, and yet it would hardly do to make more of my type. So they put me to work at A.S.T.R.A."

"And there you met the woman who was to become Lady Thanatos."

He nodded. When he spoke again, his voice had a wistful tone to it. "Everyone in the universe takes love for granted; even if they are unloved, they know there is always the possibility of love coming to them. Due to a freak combination of genes, I can feel love; but who will return love to an android? No one, I thought. And then, I met her..."

He was silent for a moment, then continued, his voice heavy. "And then the Osteomechs took her..."

I said nothing. After a time, he asked, "How much longer until we reach Vanastas, Kamus?"

"Another three days."

"She grows increasingly remote, my Lady Thanatos," he said. "She is losing touch with life, with her previous existence. I hope we find the Matrix in time... before she forgets..."

He turned and walked away from me, down the companionway. I stood alone at the rail. I put a stick of gum in my mouth and thought about it.

His story was very touching; the romantic in me was all for it. I could imagine what his loneliness had been like, and what an exalted, idealized love he must have conceived, a love close to worship, unsullied by reality or even sexual desire, since he was neuter. In other words, a feeling that bore little resemblance to real love, but which was nonetheless painful. A feeling that had sent him on the rescue trail when she was kidnapped by the Osteomechs. As I said, the romantic in me loved it; unfortunately, the detective in me was having a hard time with it. I could think of several things that struck a false note; his unfeeling description in the Maze of her conversion, for example. And I remembered what he had said to her during the carriage ride: "You will live, and when you live, so at last shall we triumph." I wondered what he meant by that.

I was still not convinced that Orpheus was an android, even a mutant android. But I was convinced that there was more going on than he was telling.

* * *

The air had turned considerably cooler as we progressed further north; we had descended to a lower altitude in search of warmer wind. Most of the aliens and natives stayed in their cabins. On the fifth night I was on deck, looking down at the low, snow-dusted foothills and moors of Hestia. Bellus and Jaspara, though not full, illuminated everything almost like daylight. My breath streamed away from me in white threads. I had been feeling increasingly gloomy the past few days, and this landscape wasn't helping matters any. Despite days, weeks, months of thought on the subject, I was no closer to formulating a plan for dealing with the Darklord. Sometimes I wondered if the best idea might be just to somehow scrape up the fare to leave the planet, to start a new business on some other world. It might be the one thing the Darklord didn't expect. I had learned long ago—or so I thought—that there were times to fight and times to run away. On another world my life would be my own—wouldn't it?

It was then that I sensed someone behind me; I turned and saw Ebony. I nodded to him, peering closely at him. "Yes, it's me," he said, interpreting my scrutiny correctly. "Ivory is currently dallying with two spice traders from the planet Diablo." He looked bored. "I believe her avowed intent is to seduce everything remotely human on his boat by the time we reach Vanastas."

"There seems to be a lack of filial affection here," I remarked.

"For good reason. I am not a prude by any means, but I believe some sense of decorum is called for. We represent a wealthy family on Greenstein's World. Our clan has always observed a tradition of primogenitive right. My beloved sister was born a bare fifteen minutes before me."

I saw the point he was making: she could make, and had

made him agree to her whims, as she had inherited the bulk of the family fortune.

Evidently I didn't keep my expression as blank as I'd hoped, for he said testily, "Well, what would you do in my place?"

"Leave," I replied.

"I wish it were that easy," he said glumly. "Our mindswapping ability is a two-edged sword. We are linked; if we remain too far from each other, madness could possibly result." He looked down at his dyed skin and the prosthetic on his hand with distaste. "So I have put up with her, and continue to." He sighed, then smiled apologetically at me. "I didn't mean to interrupt your reverie. Like you, I came up seeking a little solitude. I was admiring the boat. It's a well-constructed craft." He looked up at the balloons. "Is it my imagination, or are those gasbags organic?"

I looked up at them; the vascular bulges and striations in the exocarp were easily visible. "Yes, they are. They're the fruit of the balloon tree." He raised his eyebrows in polite interest, so I elaborated. "They're huge trees, much bigger than Earthly redwoods or the stonetrees of Shayol VI. They grow near the Inland Sea, which their root systems tap. The trees separate the water into hydrogen and oxygen and pump the hydrogen into gigantic, elastic seed pods. When they fill, they break off and rise until the thin air bursts them and scatters their seeds."

"Fascinating," he said absently. I could tell he wanted to hear no more on exobotany, so I waited for his next line.

"You travel with interesting companions," he said abruptly.

"How so?"

"The Osteomech. Those robes can't disguise the lack of flesh. I wonder why she wears a holomask. Most Osteomechs make no bones about their state, so to speak. I was unaware that they took pleasure trips."

I shrugged. "It's a free galaxy, for the most part. I'm merely their guide."

"And her companion, the android. There must be something wrong with his programming; he's almost as moody as the bone woman. I'd almost think he's not an android at all. Anyone can tattoo an A.S.T.R.A. symbol on one's forehead." He was musing to himself now. "An X-ray holo would settle it;

android interior design is a lot more efficient than what blind evolution has handed us. The date of his manufacture should be stamped on his heart-lung organ . . ."

"You seem to know a lot about androids," I said. "Do you think Orpheus is masquerading?"

He shrugged. "If he isn't, whoever programmed his musical abilities did a superlative job. I have heard him play behind the closed door of his cabin; the music is strange, but beautiful."

Further conversation was cut short by the appearance of Ivory, who wandered up the companionway. She was wearing clothes of a cloudy, misty material that shredded and re-formed in the chill breeze, and seemed designed to come apart in revealing areas. She leaned her milk-white body against me and fluttered eyelashes that could have lifted her off the deck. I caught a whiff of pheromone spray that almost stunned my glands. "Haven't we met somewhere before?" she asked me wistfully. "The Labyrinth Habitat? *Yenne Velt?* Krypton II?"

"I don't think so. If you were in that body, I'd have remembered."

She misunderstood me; she looked disappointed again, then brightened. "You don't like this body? No problem. We'll switch, Ebony and I." She turned to her brother. "Switch with me, dear."

"I don't think so," Ebony said shortly.

"Don't be difficult, dear," Ivory purred.

Ebony looked uncomfortable, but shook his head. At that point, Orpheus and Lady Thanatos came up the companionway. "Kamus,"the android said to me, "we must discuss plans for our . . . tour."

Ivory forgot about her twin and sashayed over to Orpheus. She pointed at the starburst on his forehead. "You're an android!" she said in delight. "I've heard interesting things about androids . . ."

Orpheus stepped back as if she had plague. What might have happened then was anyone's guess. What did happen was that the sky tore apart.

The two moons were at their closest approach, seeming only two handsbreaths apart, when I suddenly sensed unseen forces gathering. Darkness was in the air; how or why I did not know. There were no other Darklanders on board to cast a spell. But there was no mistaking it; even those not of the Blood could sense something wrong. The night seemed rigid with apprehension.

Ivory screamed.

She pointed at the two moons; a cloud had drifted across them, torn and ragged; it seemed to take the shape of a wailing face, with Bellus and Jaspara as cold, lidded eyes. A moan echoed across the landscape. It came again, louder; the sound of a gale-force wind.

"Brace yourselves!" I shouted.

A wind came suddenly from the south, pitching the prow downward sharply enough to cause the kragors pulling it to shriek and shy about. Then another wind struck with a boom, this one a downburst that caused one of the bag stays to snap with a sound like an arm breaking. The force of the wind scattered us like paper dolls; I hit the rail hard enough to wind me and collapsed on the yawing deck. Something that felt like a bundle of sticks landed on top of me: Lady Thanatos. Her cloak had been completely stripped from her by the wind, and her holomask had failed once again. She was lucky that no more than that failed; if the force fields holding her bones together had gone they would have been scattered over half of Hestia. She was also fortunate to have me cushion her fall, so that nothing was broken.

I lifted her off of me. Even in the chaos of the moment I could not help staring at her ivory bones, at the eerie way they moved, like something out of an ancient Earth horror movie.

No more winds struck; the tears in the sky had healed. Panic-stricken passengers boiled up from below, shouting, chattering, whistling, gobbling questions which the crew had no time to answer as they tried to repair the minimal damage to the balloon-boat. We all got to our feet. "I love this planet," Ivory said to Ebony. "So unpredictable! So exhilarating!"

"What happened, Kamus?" Orpheus asked.

"How should I know?"

"You should—you're a Darkland—" he caught himself too late. Ebony looked at me with wide eyes.

I glared at the android. "Thanks, Orpheus. Remind me to reveal one of your secrets someday."

"*Do* you have any idea what happened?" Ebony asked me.

"I'm not sure," I admitted, "but I think it was the first rumble of a supernatural volcano we locals call Shadownight." I explained briefly what it was. "For a moment there was an opening into another plane; the cosmos of Darkness."

"Does this happen every Shadownight?"

"The last time an interlunar eclipse happened over this part of Ja-Lur was before I was born, so I don't remember too much about it. I've heard that one wasn't nearly as bad as this one looks to be."

Lady Thanatos had found and donned her cloak again. Her holomask had resumed functioning, but not before Ivory had seen her. "An Osteomech!" she said. "There's a story in the latest issue of *Space-Time* holozine about them. I've often thought that making love to an Osteomech would be somewhat different . . ."

Somewhat to the surprise of all of us, Orpheus slapped her, hard. He looked like he was going to do it again, but I seized his arm and spun him away from her, though I was tempted not to interfere. Ivory looked shocked, then smiled dizzily. "How nova! A dominating android! Would you care to join me in force field bondage?"

Ebony stepped forward and took her arm. "Somehow I don't think so, Ivory," he said, leading her toward the companionway. Ivory pulled unsuccessfully at his grip on her wrist. "You people are all strange!" she shouted back over her shoulder at us.

"That's the axe calling the guillotine red," I said.

She started working over that one, but before she could decide to get mad, Ebony had her below decks.

"I'm sorry for losing my temper, Kamus," Orpheus said. He put one arm around Lady Thanatos's shoulders. "I could not stand to see that *human* speak to her so." He led Lady Thanatos, who had not said a word, away, and I was alone again, save for a few still-frightened passengers who looked mistrustfully at the night sky. Bellus and Jaspara were drawing away from each other slowly, and I realized that I no longer sensed Darkness. I felt sure that I had seen one of the first intimations of the coming Shadownight, and that there were more to come.

I leaned over the rail and looked down. The *Graywolf* was climbing again, approaching Swordcleft Pass in the Tasm

Mountains. Once through it we would be over Gargane Valley, where Vanastas lay.

All in all, it had been a very interesting voyage.

* * *

Autumn in Vanastas would make a good winter in Mariyad. Hestia was a sparsely populated nation; Vanastas would have almost fit within the boundaries of Thieves' Maze. There was no wall about the city—the mountains all about made none necessary. The Tasm range was one of the tallest on the continent, with peaks over 9,000 meters. I could see the silhouette of Darklord's Bane against the setting sun. From its foot it was supposed to look disturbingly like a stooped old man in a hood and cape. From my point of view, it just looked like the tallest mountain in the area. The winds that howled about the summit made approach by kragorback impossible. It would have to be climbed, something I wasn't looking forward to doing.

The naked rocks and snow faded out as we descended. Vanastas was low enough for trees; we came in low over evergreen forests which had been cut back almost a kilometer from the first scattered huts and cottages. A few patches of snow gleamed on the now-barren fields. The balloon-boat passed over the palace, a rustic structure of granite and timber. The city's symbol, a snarling snowcat carved from a huge log, reared on its roof. I thought about omens as we landed.

I had spoken with Orpheus; he wanted to start the expedition for the *Galactic Express* as quickly as possible, which was fine with me.

We hired a carriage that took us to the city's only hotel, the Axe and Ale Inn. Orpheus rented a room for two nights and I let the staff know we were interviewing mountain guides; I didn't say for what mountain. Then I went out to buy items for the expedition with money Orpheus had advanced me, arranging to have them delivered to him at the inn. I bought a heavier coat; my trenchcloak was no protection against the northern air. Then I returned to the inn, walking slowly down the narrow, cobbled streets. Though it was getting late, I could see outworld tourists in many of the small shops and stores. I wondered why a small city like Vanastas would draw even the few tourists it did; perhaps the quaintness and frontier atmosphere appealed to them. The appreciation certainly wasn't mutual; I saw some locals eyeing the outworlders warily. A light mist was falling, threatening to become rain; perfect weather for brooding.

I could point to no hard evidence for feeling that Orpheus was lying to me; I had only suspicions and feelings—those intuitions that form the bulwark of detective work. Lady Thanatos' story of her past bothered me, though I wasn't sure why. And Orpheus' attitude toward her still rang false at times. There had been ample evidence of a great temper lurking within him. While granting that having a loved one turned into a walking skeleton slowly losing touch with the remnants of her humanity was enough to set one's nerves on edge, I still sensed more behind it than that.

I kept on walking through the mist. I had entirely too many questions and not nearly enough answers. Thinking about Orpheus and Lady Thanatos and the others was not helping me solve my major problem—my upcoming conflict with the Darklord. If Orpheus was concealing something, it wasn't in my best interest to dig into it. I needed to get the Black Mask and head south as quickly as possible if I was going to reach Ja-Agur by Shadownight. Time was running out.

The thought of Shadownight reminded me of that manifestation on the *Graywolf*, and I felt even colder. Jann-Togah had said that this Shadownight would be strong. It looked like he meant it. How strong would it be? Too strong for even the Darklord to control, perhaps?

I didn't have time to wonder about it any further, however, because just then I heard from up the winding side street I was crossing the shouts and sounds of a fight. Before I could decide whether or not to be a hero, I saw a cloaked figure, pursued by several others, running toward me. Torchlight glinted on swords. The pursuers were shouting in Hestian. My knowledge of the dialect was limited, but I knew one of the words shouted: "Juvorkan!" It meant Darklander.

I stepped back into the shadow of a recessed doorway and spoke a Phrase: *"Hadyan meel, tos mara du!"* It was a simple spell, the best I could do on such short notice. It affected the inner ear, and it worked; too well. The world tilted for me as well, and I staggered forward, which had abruptly become "down." I collided with the cloaked figure and we both fell to the wet cobblestones, which seemed to be undulating like a sea snake with stomach flu. A brief glimpse of her body told me she was a woman.

Her pursuers were stumbling around like darklings in daylight. The one nearest me managed to draw sword and crawled toward us. I tried to unsheathe my own blade, managed it after figuring out the difference between the hilt amd my kneecap. I swung the flat of it through a puddle of dirty water, splashing it into his face; he fell over, cursing, trying to rub his eyes. I tried to stand, but I'd forgotten how my feet worked. Then, behind me, her voice said: "*Tanna rone!*" The Words stabilized the spell for her and me; the street steadied, and we ran toward the lights of the Axe and Ale Inn.

We hurried up the steps, pushed open the heavy wooden doors, and entered the warmth of the large room. I turned then to look at the Darklander I had helped.

Whatever I had intended to say went unsaid; I simply stared. Beside me, her black cloak tossed back like Darkness at bay, her hair a cloud sparkling in the rain, stood one of the last people I expected to see: Valina.

5

We were sitting at a table in the dining area of the inn, an alcove off the main room. I had my back to the wall, where I could see the huge stone fireplace, the double doors that were the entrance, and most of the chairs in which guests lounged. The room was old and high-ceilinged, the rafters and bannisters richly carved. It gave a feeling of security, but I still preferred my back to the wall.

Valina sipped spiced wine and smiled at me as I worked my way through a steak. She hadn't stopped smiling since we'd entered the inn, a half-hour before.

"What strange timing," she said. "I was just on my way to the balloon-boat port to buy a ticket back to Mariyad."

"It's not the best place for someone like us these days," I said. She lost the smile then, and I regretted my words.

"I know; I was planning on buying passage across the Eastern Ocean. It would have taken my last dechel, but it would have been worth it if I could somehow escape Shadownight..."

I shook my head. "You're a Darklander; you know better than that. Shadownight affects all of Ja-Lur; at least, all the lands I've ever heard of. An eclipse is only seen over a certain part of a planet, normally, but Shadownight is more than a matter of orbits. The only way to escape it is by going offplanet."

"I can't afford that." She sighed and looked at me. "You have a bad habit of being right, Kamus. So, tell me—where are you going to spend Shadownight?"

I told her. She looked stunned. "You can't be serious!"

"I wish I weren't."

"I'd assumed you'd given up that mad vendetta against the Darklord! Kamus, you haven't got a chance! He could crush you any time he wants!"

"You're really building up my confidence. I know the odds aren't good. Terrible, in fact. But I've got to try. That's why I've come north."

She wanted to know more, so I told her about Orpheus and Lady Thanatos, about the Black Mask and the *Galactic Express*. She had heard of the Black Mask, of course; I saw her eyes gleam with interest when I said that Orpheus Alpha professed to know where the talisman was. The question of whether or not I could trust her occurred to me, but I ignored it. I needed badly to confide in someone.

She leaned back in her chair, black cloak wrapped around her, and stared at me in disbelief. Claiming to have met Jann-Togah was only slightly less fantastic than claiming to have met Mondrogan the Clever.

I asked what had happened to her. She had gone north from Mariyad, travelling by various means. She had not found the peace and pain-ease she had sought in the North; I hadn't thought she would, and neither had she. What she had hoped to find—and hadn't—was a lessening of suspicion and paranoia toward possible Darklanders. But, though I was the only other Darklander she had encountered in her months here, she had seen plenty of persecution toward those suspected of the Blood.

"The outlying districts . . . the mountain communities," she said, shuddering. "Some of them have just gone mad, killing anyone who isn't fair-skinned . . . if my hair had been black, I'd be dead now."

So she had come to Vanastas, where she had hoped to find more civilized behavior. But as the time of Shadownight drew closer and supernatural happenings became more frequent, the city folk began looking for scapegoats also.

"Those who attacked me called themselves the Darkness Destroyers. They are a vigilante group. Two weeks ago a tourist—an Earthling from the Oriental Alliance—was found dead by their hands. His eyes and ears had been mutilated . . ."

I nodded. His sight, smell, and hearing had been savaged, no doubt with a tool made from a dead man's bone, to prevent his spirit from finding his murderers. It was an old superstition; I had been threatened with it more than once.

The sound of an argument from the common room interrupted her story. I looked up and saw, to my surprise, that Ivory and her brother had also stopped in Vanastas. They were sitting at a table not far from us.

"That's a disgusting suggestion!" Ebony shouted. "That's worse than what you did to that poor little monkey on the Ghost Planet!"

Ivory shrugged. "I just wanted to try something different." Ebony turned away from her in a rage. Ivory looked sadly toward what was evidently the object of their discussion—a public phonecub tethered to the bar. I shuddered and returned my attention to Valina.

"I almost envy you, Kamus," Valina said softly. "At least you've got a goal to work toward, however hopeless it may be. All I can do is try to stay alive. I hope you survive this. More; I hope—ridiculous fantasy!—that somehow you bring the Darklord down. I have no cause to love him either."

She had lowered her voice when she said that, but she did say it. I knew it took considerable courage for her to speak thusly about someone who was almost a god, and who had little sense of humor. Right then I wanted to ask her to help me; to come with me on the long trip south, to the Black

Desert and beyond. I almost did ask her. But she was right—it was not an easy quest, and I could not ask her to go with me simply because I was scared. And I did not really know her . . .

She looked at me then and smiled as though she had read my thoughts, which I didn't entirely discount. "I've thought about you quite a bit, Kamus," she said.

I didn't know what to say to that. I wasn't sure if I had thought quite a bit about Valina or not. Our relationship had hardly been cordial, for the most part. I told myself that was because of the geas that Kaan Ta'wyys had laid upon her, but it made no difference. I knew I had to be careful who I put my trust in; I suddenly regretted telling her of my quest.

I don't know if my silence hurt her or not, for a shadow fell over the table, and I looked up to see Orpheus and Lady Thanatos. "You have a talent for disappearing, Kamus," he said. "No matter. Everything is ready; the jemlas are saddled and the equipment packed. We could leave tonight, unless you wish to sleep, in which case I will take the jemlas to the stables." Then he looked at Valina. "Who is she?"

He didn't find out until later, because just then the large double doors of the Axe and Ale Inn were hurled open, and the same group of vigilantes that had attacked Valina earlier burst in amidst a flurry of snow. "There they are!" one of the Darkness Destroyers cried, pointing at us. Valina and I stood.

"All we want are the Darklanders," the leader said loudly, is voice echoing in the suddenly silent room. He pointed at Valina and me.

Valina raised both of her arms; whether in a spell to stop them or in fright I never knew, for the instant she did, Lady Thanatos collapsed with a dry rattle, shockingly loud. Her robe parted and the holomask vanished, revealing the pile of bones for all to see. "No!" Orpheus shouted, dropping to his knees beside what was left of Lady Thanatos. I noticed his expression; it was not shock or horror, but more like rage. The mandate was working full strength again, and had finally shut off her power.

But that wasn't how it looked to the locals. To them, Valina had just turned a living woman into a skeleton. With howls of fear and wrath, the Darkness Destroyers and other Vanastans charged toward us, and I found myself in the middle of the latest of a long line of tavern brawls.

"How exciting!" Ivory cried. "Frontier justice!" Then a sword whistled by her, shaving a lock of white hair from her scalp, and she dove under a table with a whoop of fear.

I heard the innkeeper shouting protests, with no one paying much attention. Orpheus fired his blaster, with no result. I drew sword. One husky, bearded fellow thrust at me; I parried, pricked his hand with my swordpoint to loosen his grip and kicked the blade from his hand. It skewered a roast two tables away. Another vigilante stumbled over Lady Thanatos' bones, scattering them. Orpheus kicked him in the groin. I caught a glimpse of Ivory and Ebony clinging to each other near one wall. We were considerably outnumbered; it was only a matter of time before we would be cut down. Then I heard Valina shouting Language. She was a full-Blooded Darklander and a powerful one; she did not need to enhance and stabilize her spells with potions and symbols like I did. The harsh syllables cut through the din, and all heads turned her way.

"You fear Darkness?" she cried. "Then look overhead!"

I looked up, along with everyone else. I knew what to expect since I had recognized the spell. Cries of fear and terror began as the corbels beneath the ceiling, carved in the shape of darkling gargoyles, shuddered and seemed to come to life. Grinning mouths howled, and taloned hands clawed the air as though trying to pull their bodies free of the walls.

The locals fled like royalty from a revolution. "Hurry!" Valina shouted to us. "The spell won't last long!" Which was true; already the wood was reasserting itself, and the creatures stiffening again. Only because the wood had once been alive had she been able to weave such an illusion at all.

Orpheus was scooping up Lady Thanatos's bones. I pushed him toward the doors and spoke a gathering spell that pulled the bones onto her cloak, which I bundled up and ran with. Ivory and Ebony followed me. As I ran, I saw the portly innkeeper, directly beneath one of the snarling gargoyles, stagger and clutch his chest. The blood drained from his face, and he fell to the floor. There was nothing to be done for him, so I leaped over him and burst out the doors.

Outside, it was snowing harder. Orpheus had already mounted his jemla; I leaped onto another, hugging the bundle of bones to my chest; there was always the chance that the stasis cell had worked. Valina mounted the third jemla.

Across the street, under a streetlamp, the mob was busy collecting its courage. "There they go!" one shouted. They pushed toward us through the snow.

I turned my jemla and saw Ivory and Ebony in the street, looking frantically for an escape route. "Take a jemla! Follow me!" I cried to them.

"I've never ridden anything alive before!" Ivory shouted.

"Think how nova it will be!" I shouted. "And hurry!" I grabbed a potion vial from my pouch, hurled it into the air and spoke several Words. It ignited; instead of the spectacular flare I had expected, it was a rather fizzling burst of orange light, but it dazzled or frightened several in the forefront of the oncoming mob; they fell in the slush, and others tripped over them.

"Come on!" I shouted to the twins, who had succeeded in mounting two jemlas. They could no more spur them to a gallop than they could jump them into hyperspace, however, so I spoke two Words that stung the animal's rumps. That did it; the twins hung on for dear life as the jemlas raced out of town, and I followed as fast as I could. A couple of arrows whizzed past my head as I rode past the last guttering light and into the dark snowstorm beyond.

* * *

Valina and Orpheus were waiting in the darkness beyond the edge of town. Without a word, Orpheus turned his mount toward the starlit silhouette of Darklord's Bane, and the rest of us followed, riding recklessly through the fields, avoiding the lights of the peasants' huts, until we entered the woods. They were as dark as a nightmare; I spoke a Word and a flickering green light kept pace with Orpheus. And so we rode for some time, the snow-laden branches thrashing and soaking us.

After several hours, the ground began to slope sharply upward. I caught up with Orpheus and said, "We'd best shelter for the night while there's still forest about us."

"How shall we find shelter in this blackness?" he asked.

"That's easy." I spoke several Words to the Dark light above me and it dipped and floated off into the night. We followed, and after a time came to the valley's edge. There was a cave there; damp and deep, more than large enough to shelter us and the jemlas. I gathered a pile of wet wood near the entrance and coaxed it into fire with another spell; Valina's Darkness at the inn had left her too tired to help.

In the flickering yellow light, Orpheus looked at the bundle of bones I had laid down. His face was pale, but without expression. I knew what he was thinking: now we would learn if the stasis cell had preserved Lady Thanatos' mind.

He opened the cloak on the damp rock, revealing the jumble of bones. Ebony looked at them nervously while Ivory clung to him, wide-eyed and at last at a loss for words.

Orpheus took his kithara from his chest pack and began to play. The strange, halting notes vibrated in the cave. The wind outside gave eerie counterpoint. The bones, pale against the dark cloak, seemed to move slightly. "No," whispered Ivory. "This is too strange, I don't—" Ebony made a sharp silencing sound. Ivory bit her lip and watched as though hypnotized.

Thunder sounded distantly as Orpheus played on. Then, with a resounding clatter, the bones flew together, femurs snapping into pelvis, tibiae fitting to fibulae, ribs aligning like Orpheus's pale fingers strumming the strings. Vertibrae strung themselves like beads onto the cable that extended from the brainbox. The entire assemblage was over in a moment. The skeleton sat up. The skull turned, as scanners in the eyesockets looked at us. I looked at Orpheus. He was leaning forward, fingers still on the strings, staring intently, willing her mind to be intact.

"Orpheus?" The lower mandible moved as the voice sounded—an atmospheric touch programmed by the Order of the Osteomechs. "What happened?" she asked.

Orpheus swallowed, relaxing only a tiny amount. "It appears that the stasis cell worked, though we must test your memory and reflexes to be certain." He held out his hand—she took it after a moment. "How are you called?" he asked her.

"Lady Thanatos."

"What are you?"

"An Osteomech."

Orpheus Alpha lead her toward the rear of the cave, still asking questions, beginning, I could tell, to believe that her mind had survived the shutdown intact. I took a deep breath and, hearing my joints crack, realized how tense I had been.

I stepped to the mouth of the cave. The fire was warming up the interior nicely. I looked out at the wet night, thinking about the fact that Orpheus had only brought enough provisions for two, which wasn't good, as there were now three extra in the party. A slight eddy of wind brought mist swirling around me, and I shivered. I was tired, cold, and lost, my companions—for the most part—people I didn't particularly trust. I could see no good end to this fiasco.

I realized someone was standing behind me, turned and saw Valina. She smiled at me.

"Feeling better?" I asked.

"Much." She stood beside me, looking out at the night. "That was as close an escape as I've had since last we were together."

"No one ever said I don't know how to show a lady a good time."

She smiled again. "Don't take all the credit, Kamus. It was I that put a spell of mock-life on those sculptures."

I nodded, then abruptly recalled the innkeeper's reaction to that spell. Valina frowned at my change of expression. "What is it?"

I told her. She shrugged. A pity, of course; yet I can hardly be held responsible for his weak heart." She gazed out into the black forest again, evidently dismissing the subject. I felt slightly nonplussed. It was true that she had not intended to kill the innkeeper, but the casualness of her reaction shocked me slightly. Death is more common on Ja-Lur than on most worlds, but it has never grown that common to me. I'd been the inadvertant cause of death before, and I'd never been able to shrug it off; it always upset me. I hoped it always would; to feel otherwise was to give in to Darkness.

I might have pursued the subject, but she spoke first: "This is a bad situation, Kamus."

"You're telling me."

"Worse than you think; the Darkness Destroyers will not be content with running us out of town. They may send a posse after us, to kill us or bring back proof of our deaths. We have only one choice—we will have to begin our climb up Darklord's Bane immediately. They won't pursue us into ice giant territory."

"I don't blame them. So it looks like all of us are going on Orpheus's quest." I had been given a few pointers on mountain climbing on Earth by Thea Morn, and I knew that a good sleep the night before was essential. Valina and I put a shielding spell on the cave to keep the night life out and keep the fire from being seen, and agreed to take turns waking up to maintain the spell. Then we all spread our bedding out, except Lady Thanatos and Orpheus, and turned in.

I tried to sleep, without much success at first. There was too much I didn't know about everyone here for me to be comfortable. I was wondering if it was entirely a coincidence that Ivory and Ebony were on this expedition now also. Why had they gotten off in Vanastas, hardly one of Ja-Lur's tourist traps? Ebony had muttered something about Ivory wanting to hunt snowcats. I didn't give them much hope of that, unless their finger prosthetics had laser cannon attachments. And my meeting with Valina was almost too pat to be believed. Had it been engineered? If so, by whom? Valina? Or the Darklord? And why?

"Paranoia is an occupational hazard in my line of work." I had heard those words from someone not too long ago. I tried to remember who had said them, but I was too tired, and too many events and dangers had gotten in the way. Still, the sentiment was one I knew I should keep in mind. To suspect everyone was no way to live.

But as I finally fell asleep, my last thought was of how Valina's interest had quickened when I had mentioned the Black Mask.

6

The next day we began climbing Darklord's Bane.

Orpheus and I had purchased ice axes, ropes and other equipment for climbing. There were crampons made from the dagger-sharp teeth of snowcats, and pitons of ironthorn. Luckily we had bought spares, so the entire party could be outfitted. We rubbed an ointment made of jennin leaves on our skins to protect them from the reflected light of the dull sun.

We rode at first, up rocky, snow-patched terrain, leaving the trees behind, crossing rivulets of melted snow. Orpheus was our guide. As he had promised, the android was leading me first to the Black Mask. It was important to more than just me now—we might need its aid to leave Hestia alive.

It was fairly easy going. The air was crisp, the sea-blue sky was empty save for a few black specks circling in the distance. I thought at first they might be bloodbirds, scavengers, but realized after a moment that they were riderless wild kragors that lived on the lower slopes.

Lady Thanatos had seemed unaffected at first by the power loss. Her memory and functions, according to Orpheus, were intact. But as the day progressed I began to wonder. She seemed more reserved than ever, often not answering when Orpheus or I spoke to her. She refused to activate her holomask, and rode with her cowl thrown back and her ivory skull gleaming proudly in the sun. Orpheus was obviously upset by this, and just as obviously unsure what to do about it.

That night we spent on the slope, under the clear, cold stars. Orpheus shot a smurf, which helped stretch our supplies. Valina and I again took turns maintaining a spell to keep some of the cold wind back and to protect us from predators. The spell would vanish at daybreak, but by then we would be moving again. None of us spoke very much; even Ivory seemed subdued. The outline of the mountain, looming over us, now looked very much like an old, bent, cowled man, leaning on a walking stick. He seemed to glare down at us with infinite malice. I wondered why the mountain had been named Darklord's Bane, instead of something more appropriate to its shape. It could not be because of the possibility of the Black Mask being hidden there, for I knew of no legends to that effect—only Orpheus's statement. At any rate, though the peak was not difficult to climb, fear of ice giants had been sufficient to keep all but the most brave from attempting to scale it and reach the *Galactic Express*.

Valina had pitched her bedding near mine, though the lack of privacy kept anything from developing. I was not sure that I wanted anything to develop; I still had decidedly mixed feelings about her. Was she near me because she wanted me, or for some other reason? I remembered how she had tried to use me to find the *Synulanom*. True, she had been under a geas then. But I remembered her last words to Kaan Ta'Wyys: "... Together we can rule all of the North, we can challenge the Darklord himself!" She had not been ensorcelled when she said that.

If Valina sensed my state of mind, she gave no sign of it. We lay close together, not speaking.

Lack of privacy had not inhibited Ivory; unable to interest Orpheus or me in such sexual gymnastics as the Denebian Planetbuster, she had turned to Ebony for solace. He was less than comforting, at last pushing her away from him roughly.

"You're responsible for us being here!" she hissed at him, her mood turning with childlike quickness to anger. "Well, remember, I still have say over your future, Ebony! It won't be a profitable one, I promise you that now!"

Ebony said nothing, but if looks could maim, Ivory would have made the climb in a basket.

By midmorning of the next day we reached the main slope of the mountain. "We can ride no further," Orpheus said. He pointed to the Walking Stick, the huge, snowcapped spire of rock that looked like the old man's cane, which rose to one side of the main peak, whose snowslopes were too riddled with crevasses to be climbed safely. "That is our destination. The Black Mask lies in an ancient temple near the spire's summit."

"You never have told me how you know," I reminded him.

"When we find the Black Mask—then I will tell you."

Lady Thanatos laughed cavernously at this, and Orpheus's gaze jerked toward her. "Why do you laugh, dearest?" he asked in a dangerously soft tone.

"I laugh because I have heard you say such things before, Orpheus." There was mockery in the graveyard voice. "You have said much the same to me. When we find the Matrix and I am refleshed, then will my memory be returned to me. Then once again I will be happy, young and full of life. But you want this for yourself, Orpheus, not for me..."

"I want it for more than myself," Orpheus said, teeth clenched. Then he pulled his kithara quickly from his pack. Lady Thanatos laughed; her laughter was cut short by the strum of the strings, which collapsed her into unconsciousness. Orpheus then struck another chord, and the skeleton fell apart.

We watched, shocked, as Orpheus packed the bones and the brainbox in his jemla's saddlebags. "What did you do to her?" I asked.

"I deactivated her force fields," Orpheus replied shortly. "It was the best thing for her." He remounted and rode upslope. The rest of us followed slowly. If I had any lingering belief in Orpheus's love for Lady Thanatos, I left it behind there.

Not long after, we reached the loose rock at the base of the Walking Stick. Orpheus repacked Lady Thanatos's bones, distributing them among his and my packs. We left the jemlas in an isolated, protected grove, near grass and water, and began the climb up the Walking Stick.

"Don't hug the rock," I advised the others. "Trust the rope to keep you from falling." The spire was not quite vertical, and the surface was broken and pitted, giving us numerous hand- and footholds. I led, followed by Valina, Orpheus, and the twins. Surprisingly, none of us were terribly bad climbers; Orpheus, though slim, was wiry and did not tire easily. Valina's endurance had been increased by the semi-fugitive life she had lead. Even the twins managed; genetic and physical conditioning on Earth had kept them in shape. Still, we set a slow pace, and the climb took most of the day.

I found myself enjoying it. The air was cold and fresh, the physical exertion pleasing. My world became the rock face before me. For the first time in a long while, I had an adversary that was no more or less than what it seemed.

After four hours of climbing and resting, we reached a wide, snow-covered ledge. The Walking Stick still rose above us for another fifty meters. A thin arch of stone stretched from the ledge to the main body of the mountain. The arch was barely two meters wide, slick with snow, and beneath it was nothing but air for a long way.

Though the spire was protected from the winds by the bulk of Darklord's Bane, short, cold buffets of air struck us, foretastes of what it would be like on the main slope. "We have to cross that to reach the *Galactic Express*?" Ebony asked, looking dubiously at the natural bridge.

"It is the only way," Valina said.

"We'd better camp here tonight," I said. "It's getting dark, and it's already colder than an ice giant's—"

"Kamus!" Orpheus called. He had been exploring the far end of the ledge. "I've found the entrance!"

It was a vaulted entrance, constructed of massive blocks of stone. Valina and I looked at it. Darkness had been invoked here, many times; after ages, the residue of power was still faintly detectable. It had no doubt been built in the Elder Ages. It was all but buried in snow. Valina and I spoke the same spell and the snowfall of years hissed and melted, and rose in steam away from the entrance, revealing the dark interior.

Orpheus lit a torch from his pack, and the others followed us into the temple. As had happened before in Kaan Ta'Wyys's castle, we were drawn by the essence of powerful Darkness to its source. The winding passage was cold and festooned with stalactites and stalagmites that had formed since it had been built. Doors lined it at irregular intervals, some opening into dark, unknown chambers, some closed, some walled shut. We followed the Dark lead. For the first time since I had set foot on the *Graywolf*, I knew I was going to find the Black Mask—the one thing that could help me defeat the Darklord.

We turned into a small chamber. There were several bound chests on the floor, the wood preserved through the ages by the cold. Valina and I reached for the right one together.

There was no locking spell on it; as we lifted the lid, I heard something fall from it. It was a ring; I picked it up and put it in my pouch without looking at it. I had no eyes for anything except what lay before me in the now-open chest, on a cushion.

The Black Mask looked like nothing spectacular: merely a small plain cowl that covered the upper half of the head and the eyes. It was made of black silk, and the eyeslits were covered with what seemed to be faceted obsidian. I picked it up and put it into my pouch, resisting the frightening temptation to look through it. I caught a glimpse of Valina's face as I did so; she was staring at it as if it were the Holy Grail. "We found it," she whispered. "What luck! What incredible luck!"

We started back down the corridor. As we approached

the entrance I said to Orpheus, "So you were right. *Now* will you tell me how you knew it was here?"

He smiled slightly, then looked slightly perplexed. He said, "You will understand why I did not tell you before; you would never have believed me. The fact is, I—"

He never finished the sentence, because, as we stepped out of the temple entrance, we were attacked by an ice giant.

All of us nearly died then. As I felt the last rays of the sun on me, there was a roar louder than a blastoff, and something knocked the wind from me and sent me sprawling into a snowbluff. I felt myself sliding, and managed to grab an outcropping of rock just as my feet went over the edge. I pulled myself to safety, looked around, and saw the ice giant. He was at least seven meters tall, a pallid white in color, and had hair and a beard as stiff and spiky as icicles. He was dressed in snowcat hides, clumsily stitched together. He looked annoyed. He swung another blow with his fist down at the rest of the group, who ran in various directions to dodge it. Valina retreated into the temple. The twins ran toward the stone bridge, across which the ice giant had evidently come. Orpheus slid into concealment in the snowbank beside me. "Impossible," he said, staring at the ice giant. "The square-cube law—"

The ice giant crouched before the entrance and groped inside. "Never mind the square-cube law!" I said. "He's after Valina!"

Orpheus aimed his blaster at it, and fortunately the mandate was not working, because the blaster was. A thin red line drew itself between the ice giant and the raygun. The giant roared and slapped at his side where he had been hit, as though swatting an annoying insect. Then he returned his attention to the entrance. I shouted a spell that should have immobilized him, but nothing happened; either I had gotten it wrong or the mandate's malfunction had damped my abilities. The ice giant stood up with Valina grasped in both hands like a large doll. She was struggling weakly; the grip was no doubt tight, allowing her no breath with which to shout spells. The ice giant slung her over his shoulder and began climbing up the rest of the spire.

I ran toward the rock wall and started climbing up after him. Orpheus grabbed me and pulled me around to face him. "You can't save her that way! You have powers—use them!"

I looked over his shoulder and saw a wild kragor winging slowly by. "You're right," I told Orpheus. "There's one chance."

He released me. I took powder and potions from my pouch and formed several geometric shapes in the snow with lines sprinkled. Then I spoke the Words of a docility spell, forcing myself to empty my mind of all other thoughts, to concentrate only on getting it right. I closed my eyes and put everything I had into it; there would be no second chance.

A gust of cold wind about me, and a beating of wings; when I opened my eyes the kragor had settled onto the ledge, head bowed submissively.

I vaulted onto its back and took off in a flurry of wings and snow. Below me Orpheus watched, as did Ebony and Ivory on the Walking Stick ledge. Then I pulled away and up, cold thin air beating against me.

The ice giant had reached the top of the Walking Stick, a knob of rock less than three meters across. He still held Valina in his hands. He roared as I circled him, but did not release her. She was struggling feebly in his grasp.

I pulled on the crest of horns on the kragor's crown, swooping closer. The ice giant released one hand to swipe at me. He missed and resumed his grip on Valina.

Below, I saw that Orpheus had his blaster aimed at the giant, but knew he could not fire for fear of hitting her. For the same reason, I was loathe to try a spell, but I knew that I had to. I crossed my fingers for luck and spoke the Words to a doubling spell. It worked; suddenly, there were two Kamuses on two kragors flitting about the ice giant.

My double dived in close; moving quickly for a creature so large, the ice giant released Valina and struck out at it. The movement of the air shattered the fragile illusion, but in the darkness, the giant thought it had swooped below the edge of the rock. He kneeled and peered over the edge. There was a flash from below, and a red beam seared the snow by his head. The giant reared back, howling, temporarily dazzled. I had landed the kragor behind him; now I jumped off and pulled Valina to her feet. She was conscious enough to walk. But the sound of the kragor's wings alerted the giant. He turned, let out a gravel-making growl, and stepped forward. I threw my sword at him; it was all I had time to do. It stuck in his big toe. With another howl of pain he seized his foot, hopping about—and toppled over the side.

We hurried to the edge and looked down. The ice giant had slid down the steep slope to the ledge, sprawling there in a cloud of rocks and snow, very nearly going over. He climbed to his feet again, making sounds like a volcano. Perhaps he intended to climb the spire again, but his attention was distracted by the sight of Ebony on the middle of the natural bridge.

It all happened very quickly. From where we stood, we could see Ivory, hiding behind a jumble of rocks near the temple entrance. The ice giant moved past her, started out across the bridge toward Ebony.

"Run, Ebony!" Ivory shouted.

Ebony, panicking, tried to retreat, but slipped and nearly fell off the bridge. The ice giant reached for him, seized him, lifted him. I could see Ebony's eyes clearly as he stared at his sister.

Ivory clapped her hands to her head. "No, Ebony—*no!*" She screamed. But she could not prevent what happened. Even from our position far above her, I could see the changes take place in her face, the expression changing from one kind of horror to another. Then a red arc of power struck the ice giant in the back of the head; he roared, staggered, and fell once more, this time toward a landing he would not rise from. And Ebony's body went with him.

Valina and I climbed down carefully. Orpheus met us. "From where I was shooting, I couldn't see Ebony until it was too late," he said. "But he was dead anyway."

"No," I said. "You're wrong about that," and I looked over at the rocks, at the white form of Ivory, still and silent. The others looked too, and saw what I meant.

Ebony had mindswapped at the last instant. In the fear of death, he had forced Ivory's mind into his body before it had been crushed by the ice giant. Now, in his sister's body, he sat staring at the chasm into which he had hurled her.

7

"My cloak was caught on a stalagmite near the entrance," Valina told me. "I couldn't get beyond the ice giant's reach." She was breathing in shallow, painful gasps, but no ribs seemed to be broken or any internal injuries suffered. Relieved on that score, I crossed to where Ebony, now in Ivory's body, sat in the snow, rocking slightly. I stood looking down on his female form. He had saved himself at the expense of his sister's life, and judging by the fetal curl he sat in, he probably would have been better off dead. A drop of saliva gathered on the pale chin and fell, burning a hole in the snow. I looked away. I had not been particularly fond of Ivory, but she had deserved better than this.

"I will go mad," Ebony said, suddenly and clearly, in that voice that was his sister's and yet his also. He looked up at us, his gaze terribly calm and certain. "There is no question of it. We were linked, you see . . . where one mind goes, the other follows. I will go mad, soon. Very soon." He looked down at himself, running his hands over her body. "Ivory always kept this body in splendid shape. I've always admired that, always enjoyed the times I spent in it . . ." He began to sob, the harsh sounds echoing in the mountain stillness. "I didn't mean to!" he cried. "I know she said she was going to cut me off, but she always said that . . ." He began going through his sister's chest pack. "She carried a lot of drugs . . . there must be something in here that can help me . . ." he rummaged through it with increasing urgency, pulling out items like vibrator attachments for her prosthetic finger and ultrasonic facial cleansers, and tossing them into the snow. Valina crouched beside him and held the feminine white hands, stilling them. He looked vacantly past her.

I looked at the darkening shape of the mountain. "We'll have to camp in the temple tonight. It's too dark to go on."

"The way is very easy from here," Orpheus said. "We could reach the *Galactic Express* in a few hours."

"We could also run into more ice giants at night. This place is easily defended, so long as we keep an eye on the bridge."

Orpheus shook his head. "I want to move on. After all, I am paying you—"

"So you are," I told him. "And you'll get what you pay for. I'll see you safely to the *Galactic Express*. Only not tonight. If for no other reason than that Ebony is in no shape to travel now."

"You owe me better treatment than this," he said in a low voice, his face dark with anger. "I led you to the Black Mask, I helped you save Valina. You don't understand how important this is!"

I picked up my sword where it had fallen from the ice giant's toe. "I have a few ideas about it," I said. "One of them is that you don't love Lady Thanatos at all. You have other plans for her." It was a blind thrust; I'm not sure what made me say it. Maybe I had been subconsciously putting things together over the course of the journey. But the remark had its effect; Orpheus grew pale and stared at me, searching my expression. I said nothing; it was his move.

His gaze fell. "We will talk later," he said. "I must reassemble Lady Thanatos. It is not good for her brainbox to remain comatose for so long. If you would be so good as to unpack . . ."

We did so, and Orpheus retrieved the bones and began to play his kithara. Within moments, Lady Thanatos stood before us again and the situation was explained to her.

When she spoke, her funereal voice almost seemed eager. "Shall I really have a body again, then? It is hard to believe . . . it has been so difficult to keep hoping." She looked at her skeletal frame. "To think there are those who seek this . . ."

"We all have strange goals," Orpheus said dully. He did not sound like a happy android. Lady Thanatos looked at him with an eyeless gaze for a long moment. Then, hesitantly, she took his hand in what was left of hers. "I am . . . grateful, Orpheus," she said.

He did not answer, merely turned away and entered the temple of the Black Mask. I watched him disappear into the blackness, wondering if my words had caused his change in attitude. He acted like he had been defeated.

I did not know why, but I knew I was right. Orpheus Alpha did not love Lady Thanatos, or the woman she had once been.

* * *

I awoke just before dawn, after dreams of haunting music. I sat in the cold wind that eddied into the temple entrance. The others slept just within the temple. Valina and I had set up the usual protection spells against dangers from the outside. But still I felt uneasy, as if something was wrong. I sat looking down at the nighted wilderness. Against the gray horizon I could see a line of darker gray; a storm was moving in. I decided to waken the others so that we could get an early start.

But just then there was the rustle of a cloak behind me, and, as she had done on previous nights, Valina joined me. The cloak's rustle sounded stiff, almost crackling, I noticed; it had seen better days. So had we all.

"I have something that might interest you," she said. From within her cloak she pulled a sheet of pliable plastic, perhaps twenty centimeters by ten, with a row of pressure-sensitive controls along the bottom—a holozine. I looked at the logo and realized it was the latest issue of *Space-Time*, the one that Ivory had mentioned on board the *Graywolf*.

"It was one of the things Ebony threw out of his sister's pack. I saw mention on the cover of an article—"

"—about the Order of the Osteomechs," I finished, reading the cover. "Thanks—that was quick thinking." I pushed the SCAN button on the holozine, and a succession of three-dimensional images flickered rapidly over the screen. I stopped it at the article. The image was a window open onto a barren world under a black, starless sky. A translated voiceover told us that this was the world of the Osteomechs. Then the scene changed, showing a white-haired woman in her sixties.

She had obviously refused any sort of rejuvenation shots. Her face bore a brooding, introspective expression.

"This is Cathrael Avery, one of the leading research scientists at A.S.T.R.A.," the narrator said. "There is reason to believe that she has voluntarily joined the death-worshipping cult known as the Order of the Osteomechs..."

We listened to the details. Cathrael Avery had been instrumental in developing pseudoplasm and the Matrix incubators. According to the article, she had always been a moody woman, obsessed with the concept of death, refusing to take rejuvenation shots. She had disappeared seven Earth weeks before from A.S.T.R.A.'s deepspace research facility. Co-workers said she had spoken of becoming an Osteomech.

There was more information about her work and life, including the fact that she suffered from Osteomycosis Peri, a rare bone fungus. "It's her," I said. "It has to be."

"But didn't Lady Thanatos say she had been a young woman?"

"That's what Orpheus told her." I thought for a moment. Lady Thanatos' story of her past had troubled me, for reasons I had been unable to name. But now, with the information in the article, things fell into place. I snapped my fingers. "She wasn't young, and I can prove it."

"How?"

"Let's wake them up and I'll show you."

But when we went down the length of dark corridor, all we found was Ebony, whimpering in his sleep. Orpheus Alpha and Lady Thanatos were gone. "Well," I said, "they've either gone further into the tunnel, which doesn't seem likely, or they've sneaked past us somehow."

"I'm usually a light sleeper," Valina said. "But I slept strangely this night. My dreams were full of somber music..."

I looked at her. "That explains how they left," I said. "Evidently, Orpheus can strum humans to sleep as well as Osteomechs."

"But why?" Valina asked. "Why is he suddenly so eager to reach the *Galactic Express*?"

"I think he's afraid that I've figured out why he wants to reflesh Lady Thanatos in pseudoplasm. The irony is that I hadn't; not until I read that article and realized who Lady Thanatos really is. But Orpheus thought I had, and so he's taken Lady Thanatos to the *Galactic Express*. We should be glad he's an android, albeit a mutant one; his conditioning was still strong enough to prevent him from murdering us while he had us drugged by his music. Let's go! If I'm right, we've got to stop them!"

We packed hurriedly. "What about her? Or him, rather," Valina asked, indicating the still-sleeping Ebony.

"We can't leave him here," I said. "But we can't keep an eye on him all the time, either."

"This may help," Valina said. She squatted down beside Ebony and shook him into wakefulness. As the pink eyes opened, she muttered a Phrase of Darkness into his ear. Ebony stood, his sister's body quiet, eyes hooded.

"Good idea," I said. "I hope it keeps." Obedience spells don't always last in disturbed minds.

"We have no choice," Valina said. "Let's go!"

The east was the color of dark wine. The air was cold and ominously still. The line of clouds now had swelled over half the sky, dark gray billows that flickered occasionally. "That storm's coming in fast," Valina observed.

"That isn't all that's coming in," I replied, and pointed down the main slope of the mountain at six or seven dark shapes toiling over the treacherous snowbanks. Valina gasped. "How can they climb that unstable surface? Who are they?"

"Osteomechs," I said. "They've been pursuing Orpheus and Lady Thanatos. They almost caught us in Mariyad."

"They may catch us here. They're light enough and strong enough to climb quickly," Valina said.

We crossed the bridge and found the tracks of Orpheus and Lady Thanatos. They headed up a snowfield toward the summit.

Dawn came as we climbed, adding a bit more light than the moons had. After an hour of climbing, we stopped for a quick breakfast of pemmican, then continued on. We could no longer see the pursuing Osteomechs, but I had the feeling they hadn't turned back.

The route Orpheus had taken led around the north shoulder of the old man and up toward a narrow chimney. Once we rounded the shoulder, we were in wind colder than the dark side of Bellus, a steady, dehibilitating assault that slowed us and made icicles of our tears. I wondered how Lady Thanatos's skeletal weight had remained on the slope.

Measured in eons, it wasn't too terribly long before we reached the chimney. We wedged ourselves inside, panting and recovering slowly from the wind. Then Valina and I inched our way slowly up the narrow fissure and belayed the complacent Ebony up.

I noticed it was growing steadily darker as I climbed, and when I looked up at the crack of sky I saw why; clouds covered the heavens, darker than a blind man's dreams. We struggled out of the crack and into still, cold air. The wind was cut off by the peak, which formed the hooded head; we stood now on the hunched, snow-covered shoulder, a snow-filled depression. The wind howled and whistled like drunken banshees around the peak. We stood on the silent snowfield, staring.

In the middle of the snowfield was the *Galactic Express*.

Lightning flashed in the distance, and thunder came entirely too soon after it. I stared at the ship. I had never seen a spaceship like it. It was not particularly large, perhaps a quarter of a kilometer in length and four stories high. It had evidently landed quite gently, almost like settling into a berth. The years' snow had drifted about it, but not buried it.

It had obviously been a luxury liner, designed for elegance and nostalgia. It had the traditional rocket shape, with huge, scalloped dorsal and stern fins. Rows of portholes lined its sides, and six huge, half-irised oval viewports told of an observation deck. All necessary external equipment, such as antennae, lifepods, proximity sensors, and so on, had been integrated into the sleek design.

The several years it had spent on Darklord's Bane had not been kind to it. The flared rear thrusters had once gleamed like chrome; now they were dulled and scarred by storms. The needle tip of the nose had broken off, and the point, still sharp enough to prick a finger, stuck out of the snow.

The tracks led from the fissure toward one of the closed airlocks.

Ebony began to giggle. I looked at him—was the spell beginning to wear off? A spatter of freezing rain passed swiftly through the crater, rattling almost like hail on the ship's hull. We hurried toward the entrance.

"Can you open it?" Valina asked me as I investigated the locking mechanism.

"I'm not sure . . . it depends, of course, on whether or not the mandate is functioning—"

A red line of light struck between Valina and me, scarring the dull surface of the airlock. I smelled vaporized metal as I dived behind a snowdrift, followed by Valina. "I don't think it is," she gasped. She pulled Ebony down as the mindswapper turned to look in surprise at the Osteomechs, who were climbing out of the fissure like the dead leaving the grave. The one who had fired before aimed its blaster again.

"Ulom ged! Vela wer tasan ti!" I shouted. It was supposed to be a reverse of the spell Valina and I had used to melt the snow of the temple of the Black Mask. Instead, the snow rose in flurries about the Osteomechs as a small whirlwind formed, blinding their videoreceptors. It did not sweep them off their feet; I assumed they wore weights to keep from being blown away on their climb. But it did disorient them momentarily.

"Fine, I'll take what I can get," I said, as we ran back to the door. I tried several digit combinations on the airlock's code panel, none of which worked.

"Perhaps this will serve," Valina said, speaking a spell of opening. The hatch slid slowly to the side with a hiss of musty air. Valina pushed Ebony inside and climbed in, and I followed, closing the airlock behind us. Valina applied a locking spell to it, which I seconded for good measure. "That should hold them for a time," I said.

We repeated the operation on the inner hatch, and were inside the *Galactic Express*.

It was much warmer inside. We were in one of the service corridors, garishly lit by banks of longlife emergency lights. Just inside the ship was a dried, mummified corpse of a crewman; he had died with his hands on the airlock controls, which, at the time of the crash, had been inoperative. We hurried down the narrow corridor and found an open door that led to what was evidently an auxiliary engine control and monitor station. Another door on the other side led out.

Valina was breathing hard; the past forty-eight hours, and particularly the last push toward the summit, had taken a lot out of her, and the spell-casting hadn't helped. I wasn't in much better shape myself, but we had no time to give in to fatigue. I looked about the room; it was small, with several mummies strapped into chairs before control consoles. The air was close and fetid. Tools were scattered about on the floor. "We haven't got much time," I said. "We've got to find Orpheus!"

"How?" Valina asked. "These controls are incomprehensible to me."

"Me, too." I steered Ebony toward one of the control panels. "Can you use this equipment to locate Orpheus?" I asked him.

"I can," he answered in the dull voice of the spellbound. "As long as the mandate hasn't damped the ship's power reserves."

He ran his sister's delicate fingers over several buttons. An overhead lifescan screen flickered with static, and an electronic tone sounded. Ebony said, "He is on monitor." We looked up at the screen; Orpheus, his back to us, crouched over a coffin-like black box with a set of crystalline controls on the front of it. There was a clear panel inset at face level, and I could see Lady Thanatos's skull within.

We could see little of the background; some ornate furniture and part of a wall mural of a gas nebula. "Where is he?" I asked Ebony.

"This equipment is not functioning right," Ebony said dully. "I can't get a location reading."

Orpheus finished making adjustments on the Matrix, and straightened. "Try to get a fix on him!" I said. "I'll keep him occupied!" I pushed the microphone button. "Orpheus!" I said.

Orpheus turned toward the monitor screen at his end and stared, shocked. Then he made an attempt to regain his composure. "Hello, Kamus. As you can see, I reached the *Galactic Express* without your help. I thought it for the best, since you obviously did not seem disposed to help me further. Soon, Lady Thanatos will be reborn."

"Reborn as what, Orpheus?" I asked. "As Cathrael Avery? Or as your puppet?"

He still tried to bluff, though he looked like he had been hit with a mace. "I don't know what you mean. Lady Thanatos—"

"Is Cathrael Avery, a research scientist for A.S.T.R.A., until she joined the Order of the Osteomechs voluntarily."

"You must be mad, Kamus," Orpheus said. "Lady Thanatos told you her history herself. She was a young woman on Carcosa—"

"Did you know I've been to Earth, Orpheus? As part of a cultural exchange program? I studied some medicine there, among other things. Lady Thanatos's skeleton is not that of a young woman. Her coccyx has ossified, something that only happens in older women."

"I don't know what you're—".

"You want more proof? As Cathrael Avery, she suffered from a bone fungus. She still has traces of it."

Orpheus evidently realized he could no longer bluff. "How did you know?"

I told him; I wanted to keep him talking until Ebony could get a fix on his location. "I must have noticed the ossified coccyx when she fell on me during that pre-Shadownight manifestation on board the *Graywolf*. That was also where I saw her illuminated in the black light from an outworlder's clothes. Ultraviolet makes some fungi floresce." It wasn't until after I read the article in the holozine, however, that it began to make sense.

I heard a distant crash, and a muffled sliding sound from down the corridor. Valina looked warily around the hatch opening. "The Osteomechs are in the airlock," she said. "They're working on the inner hatch."

I looked at Ebony; his sister's body was trembling, the eyes wide as he stared at the bodies of the crew. "Dead," he said, his voice breaking. "They're all dead. Like Ivory. She's dead, in my body. We're both dead."

Valina stepped quickly to him and spoke the obedience spell to him again. He returned to his work, but I could tell the spell would not hold long.

I looked back at Orpheus. "You plan to return Cathrael Avery to A.S.T.R.A., reprogrammed as a champion for androids' rights. She'll see that all androids produced by A.S.T.R.A. have full emotional range and free will, just like you do—am I right?"

"Close enough. As long as A.S.T.R.A. and the Homunculi Corporation produce androids, they will deny them their rights as thinking beings! I will give to the androids what was given to me by accident: the ability to fight!"

"I agree with your cause," I told him. "But this isn't the way to do it. If you destroy Cathrael Avery's personality and give her a new one, it's murder, Orpheus."

"She chose death—chose to be an animated skeleton! I

have a right to use her for the greater good! You can't stop me, Kamus! The Matrix is already activated, and I have programmed it to self-destruct afterward."

I glanced at the scan display Ebony was operating. Various sections of the ship flickered on the screen in strobing succession. Then, suddenly, it froze on the same image as the one on my monitor, and a printout flashed across the bottom: OBSERVATION DECK.

I switched off the monitor and asked Ebony, "You know about androids. Is there still time to stop his reprogramming of Lady Thanatos?"

"Perhaps... the incubation will take an hour. We can cancel the programming if we reach it before then."

Then, suddenly, there was another crash, much louder this time, from the corridor. I leaped to the hatch and looked out; the inner airlock had been opened. Lightning flashed outside as the Osteomechs poured into the *Galactic Express*. I jerked back into the room as rayblasts flickered down the corridor. "Company!" I called to Valina.

We dodged behind a console as one of the Osteomechs entered; its raybeam singed our hair. I had pulled Ebony along with us, but suddenly he stood, staring at the Osteomech, who stood with cape and mask discarded. "It's death!" he screamed, and ran straight toward it. Surprised, the Osteomech fired and missed, the blast shattering the readout panel of a tau scanner. Then Ebony hit the bony figure with his sister's body, knocking it off its feet. The Osteomech hit the wall skull-first, shattering the bone and smashing the brainbox within. Its bones scattered across the deck. Ebony turned and ran through the other door, his footsteps fading away to silence.

The Osteomech's raygun had landed near us; I jumped for it, got it, and made it back just as another skeleton came through the door. I shot at it—the ray sliced through its cervical vertibrae, and the bones clattered to the deck. I felt little compunction about killing these creatures; they had given up their lives long before.

We ran for the door Ebony had used, and made it just in time; other Osteomechs were right behind the first two. Valina and I ran down another curving corridor and toward several lift tubes. We slid beneath them and were sucked up to the next deck.

More long-dead crewmen and passengers, both human and alien, were lying about. The air smelled like a tomb. We hurried through the mouldering remnants of the hydroponics section, past the storage bay area, and up a frozen escalator.

We were now on one of the passenger decks. We passed richly-stained simuwood walls with art-deco designs and doorways leading to luxury staterooms. Then we turned a corridor and found ourselves in a dead end: the ship's crash landing years before had shattered several decorative synstone pillars across the passageway.

In the hallway's silence I could hear the dry whispering of animated bones searching for us. "We've got to do something," Valina said. But she hesitated, and I knew why. Strong spells must be spoken loudly, and that would lead them to us. They could shoot faster than she could speak. Also, we were both exhausted; a strong spell might backfire on us if said improperly.

Still, something had to be done. "Try a scattering spell," I suggested. As I spoke, two skeletons stepped into view around the corner. I fired at one, dropping it while Valina shouted *"Dana sani malem kow dia!"*

The scattering spell worked; the Osteomech literally flew apart with explosive force. Valina slumped against me, and from down the corridor I heard more of them approaching. They were coming in force, and we were trapped.

I looked around desperately, and then saw that one of the fallen pillars had partially blocked a door marked "Transportal." I thumbed the intensity switch on the blaster to melt and aimed it at the end of the pillar; it grew hot, then ran into slag. I pulled Valina forward and tried the door. It was stuck; I kicked it, and it burst open. Within was an intership transportal arch, for emergency travel between decks or from one end of the ship to another. I quickly programmed it for the observation deck.

"What is this?" Valina asked.

I told her. "If it works, we'll be on the observation deck. If it doesn't. . . we won't be anywhere, and won't care. Come on!" I could hear sounds like dice rattling outside the door. The Transportal's screen shimmered within the arch, and we stepped through together.

We stepped out onto the observation deck. It was a huge area on the ship's top deck, the entire ceiling a tinted transparent dome. Luxurious force couches and chairs were everywhere. There was a dancing floor, and a game area, including a four-D pool table and a galactic pinball machine. There were more mummified corpses, but not many. I noticed these things very quickly; what interested me far more was the sight of Ebony; his sister's recumbent form was on the floor in front of us.

At first I thought he was dead; then I saw him breathing, deeply and regularly. He was asleep!

Nearby him was the Matrix, humming softly. We saw no sign of Orpheus.

Then we heard him say, "I've been expecting you."

He started to play his kithara.

With almost the first note, I felt dizzy, soporific. I tried to say something, to speak a spell, but my tongue felt as heavy as a whale. I turned and saw Orpheus step out from behind the transportal, a smile of triumph on his face. I had been right about him putting us to sleep in the temple. I wished I hadn't been.

He took the gun from my hand and threw it across the room, then stepped away. I felt myself falling. I tried to crawl across the light year or so of carpet that separated us, but the music was filling my ears and my mind . . .

It stopped. I was on my hands and knees; I looked up and saw that one of the Osteomechs had come through the Transportal. Unaffected by Orpheus's music, which was meant for humans, it had grabbed the kithara from Orpheus and broken it. Orpheus backed away from the Osteomech. I struggled to my feet and put everything I had into a kick that broke the skeleton's backbone. It collapsed. I spun toward the transportal, saw another Osteomech halfway through the interface and swung my hand against the control panel, scrambling the coordinates on this arch. As if bisected by a raybeam, half of the skeleton fell to the deck.

"It'll take them a moment to reprogram the arch from their end," I gasped. I turned and saw Orpheus crouched by the Matrix, sobbing. I also saw Ebony getting to his feet, looking dazed. "What's happened?" he asked. He sounded lucid. "I heard music . . . I feel like I've slept for years . . ."

Orpheus's playing seemed to have cleared his mind, at least temporarily. "This place will be filled with Osteomechs in a few minutes," I told him. "We've got to get out of here."

I looked across the deck and saw the entrance hatches to several lifepod silos; their exit ports rose above the viewing dome outside. "Help me get the Matrix in one of them," I told Ebony. Together, he and I began pulling the box containing the re-forming Lady Thanatos across the carpet.

"It's too late," Valina said. She pointed at the transportal arch. "There they are."

As I looked, the last of four Osteomechs entered through the arch. None held rayguns; they wore swords instead.

"Orpheus, your blaster!" I whispered to him. The android still looked dazed by his unexpected defeat. He drew the raygun, held it ready.

No one moved, no one spoke, for a long moment. Then one of the Osteomechs said, "Deliver unto us the Lady Thanatos." The voice was even more lifeless than Lady Thanatos's had been.

Orpheus looked pale, but shook his head. "She is no longer one of you," he said.

"She is to be our priestess," another said soullessly. "The leader of our kind."

"She would have been that to my kind," Orpheus said, with a catch in his voice. "But no more."

"Then there is nothing else to do," said the first skeleton, "except experience the totality of death." He drew his sword, as did the rest of them. They charged toward us with hideous cries. Orpheus pressed the firing button, but there was only a dull buzz. He looked at it in shock.

"The mandate?" Valina asked.

"No! It's out of power!"

"What timing," I said, and then they were upon us.

I parried the first cut, barely deflecting the point from my ribs; though my opponent was light, its forcefield musculature made it very strong. The fury of its attack and its unnerving appearance forced me back.

From the corner of my eye I saw Valina, exhausted as she was, grab a femur that had been amputated earlier by the Transportal and use it as a staff to fend off the attack of another Osteomech. Ebony, weaponless, pushed a force chair in the way of the third and ran. Orpheus hurled his useless gun at the fourth one, chipping off a rib, then turned and ran, pursued by the sword-wielding nightmare.

My opponent swung a whistling slash that I ducked

beneath. The blade hit part of a sonic sculpture, and the resulting tonal vibration shook the Osteomech like a dead tree in the wind. I stepped behind it and pushed it toward the galactic pinball machine. It crashed through the hemispheric covering and a cacophony of sirens and explosions sounded, lights flashed and miniature stars went nova. A runaway spaceship lodged in the Osteomech's ribcage, and a comet shattered against its skull. It collapsed into a pile of bones under a sign that flashed BONUS GAME.

I turned toward the others. I saw Ebony dodge a sword-thrust, roll over on the deck and come up with the blaster that Orpheus had taken from me and thrown away. He fired, and a beam of red light struck the skeleton, decapitating it. The Osteomech fell apart as its forcefields collapsed. Ebony picked up the skull and hurled it at the one menacing Valina; it struck the other's occipital ridge, and both skulls shattered.

I looked about for Orpheus and saw him running toward the lifepods, pursued by the last Osteomech. He climbed into one of the pods and activated the hatch, but he was an instant too late—the Osteomech leaped in with him, and the hatch closed. In the circular viewport on the hatch I could see the two of them struggling in the narrow confines of the lifepod. I ran toward it, but suddenly the deck shook with a muffled roar and the lifepod hurtled away from the *Galactic Express*.

We stood amid the strewn bones, Valina, Ebony, and I, looking up at the storm that still raged outside. The lifepod dwindled to a tiny speck. I had an instant's vision of them flying forever through the vastness of space, Orpheus battling the nightmare marooned with him as he had battled the nightmares within him for so long. In that instant, also, I wondered if I had done right in stopping his self-appointed holy mission.

Then Valina cried, "There!" and pointed upward into the clouds. "It's coming back down!"

It was, falling like a silver meteor back out of the sky.

"He's coming too fast," Ebony said. "He hasn't fired his retros! If he hits us—!"

I ran to the Transportal. There was only one chance; to use the arch to take us across the ship, out of range of the explosion the lifepod's crash would cause. Forcing myself to be calm, I set the intership coordinates for the engine room.

"Jump through it!" I shouted to Valina, as Ebony and I lifted the Matrix to carry it through. We ran toward the arch, and reached it—too late. I felt the observation deck lift and buckle beneath my feet as we fell toward the arch's shimmering interface, heard the thunderous crash of the lifepod striking the *Galactic Express*. The last thing I saw was the interface breaking into rainbow fragments, and then someone pulled the planet out from under me and I fell into the blackness of space.

* * *

I sneezed.

I had been dimly aware of my nose tickling for a century, it seemed. I was hoping for a sneeze, as it would be a good sign that I was somehow still alive. The sneeze finally came, and when it did, it lifted my head out of the warm grass it had been lying in and rolled me over on my side.

Warm. Grass. Wait a minute, something was wrong here. I was a detective, I should be able to figure this out . . .

I opened my eyes and looked up at fleecy clouds. In the edge of my vision the crystalline spire of a ship from the Pandora System glittered in the dim late afternoon sun. I raised up on an elbow—probably the bravest thing I've ever done, considering how my head was suddenly feeling. Things whirled, then steadied.

I was lying in a small patch of grass near the edge of the spaceport landing field.

I looked around. Nearby was a shuttle Transportal, designed to ferry passengers to the Terminex. Its interface shone enigmatically. Lying beside me were Valina, Ebony, and the Matrix, still humming imperturbably as it proceeded with its work on Lady Thanatos as programmed by Orpheus.

There was no one about. The buildings of the spaceport were dark, and there was no activity on the field.

Memory of what had happened came back. I crawled over to Valina, put my ear to her mouth and pressed my fingers against her wrist. She was alive. Her eyelids fluttered. I exhaled in relief.

Ebony sat up, holding Ivory's pale head in his hands. He stared down at his sister's body. "Ivory," he said, in a low tone. He looked at me, blinking in wonderment. "I'm not insane," he said. "I thought I was going mad."

"Maybe Orpheus's music cured you," I said. "Or maybe you only hoped you were going mad."

He nodded slowly, then looked around us. "What happened?"

I shrugged. "Your guess is as good as mine. I'd say the struggle between Orpheus and the Osteomech caused the lifepod to go out of control. It hit the ship and there was an explosion, but I don't think it was strong enough to blow us back here."

"Maybe it was," Ebony said. "We were hurled into the Transportal. I saw the interface break up; it looked like a power surge hit it, because of the crash. Then we fell into it . . ."

"And now here we are, sitting by another Transportal," I said. "Neither one of them had the power it would take to transport us from Darklord's Bane to the spaceport."

"It had to be the power surge," Ebony said. "A one-in-a-billion chance, but there's no other explanation—"

"Yes, there is," Valina said. She sat up and looked at me. "You know what it is, Kamus."

I knew. The Darklord could have moved us through Darkness, as he had moved Taqwatkh from the scene of his crime to the *Yith'il*.

I closed my eyes. I knew which was by far the more likely of the two explanations. I also knew which I would rather believe, which one I would cling to until proven wrong. I did not want to believe that the Darklord had saved me from the inferno on the observation deck of the *Galactic Express*. If he had, that meant he knew I was on Darklord's Bane, and why. And that meant he knew I had the Black Mask.

I opened my pouch and looked in it. The mask was still there. I had not yet looked through it. I dreaded now the time when I would; I dreaded what I might see.

There was something else in my pouch; I reached in and brought out a ring. It sparkled in the fading light. It was a ring carved from a black stone shot with gold sparkles. On it was the caricature of a laughing face. One horn sprouted from the left temple. I had seen that stylized face before, most recently on the ancient parchment of the *Synulanom*. It was the sigil of Mondrogan the Clever, the half-breed Darklander of long ago. On impulse, I slipped it onto my finger. It fit.

I had found the ring on the chest that contained the Black Mask, and had kept it without looking at it. Now I stared at it, not knowing what to think. Had Mondrogan been in that ancient temple? According to the stories, he and others had hidden various Elder Objects from the Darklord during the Dark Wars. Had he hidden the Black Mask there?

"What will you do now, Kamus?" Valina asked softly.

I shook my head. "A lot of thinking," I said.

I had promised myself that I would not be the Darklord's pawn. But did I have a choice—had I ever had a choice? Had I been played for a fool by him again? And were more people—Orpheus Alpha, Ivory, the innkeeper and, yes, even the Osteomechs—dead now because of my quest?

It seemed to me now that I had never had a choice. My decision to seek him out had not been mine, it had been his.

There was only one way to escape him; to leave the Darkworld. Only by putting hundreds of parsecs of space between him and me, only by going to a world where Darkness no longer held sway would I be free of him. Let Shadownight come, let Sanris and the others go unavenged, let what was left of my career vanish like a darkling in daylight.

At the moment, it seemed the only sane decision.

I looked at Ebony. He sat quietly, crosslegged. His sister's face seemed sane, though haggard. He was looking at the Matrix.

I looked at it too, and suddenly my mind snapped into gear again. "How much time is left before Lady Thanatos's reprogramming is completed?" I asked him. Ebony leaned over the Matrix and pressed several controls. The humming stopped. "It's good you spoke," he said quietly. "I stopped it just in time; another few minutes and she would have risen, and the Matrix would have self-destructed."

"Can she be reprogrammed with her original mind?"

"It's possible," the androgynous voice said.

I breathed a sigh of relief. "Good. At least that much will be done."

"I'm afraid not," Ebony said. And suddenly the blaster he had used on the *Galactic Express* was pointed at us.

I stared at him in disbelief for a moment. Then I sighed, feeling all my exhaustion overwhelming me. "Let me guess," I said slowly. "You want the Matrix."

"And the pseudoplasm. That's right, Kamus," Ebony said. "I wanted to get out from under the threat of disinheritance that Ivory held over me. I was offered a great deal of money by the Homunculi Corporation if I would find these things on the *Galactic Express*. The Corporation is tired of being number two in the android business. Now they'll have what they want, including the mind of an A.S.T.R.A. scientist."

"I should have seen it sooner," I said. "Your knowledge of androids, your willingness to go with Orpheus and the rest of us . . ."

"Exactly," Ebony said. "Ivory had no idea, of course; I convinced her it would be 'nova' to go. I did not intend that she should die. I merely wanted to be free of her financially." He gestured with the raygun. "Stand up, both of you."

Valina and I stood. "The blaster may not work, you realize," I said.

"I doubt that you want to take the chance." He stood also, and seized the Matrix by a handle near one end. His sister's body was strong enough to drag it. "Keep your backs turned while I use the Transportal. I have a spaceship to catch."

"What do you think they will do to her?" I asked him.

"Reprogram her, most likely. Corporate competition is as ruthless as war and she's supposed to be wandering some lifeless planet as an Osteomech."

"They'll take away her past," I told him. "They'll take away her mind, and change it for their purposes. Remember how it felt when you thought you were losing your mind, Ebony?"

He hesitated; I saw indecision in the beautiful white face. "She doesn't deserve that," I said. "Let Cathrael Avery make her own decisions; let her live and die in her own body, with her own mind, or not—but let it be her choice."

He drew a ragged breath. "I didn't do that for Ivory; why should I do it for her?"

"*Because* you didn't do it for Ivory," I said. I stepped toward him. The raygun was still aimed at me. I told him, "In a moment of weakness, you took a life. Now give one."

He closed his eyes for a moment, in pain; I reached out and took the blaster from his sister's trembling hand. He fell against me, shivering. "What should I do?" he asked plaintively.

I turned him toward the Matrix. "She wanted to be an

Osteomech," I said. "But a lot has happened since then. Restore her to what she was; then it's up to her."

He nodded and put his small white hands on the controls.

We sat together as the afternoon became evening, waiting for the Matrix to do its job. I saw very little movement around the buildings or the few ships on the landing plates; it seemed as if the spaceport was largely deserted. It was quite a difference from the thriving business it had been doing a week before.

"Kamus," Valina asked, "I understand how you figured out who Lady Thanatos was; but how did you know what Orpheus intended for her?"

I shrugged. "Feelings, mostly. Intuition. The way he spoke to her and treated her. A few clues; he'd told her he couldn't get a new body for her from A.S.T.R.A. because it was too expensive. A.S.T.R.A. would probably have donated an android form free, for the favorable publicity it would have engendered. He wanted to put her into a Matrix he could reprogram. When he learned of the one on the *Galactic Express*, he saw his chance.

"Then there were his reactions to the humans and outworlders around him. He hated and resented them for their attitudes toward androids. He had a right to. He wasn't just feeling that for himself; he was feeling it for all androids." I was quiet, then, thinking about it. Orpheus Alpha's desire for android emancipation had been a noble cause, no doubt of that. I wondered again if I should have interfered. He had kept his word and delivered the Black Mask, though he had never told me how he had known it was there. And in return, I had helped to ruin his dream.

But his wasn't the only dream that had been ruined. I had finally realized that, no matter what I did, no matter where I went, the Darklord was a move ahead of me. There was only one decision left to me, then. I looked toward the west, where the faint outline of Jaspara was just rising. In a moment, Bellus would rise in the east. Shadownight was only a week away; I doubted I could reach Ja-Agur in time. Very well, then, I thought; let it come. When it did, I would be on the other side of the galaxy. No shadow could reach that far.

I looked at Valina, and wondered if I wanted to ask her to come with me. I still felt wary of her. I had always listened to my hunches before, but lately they had not been doing too well.

"Paranoia is an occupational hazard in my business." Now I remembered who had said that: Daniel Tolon. I knew how he felt.

Valina felt my gaze on her, looked up, and smiled at me. I smiled back. She had stood by me, had helped me find the Black Mask and the *Galactic Express*. The least I could do in return would be to help her escape Shadownight.

A soft chime sounded from the Matrix, and the lid of it evaporated in a cloud of black smoke. Within was an android body with the features of Cathrael Avery. She blinked, opened her eyes, and slowly sat up.

"Hello," I said. I put my trenchcloak about her and helped her step from the Matrix. As she did so, it also dissolved and turned to smoke. It had self-destructed, as Orpheus had said it would.

She looked up at Ebony, Valina and I. "What happened to me?" She said slowly.

"It's a long story," I said. "I think you'll find it interesting. You may even find a cause worth pursuing in it; someone else did. While we're talking, we might as well walk to the spaceport. I think we've all got somewhere to go."

PART FOUR

The Man with the Golden Raygun

I

When I first saw Polaris Lone, he was standing on a high observation platform at the Unity Spaceport, looking down at the spaceships far below. The last time I saw him he was also on a high place, looking down. In between those times a lot of events took place, all of them bricks in a wall that separated me from all that I had been before.

Cathrael Avery, formerly Lady Thanatos, had boarded a Unity patrolship that would take her back to A.S.T.R.A. Perhaps, after she arrived there, there would start to be some changes in the current status of androids. Her tenure of living death as an Osteomech had cured her of her morbidity and desire for death. She had been impressed and touched by Orpheus Alpha's holy cause, even though she would have been the victim of it. And she was an android herself now, her personality housed in a brain of pseudoplasm rather than crystallized filaments. I hoped she had a different view on the matter.

Ebony had also gone; he intended to return to his family and confess his crime.

As for myself, I wasn't sure what to do. Only a day before I had fully intended to buy a ticket for myself and Valina on any ship for as far as we could go away from the Darkworld and its Darklord. But that was before we learned that there were now very few ships landing or leaving the Spaceport. The chaos brought about by the impending Shadownight had caused numerous equipment failures and several crashes. The Unity had declared Ja-Lur off-limits to outworlders until the crisis had passed.

Valina watched me as we walked slowly down a soft-lit

corridor that paralleled the landing field. I had told her of my intention to leave Ja-Lur. She had seemed quite taken aback. Then we had learned that very few ships were willing to risk blasting off, and those that were, were asking exorbitant rates, far beyond my meager savings.

There seemed to be no choice but to return to my original plan, I told her. "After all, we can't walk to another planet. I don't know how we can possibly reach Ja-Agur before Shadownight, but going south is better than staying here. The way this thing is shaping up, it makes more sense to keep moving. At least, that's how I see it. You may want to take your chances and stay in the Northern Nations, but I can't show my face in Mariyad again, because I left my belongings in the Maze. Just a few grimoires and potions, but enough to mark me as a Darklander. If word's gotten about I'll be as welcome as a barbarian at a palace ball."

To my surprise, I was almost relieved to find myself still on my original course. My decision to run had been a weakness, an abandonment of the moral code I had adopted when I first became a private eye. I couldn't do that. That code was more than just trappings, like my trenchcloak. Darklanders live with Darkness, with the possibility of being corrupted by the power in their Blood. There are ways to fight it; this was my way.

If I admitted defeat to the Darklord, I admitted defeat to the Darkness within me.

"I'd like to go with you," Valina said. She looked at me. I tried to meet her gaze, but could not. "You still don't trust me," she said; I could hear the hurt in her voice, the reproach. I did not answer. It was true. Try as I might, I could not forget how she had wanted to share the power of the *Synulanom* with Kaan Ta'Wyys, even after he had released her from his geas. She was a powerful Darklander, and would make a good ally—if she would remain my ally.

But how could I be sure of that?

I looked away. Standing on an observation platform not far down the corridor was a man dressed in a suit of shiny black flexarmor. He was tall, compactly built, and, though evidently just sight-seeing, seemed waiting for someone or something. He glanced at me, and our eyes met; his had a unique color; the gold of ancient treasure. As he shifted position, I saw another flash of gold at his hip: a golden blaster. He looked at me levelly for a moment, then turned away.

Valina said distantly, "I can't force you to believe me, Kamus. That's one thing of which I'm incapable. I wish you well in your quest. May we both survive Shadownight."

She turned and started down the curved corridor, passing the man in black. I watched her go. Perhaps I was right, but even so, I did not want her to go. She was the only one I had who understood and sympathized. Without her, I would face the unknown alone.

I opened my mouth, and perhaps I would have called her back. Except that several interesting things happened.

A humanoid alien, tall and slim, with milk-pale skin and fleshy antennae which rose from where a man's ears would be to several inches over his head, walked past me and down the corridor. He was wearing a green onesuit, and a green glove on his left hand. I couldn't place his planet of origin, which wasn't surprising, considering the number of planets in the Unity. There was nothing about him that seemed unusual, except that he was gloved only on his left hand.

As Valina passed the man in black, he turned to watch her. Again, nothing unusual; despite privation and hardship that should have made her look like something the darklings dragged in, Valina was still improbably beautiful. The alien altered his course slightly, moving toward the man in black, who did not see him. As Valina passed the man in black, the pouch hanging about her waist came loose and dropped to the floor. She heard it, and turned to pick it up at the same time that the man in black knelt to retrieve it. As he did so, I saw the alien pull the glove from his left hand. The left hand was not pale like his right. It was red, and it glowed.

Valina saw the alien move swiftly toward the man in black, glowing hand upraised to strike. I saw it too. She and I both shouted, "Look out!"

The man in black moved quickly and fluidly, diving to one side. The alien struck down with his glowing hand, knife-edge style. The hand sliced through the tiled floor like a laser through butter, with a crackling sound and a series of blinding sparkles trailing behind it. It left a trough dug in the floor.

The alien leaped at the man in black again, his hand trailing energy. The hand itself was somehow difficult to look at; like a black light, it was hard to focus on. The man in black was on his feet and had the golden blaster in his hand. The alien waved his crackling hand in a circular motion, leaving a trail of energy like a shield before him. A ray of golden light burst from the blaster, hit the energy shield without visible effect and was gone. He leaped forward before the man could fire again, knocking him off his feet. They went down, the man in black holding the alien's wrist in an attempt to keep the glowing hand from touching him.

"*Dana sani shevashet mone!*" Valina shouted. It was a variation of the scattering spell. The two of them flew apart, and both landed sprawling. The alien staggered to his feet, facing me, confused and angry. He glared at me; his eyes had no pupils, but seemed filled with a milky fluid containing black specks. He stood for a moment, indecisive, and I reached quickly into my potion pouch and pulled out a vial of moonflower pollen. "Here—catch!" I said, and tossed it to him. Reflexively he caught it in his left hand to disintegrate it; the vial vanished, but not all of the pollen did, and what remained surrounded him in a cloud. The alien sneezed, staggering backward. The man in black stepped aside, planted one boot firmly against the alien's tailbone and shoved him toward the observation port. The alien fell forward and put out both hands to catch himself; a large portion of the platform's safety bubble disappeared, and the alien fell with a fading cry toward the plasticrete far below.

The man in black looked through the half-vanished bubble. I could hear the siren of a robot ambulance far below. Then he looked at Valina and me, and I got my first clear look at his face. It was a lean, almost cruel one, seamed with a long white scar that ran down one cheek. His golden gaze appraised us, quickly and coldly; then evidently he decided we constituted no further threat. He grinned. Even with the grin, it wasn't a face I would want to see in my mirror. "Thanks for your aid," he said, extending a black-gloved hand to me. "Things might have gotten out of hand otherwise."

I winced slightly; a pun at the expense of someone's death isn't my idea of humor. The man shook my hand with a strong grip, then took Valina's. "My name's Polaris," he said. "Polaris Lone." He had a slight accent that I couldn't quite place, though it was definitely outworld. About then, a security team came around the corner, blasters drawn. Polaris Lone looked at them. "This will take some explaining, I expect," he said to us. "I hope you won't mind waiting a moment."

"Not at all," Valina said.

Polaris Lone joined the security team and spoke to a sergeant, a large, burly fellow whose face had all the sympathy of a stone gargoyle. Polaris said one short sentence, too low for me to hear, and showed the sergeant a card which he took from his chest pack. The sergeant's eyes went wide.

Polaris rejoined us. "Everything's set right," he said as we walked down the corridor away from the security team. "I'm sorry," he continued, "but I didn't get your names."

I introduced myself and Valina. Though Polaris seemed to have recovered completely from the unexpected and unexplained (to us, anyway) attack, I hadn't. I've gotten used to death over the years only in that I've learned how to roll with the inevitable trauma the sight of it always causes.

I glanced at Valina. She, too, seemed slightly pale. In a way, I was glad to see that. It made more of a bond between us; forged more common ground, and gave me just a bit more hope that I could trust her when Darkness fell about us. For she had evidently reconsidered leaving me.

Polaris's eyebrows had gone up slightly at my name. "I've heard of you, Kamus," he said. "Well, after your help, the least I can do is buy you both dinner."

"That's most kind of you," Valina said.

"Come along, then," and he set off down the corridor without looking back, his spine straight as the golden beam of his blaster.

I glanced at Valina. She was watching him go as though hypnotized by the play of the soft lighting on his shiny flexarmor. "Who do you think he is, Kamus?" she asked, without taking her eyes off of him.

"I don't know," I said. I wondered if it was in our best interests to follow him. I did, however. After all, he had offered dinner, and I was hungry.

But I did notice that we were walking north instead of south.

* * *

We dined at the restaurant in the Galactic Arms, the spaceport's luxury hotel. Polaris Lone treated us to quite a meal: flambéed hurkle with Liebfraumilch 2117; roast stuffed jessipeel from the planet Aloha, and sautéed loin of mara with Saurian brandy. It was a far cry from half-frozen pemmican and melted snow; or, for that matter, from my diet on the best of days.

Valina had been accustomed to such elegance once, being a high-born slave. She had visited one of the several powder rooms for ladies of various species, and, with a little help from spells that now worked within the spaceport, had come out looking like she had spent the past week as an overlord's guest, rather than battling androids, ice giants, and Osteomechs. I could have cleaned up also, but, outside of some perfunctory washing, decided to go as I was, tattered trenchcloak and all.

Polaris, despite his rather utilitarian dress, was obviously comfortable and at ease in the posh surroundings. I said, "You seem to lead an exciting life, Mr. Lone."

"Polaris, please. You mean the fellow with the contained antimatter hand? I think that was the residual of a bit of unpleasantness on a Dyson sphere called the Blackstar a few months back. Some people carry grudges, you know." He changed the subject. "If I've heard aright, you're not exactly a dull sort yourself, Kamus. You're from Earth, are you not—sort of a private eye transplant?"

"Not exactly," I said, and went on to explain how I had gotten the idea of becoming a detective from old Earth culture. This led him to ask me about some of my cases; I outlined them briefly, then asked, "And what do you do for a living?"

He shrugged. "Oh, a bit of this and a bit of that. Sort of a freelancer, you might say; on the Blackstar, for example, I found myself on the wrong side of a revolution, and had to make sure it became the right side."

"What brings you to Ja-Lur?"

He shrugged. "I needed a vacation, and thought someplace out of the way would do nicely."

I didn't need a meteor to fall on me to realize that he didn't want to talk about himself. "But I seemed to have arrived at the wrong time," he added; "Immediately after planetfall I am informed that this world is declared restricted, and all offworlders are requested to leave as soon as possible. Something to do with an approaching phenomenon called

Shadownight. As natives, perhaps you can explain this to me?"

I glanced up through the crystalline roof of the restaurant. Overhead, in the night sky, the cresents of Bellus and Jaspara were moving toward each other. I recalled the strange event on board the *Graywolf*. It was likely that every night, somewhere, were reverberations of the approaching Shadownight. And Jaspara had not even begun to eclipse Bellus.

"It's difficult to explain," I said to Polaris as he signalled the robot waiter for the check. I told him about the cosmos of Darkness that overlapped ours, and how the focal point seemed to be the eclipse called the Bloodmoon.

"Fascinating," Polaris said. "And this Darklord, though he has never been seen, rules the planet?"

"When you're the most powerful sorcerer in a millennium, certain things come easy."

"I have heard of this Darklord, of course," Polaris mused. "In fact, I rather thought I'd have a look at the Darkland. None of the tours include it, so I thought I'd go south in my flier."

I said cautiously, "You know, of course, that the Darklord frowns on uninvited guests."

"I've gathered that he's a bit insular."

I felt Valina's gaze on me, and knew what she was thinking; if Polaris Lone had a flier and was willing to take us, we could reach Ja-Agur in plenty of time for Shadownight. I thought about it. There seemed little question that he would be a good ally in a fight, if it came to that. Yet I did not feel entirely comfortable about him. It seemed I had little choice, however, if we were to be beyond the Black Desert in a week. Surely there would be no harm in hitching a ride with him that far. After that, we could part company.

"In that case, since you're going that way," I said, "would you consider dropping us off in Xikree? It's a small village in the south of the Black Desert."

"No problem at all; glad of the company. Pleasure trip?"

"Not exactly." I said no more, and he did not press me. I glanced at Valina; she seemed quite pleased for someone who had done her best to talk me out of my quest.

Polaris paid the check, and we left the restaurant, taking a slidewalk to the landing field, where Polaris said a planet skimmer had been held in his name. This gave me something else to wonder about: how did he rate the use of a flier on a restricted world?

The slidewalk took us and several others out of the Terminex. Since last I had looked at the sky, dark clouds had covered the stars. "It looks like rain," Valina said.

She had scarcely spoken when it did begin to rain, but not the way any of us expected. A few wriggling shapes, black against the white plasticrete, fell from the sky. I looked closely at one. It was perhaps two inches long, a tiny humanoid shape, with a horned head and a forked tail. It leaped to its feet after landing and quickly scuttled under a plant. "It seems to be raining imps," I said to the others. Polaris looked about with a slight, incredulous smile. Valina, who knew more about the workings of Darkness, looked worried.

A few others on the landing field, both human and outworlders, looked about them with the same disbelief. The rain of imps grew heavier. One outworlder, a catwoman from Felix VII, hissed when several imps fell into her long, silken fur. Another imp began climbing up Valina's cape; she shook it free with an expression of distaste. "Perhaps we'd better go back inside," Polaris suggested.

That was easier said than done, however; when we turned back to the Terminex, we found the automatic doors had failed. "Get used to this," I said to Polaris. "The Darklord's mandate is about as stable these days as a trunkful of Californium."

The demonic rain was increasing; the landing field was littered now with small, writhing, scurrying shapes, and I could hear cries of panic and disgust as the imps attacked people, giving them painful bites and scratches with tiny teeth, nails, and horns. "We'd better make a run for the flier," said Polaris, "since the alternative seems to be being nibbled to death." I agreed wholeheartedly; he seemed in no particular danger so far, as his flexarmor resisted the imps' efforts. But Valina and I had already suffered several bites. To make matters worse, they were venomous, raising painful welts like bee stings.

We ran across the field toward the berth of Polaris' flier. I held my trenchcloak over Valina and myself; neither of us were ready to try even a simple spell during this time of encroaching Darkness. Imps slid down curving ramps, rose in clouds up lift tubes, and overflowed from dish antennae, all of them scuttling about with the abrupt stop and go motion of lizards. Individually, they seemed to be voiceless; yet from all over the field rose a shrill, grating keening, like a tape of crowd noise played at very high speed. As they thickened underfoot, we could not avoid stepping on them; the crushed bodies filled the air with a stench.

"Here!" Polaris shouted, finally. We had reached a U-shaped berth near a landing plate occupied by a crystalline starship almost covered with imps. Polaris's flier was likewise crawling with the creatures. He drew his raygun. "I'll have to burn them away from the hatch," he said, and fired. Or, rather, he tried to; the blaster did not work. Polaris looked at it in disbelief.

"It's the mandate," I said, hopping from one foot to another as I shook off the imps. They were fast becoming a very real danger; as numerous as army ants, and even meaner. I looked at Valina. "We'll have to try a spell!" She nodded, and together, dancing about like particles in a cloud chamber, we spoke in unison the words of the scattering spell.

At first, we thought it had worked; the myriad imps slid off the fuselage of the flier. But instead of scattering, they scurried together, forming a writhing pile which grew larger very quickly. They came from all directions, hurling themselves on top of those underneath, climbing up as the pile grew bigger, until it was as tall as a man, then taller, and the imps on the bottom must have been crushed and suffocated by their fellows' weight. Valina and I stared in fascination as Polaris threw open the gull-wing hatch. I didn't know what was going on, but I knew I didn't like it.

I liked it even less when the huge pile of imps quivered and seemed to solidify. It was now more than twice as tall as me. Its lower part split into two log-thick parts, and appendages sprouted from either side. Two red eyes were suddenly blinking down at me. A tail the size of a tricorn snake whipped the night air. And still it was growing. One clawed hand struck down at me. I ducked, grabbed Valina. "Looks like they've discovered teamwork," I said, as we climbed up on the wing and into the cockpit.

Polaris manipulated controls and the flier rolled out of

the berth. He started to taxi forward, but the flier suddenly jerked to a stop. "What in—?" Polaris said; then he looked behind us, as did I.

A black, taloned hand, huge and gnarled as a tree stump, had gripped the tail assembly. The flier's wheels spun against the plasticrete. "I think he wants us to stay," I said.

"So it appears," Polaris said. "Let's see if we can't make things hot for him." He activated the rear auxillary thrusters, and a blast of chemical flame singed the giant Darkling's hand. With a howl that probably shattered glass for miles around, the monster released us. The flier lurched forward, then accelerated smoothly as Polaris engaged the primary repulsor drive. The ground dropped away from beneath us; in a moment, we were high over the spaceport, banking in a steep turn, the still-raining imps splattering against the flier.

Valina gripped my arm; at first I thought it was nervous reaction to her first flight in an outworld vehicle. Then I saw through the cockpit bubble what she saw. The darkling was still growing as the rain of imps continued to contribute to its mass. It was as big as a spaceship now, and rapidly getting bigger. Lambent red eyes, each the size of a witch's cauldron, glared at us.

"We have to do something to stop it," Polaris said tightly. "It'll destroy the spaceport."

"The Black Mask, Kamus," Valina said in a low voice. "You must use it."

I thought of the Elder talisman, still in my pouch. If I put it on, it could show me the underlying nature of this manifestation, and the way to defeat it. But there was also the possibility that what I saw through the Mask would be too much for me to handle. Was I strong enough to resist the visions of Darkness that I might see?

"Something must be done quickly," Polaris said. "I have no weapons on this flier."

I glanced up at the cloudy sky. The two moons were drawing apart; the rain of imps had almost stopped. The gargantuan darkling might be weakening, but it was still capable of making high-technology mulch out of the spaceport. An arm like an ebon sequoia reached out; one huge hand snapped off the spire of the crystalline ship with a sound like a thousand bells. The darkling struck at us; Polaris banked sharply, but the wind from the huge club almost sent us into a spin.

I took the Black Mask from my pouch and, holding my breath, put it on.

At first, I saw no difference in anything. My vision seemed sharper, however; clearer in a way that had nothing to do with light. I looked down at the darkling and, though it was night and the clouds obscured the moons at the moment, still I could see the creature clearly. Its body was black and glistening, but the skin, though smooth, seemed stitched with innumerable hair-fine lines, like delicate filigree.

The flier circled again, Polaris increasing his range as the darkling grew steadily bigger. It reminded me of my fight with the ice giant atop the Walking Stick of Darklord's Bane, save that this creature was already ten times bigger and still growing. No simple doubling spell or the like would stop it. I stared down at it, searching for some clue to its defeat.

Then I noticed something as our orbit took us behind it. At the base of the darkling's skull was a dim red glow, duller than the glow of its eyes, as if I were seeing it beneath a layer of skin. When I saw it, I knew what had to be done. It didn't occur to me to wonder where the knowledge came from, or if I should question it. I was seated next to Polaris in the front of the cockpit. The flier had dual controls. I seized the sticks and said, "Leave it to me."

Polaris relinquished control immediately, and immediately I dropped the flier's nose, heading us straight toward the darkling's neck.

Some effort had been made on the ground to mount a defense against the monster; red raybeams licked upward, scoring the thing's legs. But it was like trying to erode a mountain with a water pistol; all they did was attract the darkling's attention. Still, that was enough; it kept the behemoth distracted while I sent the flier screaming, full-out, toward that murky third eye.

Valina said nothing, though her grip on my arm was tighter than a publican holding his moneypouch. Polaris simply said, "I do hope you know what you're doing, Kamus."

So did I. The darkling filled our vision, and then the nose of the flier stabbed into the dim red oval that I and no one else could see.

We felt only the slightest resistance, like plunging through a mountain of paper. There was a crackling, tearing sound, and then the night sky was before us as I pulled the flier's nose up. I came around again, in time to see the giant darkling falling apart, disintegrating into its millions of component parts; the imps that had come together to form it. They fell back to the field, scattering like roaches in the Maze. I leaned back, limp with relief.

"Well," Polaris said, "our large friend seems to have gone to pieces. Well done, Kamus."

"The spaceport personnel should be able to deal with the imps," I said. "They'll vanish at daybreak, anyway."

Valina, in the seat behind me, said, "Take off the Mask, Kamus." I sat up at her words; I had forgotten I had it on. It had worked; somehow, it had shown me the place to strike. I reached up to remove it, glancing back as I did at Valina.

I caught a glimpse out of the corner of my eye of her just as I pulled the mask off, and I felt like I'd plunged into liquid oxygen. What I saw, only for an instant, was a nightmare's distortion of her face: the head subtly elongated and lupine, her eyes narrowed, lips blood red, ears and teeth just slightly pointed. It was an almost subliminal flash, received while in the act of removing the mask; I was not even sure I'd really seen it. Then I was blinking in the reflected instrument lights of the cockpit, looking at Valina, who looked back at me in concern.

"Are you all right, Kamus?" she asked. "You look like you've seen—" But she did not finish the sentence, and was it my imagination, or did she become slightly paler in the wan light?

We were both silent for a moment. "It's nothing," I said, "battling giant darklings always upsets me." But still she watched me, eyes wide and dark—and frightened.

I settled back in my seat, watching the night land blur beneath us. Polaris was going south, and already the grasslands of Adelan were behind us. Already we had covered a distance that would have taken hours by balloonboat, or a day on foot. At this rate, we would reach Ja-Agur in plenty of time for Shadownight.

The thought gave me no particular satisfaction, however. I huddled in my trenchcloak, cold despite the comfortable warmth of the cockpit. In my mind one thought cycled, over and over: the Black Mask shows things as they are.

2

In another two hours we were over the Inland Sea. Our course would take us very near Kadizhar, the island on which I was raised. At another time, under very different circumstances, I might have been tempted to pay a visit for old times' sake. But now I had several other things on my mind. I had asked Polaris to put us down in Xikree, one of the few villages beyond the Black Desert. I had no desire to arrive in Ja-Agur in so noticeable a vehicle as a Unity planet skimmer. We would cross the rest of the obsidian sands and the Mountains of Darkness some other way. Our only chance lay in doing the unexpected—if anything could be unexpected to the Darklord.

Since the evidence seemed to indicate that the Darklord knew I had gone to Hestia in search of the Black Mask, it seemed logical that he knew I had it. For that reason, I was tempted to throw it away—again, in an attempt to do the unexpected. I did not, however. It had helped us once, and might do so again. But I hoped the need for it would not come up. I could not rid my mind of that momentary nightmarish vision of Valina. I still could not be sure if I had imagined it or not. But I could not, at the moment, bring myself to don it again to be sure.

Valina said nothing more; when I glanced back a few minutes later, I saw that she had fallen asleep. I was tired, myself; casting spells and fighting for one's life can be draining. But I could not sleep. I watched the flickering lights of the instrument panel. Polaris said nothing, concentrating on piloting the craft. I watched him. I had so many unanswered questions concerning him that I didn't know where to start asking. He had led us to believe that he was a mercenary, a soldier-of-fortune, and that he was going south for a lark. I believed that the way I believed the Darklord was Santa Claus. But, I told myself, perhaps I wasn't giving Polaris Lone enough of a chance. He probably had more reasons than he was telling for being on Ja-Lur, but that did not mean he couldn't be trusted. I thought once again of Daniel Tolon's statement. I did not want paranoia to become such second nature to me. Perhaps, if I asked him a few questions, he might be more informative . . .

I was about to speak when my head struck painfully against the headrest and I felt the hurkle try to climb up my throat. I quickly sized up the situation—we were falling. I looked out the window. There was nothing but water below us, which would at least be softer than land. "Hang on," Polaris said levelly. "I'll try to glide in."

I began to chant the Words of a spell that might ease our impact. Valina awakened and joined in. We barely finished it in time; our speed slowed and the craft levelled slightly, but we still hit like a mace against a shield. A bonejarring crash and splash was repeated twice, and then everything was still, save for the gentle rocking of the ship and the not-so-gentle pounding of my heart.

Polaris pressed the start code, but we heard nothing—not even the electronic tones that indicated transmission. "I take it this is your unpredictable mandate operating again," He said. "The crash seems to have permanently damaged the controls. Most annoying, this on-again, off-again state of affairs."

"It seems to be happening less now than when it first began," I said. "The closer we come to Shadownight, the more the mandate stays inactive, instead of flickering on and off."

"Cold comfort to us at this point," Polaris observed.

Fortunately the hatches had emergency mechanical latches. Soon we were all sitting on the roof of the floating flier. A dim gray light in the east suggested dawn. Polaris looked about us, then pointed to the southwest. "There seems to be an island in that direction."

I looked off into the darkness. "What did you do—smell it?"

"Not exactly," Polaris replied. "I have rather good night

vision, thanks to infrared contact lenses. They have limited magnification powers, too."

"It figures," I said. "Well, the island is called Kadizhar. If we can reach it, we can hire a boat, if the flier can't be repaired."

"The problem is reaching it," Valina said.

I looked at the shiny metallic surface I was sitting on. A small knob was rubbing against my ankle. I pulled on it and raised a telescoped length of sturdy antenna to a height of two meters. By using spare wire in the tool compartment and my sword as a crossbar, we fashioned a sail out of Valina's cloak.

"Very resourceful," Polaris commented. "But I'm constrained to point out that there is no wind to speak of."

"There will be." I looked at Valina. "Do you feel up to it?"

"With your help."

We both faced the north, and with the aid of gestures and a vial of cloudsilk thrown into the air, spoke the Words of a wind spell. A breeze began almost before we finished speaking, and quickly grew to a stiff wind. The makeshift sail billowed out and we began to move southward slowly.

"This is amazing," Polaris said. "All you have to do is speak to make it so?"

"For simpler spells, yes," I told him. "More powerful spells, those with more far-reaching effects, require some aid; proper use of potions and talismans, laying out of symbols and so forth. Of course, you have to be a Darklander for any of it to work; otherwise, the Words are just words."

Polaris looked thoughtful and said no more. We sat somewhat precariously on the flier as it drifted southward. Fortunately, the sea was fairly calm. Still, it was a slow and tiring ride, and the sun was sinking toward afternoon when we entered the harbor of Kadizhar.

For my part, I did a lot of listening, while Valina and Polaris conversed occasionally in low tones. I heard some of what he told her; he had evidently led quite an interesting life. He had been, among other things, a terraformer, an asteroid miner, and a singularity scout. He had helped overthrow the oppressive Technocratic regime of the Crimson Nebula, and had worked with the Worldbeaters, an elite corps that stopped Dal the Merciless's plan to rule the Chan Gen system with his solar lens.

Valina listened as though ensorcelled while he talked about far-flung worlds and evil tyrants. She obviously believed every word. Not that I was all that skeptical; there was something about the quiet, almost modest way he spoke that made me accept even the taller stories. He was always vague and non-committal about his own part in these adventures, skillfully turning away questions about that. He was merely, he claimed, a galactic jack-of-all-trades with a penchant for getting into adventurous situations. I was sure that he was more than that. But I wasn't sure if I wanted to find out what he was.

* * *

Kadizhar was a mountainous island, with more vertical surfaces than horizontal; it had one small town whose quarried stone buildings clung to the rocky cliffs that plunged down toward the clear blue water. There were few ships in the harbor when we docked; as we sailed in, sailors stared and children chattered with excitement, merchants and tradesfolk stroked chins or pulled beards. We made quite a stir. Outworld technology wasn't seen too often outside the Northern Nations. By the time we had drawn up to the docks, it seemed the whole town had come down to the waterfront; old and young, rich and poor crowded to see the strange ship and its strange crew. I spoke with the owner of a boathouse and managed to buy space there in which to berth the flier. Once it was out of sight, and the smooth, salt-stained doors locked, most of the crowd began to lose interest, though enough still clustered about us as we moved along the wharf, offering all manner of services for a few dechels, or begging Polaris to show them some outworld magic. There were also those who stood back, huddled in cloaks and doorways, muttering and looking askance at us. The increasing terrors of Shadownight's approach had not made strangers welcome in most of Ja-Lur's cities.

A quick investigation of the flier proved that it would not take to the air again without more repairs than we could perform. A boat would have to be bought to take us across to the Wall of Thunger, the only scaleable area of the sheer cliffs that separated most of the Sunken Jungle and the Black

Desert from the Inland Sea. We were given the name of one Seskin, a shipowner with reasonable prices. To buy a boat would put a serious dent in my savings, but there was no other way off the island; no one was willing to rent a boat or ferry us to the inhospitable southern shore.

We made our way up the winding, narrow streets. Kadizhar had not changed much since the last time I saw it, almost twenty years before. I had spent most of an unhappy childhood and adolescence here. My mother never quite recovered from the trauma of her rape on the last Shadownight by a Darklander. She tried very hard to love me and to convince herself that I was completely human, but she was always somewhat afraid of me. When I was ten she died—peacefully, I hope—in her sleep.

"Delightful little village," Polaris said, in the tone of someone who has just discovered an interesting tide pool. "Ah, now, *this* is striking!"

We had just entered the village square, and Polaris was referring to what was probably Kadizhar's single attempt at art: two bronze statues, green and white from sea air and gulls' droppings. "What is the scene of, Kamus?" Polaris continued.

"It depicts a battle between Mondrogan the Clever and a darkling, which supposedly happened on Kadizhar in the distant past," I said. We walked around the statues, admiring them. It had been a long time since I'd seen them, and I was surprised and slightly gratified to find that, instead of seeming smaller and more tawdry compared to my memory, I was more impressed than ever by them. Mondrogan was posed in the act of hurling a potion vial at the snarling darkling. Though weathered by time, the details were still extraordinary, perhaps captured by some ancient form of lost-wax casting. I looked up at the sardonic face of the half-breed Darklander. From his tousled hair one lone horn sprouted, curving up from the left temple, just as it did on the stylized drawing of the ring I wore. The fake horn had been Mondrogan's way of bravely—or foolishly—flaunting the fact that he was a half-breed.

"I have never seen a rendering of him before," Valina said. "He was a handsome man." It was true; his face, though slightly elfin, had sharp lines of character, high cheekbones, and piercing, deep-set eyes. He looked oddly familiar to me.

I wondered, as we continued on our way, if he had known who his Dark parent had been. He, too, had fought against the Darklord, a millennium ago. No legends told of his final fate. I felt a kinship for Mondrogan the Clever. I hoped I would be more clever than he had been when the need arose.

Occupied by my thoughts, I suddenly realized Valina had spoken to me.

"I said, this is not the route we were told would take us to Seskin's house," she pointed out. I looked about and realized she was right; in my reverie, I had followed a route learned many years before, and now stood before a small door, painted a weather-beaten orange, in a tiny court. I stared at it, shocked by its sudden appearance, and trying to feel some measure of pleasurable nostalgia. For it was within this small basement dwelling that I had done the majority of my growing up.

I lived from hand to mouth until I was fifteen, running errands around the docks, stealing... a hard existence. I grew up fast. I had no clue to the potential power within me until, having entered here, the house of a charlatan, in search of food, I came upon several scrolls wherein he had laboriously copied spells of Darkness. My mother had taught me to read the bastard Adelanese spoken about the Inland Sea, but this writing was totally different. Yet, to my astonishment, I found that I could read it; just barely. I'll never forget what happened when I read one of the spells out loud. The long, sinuous leaves of a serpent plant nearby began to writhe about, reaching greedily for and waving knives and kitchen utensils. I watched in terrified fascination, knowing that I was somehow responsible. Then the door behind me opened and there stood Dessus the charlatan, watching with as much wonder as I. He, too, knew I was responsible.

He was a kindly old man who eked out a starveling existence by preparing love potions, headache remedies and the like for the more gullible folk on Kadizhar. He was always willing to listen sympathetically to their troubles, which was why he was allowed to remain on the island, though his remedies seldom worked. He recognized that I had Dark Blood, and undertook to teach me the rudiments of the Language of Darkness.

I had just reached manhood when the Unity of Planets

made contact with Ja-Lur and the spaceport was built outside Mariyad. The possibility of traveling to other worlds fascinated me, and when I heard that a few Ja-Lurians would have the privilege of doing so if picked for the cultural exchange program, I applied, without any hope of success. After all, I was barely literate, uneducated, and the only talent I had I could not demonstrate for fear of being lynched. Yet I became one of the select few. I never learned the reason why. Now, staring at the ancient building where Dessus had once lived and taught me what little he knew of Darkness, I wondered if I ever would know. There was a lot about my past that was still a mystery to me.

Dessus had died the year before I left for Mariyad, of a fever that all his panaceas and all my fledgling powers had been unable to cure. He had told me once that his greatest fear had been of dying unmourned. I made sure that didn't happen; the people whom he had aided, more by kind ear and tongue than by cantrips and potions, all contributed what they could to give him a good funeral.

"Are you all right, Kamus?" Valina asked me. "You're very quiet."

The small orange door creaked open and an old woman peered out. "You got business here?" she asked brusquely.

"No," I said. "None." I turned away and led Valina and Polaris out of the court. Valina looked concerned, and Polaris wore a quiet smile.

* * *

Seskin's house was not far from there. He turned out to be about as reasonable as a starving sandcat, and we ended up with a small, single-masted skiff, a map that supposedly showed a safe route through the Sunken Jungle, and a very flat money pouch.

On top of all that, when we returned to the boathouse to load what little belongings and equipment we had onto the skiff, we found a picked lock and an enterprising young thief in the process of ransacking the flier. He saw us, and his face, under several layers of dirt, went white. He had a lean and wolfish body, and a face left ravaged by pox. His teeth were like toppling gravestones. He was perhaps half my age, and looked older than me. I remembered similiar times as a youth, searching and stealing for food and shelter on these docks, and felt sorry for him. I was about to tell him to drop what he had and leave, but before I could speak, Polaris shouldered past me and faced him.

The youth, realizing there was no way out except past us, drew a dull and notched sword, but before he had it clear of the scabbard Polaris's golden blaster was pointed at him. The thief stood very still; almost certainly he had never seen a ray gun before, but knew what they could do.

"That won't work," he said in a quavering voice. "The mandate—"

"Might be in effect," Polaris said quietly. He had a very slight smile on his face. "Then again, it might not be. I understand it's hard to tell, these days. So you'd best ask yourself: Do you feel lucky?"

The youth, his teeth chattering like a fever victim's, dropped his sword and turned to leap into the water, but a blast of golden energy scorched the planks before him and he fell backward, wide-eyed but unhurt. Polaris holstered his blaster.

"Now get out of here," he told the thief, "and think twice before you steal again."

The boy ran. I looked at Polaris angrily. "That was nothing less than torture," I said.

He looked at me in surprise. "Nonsense. I just put a healthy scare into him. Perhaps it will save his hide at some later date."

"After all, Kamus," Valina said, "he *was* robbing us."

I started to speak again, but swallowed it instead. Polaris looked at me for a moment, then shrugged and turned toward the flier, and the several tools and food items that the thief had scattered on the dock. Valina quickly moved to help him begin transfering them to the skiff moored outside, and after a moment, so did I. Nothing more was said about the incident. I had the feeling that Polaris forgot it almost immediately.

I did not forget it, however. I remembered the slight smile on Polaris's face as he had held the raygun on the boy. Perhaps my anger had come more from my distrust of Polaris than from any feeling of empathy for the youth. But I felt sure of one thing: the cat-and-mouse game had not been due to Polaris's concern for the thief's morals. He had enjoyed doing it.

3

The voyage across the rest of the Inland Sea took the better part of two days. Valina and I kept the sails filled as best we could with whatever small wind was available, parcelling our strength for other things, such as the slight possibility of sea serpents. Valina picked up techniques of sailing quickly, and Polaris had had nautical experiences on other worlds. We pushed steadily on toward the southern coast and the Wall of Thunger.

I spent much of the voyage sitting at the prow, chewing gum, watching the sea monkeys playing in the water when I wasn't staring at the horizon. The temperature grew steadily warmer as we moved southeast. I watched the straight line that separated two almost-identical shades of blue, and waited for land to show. Beyond the Wall would be the Sunken Jungle, and beyond that the Black Desert, and beyond that...

It seemed impossible to reach the Darkland in time now. But for some reason, I was no longer worried. I thought of how I had wanted to flee the Darkworld only days past. If a ship had been available, I might very well have. But I knew that sooner or later I would have returned. I could not leave this matter unsettled, if for no other reason than my own curiosity. But there was more to it than that, of course. I remembered what Jann-Togah had said when we parted company outside the Mariyad gate: "My father fears the loss of his power, and he will do anything to prevent that." Anything means just that, when one speaks of the Darklord: a spreading of Darkness such as had happened a thousand years before, on the first Shadownight, when he had attempted to conquer the planet.

He had been beaten, but just barely. Among those who fought him had been a crafty wanderer, born of Darklander and human. I looked at Mondrogan's ring on my finger. Perhaps he had hidden the Black Mask centuries ago, from the Darklord. And now I had found it, due to a number of strange happenings and lucky breaks.

How much of it had been luck? My short stay on Kadizhar, my brief return to Dessus's home, had made me think about my past a lot. It seemed now that, ever since my return to Ja-Lur from Earth, a pattern had been woven. I had been pushed and pulled this way and that by what had to be more than happenstance and coincidence; even the sporadic failures of the mandate now seemed to me designed to specific ends, instead of merely random chance. But why?

I had blamed it on the Darklord. But perhaps some grander design was at work?

The idea seemed the height of conceit. And yet . . . I could not help but notice the parallels between Mondrogan the Clever and me. He had fought the Darklord, and helped stop him. Perhaps I was intended to do the same?

I shrugged. I had little proof one way or another . . . it was certainly more comforting to believe this than to think of myself as the Darklord's puppet. I would find out soon enough.

* * *

Little happened in the way of Shadownight phenomena on the two nights we spent at sea. The first night, as the nearly-full Bellus and Jaspara drew nigh, we were treated to a calvacade of illusory attacks by what seemed to be the phantoms of various sea monsters, most of which had been extinct on Ja-Lur for millions of years. Polaris wasted several golden bolts of energy before we realized that the beasts, fearsome as they appeared, were as tangible as foam.

The second night the occurrence was also of a visual nature; the sea seemed to turn to fire. Phosphorescent waves shattered like liquid light against our hull. As the moons passed zenith, the intensity increased until we were all forced to blindfold ourselves; it was like sailing on the surface of a sun.

I did not speak much with either Valina or Polaris during those two days. Valina tried several times to engage me in conversation, but I remained introspective and taciturn. She gave most of her attention to Polaris, which increased my feeling of distance. My dislike of him had not lessened since the incident in the boathouse, and his usefulness in every situation and air of quiet superiority didn't help matters any.

One night, when they were both asleep, I put on the Black Mask again and looked at Valina. This time she appeared unchanged through it; whether that was due to her being asleep, or my imagining that her appearance had changed before, or something else entirely, I had no idea.

* * *

At last the Wall of Thunger rose into view over the southern horizon. By mid-afternoon we beached on a short stretch of sand that ended against a sheer wall of rock which towered almost five hundred meters above us. The top of it was wreathed in mist from the humidity of the Sunken Jungle. The Wall ran for hundreds of kilometers along the southern shore of the Inland Sea. It was not more than thirty meters wide at some points, and it held back the sea from the Sunken Jungle, a huge, roughly circular depression perhaps a hundred kilometers in diameter and almost two hundred meters below sea level.

Valina stood before the wall and looked up. "It will be a difficult climb," she remarked. "Much worse than the Walking Stick."

"Perhaps not," Polaris said. "I've had some experience at mountain climbing. Olympus Mons on Mars, for example . . ."

"Why does that come as no surprise to me?" I asked rhetorically.

"And I also have this." He held up his arm and indicated a tiny lump on the sleeve of his flexarmor, just over the wrist. He pointed up the Wall and flexed his arm. A monofilament line shot from the lump, visible only by being white against the dark rock, and hit the wall. Polaris tugged on it to demonstrate its anchorage. "Very high adhesion factor."

"Do you have any other tricks up your sleeve?" I asked him.

"Up my sleeve, in my belt, boots, gloves . . . this suit is wired to my nervous system."

So he was a cybernaid; I had suspected as much. Luckily for him, his cyber suit only augmented his abilities; when the mandate caused it to fail, he was reduced to the status of the rest of us, but not crippled.

Using the exoskeletal strength that was another aspect of his suit, he held onto both of us and we rose slowly up the wall, using our legs to keep us away from the rough surface, as he rewound the line. The end of it had anchored almost halfway up; We stood precariously on a small ledge while Polaris fired it up into the mists again.

"What happens if the mandate happens to take effect now?" I asked as we rose again, the mist closing about us.

"Try not to think about that," Polaris said.

Fortunately, it didn't. In a matter of minutes we stood on the edge of the Wall of Thunger, looking down into the misty depths of the Sunken Jungle. The forest canopy stretched out below us. Orange apes chattered faintly in the trees, and flocks of birds could be seen. Far away, in the mist, I could make out the immense girth of a balloon tree; its giant, lighter-than-air fruit tugged at its branches.

"Do we have to go through this?" Polaris asked.

"According to the map, it's the quickest way," Valina replied. "To the east or west the ground is broken and shattered, full of chasms, and beyond that, uninhabited and waterless leagues of sand."

"And down there is a jungle full of land kragors, tricorn snakes, jungle cats, mosquitoes the size of bloodbirds, and barbarians," I said. "Not a pleasing choice."

It was the only choice we had, however, and so Polaris lowered us into the mist.

Crossing the Sunken Jungle wasn't a bad experience compared to, say, falling into a black hole. The mist and humidity wrapped around us like passionate ghosts, and before we were out of sight of the Wall even Polaris was sweating; something I wouldn't have thought possible, considering the immaculate appearance he always managed to present. We moved slowly through the oceanic air and the tangled undergrowth. The jungle was filled with sinla vines, a creeper similar in its enthusiastic growth to earthly kudzu. Polaris's golden blaster served as a machete; after each slashing ray of light the cacophony of jungle sounds would stop in shocked silence, then begin again. He also used the strength supplied by the exoskeletal reinforcements in his flexarmor. We tried to follow Seskin's map as closely as we could; it instructed us to follow a ridge of lava. The ridge not only ran in a relatively straight line across the Sunken Jungle, but it also was considered taboo ground by the Kragor Tribe, and so we would not be troubled by them as long as we stayed near it.

Valina periodically recited a protection spell to keep the smaller annoyances and dangers from us. It was necessary, for life was everywhere, and little of it was friendly; tricorn snakes entwined treetrunks, tiny winged leeches sought any exposed skin, and spiders the size of sandals scurried underfoot.

We had gone perhaps half a kilometer when the myriad buzzings, hissings and other sounds were overwhelmed by a saurian roar that sounded too close and too angry for comfort.

We stopped. "What was that?" Polaris asked.

"Nothing small," I replied. Then we caught a glimpse of an indistinct gray form with a spiked back moving through the mist, eastward.

"Let's go west," I suggested.

After several more grueling hours of a roundabout route, we at last came to higher ground near the lava ridge. We found something that vaguely resembled a dry area, and bivouacked. Polaris's gun and suit were both in need of solar recharging, and Valina was exhausted from the effort of the trek and of maintaining the protection spell. I took over maintaining it; my weaker powers would serve while we were encamped.

I found enough edible fruits and tubers to make a meal of sorts, and afterward sat near the edge of the area enclosed by the protection spell, listening to the jungle noise and wondering how I was going to sleep. Dusk came. I wondered what form of strange and surreal happenings this night would bring, if any. There was but a week left before Shadownight, and we still had to cross the Sunken Jungle, most of the Black Desert, and an unknown part of Ja-Agur. It seemed impossible to make it on time, and yet we had already come farther in three days than I would have believed.

Valina sat down beside me, her gray cloak, now much the worse for wear, gathered about her. "We have not spoken overmuch, Kamus," she said, and coughed.

"Correction," I said; "*I* haven't spoken overmuch. You've spoken quite a bit—mostly to Polaris."

She raised an eyebrow. "Does this bother you?"

I glanced at Polaris, who sat with his back turned a little ways from us. "Frankly, yes," I said in a low voice. "I think he's slipprier than a sea snake, with a personality about as deep as a quantum level. I realize he's been very helpful to us, but I don't think he's doing it out of the goodness of his heart."

"Why, then?"

"I'm not sure. I just have the feeling that this is no pleasure jaunt for him."

She gave me a look of anger that I remembered from my office, months ago. "I think the plain and simple truth is that you're jealous of him," she said quietly, and started to stand up.

I grabbed her cloak with my hand to stop her. There was a crumpling sound, like old parchment being crushed, and she jerked the gray cloth from my grasp. Nevertheless, she sat down again.

"I didn't mean to lose my temper," I told her. "But I'm convinced that there's more to Polaris than he says."

"Quit hiding behind your ridiculous Earth fantasy," she said, in a low, scathing tone. "You know there's no mystery here. You simply resent his ability to take charge, his competence, knowledge, and gallantry."

"I've seen more gallantry in berserkers."

"You mistrust everyone," she said, and walked away. She sat down beside Polaris and spoke with him. In a few moments they were chuckling quietly, no doubt over one of Polaris's witticisms.

I sat there, brooding. It was true to an extent that I resented Polaris's upstaging of me. But there were also too many unexplained things about him for me to trust him. And it was also true that I could not bring myself to trust Valina completely.

It seemed that, by various imperceptible means, I had come to be alone in my quest once more. I thought again of Daniel Tolon's words about paranoia. But I also thought of Jann-Togan's warning about a danger from the north. I had wondered before if the danger might have been the Black Mask. But now, for the first time, I wondered if it might be Valina instead.

Though I could not see the sky, I could tell that Bellus and Jaspara had risen. The sense of Darkness was unmistakable. Every night for the past week, I had felt it growing from imperceptibility, stronger with every turn of the planet. I spoke the protection spell again, hoping that the rising tide of Darkness would not twist it into something dangerous. But nothing happened that night—at least, not to us. Though, as I finally fell asleep, I had no doubt that torment and terror were falling like rain over large parts of the Darkworld.

* * *

After a night that was expiation for more sins than I could ever commit, I was roused by a green, wet dawn. We continued our route down the lava ridge. As usual, progress was slow, made more so by a brief but torrential shower that soaked us during mid-morning. Valina was not feeling at all well; her exertions of the past two weeks, combined with the pestilent surroundings, had weakened her resistance. It was not going to be a good day. I was sure of that a few minutes later when the rain stopped and we were captured by jungle barbarians.

They stepped out of the jungle about us, at least ten of them, all tall, dark, and looking capable of beating ogres two falls out of three. Nine of them had arrows trained on us. I glanced at Valina, warning her without words that there was no chance of completing a spell in time.

"I thought you said there was no danger as long as we followed the ridge," Polaris said to me.

"Not from the warriors of the Kragor Tribe," I said. "Unfortunately, these fellows are from the Junglecat Tribe."

It was true; all our black-maned, scowling captors wore loincloths or togas of spotted junglecat hide, with the snarling totem tattooed on their chests. This was the tribe that Ult had belonged to. Remembering his general attitude didn't increase my optimism.

The leader was a giant with a patch of hide over his left eye, most of his left ear missing, and not enough unscarred skin left to cover a hand drum. He wore a necklace of long saberteeth and held an obsidian axe. He came forward and stopped in front of us, looking us over, his face impassive.

"Perhaps you should offer him beads," Polaris suggested dryly to me.

"That won't be necessary," the barbarian said. He spoke in well-accented Adelese, his tone quiet and slightly sardonic. We stared at him in surprise, and the faintest ghost of a smile creased his face. "We're quite overstocked on beads currently."

* * *

The march back to the Junglecat village took most of the day. During it, Thon, the chieftain, told us about himself. He had also been a wanderer, like Ult, and had also been captured by a Darklander. But instead of becoming a slave, Thon had been the subject of various experimental spells for increasing intelligence. Finding that the spells worked to an extent upon Thon, the Darklander had tried them on himself, but succeeded only in inducing a mood of such morbid introspection and existential *angst* that he committed suicide, leaving Thon with an insatiable desire for learning and a castleful of books.

The barbarian had read, traveled, and studied in the Northern Nations. Eventually, fed up with what he felt was the hypocrisy of civilization, he had returned to the Sunken Jungle.

We sat, our hands bound behind us, on crude wicker furniture in a large grass hut. We were surrounded by guards who kept arrows aimed at us, insuring Thon a captive audience as he spoke.

"Granted, it grows boring here at times," he told us. "But look at the positive aspects—I'm regarded with awe and reverence because I've taught my people new and useful things. My every whim—within practicality, of course—is granted enthusiastically. Isolation is a small price to pay, though I must admit I'm grateful for this chance to hear news of the outside world."

"We'd like to stay and chat for awhile," I told him. "But we really do have to be going soon."

"Oh, I'm afraid that's not possible," Thon said in a tone of genuine regret. "You see, Grigor, our shaman, has convinced the people that your sacrifice would be appeasing to the Darklord, and that it would ameliorate the worst effects of the coming Shadownight." He sighed. "Pity . . . I so seldom encounter civilized people with whom I can exchange ideas and conversation. Still, a good leader knows when to bow to the will of the people."

He stood and opened a small woven basket, and from it

took what seemed to be three lengths of thick brown rope; or so I thought until I saw them coiling and flexing slowly, sluggishly, in his hands.

Valina murmured, "Soundsnakes!"

I glanced at the guards. They stood like statues, each holding an arrow notched and drawn. The bows were heavy, but the guards showed no sign of strain.

Thon laid the soundsnakes out in a row on the packed dirt floor, then took a brand from a smoky fire near the entrance. "*Jinta kwol*," he murmured. "*Sinald dammi, maldoz, ghoor, tas zule . . .*" and so on, chanting a long and meaningless string of Darkness. Each time he spoke a Word, he touched the smouldering brand to one of the soundsnakes, which coiled and tightened in agony. Then he picked them up and draped them around our necks. The cool, dry skin of the snakes coiled snugly against our windpipes, comfortable as nooses.

"That should prevent you speaking Language," he said. "Well, it's been most pleasant chatting with you; I only wish we could have prolonged it somewhat. But the moons are rising, and I must see to the ceremony, which will take place in a few hours." So saying, he lifted the kragor hide which served as a door and left the hut.

Polaris looked down at the snake about his neck. "What in the galaxy is this for?"

"Speak softly," I cautioned him. "It's a soundsnake." I could feel the creature tighten ever so gently about my throat as I spoke in a whisper. "They respond to various speech patterns, and they're easily conditioned. You heard Thon speaking Darkness as he burned them. He wasn't reciting a spell; he was just repeating Words he had heard at random. The snakes are now conditioned to contract if we say a Word of Darkness. Before Valina or I could complete a spell, they'd strangle us."

"You do have some very remarkable animals on this world," Polaris said. "I could easily rid myself of this thing, but I doubt I could stop all of those arrows from hitting us."

"How do we get out of this?" Valina asked.

I swallowed, feeling my Adam's apple move against the soundsnake. "I don't know if we can," I said.

* * *

Though the hut had no window, I could sense when the two moons of Ja-Lur were reaching zenith. The soundless throbbing in my blood that signalled the rise of Darkness was unmistakable. Thon came back into the hut and said, "Please follow me." The guards herded us out.

The Junglecat village was a small one; concentric semicircles of huts constructed of speargrass and sinla vine, facing a small open area. A meager spread of tilled ground was faintly visible beyond the huts, and beyond that a wooden stockade. Three stakes, surrounded by piles of brush, had been raised in the center of the compound. A small stone altar stood before them.

The guards ushered us forward. We tripped several times over the snaky sinla vines that had grown even across the bare ground of the compound. The area was lit by huge torches that cast a baleful light. The assembled tribesfolk, men, women, and children, crowded close, pushing for a better view.

I looked up; the moons were approaching each other. They were gibbous; in another three nights they would be full.

Polaris's gun was taken from him and laid on the altar, as was my potion pouch. I thought of the Black Mask within it, useless to me now. I thought about how far I had come, and how absurd it seemed to die here at the hands of barbarians. True, I had had no guarantee I would see this through to a successful conclusion. Quite the opposite, in fact. But I at least wanted my death to be meaningful. I felt my heart beating like the drums that had started beyond the torches, felt the power I had, sporadic and uncertain thought it might be, demanding to be used, surging like adrenalin. I looked at Valina and saw she felt the same way. She opened her mouth; I knew she was going to speak. Better to die in an attempt at freedom than to be slaughtered like a sheep. I caught her gaze and shook my head slightly, then looked up at the approaching intersection of Bellus and Jaspara. She understood and nodded; she would wait, as would I, until it would do the most good. The heightening Darkness about us might work for us, or it might not, but that was a chance we would have to take.

Tribesmen approached with ropes to bind us to the posts. I looked up and saw that the moons were touching, beginning to form intersecting discs. The drums grew louder. Under their cover I told Valina in a low voice what my plan was. She nodded, and together we began to silently mouth the spell I had in mind. We made no sound, spoke no Word of Darkness out loud. The snakes about our throats did not tighten. But, aided by the Darkness in the air about us, the pantomime worked.

As my arms were seized to be bound, one of the sinla vines that covered the clearing suddenly quivered, then jerked about the ankle of the man behind me. Off balance, he staggered and fell. Another vine snapped like a whip against the arm of one holding a torch. He dropped it with a cry; it landed against one of the grass huts. The damp speargrass began to burn, slowly and with much smoke. Still, it was a fire, and that was enough to start a panic.

I saw Polaris flex his shoulders, and wedges of sharp blades sprang free from his wrists, slicing through his ropes, then fanning out to surround his hands like sharp metal fingers, extending beyond his fists. He tore the soundsnake free of his neck. A barbarian lunged at him with a spear; Polaris brushed it aside with one hand and punched the other toward the barbarian's throat. I saw him grin as the blades were stained red.

An arrow whistled past my ear; I ducked, pulling the soundsnake from about my own neck as I did so. The smoke from the fire was rapidly filling the clearing, making the aiming of the arrows difficult; still, they were coming too close for comfort. But the sinla vines were also at work, weaving and rising like snakes, tripping warriors as they rushed forward to attack, as well as others who tried to run.

Valina removed her soundsnake and cried *"Alalen yok tinnece!"* Her voice rose above the clamor and confusion. She coughed in the middle of the spell, but it still worked—we heard staccato crackings as spear and arrow shafts broke in two.

Thon grabbed Polaris from behind in a a bear hug. "A noble effort, outworlder," he said. "But I have you now!"

"This will come as a shock," Polaris replied, "but you haven't," and Thon shouted in agony as he was suddenly hurled backwards from Polaris. I smelled burning flesh and felt my hair crackle with electricity even in the damp air. Polaris's suit had delivered what had to be a fatal charge to the barbarian chieftain. Thon fell to the ground, his arms and face burnt.

Polaris grabbed his gun from the altar and tossed me my potion pouch. "Time to go," he said, and aimed the golden beam in a wide swath that burned a route through the writhing vines and the stockade, toward the dark jungle. We ran toward it.

Polaris used his blaster both as a light and a machete as we stumbled through the jungle. Behind us, I could hear the war cries and curses of the Junglecat Tribe as they took up pursuit.

We soon came to a relatively open area, and stopped. Valina and I were feeling weak from the exertion and the spelling. "We won't be able to outrun them," I gasped.

"I've got a few more weapons in reserve," Polaris said calmly. "Let them come."

"You won't be able to wipe out the whole tribe," I told him, "much as you might like to." He looked at me sharply at that, but I turned away, looking around the clearing. At its far end, in the light of the separating moons, I saw the grotesque shape of a balloon tree. "If only we had a basket to travel in!" I said. "But we can't construct one in time!"

"We can," Valina said. "There are vines, and I know a weaving spell that might work. But it will take time. You two will have to hold them off." She coughed again.

I looked at her. "Are you up to it?"

"I'll have to be, won't I? Give me your potion pouch—I will need help."

I hesitated only a moment, thinking of the Black Mask. Then I handed it to her. She ran across the clearing and stopped beneath the balloon tree. In a few moments I could smell the musky scent of spidersilk powder, and heard her beginning the spell.

There was a sound of crashing in the underbrush. "They're coming," Polaris said. "Let's get into the jungle; I'll try to pick them off."

"There's an easier way," I said, "though I realize it won't be quite so fulfilling for you. May I?" and I took his raygun from his hand. I fired several shots into the network of vines and creepers that wove from tree to tree. Several large branches and vines fell like a huge net, just as the first of the tribe came into view down the narrow trail we had made. The vines entangled them; they fell, and those behind them fell over them.

But others were coming from other directions, and they would reach the clearing in a moment. We retreated to where Valina soood. The basket was forming, although slowly, the vines interweaving like trained snakes. Other vines rose up from it and slid over the smooth surface of one of the huge balloons, tethering the basket to it.

An arrow struck the massive trunk of the balloon tree. "Into the basket!" Polaris said.

"It isn't finished!" Valina replied.

"Maybe not, but we are if we stay here," I told her. We all climbed in as several barbarians burst into the clearing. Polaris severed the balloon's thick stem with a slash of his golden beam, cauterizing it, and, with a lurch, we rose up through the branches. Several arrows were fired after us, but none hit the balloon, and in a moment, we were out of range, successful once again in the latest of a long series of narrow escapes.

4

We ascended quickly to a dizzying height and began to drift southward. Overhead, Bellus and Jaspara drew away from each other; the time of madness was over again for another night and day.

The basket rocked and shifted beneath us; the incompleted spell had left it poorly tethered to the gasbag, and, in addition, the vines comprising the basket were not tightly woven. Moving carefully, Polaris used lengths of his monofilament line to help secure the attachments as best he could, but it remained a somewhat precarious situation.

When Polaris had finished, he looked at me and grinned. "Well," he said, "that last episode was rather exhilarating, wasn't it?"

I took a ragged breath of cool air. "Perhaps for you," I

told him. "But then, I've noticed that you take death a bit more casually than I."

He raised an eyebrow. "Might I remind you that those barbarians were bent on our destruction?"

"I'm not saying they weren't. I'm just saying that I don't enjoy killing."

"And that I do?"

"Well," I replied, "if the headsman's hood fits, wear it."

For a moment, those calm golden eyes flashed as hot as stars. Polaris looked very dangerous indeed then, and the basket seemed much too small. Then Polaris laughed.

"An interesting attitude for someone in your line of work," he said, his voice amused.

I held onto my anger. "It's the only attitude possible. You can become what you fight against very easily."

Polaris looked down at the misty landscape. "There are times," he said softly, "when that is necessary."

I did not say anything more; my eyelids were suddenly as heavy as visors. I wondered if I should sleep with Polaris awake, but I had little choice; I was snoring before I sagged to the floor of the basket, where Valina was already asleep.

* * *

I awoke at dawn. We had left the Sunken Jungle behind. Though the sun was just rising, spreading dull red light, it was already warm. I pulled myself to my knees, carefully, trying to avoid rocking the basket, and looked over the rim. We were floating over the sands of the Black Desert. The ebony dunes stretched as far as I could see in all directions, broken occasionally by a monolithic basalt outcropping.

Valina was still asleep. I looked at her; her skin was slightly flushed, and felt warm to the touch. Still, she seemed to be sleeping soundly, and her breathing was regular. I hoped she would be all right.

Polaris sat beside her, polishing his raygun. "Hungry?" he asked with a smile. He seemed to have forgotten, or was ignoring, my accusation of last night. He pulled from his chestpack a food bar that smelled like ambrosia with nuts. "This should satisfy your metabolism as well as it does mine; the nutrients have a wide digestion base. I've often wondered at the preponderance of human beings on various planets in the galaxy. Goes against all the laws of random selection, you know."

I chewed on the bar; it tasted better than it smelled, if that were possible. "I didn't think you put that much stock by laws," I couldn't help remarking. Once again, he chose to ignore me.

"We are making quite a good pace," he said.

I looked over the side again. Far below, a dark dot moved against the darker sands; a solitary hunting sandcat. There were no other signs of life about.

"At this rate," Polaris asked, "how soon can we expect to reach the Darkland?"

"Not more than another day if the wind keeps at this level." I chewed, thinking about the wind; as far as I knew, it did not blow toward the southwest at this time of year. But I could be wrong.

I could feel nervous excitement within me. There was a chance that we would reach Ja-Agur by Shadownight after all. There was no way to formulate a plan after that; I would simply have to play it by ear. It seemed, also, that Polaris Lone would be with Valina and me. I wasn't too happy about that idea.

Valina stirred then, opened her eyes, and sat up. The basket creaked alarmingly, and cold air rushed in from gaps in the weaving that appeared suddenly. "Easy!" Polaris said to her. "I'm afraid we've put all our eggs in a rather unsafe basket." He smiled down at her and offered her a food bar. She accepted it with a smile that seemed more than just gratitude. I turned away to hide a grimace, telling myself that I was not so much jealous as disappointed; I had hoped that Valina would have better taste than to like Polaris Lone.

It grew quite warm quite quickly. The heat made the balloon rise to a dangerous height, even with our weight. Valina and I huddled in the shade cast by the gasbag, while Polaris kept an eye on the rigging and the basket's construction as best he could. Despite the black, full-length flexarmor he wore, he did not seem overly discomfited; perhaps he was used to hotter climates on other worlds, or perhaps the circuits of his cyber suit provided cooling.

What little conversation there was took place mostly between Polaris and Valina. I watched the kilometers pass.

During the afternoon it began to cool a bit, and the balloon lowered to within a couple of hundred meters of the sands. At one point we saw several moving forms below us. They were Rumphs, members of one of the nomad tribes that roamed the Black Desert; when they saw us, they spurred their desert jemlas into a gallop, shouting and firing arrows at us. Polaris stepped to the edge of the basket, hand reaching for his blaster. I grabbed his wrist, my movement causing the basket to rock dangerously.

"Take it easy!" I said. "We're safely out of range. Besides, they're just having fun. If you kill one of them, the rest will pursue us all the way to the Darklord's doorstep."

"I was merely going to fire a warning shot," he said. "Don't you trust me?"

"About as far as I can shot-put a planet," I said. I was trying to goad him, possibly not a bright idea in our current situation, but I had had it up to my nonexistent horns with Polaris Lone. He refused to be goaded; he merely shrugged. "Pity you feel that way, since circumstances have made traveling companions of us," was all that he said.

Valina, however, had quite a bit to say. She clutched the vines that formed the rigging, her gray hair whipped by the wind. "Kamus, you're being a fool! Can't you see that Polaris can help you against the Darklord?" Her voice was hoarse and cracked.

Polaris arched an eyebrow at me. "Good manners have kept me from asking the purpose of your journey, but I'm afraid this piques my curiosity." He had to speak loudly to be heard over the wind. "Do you intend to challenge the Darklord?"

"With your help he could," Valina told him.

"That's absurd," I replied. "My only chance is to sneak in unobserved during Shadownight. Polaris is about as unobtrusive as a meteor."

"What does it matter?" she shouted over the wind's rising wail. "We have the power! We have the Black Mask and the—"

She stopped, suddenly in a fit of coughing. I was about to ask her to finish her sentence when the basket shuddered violently as one of the sinla vine riggings snapped. Intent on our discussion, none of us had realized the extent to which the wind had risen; we were now being blown at such a speed that the black sands below seemed a blur. We held on to the edges of the basket, which now trailed behind the balloon at a slight angle. I looked behind me, toward the southwest, and saw a jagged, irregular horizon ahead: Ja-Hedage, the Dark Range. The mountains that marked the boundary of the Darkland.

It was no longer possible to talk, or to do anything except hang on. The sun went down, and the twin lanterns of Bellus and Jaspara lit the sky, and still the wind blew. I wondered if it was the Darklord's doing, as I had wondered about so many things before. At any instant we expected the basket to come apart. Valina and I spoke binding spells to hold it as best we could, but it was obviously only a matter of time. We were among the black peaks of Ja-Hedage by the time the moons were high in the sky. They were not tall; a thousand meters or so at most. But their sheer, slick sides and almost-needle points made them nearly impassable on foot.

The wind whirled us through them in a spectral roller-coaster ride that lasted almost an hour. Time after time it seemed inevitable that we would be crushed against a wall of rock or impaled on a spire. At one point, Polaris blasted a knob of stone into fragments only moments before the basket would have collided with it. But, though we were buffeted about and flung against the walls several times, the basket held.

Then we were shot like a stone from a sling through a final narrow pass, and the mountains dropped away behind us. Before us was a land that looked, at least in the moons' cold light, even more barren than the Black Desert had been. I saw occasional stunted, twisted trees, white stretches of salt, low hillocks of sparse grass. The feeling was that of ancient, unchanging desolation. The sight of it was depressing, even repulsive—and yet, deep in my mind was a strange sense of déja vu, as if I were somehow coming home to a birthplace all but forgotten. I could see in Valina's eyes that she felt the same way.

The wind began to die abruptly. The balloon sank, so quickly that I thought there was a leak in the bag. The desolate landscape rushed up toward us. I caught a single glimpse of a lone man standing motionless on a sandy rise, his arms folded. Then the spell-woven basket came apart into streamers of vines. We clutched at them as we were dragged through the scratchy brush. I rolled over several times and came up with cold sand in my mouth.

The balloon was still rigid, full of gas, yet I saw it strike the ground like a lead dirigible and lie heavily on its side. I struggled to my feet, as did Valina and Polaris. We had landed less than ten meters from the man, who watched us with amusement in his dark eyes and a sardonic grin. I remembered that grin. He wore a red kilt and a feathered belt with an unscabbarded sword thrust through it, and a dark cloak.

Valina met his gaze and went pale. I knew she sensed the aura of his Dark power; it was strong enough to fry eggs on. Polaris could not sense it, but he knew the man was somehow responsible for bringing us down. He gripped his blaster.

The man ignored both of them. "Kamus," he said to me, inclining his head. "So nice to see you again."

I said nothing, at first. "Do introduce us, Kamus," Polaris said in a dangerously soft tone.

"Take your hand off your raygun," I told him. "It would bother him less than a water pistol. Polaris Lone, may I present Jann-Togah, son of the Darklord."

5

"I think," I added, looking at Valina, "that Valina has already recognized you."

Polaris said, "I've heard of you. So, the prodigal is returning."

Jann-Togah spared him a glance that would have frozen brimstone. Polaris, though he did not look cowed, nevertheless said nothing further as Jann-Togah looked at Valina. I saw his eyes narrow slightly, and wondered what his vision, more attuned than mine to matters of Darkness, had seen. But his voice was courteous as he said, "I sense you are a Darklander.

You were wise to come here; our kind are not welcome elsewhere on Ja-Lur currently."

Valina straightened her shoulders, throwing off her fear like a cloak. She was not the sort to be staggered by anything for long. But when she opened her mouth to reply to him, the only sound that came out was a squeak like a rusty gate. Her eyes went wide, and she put one hand to her throat. Tears of pain came to her eyes as she tried again to speak.

"Easy," I counseled. "It seems that your illness, and all the spelling and shouting, has given you a first-class case of laryngitis."

Her reaction seemed rather extreme; she almost went into shock. "Take it easy!" I said again. "You'll be alright in a few days." This did not seem to comfort her. Jann-Togah put his fingers on her throat, feeling it, and nodded. "Kamus is right," he said. "Don't be upset; when there is time, I will speak a healing spell." She looked at him with gratitude. Jann-Togah looked at me again.

"Fancy meeting you here," I said.

He gave a smile at that. "I'm glad you survived your balloon trip intact."

"Thanks to you, I'm sure. I thought someone had called that wind from Darkness. You might have been a bit more gentle with the landing, though."

"Forgive me," he said dryly. "When I sensed the Black Mask from the other side of the desert, I found it hard to contain my patience. I had thought, you see, that the approaching Shadownight would make it easier for me to breach my father's barrier. But I underestimated his power once again, and so I have been here for weeks, seeking a way to continue."

I looked at the bleak land before us; no different, as far as I could tell, from where we stood. "I don't quite see what the problem is."

"You see only wasteland. I see only mist: a thick fog, with occasional vast and darksome shapes moving in it. That is the barrier my father has placed here for me. Should I be so foolish as to enter it, I would lose my powers and my way within ten steps, and make a meal or something best left unnamed within another ten, quite likely. Or so matters have been. But now things have changed. I don't know how you came about the Black Mask, Kamus, nor do I care overmuch. All that matters is that it will show me the way through my father's barrier." He held out his hand. "If you would be so kind."

He was right, and I knew it. I had brought the Black Mask to Ja-Agur to be used against the Darklord, and who could use it better than the Darklord's son? Besides, he could take it from me whether I resisted or not. I took it from my potion pouch and handed it to him. I heard Valina gasp as I did so.

Jann-Togah put the mask on. It seemed to fit perfectly; there was something very right about him wearing it. It covered the upper half of his head like a cowl, the faceted eyepieces gleaming darkly. For a long moment after donning it, he stood motionless, staring through it, seeking the vision he wanted from Darkness. Then he released the breath he had taken. I glanced overhead. The two moons, now almost full, would soon pass in near-total eclipse. I felt a prickle like electricity on my arms and spine. Force waited to be released. It was the night before Shadownight.

Jann-Togah turned toward the south, lifted his head with the surprised air of someone finally seeing something that had been in plain view all along. Then he looked at us. "Come," he said. His voice was rich with anticipation and a deadliness that made me shiver. "We must be through the barrier before the moons merge. Once in Ja-Agur, my full power will return to me, and we shall need all of it."

We started forward. "What do you see?" I asked him as I fell into step beside him. I had received no thanks, nor had I anticipated any; as soon expect mercy in the Maze.

"I see the way through the mist," he said impatiently. He said nothing else, but I noticed that the route he led us by was winding and circuitous for no apparent reason. He would walk over copses and through brambles, and then detour around open, level spaces. Polaris was at first minded to take his own way, but I told him, "I don't know whether Jann-Togah's bane applies to us or not, but that fancy suit won't do you much good against things you can't see." He decided to play it safe.

As we walked, I could sense Jann-Togah's power increasing; every step he took seemed to stoke the fire within him. It was difficult to tell how far or how long we walked. The double shadows cast by the moons slowly merged, and the dead light seemed to intensify, as did the dark tension in the air. Looking up, I saw that the almost-total eclipse had begun.

The ground shook slightly beneath us. Jann-Togah stopped. "We must wait," he said. "This is the beginning of the madness."

"You're telling me," I said. The world seemed to be holding its breath. Then, abruptly, we felt cold gusts of wind begin, short and regular, like something panting.

Far away, a dark jagged boulder suddenly exploded like a shrapnel bomb. We dropped to the ground. "This simply isn't possible," Polaris said.

"Glad to hear it," I replied, as Jann-Togah's cloak tore free from his shoulders and hurled itself into the sky, assuming a batlike shape as it flew away. "Look out, Kamus!" Polaris shouted; he whipped his raygun out and fired over my shoulder. I turned to see a huge sandcat leaping at me, fangs bared, its snarl like sailcloth ripping. The beam passed through the cat harmlessly, then seemed to sag, waver and diffuse, like wine in water. Jann-Togah made a Sign and the beast dissolved into black motes just before it would have impaled itself on my probably-useless sword. I never knew if it was real or not.

The ground shook again. A funnel-like aperture opened suddenly in the sand beside us. It looked oddly soft, as if the ground had somehow become fleshy. I was off-balance; I began to slide down the slope toward the opening, which had suddenly developed huge teeth, and was champing like a mouth. Valina threw herself forward, stretched a hand toward me and caught my wrist just before I slid out of reach. Then Polaris helped her pull me out of the pit, which closed sullenly.

Overhead, the moons formed a figure eight on its side: the sign of infinity. I hoped it wasn't to be taken literally.

We huddled together on a low hillock, clasping hands to share our energy. Jann-Togah extended his left arm in a Gesture and turned quickly in a circle; a dark line of power scorched the sand, following his movement and enclosing us in a circle of protection. "This will not be enough," he said in a low voice, and turned to Polaris. "Have you any defenses?"

"I can lay a force field about us, assuming the mandate

allows it. But it will drain my power almost completely."

"No matter—do so, and quickly! We need it!"

Polaris made no visible move, but the cold gusts of wind suddenly ceased about us, though we could see spurts of sand kicked up beyond the boundary Jann-Togah had laid. The small rise we were on, little more than three meters across, was relatively stable, but the ground around it shook like a behemoth with palsy.

Valina shook Jann-Togah's shoulder, pointing urgently at her throat. I knew she wanted her voice back so that she could help with the defenses. But Jann-Togah could not spare the time for a healing spell now. I looked up and saw shapes fleeing across the elongated double moon. Hail suddenly rattled off the force field like a cannonade, and we could see frost forming on the gnarled trees outside. It did not last long, however; it melted, and the puddles began to steam. Clumps of grass withered and blackened in the heat.

I felt Valina grip my arm; I turned and looked at where she was pointing. The land there sloped down into a wide salt flat, in which cracks were now opening like a sun-baked river bed. And from these cracks, wraiths appeared; shadowy, dim and mist-like, wearing the armor and trappings of ancient times. They fought soundlessly, and I knew I was seeing a recreation of a battle that had taken place during the Dark Wars, ten centuries before.

I watched Polaris during the worst of it, as he held grimly onto us, unable to contribute spells, only able to supply animal energy. For the first time, the only time, I saw fear in his face. It filled me with gratifaction; I hate to admit it, but it did. It was a partial recompense for what came later.

Overhead, the stars seemed to pulse in the sky. Strange auroras danced. In the midst of the pyrotechnics I saw—or thought I saw—a Unity patrol cruiser flash across the heavens and plunge out of sight beyond the horizon. But I could not be certain of it; at that point, I could not be certain of anything.

Jann-Togah still wore the Black Mask, and through it, evidently, he could see much that we could not. Several times he turned and made a Sign of defense against a part of the force field where I saw nothing. Once, however, I saw the imprint of clawed feet in the sand.

I was feeling very helpless during all this. I knew no

spells potent enough to help, and would not risk using them if I did. I gripped my sword and waited for it to be over.

Beyond the force field, it began to get dark. The starlight faded; only the hourglass shape of the moons still shone. Darkness that was more than the absence of light, that was almost a tangible flood, surrounded us. Within the force field light remained. Then, close enough to my elbow to make me jump, I heard the beating of batlike wings. I whirled and saw, pressing against the energy wall, a face with fangs and red eyes. Valina gasped; even Polaris swore in fear. The darkling was only a dim shape beyond the light, but it was a very large dim shape. It swung a heavy, knobbed tail at the field. There was a dazzle of lights and a crackling sound as it struck. Polaris groaned and staggered; I realized that the blow had reverberated in his nervous system, connected to his cyber suit. The tail struck again, quick as a whip. Jann-Togah turned, but too late; the second blow shattered the field. The last thing I saw was Polaris dropping to the ground, unconscious from the backlash. Then, with a roar as powerful and ancient as the sea, Darkness was upon us.

The only light was the parting eclipse above me, which illuminated nothing. The Darkness was so thick I felt like I was suffocating. It was rife with foul smells, and distant screams that made torture sound tame. The ground quaked. I staggered forward, buffetted by the temblor and the gale, immediately and totally lost. I felt my sword torn from my hand.

Then I heard a hoarse croak, which I knew was Valina trying to scream. I tried to spell up a light, but couldn't get a spark. But light did come—it blazed up behind me in a cold, actinic glare that sprang from Jann-Togah's upraised hands. The Darkness was pushed back, but with difficulty. He staggered, as if holding up a great black curtain.

"Kamus!" he gasped. "Help . . . them . . ."

I turned and saw before me the darkling that had shattered Polaris' field. It was one of the larger darklings I'd ever run across; big enough to hold Polaris and Valina each in a taloned grasp. Polaris was still unconscious; Valina was struggling feebly, unable to shout spells. The darkling grinned at me. It had a brace of horns around its head, and a horned carapace that encircled its throat.

"Farewell, fool," it said to me in a howl like the gale. "My master has need of these two!"

The wings began to flap. Sand and dust whirled. I inhaled to shout a spell, and choked on a lungful of dust.

The darkling rose from the ground.

I did the only thing I could do. I ran forward and leaped at it.

I managed to grab one of the horns that ringed its neck. As we rose into the night, I swung my free fist with all my might at its leathery chin, knowing the darkling would not feel it.

I was wrong. It did feel it.

The darkling screamed in pain, and I saw a red flash as my fist connected, felt heat on my knuckles. Its body convulsed and shook me free. I fell; I had an instant to realize that the darkling had dropped one of its prisoners; then I made an impact crater in the sand and forgot about everything for awhile.

* * *

I awoke coughing, my nostrils filled with something that smelled worse than darkling's breath. A crushed stim-cap was being held under my nose by a black-gloved hand. I focused on the hand's owner and saw Polaris.

"Feeling better?" he asked. His tone was faintly mocking.

I pushed him aside and staggered to my feet. "Just wait until I wake up first sometime." Overhead, Bellus and Jaspara had separated. Our surroundings were back to their normal, dismal state. Jann-Togah sat to one side, looking very tired, the Black Mask a shapeless lump of cloth beside him.

There was no sign of Valina.

I looked at Polaris. He said, "I'm afraid the thing only dropped one of us."

I was tempted to say that it had dropped the wrong one, but I didn't. After all, Polaris had tried to stop the sandcat.

I turned away from him and looked at Jann-Togah. "What happened?"

"As he said. You attacked the darkling, and somehow caused it injury—"

I was about to tell Jann-Togah that all I did was strike the creature, but I kept quiet. I had suddenly become aware of something.

"—and you and Polaris fell. The darkling flew south with Valina, presumably to my father's citadel."

"He knows that we're coming, then."

"Not necessarily. At any rate, he does not know where we are," Jann-Togah said. "My powers are full now, and I have the Black Mask. I can spread spells of confusion and diffusion, which may keep him from pinpointing us in time."

He stood, wearily. "We must continue. We have only the rest of tonight and tomorrow to reach the Dark Spire."

We started southward under the light of the setting moons. As we walked, I slipped the ring of Mondrogan from my finger and into my pouch. I had not told Jann-Togah that I had injured the darkling by punching it, because I had remembered that I wore the ring on that hand. Had it somehow caused the darkling pain when it touched the creature? In other words, was it, too, a talisman? Since I had worn it, I had sensed no power invested in it, but that was easily explained: I had found it with the Black Mask, and the Darkness surrounding that could mask a talisman of lesser potency. My powers might not be able to distinguish between the two, but Jann-Togah's probably could, if his attention were called to it. I thought it wise to keep the ring a secret for now.

But if the ring was a talisman—why? I had never heard of it, but then, my knowledge of Darkness couldn't fill a belly dancer's navel. I would have to know more about the ring before I could properly use it. Strangely, though, it seemed to me as if I did know the reason behind its power—as if I had all the parts of the mosaic, but could not quite put it together. I was too tired to think clearly; my mind kept dancing. There were too many things to think about. The kidnapping of Valina by the darkling, I only gradually began to realize, might mean worse than her death, if she was in the hands of the Darklord. I tried to feel the proper amount of horror at this, but I was still too shocked by its suddenness. One emotion I did feel, however, was guilt. I should have kept her from coming, I told myself. But I had been afraid to go south by myself. It did little good to remind myself that she had made her own choice—she had wanted to come. I still felt responsible. Though I had been suspicious of Valina, I had not disliked her.

And so it went, through the rest of the long night; guilt and recrimination, mixed with the dazed memory of Shadow-night's eve. How much of that phantasmagoria had been real and how much illusion? The glimpse I had had of a Unity patrol cruiser—had it really fallen across the sky and below the southern horizon? Had I really seen armies dead for a thousand years battle again?

I had no answers. I followed Polaris and Jann-Togah, my step sprightly as a zombie's as the sun rose on the last day before Shadownight, and I could not escape the feeling that I was on a death march.

The sun rose, the color of magma. Ja-Lur is dark compared to most worlds of men, but today seemed as though a film were cast over the landscape. Polaris had to use the infrared powers of his lenses to help him see.

By mid-morning we came to a wide, slow-moving river that came from the west and continued on in a wide curve toward the south. No plants grew on its banks, and I could see no signs of life in the black waters. I did not need to be told that this was Ja-Kanak, the Dark River.

We built a raft from the stunted trees of the wasteland, binding it together with Polaris's monofilament line. His suit had recharged during the morning, and his exoskeletal strength, combined with Jann-Togah's powerful muscles, accomplished the job in fair time. The current moved us slow but steadily. There were areas in which the river flowed obviously uphill. Jann-Togah said it supplied the Dark Spire, his father's citadel, with water. Hearing that, I threw my used chewing gum in it.

During our voyage, I explained to Jann-Togah what had happened since I had last seen him, and how I had gotten the Black Mask. I did not tell him about Mondrogan's ring being in the temple.

"The android never revealed to you how he knew of the mask's location?"

"No. He was going to, but we were interrupted."

He looked troubled. "It was undoubtedly my father's doing that saved you from the spaceship's conflagration. He has a plan in mind—if only I knew what it was!" He looked at me. "And you, Kamus—what was your plan?"

"I had none," I said. "I came because I felt compelled to; not only because of what the Darklord had done to me, but because of what you said he would attempt to do on Shadownight. I knew I had to do something."

"You are either very brave or very foolhardy."

"I almost ran, once—if there had been a spaceship available, I'd be in another constellation by now. But there wasn't, and so here I am."

Jann-Togah looked at Polaris Lone. "And you, outworlder—you claim to be merely along for the ride, as you put it?"

Polaris smiled lazily, and spread his gloved hands. "Curiosity, and a somewhat foolish tendency toward adventure. Added to that now, of course, is a desire to help rescue Valina."

"You make about as much sense as a sundeck on a spaceship," I told him. "You're obviously connected with the Unity in some way; you had the clout to commandeer a flier, and you hushed up that incident at the spaceport with the alien assassin easily. And you're wearing a flexarmor cyber suit with more tricks in it than a barrel of darklings; those aren't available in just any orbiting mall. It all adds up to you going south for a reason besides thrills, danger, and excitement."

Polaris seemed about to protest his innocence again, then paused. He said, "You summarize well, Kamus. All right, then: perhaps it will ease your suspicions somewhat if I tell you that my concerns here somewhat parallel yours. I see no reason to hide them any longer. You want to stop the Darklord from accomplishing certain things; so do I. This Shadownight seems a good time to attempt it."

"You are working for the Unity, then."

"I am a Unity special agent," Polaris said. "I have orders to stop the Darklord's interference with the Unity's attempt to expand contact with Ja-Lur."

"And how do you plan to do that? I assume you've gathered by now that you're not dealing with your ordinary galactic tyrant."

"Perhaps I can't stop him by myself. But with the Dark abilities of you and Jann-Togah, with the Black Mask and my technological arsenal, we cannot lose. No matter his mandate; something we have will get through to him!"

I looked at him, standing on the raft with the sun's dull glare to his right; it limned his armor in bloody highlights. He was facing me from the north. I said slowly, "Special agents have code names, do they not?"

"Usually, yes."

"And might yours be . . . Boreas?"

His face was very still. "How did you know that?"

"I was warned about a man whom the Unity would send," I said. "A man called Boreas. I was warned to watch for danger from the north. I thought the warning referred to the Black Mask, or possibly to Valina—but it didn't. It referred to you. Boreas: the Greek god of the north wind. Your name is Polaris—the North star, as seen from Earth."

He nodded. "I am Boreas. And I can help you two in your quest. Together, we can stop the Darklord."

"And when my father is defeated?" Jann-Togah asked evenly. "What does the Unity plan for Ja-Lur then?"

"This is not part of my job," Polaris said. "But I'm sure that, as the Darklord's successor, you would be treated with the proper respect—as long as you were willing to treat with the Unity.

I remembered Daniel Tolon's final words to me. I thought about what he had said of the Unity's planet scourgings, about Devil's Asteroid, about manipulations of solar systems' governments. "What if I said I'd see you in hell before helping you?" I asked.

"I'd say it's possible. We're going that way, after all." His voice was low.

"Enough of this," Jann-Togah said, his voice cutting the tension like a knife through a rope. "There will be time to discuss this after the Darklord is defeated. For now, I need the help of both of you."

He forbade further discussion of the subject, and we settled into an uneasy quiet. But I was sure now that I had been right from the start in my feelings about Polaris Lone.

* * *

The day was hot and sullen; it seemed that we and the river were the only things that moved in all the world. I fell into a kind of stupor, not sleeping, but not really awake, either. We moved slowly through an unchanging land; if all J-Agur was like this, I could understand why the Darklord wanted to extend his domain. I both yearned for and dreaded sunset and the beginning of the night—Shadownight.

The sun at last touched the western horizon. As it did, Jann-Togah pointed toward the south. We looked and saw a thin, black needle rising over the horizon, the only vertical line in a flat world.

"The Dark Spire," Jann-Togah said softly. "My father's citadel."

At the same time, Polaris said, "Our speed's increasing." And it was true; Ja-Kanak was flowing faster, carrying us toward the spire.

"Let us hope that we are not expected," Jann-Togah said. His voice was even; I glanced at him. His face was carefully set and emotionless. He folded the Black Mask and tucked it into his belt. I slipped the ring of Mondrogan from my pouch, and put it in the lining of my trenchcloak. There was always a chance that it would be unnoticed.

For the first time, we began to see dwellings: short, squat houses of adobe and brick, sitting near the banks of the river. Outside of a few rows of gardens and livestock pens, there was no sign of life. Their numbers increased, forming a small cluster about the base of the spire. The spire itself was enormous, at least a kilometer in height, with sides as straight and slick as a palace column. Ja-Kanak foamed into a huge cavern at its base. The water was touched with white, now, as it roared on its way. We hung on. There was little else we could do. Jann-Togah had kept up the spells that would protect us and the talismans from his father's notice—all we could do now was hope that it worked.

Just before we entered the cavern, we saw a long, blackened furrow on the river's left bank, ending in the silver wedge of a Unity patrol cruiser. It had crashed and slid almost to the base of the Dark Spire. So I hadn't imagined seeing it, after all.

Then, surrounded by the roar and spray of the cataract, we were swept into the cavern. The dim light of the entrance receded behind us, and we were floating in blackness.

But not for long—a Dark light came at a word from me, and showed us the high, rough ceiling and walls surrounding us. "Quickly!" Jann-Togah said to Polaris. "He will detect any major spells; you must use your abilities to stop us!"

Polaris anchored the line from one wrist about the raft, and shot the other toward the wall. It stuck, and we stopped, with a jerk that nearly threw Jann-Togah and me into the foam. Polaris stood rigid, his cybersuit part of the line that held the raft. I could see the strain it caused him—his exoskeletal strength was being stretched to its limit. Then, slowly, the line began to retract, pulling us across the current and toward the wall.

There was a narrow ledge perhaps half a meter above the water level. We scrambled onto it, getting thoroughly drenched in the process. Polaris lashed the raft to the ledge with his adhesive line so that it would not announce our presence.

We crept along the ledge for some time. The roaring of the cataract grew louder. The tunnel also grew narrower, and I knew that, if we didn't find an exit soon, we wouldn't be able to go any further.

We did find one, just in time—an arch that led into a narrow, spiraling stairway, cut from the living rock. We went up it, leaving the deafening sound of the torrent behind for an almost equally deafening silence. The spiral steps rose endlessly. I thought about the time and manpower it had taken to cut each one of them from the stone. But then I reminded myself that this was the Darklord's citadel—he was not dependent on human labor. Possibly he had raised this spire in a single night. I wondered what the Stoneworkers Guild would think of that.

This was the Darklord's citadel—the thought cycled through my mind, over and over. Already I had come further than I had thought I would, but I was still a long way from winning. I wasn't even sure what constituted winning. At the moment, all I could do was follow Jann-Togah's lead.

It was a long time before we found arches leading to other levels. The place was as confusing as a minotaur's labyrinth. Jann-Togah admitted to being unsure as to our location. "It has been years since I walked these passages, and many of them I never walked."

We were on a landing near one of those corridors, hiding behind the stone arch. Four Darklanders, the first we had seen, suddenly came into view around a curve in the corridor. They were all wearing shapeless black cloaks. "I have an idea," Polaris said . . .

The cloaks were large enough to conceal Polaris' suit and my trenchcloak. As long as no one got close enough to realize that one of us had no aura of power, while another's was strong enough to supply a regiment, we stood a chance of being unnoticed. The guards we had left stunned by Polaris' beam in the stairwell, wrapped up with line. Jann-Togah had insisted that they not be injured—they were, after all, his potential subjects. I thought I detected disappointment in Polaris's reaction.

We continued on down the corridor as Jann-Togah searched for a landmark. We did not have much time—the moons would be rising soon. Even within the spire, we could sense that.

The corridor that we followed led upward at a considerable angle. I estimated that we had to be high above the base of the spire by now. In another moment, we found out just how high.

As we rounded another curve the wall on the right side suddenly fell away in a large arching balcony. The scene it opened upon was a gigantic crater, surrounded by sheer walls well over a hundred meters high, all of glistening black rock. Above their uneven rim the stars shone, and the moons, now full, had just cleared the walls.

On the floor of the crater Darklanders were lining up in ranks. There must have been several hundred of them, and more were joining all the time. Huge braziers lit the scene. They faced a large dais that stood in the center of the crater. It was empty, but I knew it would be occupied soon—by the Darklord.

"What are they doing?" Polaris murmured, staring down at the gathering throng.

"Preparing to join their power, even as we did to hold off the terrors of last night," Jann-Togah said. "My father will soon join them, and, at the time of the Bloodmoon—"

"You three! What are you doing away from your posts?"

We turned and saw five more guards approaching us. They carried leather slings.

Jann-Togah started to say something, perhaps intending to talk our way out of it. He never got the chance, however, for Polaris whipped out his blaster as soon as he saw the guards. The guards scattered, and their slings made venomous sounds in the air. Jann-Togah tried to Gesture, but a padded missile from one of the slings struck him on the forehead, and he staggered back, dazed. Polaris's draw was impeded by his cloak, and another missile dropped him. I remember getting my sword halfway free before most of the galaxy exploded inside my head.

6

The cell I woke up in could have been any cell in the Mariyad Garrison; I've seen enough of them to know. It was a small, square room, the walls and ceiling of jointed black stone. There was a mattress on which I lay, a stool, a chamberpot, and nothing else. The door was also stone, hung on massive metal hinges. I saw all this by conjuring a Dark light.

I lay there for a time after awakening, my mind full of thoughts about Polaris Lone that involved boiling oil and molten lead. The hotheaded fool was responsible for this.

I crossed to the door and pushed at it. It didn't budge, which didn't really surprise me. I hesitated, then spoke the strongest spell I could handle without help from my missing potion pouch, taking the chance of a psychic backlash. It should have at least put a dent in it. It didn't. I tried a trick I had used long ago once, and attempted to rust the latch with another spell. I might as well have been reciting poetry.

I sat down again, wondering if now was the time to resort to panic.

There was no way out. I had gambled, and the Darklord had taken the dice. I thought of Valina, and Sanris, and all the others who had had their lives changed or ended because of me and the Darklord's actions against me. I felt I had let them all down. I had also let myself down.

I thought of the places I had seen, the things I had done. I felt nostalgia for my old office overlooking the Maze; an emotion I thought I'd never feel. I remembered the winding, sunlit streets of Kadizhar, which I had just seen recently after so long an absence. I had played as a child under the shadow of Mondrogan's statue . . .

Perhaps there was still hope; perhaps Jann-Togah or Polaris could do something. I did not particularly trust either of them, but we were allies against a common enemy, and they had more power than I. I wondered if Jann-Togah now languished in another cell. Even if he could somehow defeat the Darklord, could I expect any more mercy from him? Like father, like son, after all.

Like father, like son . . .

I sat very still and thought about it. I fitted pieces that I had not known I had together into a finished picture, and looked at it carefully from all sides.

My potion pouch and my sword had been taken from me, but they had left me my greatest weapon—the deductive training that I had learned, slowly and with many mistakes, in the course of my career.

I felt in the lining of my trenchcloak, hardly daring to hope—and found the ring. I put it on my finger. The stylized face grinned at me. "Keep grinning," I told it. "Things won't be funny much longer."

I turned toward the door again and spoke the spell of opening. I would have to take the chance of it being more than I could handle. I needn't have worried. I added a single Word to the spell's end, and at the same time I hit the door with my ringed fist.

The door shattered outward as though hit with a catapult's load, revealing a deserted corridor. I felt no exhaustion reaction; if anything, I felt exhilarated. I had been right; there was still a chance.

* * *

I followed the corridors. I let the power that I now controlled extend my awareness, searching for Jann-Togah's powerful aura. Unless the Darklord had concealed it, I would find him. I didn't think he would expend the power to do that, not this close to Shadownight.

But I found Polaris Lone first. From behind a huge door I faintly heard his voice, speaking over a babble of many others'. I called to him, warning him to stand away from the huge stone door. Then I spoke the Breaking Spell again and struck the door. It collapsed in a cloud of powdered stone.

Beyond stood Polaris, wide-eyed, with at least a hundred outworlders of various species in the huge chamber. It seemed that I had also found the crew of the cruiser that had crashed.

"How polite of you to knock first," Polaris said.

I was about to answer him when I saw a face I recognized. "Daniel!" I said in amazement. "Daniel Tolon!"

The sandy-haired Unity agent pushed to the front of the crowd, and we clasped hands. "Kamus! Why are you here?"

"No doubt for the same reason you were on board that cruiser—in an attempt to stop the Darklord before Shadownight. And we'd better hurry!"

"We know where they hid our weapons," Daniel said.

"Good." I turned to Polaris. "You've got one more chance to do something right. We'll need a distraction to keep the Darklord occupied while I find Jann-Togah and release him."

"Leave it to me," Polaris said. "I have done this sort of thing before, you know."

"That's what I'm afraid of," I said. "If you blow this, when they hang us, you're going first, so I can watch."

He said nothing further, merely started down the corridor. The Unity agents followed him. Daniel stayed beside me for a moment.

"You were right about him," I said, referring to Polaris.

"As far as leading a battle, however, nobody does it better," Daniel said. "I hope we both live through this. Good luck, Kamus!" Then he was gone after the rest of them.

I continued down the corridor in the opposite direction, still seeking Jann-Togah. I had a faint feeling, the barest sense of him, but as I continued it grew stronger. At last I stood before another door, behind which I knew he was.

I warned him to stand back, and made another spectacular entrance; the stone cracked in two, and the two halves fell to either side of me with a crash. Jann-Togah stared at me in amazement.

"Even I could not break that door!" he said.

"I know; I'm just full of surprises," I said. "No time to explain now, Jann-Togah. We've got to find your father."

We hurried through the twisting, rough-hewn passageways. We both had the sense of him now; as I had felt the power leading me through Kaan Ta'Wyys' castle, so now we followed the Darklord's aura. As we ran, the stone walls seemed to grow hazier, dimmer. It no longer felt as if I ran on rock, but rather on a soft, resilient material. The walls seemed shot through with glimpses of far-away lightning. Mist filled the corridor. In short, we seemed to be running through a cloud.

"Pay no attention," Jann-Togah gasped. "It is illusion; an attempt to disorient us."

Nevertheless, it grew thicker, and I soon seemed to be wading through the center of a thunderhead. I could not spare the time to attempt to disperse the spell. Jann-Togah disappeared, outdistancing me in the mist. I seemed to have lost my immunity to the reaction of casting such powerful spells. I was no longer sure which way to go—I could not sense the Darklord any more. There were no hints of corridors left; just the dark mist all about me. I took another step—and fell.

* * *

When I awoke, the mist was gone. I was lying on a cold floor. There was a faint stench in the air, somehow familiar. I staggered to my feet, took a step and slammed my hip painfully against the sharp corner of something.

My eyes were adjusting to the dark. I saw the dim square of a window, and through it an irregular skyline against the stars. Then I knew where I was.

I was back in my office in Mariyad, looking through my window at Thieves' Maze. I felt a relief that left me limp. Had it all been a dream, then? Or had the Darklord hurled me back to Mariyad, in an unexpected move?

I had struck my hip on my desk. But I had sold my desk. This room was no longer mine. I looked down at Thieves' Maze. No lights burned in its windows. No night was long enough for all the Maze to sleep. There was no sound at all from the shabby buildings. The city was still. Still, and somehow waiting.

I realized that I was waiting, too.

My door creaked like a coffin's lid. I jerked around, staring at it while reaching for a sword that wasn't there. The door creaked again, slowly opening.

"Kamus . . ."

Suddenly I felt colder than an ice giant in a blizzard. I knew that voice—and its owner was dead.

"Kamus, you promised to avenge me..."

Fingers slipped around the door's edge, and even in the dim light I could see they were swathed in mouldering cloth, caked with graveyard dirt.

I tried to speak, to think of a spell that would send Sanris back to his grave. But my tongue was magnetized by the roof of my mouth. The door opened wider. A rotting foot slid into the room.

In a moment I would see his face.

I turned and dove headfirst through the window.

I seemed to fall for a long time. I had almost given up hope of hitting the ground, when suddenly I landed on my back in the grip of two strong arms. The jolt winded me momentarily; then my vision cleared and I looked up at the impassive face of Ult, the barbarian. He sat me on my feet. "I'm glad you were under the window," I started, then broke off as I looked about. We were not on the street below my window. We weren't even in Mariyad. We were on the observation deck of the *Galactic Express*, surrounded by the calcified cyborgs known as Osteomechs. They held swords and rayguns, and their unchanging grins seemed full of a terrible joy.

"Ult!" I shouted. "I thought you were my friend!"

Ult shrugged. "What can I say, Darklander? They offered me jewels for you." He held up a pouch filled with gems. "Even a barbarian has to eat."

The Osteomechs closed in on me. I saw the Transportal arch just beyond them; I hurled myself forward. They tried to seize me, their skeletal fingers scratching my arms and face. But I broke through them and leaped through the portal.

I emerged in a bedchamber. Before me, on the floor, was a dead woman. I realized who it was and, weeping, lifted the body to the bed. "You'll sleep forever," I told her. "It was my fault—you couldn't live the life I've chosen. I should have known that." I leaned over and kissed Thea Morn—and saw her eyes open, wide in fear. I stood back in shock. "Kamus, don't!" she cried. "I'm still alive!"

But it was too late—I had already shut off the gravity generators, and I had forgotten to put on my pressure suit! Then the atmosphere of the planetoid dissipated with explosive force, and I felt myself swept out of the door. I caught a glimpse of Thea's face, the agony on it as she froze in the night vacuum, and then I was hurled into space.

I floated among the stars. Then I saw a ship beneath me; a hatch opened, and a pincer-tipped tentacle snaked out, pulled me in. Stam the cephalopod dangled me by one foot before his god, Taqwatkh, the Bringer of Lightning. Janya handed him a goblet full of elixir, which he tossed off.

"Now, Kamus," the Maltese god said with a sneer, "You will learn how strong my powers are."

"This can't be happening!" I said. "This isn't real!"

"Oh, but it is," Taqwatkh assured me. "Ask my good friend, Xidon the Flying Guard." He put his arm around the small man's shoulders.

"He's not a Flying Guard," I shouted desperately. "And he's not your friend! He's an assassin!"

Another figure stepped forward, bald, wearing long silver robes. "Then ask me—Edward Knight."

"You're not Edward Knight! You're Kaan Ta'Wyys!"

"Are you sure? Look again." The features rippled, changed again and again, showing Kaan's green hair and mocking expression, then Niano's young face, then Ratbag's pockmarks, then Orpheus Alpha's starburst . . .

"I don't know!" I cried, hiding my face in my hands. "Nobody is who they seem to be!"

"Of course," a quiet voice said. I looked up and saw Dash, my phonecub, sitting before me. The surroundings had grown dark again; I seemed to be seeing without light. Dash scratched his ear and then began to solemnly wash one of his two tails.

"I know who you are," I said.

"I expected no less." The Darklord's voice, coming from Dash, was calm, quiet, well-modulated. There was no groundshaking resonance, no sinister undertones. It was just a voice, such as one might hear any day over a phonecub.

"I expect you have questions," he went on.

I tried to recover my shattered composure. "One or two."

"Then let me save us some time; a commodity sorely needed at the moment. Shadownight waits for no one, not even me. Yes, Kamus, I wanted you to seek me. This moment was planned, not from the time you began to seek the *Synulanom*, but years before. I made sure you would be chosen to go to Earth; I wanted you to be exposed to the worlds of science and technology."

I asked the question I had been waiting so long to ask. "Were you responsible for the spell that killed Sanris of Taleiday?"

"Yes, I'm afraid so. Perhaps not the most subtle way to keep you on the track of the *Synulanom*, but at the moment, there was little time for subtlety."

I nodded. I felt no particular emotions; not even satisfaction at being right. I merely felt very weary.

The phonecub put its paws together over its belly. "I also interfered with the case of your murdered minstrel for the same reason—to spur you to seek me. I am not all-powerful; I can nudge the minds of some humans and fewer Darklanders, but mostly I work by indirection, manipulation. Also, it was important that you come to me of your own will, bringing something I needed." Dash reached behind his furry body and brought forth the Black Mask, which he dangled from one paw. "You never learned how Orpheus Alpha knew of its location," the Darklord continued. "I was able to send him the knowledge in a dream. He knew better than to tell you that—you would have guessed its origin. He did not know whether or not to believe it himself, but he was desperate for your help."

"A lot of good it did him. All those deaths are on your head, Darklord."

"All those, and millions more," the Darklord said with equanimity. "Being the Darklord is, as you would put it, no bed of houris."

"Now that you have the Black Mask, what do you intend to do?"

"As my errant son—with whom I had time to deal while you were having your nightmare—has no doubt surmised, I intend to use it in a very short time, to re-establish Darkness firmly on Ja-Lur. This will be the last chance to reverse the course our world is taking away from the Dark cosmos. The method that must be used is not pretty, alas. It requires, among other things, the psychic energy of a great many Darklanders—and the soul of at least one."

"You intend to use me as a sacrifice?"

"By no means!" The phonecub shook its head vigorously.

"No, another has been chosen for that. When that is done, I will then use the special vision the Black Mask gives to read this." The phonecub reached behind its back again, and pulled out a scroll. It pushed the parchment toward me. It unrolled partway.

"The *Synulanom*," I said.

"You do not seem surprised." The Darklord sounded disappointed. "At any rate, as you see, I intend to take no chances. Seen through the mask, the *Synulanom* will take on a whole new meaning—it will unify all of Ja-Lur in Darkness! I am not merely thinking of myself. How can Darklanders live without Darkness? I am trying to save our people, Kamus."

"Those of the Blood have survived when other worlds left Darkness."

"Survived, yes, but of what worth is that? Would a human care to survive blind, deaf and dumb? But let's not debate the matter—we've little time before the Bloodmoon. Also, I sense a disturbance in the energy of my people—I fear you've let those troublesome Unity soldiers out of their prison." Dash twitched his nose. "You are a great deal of trouble, Kamus. If I did not need you so badly—"

"What *do* you need me so badly for?" I asked. "Why did you go to all this trouble? It couldn't be just to get the Black Mask."

"True—very astute of you. You're right—I also wanted you."

Never in my life had I wanted to ask a question less. "Why?"

The phonecub rubbed its eyes. "I thought that was obvious. To become the next Darklord, of course."

7

The Darklord continued imperturbably, "I assume you realize that I am no more eternal than I am all-powerful. My life is long, but not endless. And you are to be my successor, Kamus."

The phonecub seemed to expand and recede before me; I fought back shock. The only thought I recall thinking was a line I had spoken to Polaris: "You can become what you fight against very easily."

I had come seeking the Darklord for revenge. By doing so, I realized now that I had been not denying Darkness, but embracing it.

"But—I thought that Jann-Togah—" And then a terrible thought struck me. I had never known who my father was . . . "You're not saying I am your son?"

The phonecub was silent for a moment. When the Darklord spoke again, he sounded almost hurt. "No. Merely a rarity—born of human and Darklander. But that is precisely why you are suited to inherit my mantle. Let not your lack of raw power inhibit you—knowledge matters more than strength. My power was not great when I was chosen. And I fought against the idea at first, even as you are doing. And you will have potent Elder Objects that I did not have—could not have. They will give you a world unified in Darkness for you to rule!"

"I can't let you do it" I said.

The phonecub looked amused. "Assuming you could stop me, would you really want to? Would you see this world under the rule of a galactic federation that employs thugs like Polaris Lone?"

"I would see it have the freedom to choose," I said. "Your way isn't the right way. No change, no advancement, not even one spaceport on the planet. That's stagnation. I can't let it happen, and I won't."

I pointed at the *Synulanom*. "When I went to retrieve Kaan Ta'Wyys' body for burial, the ashes of the spell were gone. You had a restoring spell spoken over them, didn't you?"

Dash clapped his paws together. "Bravo, Kamus! I am almost sorry to take you from your chosen profession. You have deduced much."

"More than you think," I told him. "I saw the *Synulanom* in its original state. It was marked with a seal that has been scraped from the parchment here." I knew I had to talk fast now, to keep the Darklord off balance. It was my only chance of escaping the fate he had planned for me—the fate he had submitted to a thousand years before. "You had that seal removed when the ashes were restored, didn't you?"

The phonecub sat quite still. "What of it?"

"You planned my education too well," I said. "You found it amusing that I decided while on Earth to become a detective. But that taught me how to put facts together. Such as the fact that you had the *Synulanom* brought to you, just as I brought the Black Mask, because you could not retrieve them yourself through Darkness."

The Darklord's voice was ominious for the first time. "Beware, Kamus, lest I reconsider you as my successor." I noticed that the phonecub seemed larger, somehow. Also, it had fangs.

"Darkness corrupts," I continued. "We all know that. There's always the danger of becoming what you fight against. Facts, Darklord! Facts such as the close resemblance between Jann-Togah, your son, and a statue I saw as a child! Facts such as the seal on the spell, and the ring that sealed the chest on Darklord's Bane!"

I was shouting now, babbling, in sheer, naked fear. The thing that had been a phonecub had swollen suddenly to monstrous size, becoming a dimly-seen titan in the mist that flowed and changed. It had more arms than a kraken, eyes that glowed like the Bloodmoon, teeth like scimitars.

"For all your power, you couldn't stand the sight of what you had been once, before Darkness corrupted you! No one knew what happened to you after the Dark Wars ended!" I screamed. "But I know! *I know your name, Mondrogan!*"

The terror that was the Darklord enveloped me. I thrust out my fist, with the ring on it. I struck nothing—the fury that surrounded me seemed to suddenly dissipate, to break apart like a cloud of dark smoke. Though there was no light, I was dazzled, blinded . . .

I stood in a vast, low-ceilinged cavern. A few candles guttered on stands. A throne rose before me, carved starkly from obsidian. It was empty. On its massive arms lay the Black Mask and the *Synulanom*.

And on the floor before the throne lay Jann-Togah.

I knelt beside him, rolled him over. He was as pale as a vampire, but he was breathing. I rubbed his wrists, and tilted his head back, and he groaned, beginning to revive.

Then I heard a rattle of chains from behind the throne. I stepped around it, and saw Valina, shackled to a column. Her clothes were torn and dirty, but she seemed unharmed. She stared at me in relief, and tried to speak, but her voice was still impaired.

"Relax," I said. There was no time to try a spell, and, the way I was feeling, I doubted if it would work. I looked about and saw the key lying on a shelf not far away. In a moment, Valina was free.

She embraced me, shivering. "Kamus," she said in a hoarse croak, "I was . . . to be . . . sac—" her throat gave out again.

"I understand," I said. So that was why the darkling had taken her.

Jann-Togah was sitting up, looking dazedly about. "I sought to take him by surprise," he said bitterly.

"The Darklord's dead," I told him. The reality of it had not really reached me yet. I had won.

Jann-Togah blinked, then raised one hand and looked at it. "My power," he said.

I realized I could no longer sense the Darkness that had been so strong within him. "He drained it from me," he said. "As I might do to a child." He looked at me with fear in his eyes. "Will it come back?"

"I don't know," I said. Then there was a sudden rumble, low enough to be felt as much as heard. One of the candles toppled. It came again, stronger. The throne creaked massively.

"Welcome to the apocalypse," I said, helping Jann-Togah to his feet. He moved listlessly. "Snap it up!" I told him. "Hear those rumbles? I have a bad feeling that Shadownight is about to bring the house down. I'd like to see it from the outside, and you know the way." I grabbed the mask and the spell.

"What does life matter now?" Jann-Togah said, his voice low and emotionless. "My power is gone."

"That's the spirit," I told him as I pushed him through the door. Valina followed us. At my urging, Jann-Togah began to move, leading us through the maze of corridors. The spire trembled ever so slightly again.

We reached the intersection of another corridor, and suddenly panic-stricken Darklanders were running everywhere, taking little notice of us. I had no idea where we were going, and neither, evidently, did Jann-Togah. We passed through a cloud of acrid, stinging smoke, and suddenly felt cold wind about us. The smoke cleared, and I saw we were standing on the rim of the crater wall at the top of the Dark Spire.

Below us, a battle was taking place between the Unity personnel and the Darklanders. I heard the babble of hundreds of spells being shouted, saw outworlders falling in a variety of ways, none of them pretty. The outworlders retaliated by raybeam weaponry and warp grenades. Swords and hand-to-hand combat raged everywhere also. The entire scene was lit with the lurid red glare of the gigantic braziers.

"We've got to stop this somehow!" I shouted to Jann-Togah.

The Darklord's son looked upward. "It will stop, now," he said.

I looked up. The red light was not all coming from the fires.

Overhead, the Bloodmoon burned.

Bellus and Jaspara were in total eclipse. The single disc overhead shone with an awful crimson light. Thunder rumbled, loud enough to cut through the din of the battle. Below, Darklanders and outworlders looked up.

And then the sky tore apart.

The heavens seemed to rend like rotten cloth, revealing Darkness beyond—a realm of strange stars and nebulae that gleamed with colors unknown in our spectrum. The Darkland groaned and tossed in response, and the Dark Spire shook like a sapling struck by an axe.

We fell to a prone position—the top of the crater wall was little more than ten meters across, and bare as an overlord's concubine. I kept my eyes on the sky.

Darklings flew through the rifts; they descended like bloodbirds, even more numerous than the imps of the rain at the spaceport. They dived on all those below. We retreated back to the safety of the kiosk from which we had emerged. The giant fire-bearing statues toppled in the quake, the burning oil from them lacing the crater floor with fire.

"Kamus!" Jann-Togah shouted. "You must use the Black Mask and the *Synulanom!*"

"I can't control that kind of power!" I shouted back.

"You defeated my father—you can do it! I have no power, and Valina cannot speak! You *must* do it!"

It was no time to argue the point. I pulled the Black Mask on over my head and unrolled the *Synulanom* before me on the shaking rock.

It was the first time that I had looked closely at it. The runes were written in an ancient, crabbed hand, arranged in various patterns. Without the mask, I knew I could not have understood one heiroglyph in a hundred. But now I could understand it all, and knew that there were parts of it I did not dare read, if I wanted to keep my mind intact. I scanned quickly over it, recognizing in passing the parts that Kaan Ta'Wyys had used against me. The Black Mask also let me see the various patterns in which the runes could be spoken, to grant control over empires—not just the Northern Nations which Edward Knight and, later, Kaan had hoped to dominate, but the entire planet.

At that moment, I had before me the power to rule the world.

But another combination of Words was also evident, and I knew this was the one I must speak. I started to read.

"DUPPIRA ALLI-TUSHNI, ASKUPPATI MACH ZULE, ANI BI'SHA . . ."

I stood, or, rather, was pulled to my feet by the power of the Words I read. My feet seemed anchored to the tossing rock. Like a puppet's arms, I gesticulated, feeling the power flowing through me.

"BOL KALATUM KUTTUMTUM, UBBIRANI GWIL EL . . . LIMDA ALAKTI DINA DINI . . ."

My voice, impossibly, dominated the pandemonium from above and below. The Words of the *Synulanom* subdued the screeching of the darklings and the screams of their victims. A darkling hurled itself toward us, but the force of the spell struck it like an arrow through a hawk, and it fell. The thunders of the shattered sky seemed to die out as I spoke the final Phrase.

"TAND DAMATH, UTRAM MER KANPA KUTULU, THOD ZU DULEMEEN BURSHUNIN, ZIRGAN GAL-KIERESH!"

I looked up—and saw that the Bloodmoon was no more.

Bellus and Jaspara were still in eclipse, but the Words of the *Synulanom* had washed the crimson light clean. There was a sound of mighty winds, and as I pulled the mask off, I saw the darklings below and above gathered like leaves in a gale and hurled back toward the cracks of Darkness. I staggered back, no longer protected by the spell's force, as the winds blew. The rushing air spun one darkling near the rim. I caught a glimpse of teeth like diamonds, eyes like rubies, claws like onyx; one taloned hand seized the *Synulanom;* the other tore the Black Mask from my hand. Then the creature vanished, with the others, back into Darkness.

I blinked looking upward in shock. The night sky had healed. The stars shone unconcernedly. Overhead, the two moons of Ja-Lur had separated.

Shadownight was over.

I was exhausted, but not so much as I thought I might be. There was also a sense of exhilaration. For perhaps the first time in my life, I had cast a powerful spell right, without the aid of potions and powders or anything save my own will.

Well, perhaps not quite—I looked down at the ring of Mondrogan, on my hand. Now that there was no other talisman about, I could sense its power, and it was considerable. I slipped it off my finger, dropped it on the stone. I did not want to wear it any longer.

I turned and looked at Jann-Togah and Valina. They both still stared at the sky, Jann-Togah's face solemn, Valina's white and stricken.

Below, outworlders and Darklanders also stood, uncertain now what to do.

"We can't let the fighting start again," I said.

Jann-Togah stirred as if coming out of a trance. He looked down at the crater's floor. "I shall speak to the Darklanders," he said. "They will fight no more if I command it."

"Don't get too close," I warned him. "If they sense that your aura of power is gone . . ."

He nodded. His gaze was bleak, but there was life in it. I was glad to see that. Even without his power, he was a born leader, and the Darkland would need him now.

He re-entered the corridor.

I turned to Valina. She was shivering; I put my trenchcloak around her. She had tears on her cheeks.

"A most touching scene," a familiar voice said.

We turned and looked at the entrance to the corridor. Polaris Lone stepped into the moonlight. For the first time since we had known him, he was less than immaculate. His cyber suit was torn, revealing thread-like circuitry; there was a bruise on his right temple, and his hair was in disarray. His golden eyes seemed to shine in the moonlight like an animal's.

His raygun was aimed at us.

"Yes, a most touching scene," he repeated slowly, approaching. "I honestly regret having to end it."

"Polaris!" Valina whispered hoarsely. "What do you mean?" The words rasped her throat; she winced and fell silent.

"I think he means to justify my opinion of him," I said, watching him.

"I have a job to do," Polaris said. "That's all. Nothing personal in it."

"Then why are you smiling?" I asked. I glanced around the bare expanse of the crater's rim—there was nothing that could serve as a weapon. I knew he could shoot before I could say a spell.

Polaris looked over the outside of the spire. "A long way down," he mused. "But don't worry—you'll be dead before you start to fall."

"Why, Polaris?" I asked. "Or does there have to be a reason?"

"I heard you recite that spell," he said. "I've seen what you're capable of. My orders were to destroy the Darklord—and any other Darklanders who might constitute trouble for the Unity." He took a step closer. "It's my job." Then he grinned. "But I do enjoy my work."

He pressed the firing button.

Nothing happened.

For an instant, no one moved. Then I leaped to one side and Valina to the other. Polaris tried the blaster again, then threw it at Valina as he jumped at me. The heavy raygun hit the side of her head; she fell, dazed, on the rim's edge.

I barely dodged Polaris's first lunge. I seized his wrist as he passed me and pulled, but he had already regained his balance—he twisted his arm out of my grasp and swung a lightning-fast hammerfist to my head. I was unable to dodge it entirely, and the world rocked like Shadownight again. But instead of jerking away as he expected, I hurled myself at him, seizing him by the waist and one leg. I expected to be electrocuted, but nothing happened—evidently his cyber suit mechanisms were not working either. I tried to pitch him off his feet, but I was too weak. He broke my hold easily and shoved me toward the edge, helping me along with a punch to my left kidney. I staggered in agony and fell on the edge. Polaris towered over me, one foot lifted.

My trenchcloak suddenly whirled through the air and draped itself over Polaris. He stumbled to one side, blinded for an instant, before wrestling free of it. I tried to rise, but someone had turned up the gravity. I saw Polaris, golden gaze mocking, step back toward me—

Then those golden eyes widened in sudden terror as he stepped on something which slid under his foot. Off balance, he tottered for a moment—then, quite slowly, graceful to the last, he fell over the edge.

He did not scream. I stared at where he had stood, wondering what he had slipped on. Then I saw it, rolling toward the edge: Mondrogan's ring. The grinning, one-horned face seemed to wink at me. Then the ring fell, to be lost forever in the sands far below.

I stood, helped Valina to her feet. "Thanks for throwing the cloak," I said. Then we started back down the corridor.

* * *

Jann-Togah, Valina, Daniel Tolon, and I stood in the cool, pre-dawn air outside the Dark Spire. The rest of the night had been spent setting up emergency treatment for the wounded. Daniel had been lucky—he had been only wounded slightly by a darkling's talons. A bandage of synflesh on his shoulder had taken care of it. He had detailed a team to investigate the extent of the damage caused to the cruiser by the Darklord's causing it to crash. They had pronounced it capable of returning to the spaceport for repair.

"My powers are returning to me," Jann-Togah said. "I can feel it." He wasn't the only one who could—standing next to him, I could sense his aura building like a house on fire.

"Do you think they will accept you as their ruler?" I asked him.

"They have no choice," he assured me. "If I cannot rule by consent, I shall rule by control—I am still my father's son."

I nodded. I wondered what he thought of the fact that he had human blood in him. The Darklord had been right: Knowledge mattered more than power, even more than blood.

He had shown no remorse over the Darklord's death. I

had told him how I had defeated him, who he was, and what had happened to the ring. "Let it lie in the sands," Jann-Togah said. "I want no part of his rule to survive him. I shall make my own reign."

"Keep in mind that Darkness is fading," I told him. "This Shadownight was one of the last surges of its receding tide. Soon the Darkland and its people will be no different from the rest of Ja-Lur."

"And you will have to deal with the Unity," Daniel said. "Just because Polaris Lone is dead doesn't mean outworlders will leave Ja-Lur. On the contrary, more spaceports will be built, now that the mandate is done with. I'm not sure if that's a good or a bad thing. It's just the way it is."

"I have learned quite a bit in my wanderings across the Darkworld," Jann-Togah said. "I think it is time for human and Darklander to know more about each other. I do not fear change."

I was glad to hear him say it, though privately I still had doubts. As he had said, he was still his father's son.

I looked at Valina. She looked back at me, meeting my gaze steadily. The application of a universal antibiotic from the cruiser's medical supplies had cured her laryngitis. "What about you?" I asked.

"I shall stay in Ja-Agur, if Jann-Togah will have me," she said. "After all, I also know a great deal about the Northern Nations. I might be able to help him." She looked at him and smiled. Jann-Togah allowed a ghost of a smile to come to him.

I sighed. "In that case," I said to him, "there are some things you had better know."

Valina glanced sharply at me, her face paling. I looked away from her eyes.

"Such as?" Jann-Togah prompted me.

"She had plans of her own from the beginning." I listened to myself wearily, feeling like an oracle compelled to speak nothing but doom. "You and I and the Darklord weren't the only ones who planned to use Shadownight."

"Don't listen to him!" Valina said angrily. "It's not true!"

"You know it is," I told her. "Do you think I don't know the real reason you went north? That I don't know where the restored *Synulanom* came from?

"When I buried Kaan's body, the ashes of the spell were gone. They hadn't disappeared or blown away—you had taken them. Later, you spoke a restoring spell to reconstitute the parchment. You kept the scroll sewed in the lining of your cloak. I felt it there, and that's what started me thinking. I'd concealed the spell that way myself.

"But you weren't willing to use the *Synulanom* merely to dominate the North, as Kaan would have done. You were after bigger game. Reading the *Synulanom* through the Black Mask would be a whole new cauldron of spells. So you went north, to find the Black Mask."

Valina said nothing, but her glare was like a radiation bath.

"You didn't have any luck until you met me—by chance or the Darklord's design. You were good—very good. You pretended reluctance, but you were willing to come with me to the Darkland, since my quest would aid yours. You planned to don the mask on Shadownight and read the *Synulanom*. But you came down with laryngitis."

Valina had grown very quiet. She watched me calmly, no malice left in her gaze. At length, she heaved a great sigh.

"How can you be so sure?" she asked, almost plaintively.

"I know *you*," I said. "I saw your reaction to losing your voice . . . your reaction to seeing the Black Mask . . . your face as you watched the darkling carry the spell and mask back into Darkness . . . and a hundred other things. I didn't have to be a detective to figure it out, or to see your personality through the Black Mask. It just helped."

Silence held as the first rays of the sun showed. Valina looked apprehensively at Jann-Togah, who stood staring gravely at the spire. Then, suddenly, he laughed a great, booming laugh—the first I had ever heard from him.

"By my father's name, I like it!" he shouted. "It's a plot worthy of me!" He chuckled at the astonishment on her face. "Don't think me that surprised, Valina. I knew when I met you that duplicity came easily to you. By all means, stay! You'll not be the Darklord, but you'll work by his side! If nothing else, you'll certainly keep me alert!"

Valina stared at him incredulously, then realized he meant it. Her smile was brighter than the sun, then, and her laughter the first joyous thing heard in the Darkland for a long time, I'll wager. I looked at her and admitted then to myself that I had been jealous of Polaris, just as I was now jealous of Jann-Togah. For all her intrigue and scheming,

Valina had been grave and resourceful, too. She may have saved my life for her own purposes, but she had saved it more than once. I knew I would never forget her.

She and Jann-Togah turned and walked back toward the Dark Spire. It was not a match made in Heaven, or anywhere near it. But I had the feeling it would last.

I wondered if the Unity would last, against them.

"Our ship is almost ready for blastoff, Kamus," Daniel Tolon said. "On our way back to the spaceport, you can tell me how you managed to defeat agent Boreas."

"I've been wondering that myself," I said.

"What do you mean?"

"You mentioned earlier that the mandate is gone. It should be, with the Darklord dead. So, why did Polaris's raygun fail?"

"Perhaps it needed recharging."

"Perhaps. . ." but I could not stop thinking of Mondrogan's ring, and how it had looked as it fell. The Darklord had once been Mondrogan the Clever, by all accounts a brave and noble man. And yet he had succumbed to temptation offered, had become the Darklord.

I liked to think that a little bit of Mondrogan had been left in the ring—and that he had been grateful to me for releasing him.

I shook my head. I had other things to think about, such as resuming my life and my career. I had made good my oath—I had confronted the Darklord, and won. I regretted having to kill him, but it had been his life or mine. Besides, in a sense, he had been dead for centuries.

I had also helped save Ja-Lur from a resurgence of Darkness, and I had avenged my friend Sanris.

So why did I feel so empty?

Why did the thought of going back to Mariyad, or some other city, of finding another dingy office and attempting to start all over again, make me as nervous as a basilisk in a hall of mirrors?

I did not want to be the only private eye on the planet any more. These past few months had taken me over much of my world, had forced me to remember and relive much of my life. When I had come back from Earth and started my career, I had thought there would be satisfaction in it. I had found little. I had seen criminals go unprosecuted, had seen death and life-in-death, had seen love rot itself into sickness and hatred. And, worst of all, I had no idea how large a part I had played in bringing all this about.

Perhaps, I told myself, I would feel different later, as I gained perspective. Surely there had been some positive aspects to all of this. Hadn't there?

"I'm not at all sure I want to go back to Mariyad," I told Daniel.

He grinned. "You misunderstand me, Kamus. I'm not suggesting that you do. They know you're a Darklander there; I checked. No, I said back to the spaceport. I think it might be a good idea for you to leave Ja-Lur for awhile. My tour of duty as a Unity agent will be over soon. I know of several worlds where people with our talents could find interesting work—worlds where you can tell the good guys from the bad guys a bit more easily."

"I could use a trip," I mused. Ja-Lur was my home—but everyone has to leave home, sooner or later. I wondered if my Dark powers would leave me, as they did the last time I left Ja-Lur, but that did not seem to matter. A change would do me good. That, and the chance to feel, for once, like a hero . . .

I pulled a stick of gum from my pouch and offered it to Daniel Tolon as we walked toward the cruiser. "Daniel," I said, "I think this could be the beginning of a nova friendship."

ABOUT THE AUTHOR

J. MICHAEL REAVES has had numerous television scripts produced and his short fiction has been published in magazines and book anthologies. One of his stories was nominated for the 1979 British Fantasy Award. He has written a novel, *I—Alien* as well as nonfiction and reviews for Warner Brothers and *Delap's F & SF Review.* He lectures on the craft of writing at various schools and colleges. He is the coauthor of the Bantam Book *Dragonworld*. He currently resides in Los Angeles.